Flight for Life

With a sudden golden movement Ramoth arched her great back. She sprang into the sky, wings wide. With unbelievable speed she was airborne. After her, in the blink of an eye, seven bronze shapes followed, their mighty wings churning buffets of sand-laden air into the faces of the watching weyrfolk.

Her heart in her mouth at the prodigious flight, Lessa felt her soul lifting with Ramoth. She, Ramoth-Lessa, was alive with limitless power, her wings beating effortlessly to the thin heights, elation surging through her frame, elation and—desire.

"Stay with her," F'nor whispered urgently. "Stay with her. She must not escape your control now . . . Think with her. She cannot go *between*. . . ."

THE DRAGONRIDERS OF PERN

DRAGONFLIGHT

Volume I of
"The Dragonriders of Pern"

Anne McCaffrey

A Del Rey Book

BALLANTINE BOOKS • NEW YORK

Dedicatory Note

Dear God,

Yes, there is a Virginia who helped me create this planet and the marvels thereon. And for whom I thank you.

AMJ

Contents

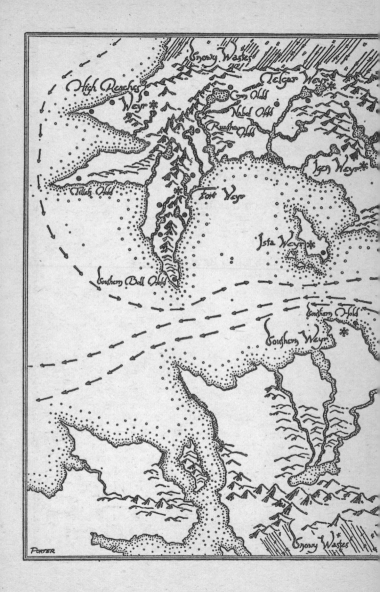

Benden Weyr

Bitra Hold

Benden Weyr

N

W E

S

Keroon Hold

Nerat Hold

Southern Current

Cove Hold

Pern

INTRODUCTION

WHEN is a legend legend? Why is a myth a myth? How old and disused must a fact be for it to be relegated to the category "Fairy-tale"? And why do certain facts remain incontrovertible while others lose their validity to assume a shabby, unstable character?

Rukbat, in the Sagittarian sector, was a golden G-type star. It had five planets, and one stray it had attracted and held in recent millennia. Its third planet was enveloped by air man could breathe, boasted water he could drink, and possessed a gravity that permitted man to walk confidently erect. Men discovered it and promptly colonized it. They did that to every habitable planet, and then—whether callously or through collapse of empire, the colonists never discovered and eventually forgot to ask—left the colonies to fend for themselves.

When men first settled on Rukbat's third world and named it Pern, they had taken little notice of the stranger-planet, swinging around its adopted primary in a wildly erratic elliptical orbit. Within a few generations they had forgotten its existence. The desperate path the wanderer pursued brought it close to its stepsister every two hundred (Terran) years at perihelion.

When the aspects were harmonious and the conjunction with its sister planet close enough, as it often was, the indigenous life of the wanderer sought to bridge the space gap to the more temperate and hospitable planet.

It was during the frantic struggle to combat this menace dropping through Pern's skies like silver threads that Pern's tenuous contact with the mother planet was broken. Recollections of Earth receded further from Pernese history with each successive generation until memory of their origins degenerated past legend or myth, into oblivion.

To forestall the incursions of the dreadful Threads, the Pernese, with the ingenuity of their forgotten Terran forebears, developed a highly specialized variety of a life-form indigenous to their adopted planet. Such humans as had a high empathy rating and some innate telepathic ability were trained to use and preserve this unusual animal whose ability to teleport was of great value in the fierce struggle to keep Pern bare of Threads.

The winged, tailed, and fiery-breathed dragons (named for the Earth legend they resembled), their dragonmen, a breed apart, and the menace they battled, created a whole new group of legends and myths.

Once relieved of imminent danger, Pern settled into a more comfortable way of life. The descendants of heroes fell into disfavor, as the legends fell into disrepute.

PART I

Weyr Search

Drummer, beat, and piper, blow,
Harper, strike, and soldier, go.
Free the flame and sear the grasses
Till the dawning Red Star passes.

LESSA WOKE, cold. Cold with more than the chill of the everlastingly clammy stone walls. Cold with the prescience of a danger stronger than the one ten full Turns ago that had then sent her, whimpering with terror, to hide in the watch-wher's odorous lair.

Rigid with concentration, Lessa lay in the straw of the redolent cheeseroom she shared as sleeping quarters with the other kitchen drudges. There was an urgency in the ominous portent unlike any other forewarning. She touched the awareness of the watch-wher, slithering on its rounds in the courtyard. It circled at the choke limit of its chain. It was restless, but oblivious to anything unusual in the predawn darkness.

Lessa curled into a tight knot of bones, hugging herself to ease the strain across her tense shoulders. Then, forcing herself to relax, muscle by muscle, joint by joint, she tried to feel what subtle menace it might be that could rouse her, yet not distress the sensitive watch-wher.

The danger was definitely not within the walls of

Ruath Hold. Nor approaching the paved perimeter
without the Hold where relentless grass had forced
new growth through the ancient mortar, green witness
to the deterioration of the once stone-clean Hold. The
danger was not advancing up the now little-used
causeway from the valley, nor lurking in the craftsmen's stony holdings at the foot of the Hold's cliff. It
did not scent the wind that blew from Tillek's cold
shores. But still it twanged sharply through her senses,
vibrating every nerve in Lessa's slender frame. Fully
roused, she sought to identify it before the prescient
mood dissolved. She cast outward, toward the Pass,
farther than she had ever pressed. Whatever threatened was not in Ruatha . . . yet. Nor did it have
a familiar flavor. It was not, then, Fax.

Lessa had been cautiously pleased that Fax had
not shown himself at Ruath Hold in three full Turns.
The apathy of the craftsmen, the decaying farmholds,
even the green-etched stones of the Hold infuriated
Fax, self-styled Lord of the High Reaches, to the point
where he preferred to forget the reason he had sub-
jugated the once proud and profitable Hold.

Relentlessly compelled to identify this oppressing
menace, Lessa groped in the straw for her sandals.
She rose, mechanically brushing straw from matted
hair, which she then twisted quickly into a rude knot
at her neck.

She picked her way among the sleeping drudges,
huddled together for warmth, and glided up the worn
steps to the kitchen proper. The cook and his assistant
lay on the long table before the great hearth, wide
backs to the warmth of the banked fire, discordantly
snoring. Lessa slipped across the cavernous kitchen to
the stable-yard door. She opened the door just enough
to permit her slight body to pass. The cobbles of the
yard were icy through the thin soles of her sandals,
and she shivered as the predawn air penetrated her
patched garment.

The watch-wher slithered across the yard to greet
her, pleading, as it always did, for release. Comfort-

ingly, she fondled the creases of the sharp-tipped ears as it matched her stride. Glancing fondly down at the awesome head, she promised it a good rub presently. It crouched, groaning, at the end of its chain as she continued to the grooved steps that led to the rampart over the Hold's massive gate. Atop the tower, Lessa stared toward the east where the stony breasts of the Pass rose in black relief against the gathering day.

Indecisively she swung to her left, for the sense of danger issued from that direction as well. She glanced upward, her eyes drawn to the red star that had recently begun to dominate the dawn sky. As she stared, the star radiated a final ruby pulsation before its magnificence was lost in the brightness of Pern's rising sun. Incoherent fragments of tales and ballads about the dawn appearance of the red star flashed through her mind, too quickly to make sense. Moreover, her instinct told her that, though danger might come from the northeast, too, there was a greater peril to contend with from due east. Straining her eyes as if vision would bridge the gap between peril and person, she stared intently eastward. The watch-wher's thin, whistled question reached her just as the prescience waned.

Lessa sighed. She had found no answer in the dawn, only discrepant portents. She must wait. The warning had come and she had accepted it. She was used to waiting. Perversity, endurance, and guile were her other weapons, loaded with the inexhaustible patience of vengeful dedication.

Dawnlight illumined the tumbled landscape, the unplowed fields in the valley below. Dawnlight fell on twisted orchards, where the sparse herds of milchbeasts hunted stray blades of spring grass. Grass in Ruatha, Lessa mused, grew where it should not, died where it should flourish. Lessa could hardly remember now how Ruatha Valley had once looked, sweetly happy, amply productive. Before Fax came. An odd brooding smile curved lips unused to such exercise. Fax realized no profit from his conquest of Ruatha . . .

nor would he while she, Lessa, lived. And he had not the slightest suspicion of the source of this undoing.

Or had he, Lessa wondered, her mind still reverberating from the savage prescience of danger. West lay Fax's ancestral and only legitimate Hold. Northeast lay little but bare and stony mountains and the Weyr that protected Pern.

Lessa stretched, arching her back, inhaling the sweet, untainted wind of morning.

A cock crowed in the stable yard. Lessa whirled, her face alert, eyes darting around the outer Hold lest she be observed in such an uncharacteristic pose. She unbound her hair, letting the rank mass fall about her face concealingly. Her body drooped into the sloppy posture she affected. Quickly she thudded down the stairs, crossing to the watch-wher. It cried piteously, its great eyes blinking against the growing daylight. Oblivious to the stench of its rank breath, she hugged the scaly head to her, scratching its ears and eye ridges. The watch-wher was ecstatic with pleasure, its long body trembling, its clipped wings rustling. It alone knew who she was or cared. And it was the only creature in all Pern she had trusted since the dawn she had blindly sought refuge in its dark, stinking lair to escape the thirsty swords that had drunk so deeply of Ruathan blood.

Slowly she rose, cautioning it to remember to be as vicious to her as to all, should anyone be near. It promised to obey her, swaying back and forth to emphasize its reluctance.

The first rays of the sun glanced over the Hold's outer wall, and, crying out, the watch-wher darted into its dark nest. Lessa crept swiftly back to the kitchen and into the cheeseroom.

From the Weyr and from the Bowl,
Bronze and brown and blue and green,
Rise the dragonmen of Pern,
Aloft, on wing, seen, then unseen.

F'LAR, ON bronze Mnementh's great neck, appeared first in the skies above the chief Hold of Fax, so-called Lord of the High Reaches. Behind him, in proper wedge formation, the wingmen came into sight. F'lar checked the formation automatically; it was as precise as on the moment of their entry to *between*.

As Mnementh curved in an arc that would bring them to the perimeter of the Hold, consonant with the friendly nature of this visitation, F'lar surveyed with mounting aversion the disrepair of the ridge defenses. The firestone pits were empty, and the rock-cut gutters radiating from the pits were green-tinged with a mossy growth.

Was there even one Lord in Pern who maintained his Hold rocky in observance of the ancient Laws? F'lar's lips tightened to a thinner line. When this Search was over and the Impression made, there would have to be a solemn, punitive Council held at the Weyr. And by the golden shell of the queen, he, F'lar, meant to be its moderator. He would replace lethargy with industry. He would scour the green and dangerous scum from the heights of Pern, the grass blades from its stoneworks. No verdant skirt would be condoned in any farmhold. And the tithings that had been so miserly, so grudgingly presented, would, under pain of firestoning, flow with decent generosity into the Dragonweyr.

Mnementh rumbled approvingly as he vaned his pinions to land lightly on the grass-etched flagstones of Fax's Hold. The bronze dragon furled his great wings, and F'lar heard the warning claxon in the Hold's Great Tower. Mnementh dropped to his knees as F'lar indicated he wished to dismount. The bronze rider stood by Mnementh's huge wedge-shaped head, politely awaiting the arrival of the Hold Lord. F'lar idly gazed down the valley, hazy with warm spring sunlight. He ignored the furtive heads that peered at the dragonman from the parapet slits and the cliff windows.

F'lar did not turn as the rush of air past him announced the arrival of the rest of the wing. He knew, however, when F'nor, the brown rider who was coincidentally his half brother, took the customary position on his left, a dragon length to the rear. From the corner of his eye, F'lar glimpsed F'nor twisting to death with his boot heel the grass that crowded up between the stones.

An order, muffled to an intense whisper, issued from within the great Court, beyond the open gates. Almost immediately a group of men marched into sight, led by a heavy-set man of medium height.

Mnementh arched his neck, angling his head so that his chin rested on the ground. Mnementh's many-faceted eyes, on a level with F'lar's head, fastened with disconcerting interest on the approaching party. The dragons could never understand why they generated such abject fear in common folk. At only one point in his life span would a dragon attack a human, and that could be excused on the grounds of simple ignorance. F'lar could not explain to the dragon the politics behind the necessity of inspiring awe in the holders, Lord and craftsman alike. He could only observe that the fear and apprehension showing in the faces of the advancing squad which troubled Mnementh was oddly pleasing to him, F'lar.

"Welcome, bronze rider, to the Hold of Fax, Lord of the High Reaches. He is at your service," and the man made an adequately respectful salute.

The use of the third person pronoun could be construed by the meticulous to be a veiled insult. This fit in with the information F'lar had on Fax, so he ignored it. His information was also correct in describing Fax as a greedy man. It showed in the restless eyes that flicked at every detail of F'lar's clothing, at the slight frown when the intricately etched sword hilt was noticed.

F'lar noticed, in his own turn, the several rich rings that flashed on Fax's left hand. The overlord's right hand remained slightly cocked after the habit of the professional swordsman. His tunic, of rich fabric, was stained and none too fresh. The man's feet, in heavy wher-hide boots, were solidly planted, weight balanced forward on his toes. A man to be treated cautiously, F'lar decided, as one should the conqueror of five neighboring Holds. Such greedy audacity was in itself a revelation. Fax had married into a sixth . . . and had legally inherited, however unusual the circumstances, the seventh. He was a lecherous man by reputation. Within these seven Holds, F'lar anticipated a profitable Search. Let R'gul go southerly to pursue Search among the indolent if lovely women there. The Weyr needed a strong woman this time; Jora had been worse than useless with Nemorth. Adversity, uncertainty: those were the conditions that bred the qualities F'lar wanted in a Weyrwoman.

"We ride in Search," F'lar drawled softly, "and request the hospitality of your Hold, Lord Fax."

Fax's eyes widened imperceptibly at mention of a Search.

"I had heard Jora was dead," Fax replied, dropping the third person abruptly as if F'lar had passed some sort of test by ignoring it. "So Nemorth has laid a queen, hmmm?" he continued, his eyes darting across the rank of the wing, noting the disciplined stance of the riders, the healthy color of the dragons.

F'lar did not dignify the obvious with an answer.

"And, my Lord—" Fax hesitated, expectantly inclining his head slightly toward the dragonman.

For a pulse beat, F'lar wondered if the man was deliberately provoking him with such subtle insults. The name of the bronze riders should be as well-known throughout Pern as the name of the dragon queen and her Weyrwoman. F'lar kept his face composed, his eyes on Fax's.

Leisurely, with the proper touch of arrogance, F'nor stepped forward, stopping slightly behind Mnementh's head, one hand negligently touching the jaw hinge of the huge beast.

"The bronze rider of Mnementh, Lord F'lar, will require quarters for himself. I, F'nor, brown rider, prefer to be lodged with the wingmen. We are, in number, twelve."

F'lar liked that touch of F'nor's, totting up the wing strength, as if Fax were incapable of counting. F'nor had phrased it so adroitly as to make it impossible for Fax to protest the return insult.

"Lord F'lar," Fax said through teeth fixed in a smile, "the High Reaches are honored with your Search."

"It will be to the credit of the High Reaches," F'lar replied smoothly, "if one of its own supplies the Weyr."

"To our everlasting credit," Fax replied as suavely. "In the old days many notable Weyrwomen came from my Holds."

"Your Holds?" asked F'lar, politely smiling as he emphasized the plural. "Ah, yes, you are now over-lord of Ruatha, are you not? There have been many from that Hold."

A strange, tense look crossed Fax's face, quickly

supplanted by a determinedly affable grin. Fax stepped aside, gesturing F'lar to enter the Hold.

Fax's troop leader barked a hasty order, and the men formed two lines, their metal-edged boots flicking sparks from the stones.

At unspoken orders, all the dragons rose with a great churning of air and dust. F'lar strode nonchalantly past the welcoming files. The men were rolling their eyes in alarm as the beasts glided above to the inner courts. Someone on the high Tower uttered a frightened yelp as Mnementh took his position on that vantage point. His great wings drove phosphoric-scented air across the inner court as he maneuvered his great frame onto the inadequate landing space.

Outwardly oblivious to the consternation, fear, and awe the dragons inspired, F'lar was secretly amused and rather pleased by the effect. Lords of the Holds needed this reminder that they still must deal with dragons, not just with riders, who were men, mortal and murderable. The ancient respect for dragonmen as well as dragonkind must be reinstilled in modern breasts.

"The Hold has just risen from table, Lord F'lar, if . . ." Fax suggested. His voice trailed off at F'lar's smiling refusal.

"Convey my duty to your lady, Lord Fax," F'lar rejoined, noticing with inward satisfaction the tightening of Fax's jaw muscles at the ceremonial request.

F'lar was enjoying himself thoroughly. He had not yet been born on the occasion of the last Search, the one that ill-fatedly provided the incompetent Jora. But he had studied the accounts of previous Searches in the Old Records that had included subtle ways to confound those Lords who preferred to keep their ladies sequestered when the dragonmen rode. For Fax to refuse F'lar the opportunity to pay his duty would have been tantamount to a major insult, discharged only in mortal combat.

"You would prefer to see your quarters first?" Fax countered.

F'lar flicked an imaginary speck from his soft wher-hide sleeve and shook his head.

"Duty first," he said with a rueful shrug.

"Of course," Fax all but snapped and strode smartly ahead, his heels pounding out the anger he could not express otherwise.

F'lar and F'nor followed at a slower pace through the double-doored entry with its great metal panels, into the Great Hall, carved into the cliffside. The U-shaped table was being cleared by nervous servitors, who rattled and dropped tableware as the two dragon-men entered. Fax had already reached the far end of the Hall and stood impatiently at the open slab door, the only access to the inner Hold, which, like all such Holds, burrowed deep into stone, the refuge of all in time of peril.

"They eat not badly," F'nor remarked casually to F'lar, appraising the remnants still on the table.

"Better than the Weyr, it would seem," F'lar replied dryly, covering his speech with his hand as he saw two drudges staggering under the weight on a tray that bore a half-eaten carcass.

"Young and tender," F'nor said in a bitter undertone, "from the look of it. While the stringy, barren beasts are delivered up to us."

"Naturally."

"A pleasantly favored Hall," F'lar said amiably as they reached Fax. Then, seeing Fax impatient to continue, F'lar deliberately turned back to the banner-hung Hall. He pointed out to F'nor the deeply set slit windows, heavy bronze shutters open to the bright noonday sky. "Facing east, too, as they ought. That new Hall at Telgar Hold actually faces south, I'm told. Tell me, Lord Fax, do you adhere to the old practices and mount a dawn guard?"

Fax frowned, trying to parse F'lar's meaning.

"There is always a guard at the Tower."

"An easterly guard?"

Fax's eyes jerked toward the windows, then back,

sliding across F'lar's face to F'nor and back again to the windows.

"There are always guards," he answered sharply, "on all the approaches."

"Oh, just the approaches," and F'lar turned to F'nor and nodded wisely.

"Where else?" demanded Fax, concerned, glancing from one dragonman to the other.

"I must ask that of your harper. You do keep a trained harper in your Hold?"

"Of course. I have several trained harpers." Fax jerked his shoulders straighter.

F'lar affected not to understand.

"Lord Fax is the overlord of six other Holds," F'nor reminded his wingleader.

"Of course," F'lar assented, with exactly the same inflection Fax had used a moment before.

The mimicry did not go unnoticed by Fax, but as he was unable to construe deliberate insult out of an innocent affirmative, he stalked into the glow-lit corridors. The dragonmen followed.

"It is good to see one Holder keeping so many ancient customs," F'lar said to F'nor approvingly for Fax's benefit as they passed into the inner Hold. "There are many who have abandoned the safety of solid rock and enlarged their outer Holds to dangerous proportions. I can't condone the risk myself."

"Their risk, Lord F'lar. Another's gain," Fax snorted derisively, slowing to a normal strut.

"Gain? How so?"

"Any outer Hold is easily penetrated, bronze rider, with trained forces, experienced leadership, and well-considered strategy."

The man was not a braggart, F'lar decided. Nor, in these peaceful days, did he fail to mount Tower guards. However, he kept within his Hold, not out of obedience to ancient Laws, but through prudence. He kept harpers for ostentation rather than because tradition required it. But he allowed the pits to decay; he permitted grass to grow. He accorded dragonmen the barest civility on one hand and offered veiled insult on the other. A man to be watched.

The women's quarters in Fax's Hold had been moved from the traditional innermost corridors to those at the cliff-face. Sunlight poured down from the three double-shuttered, deep-casement windows in the outside wall. F'lar noted that the bronze hinges were well oiled. The sills were the regulation spear-length; Fax had not given in to the recent practice of diminishing the protective wall.

The chamber was richly hung with appropriately gentle scenes of women occupied in all manner of feminine tasks. Doors gave off the main chamber on both sides into smaller sleeping alcoves, and from these, at Fax's bidding, his women hesitantly emerged. Fax sternly gestured to a blue-gowned woman, her hair white-streaked, her face lined with disappoint-ments and bitterness, her body swollen with preg-nancy. She advanced awkwardly, stopping several feet from her lord. From her attitude, F'lar deduced that she came no closer to Fax than was absolutely necessary.

"The Lady of Crom, mother of my heirs," Fax said without pride or cordiality.

"My Lady—" F'lar hesitated, waiting for her name to be supplied.

She glanced warily at her lord.

"Gemma," Fax snapped curtly.

F'lar bowed deeply. "My Lady Gemma, the Weyr is on Search and requests the hospitality of the Hold."

"My Lord F'lar," the Lady Gemma replied in a low voice, "you are most welcome."

F'lar did not miss the slight slur on the adverb or the fact that Gemma had no trouble naming him. His smile was warmer than courtesy demanded, warm with gratitude and sympathy. Judging by the number of women in these quarters, Fax bedded well and frequently. There might be one or two Lady Gemma could bid farewell without regret.

Fax went through the introductions, mumbling names until he realized this strategy was not going to work. F'lar would politely beg the lady's name again. F'nor, his smile brightening as he took heed which ladies Fax preferred to keep anonymous, lounged indolently by the doorway. F'lar would compare notes with him later, although on cursory examination there was none here worthy of the Search. Fax preferred his women plump and small. There wasn't a saucy one in the lot. If there once had been, the spirit had been beaten out of them. Fax, no doubt, was stud, not lover. Some of the covey had not all winter long made much use of water, judging from the amount of sweet oil gone rancid in their hair. Of them all, if these were all, the Lady Gemma was the only willful one, and she was too old.

The amenities over, Fax ushered his unwelcome guests outside. F'nor was excused by his wingleader to join the other dragonmen. Fax peremptorily led the way to the quarters he had assigned the bronze rider.

The chamber was on a lower level than the women's suite and was certainly adequate to the dignity of its occupant. The many-colored hangings were crowded with bloody battles, individual swordplay, bright-hued dragons in flight, firestones burning on the ridges, and all that Pern's scarlet-stained history offered.

"A pleasant room," F'lar acknowledged, stripping off gloves and wher-hide tunic, throwing them carelessly to the table. "I shall see to my men and the beasts. The dragons have all been fed recently," he commented, pointing up Fax's omission in inquiring. "I request liberty to wander through the crafthold."

Fax sourly granted what was traditionally a dragonman's privilege.

"I shall not further disrupt your routine, Lord Fax, for you must have many demands on you, with seven Holds to supervise." F'lar inclined his body slightly to the overlord, turning away as a gesture of dismissal. He could imagine the infuriated expression on Fax's face and listened to the stamping retreat. He waited long enough to be sure Fax was out of the corridor and then briskly retraced his steps up to the Great Hall.

Bustling drudges paused in setting up additional trestle tables to eye the dragonman. He nodded pleasantly to them, looking to see if one of these females might possibly have the stuff of which Weyrwomen are made. Overworked, underfed, scarred by lash and disease, they were just what they were—drudges, fit only for hard, menial labor.

F'nor and the men had settled themselves in a hastily vacated barrackroom. The dragons were perched comfortably on the rocky ridges above the Hold. They had so arranged themselves that every segment of the wide valley fell under their scrutiny. All had been fed before leaving the Weyr, and each rider kept his dragon in light but alert charge. There were to be no incidents on a Search.

As a group, the dragonmen rose at F'lar's entrance. "No tricks, no troubles, but look around closely," he said laconically. "Return by sundown with the names of any likely prospects." He caught F'nor's grin, remembering how Fax had slurred over some names. "Descriptions are in order and craft affiliation."

The men nodded, their eyes glinting with understanding. They were flatteringly confident of a successful Search even as F'lar's doubts grew now that he had seen all of Fax's women. By all logic, the pick of the High Reaches should be in Fax's chief Hold, but they were not. Still, there were many large craftholds, not to mention the six other High Holds to visit. All the same . . .

In unspoken accord F'lar and F'nor left the barracks. The men would follow, unobtrusively, in pairs or singly, to reconnoiter the crafthold and the nearer farmholds. The men were as overtly eager to be abroad as F'lar was privately. There had been a time when dragonmen were frequent and favored guests

in all the great Holds throughout Pern, from southern
Nerat to high Tillek. This pleasant custom, too, had
died along with other observances, evidence of the low
regard in which the Weyr was presently held. F'lar
vowed to correct this.

He forced himself to trace in memory the insidious
changes. The Records, which each Weyrwoman
kept, were proof of the gradual but perceptible decline, traceable through the past two hundred full
Turns. Knowing the facts did not alleviate the condition. And F'lar was of that scant handful in the Weyr
itself who did credit Records and ballad alike. The
situation might shortly reverse itself radically if the
old tales were to be believed.

There was a reason, an explanation, a purpose,
F'lar felt, for every one of the Weyr Laws from First
Impression to the Firestones, from the grass-free
heights to ridge-running gutters. For elements as minor as controlling the appetite of a dragon to limiting
the inhabitants of the Weyr. Although why the other
five Weyrs had been abandoned F'lar did not know.
Idly he wondered if there were Records, dusty and
crumbling, lodged in the disused Weyrs. He must contrive to check when next his wings flew patrol. Certainly there was no explanation in Benden Weyr.

"There is industry but no enthusiasm," F'nor was
saying, drawing F'lar's attention back to their tour of
the crafthold.

They had descended the guttered ramp from the
Hold into the crafthold proper, the broad roadway
lined with cottages up to the imposing stone craft-
halls. Silently F'lar noted moss-clogged gutters on the
roofs, the vines clasping the walls. It was painful for
one of his calling to witness the flagrant disregard of
simple safety precautions. Growing things were forbidden near the habitations of mankind.

"News travels fast," F'nor chuckled, nodding at a
hurrying craftsman, in the smock of a baker, who gave
them a mumbled good-day. "Not a female in sight."

His observation was accurate. Women should be

abroad at this hour, bringing in supplies from the storehouses, washing in the river on such a bright warm day, or going out to the farmholds to help with planting. Not a gowned figure in sight.

"We used to be preferred mates," F'nor remarked caustically.

"We'll visit the Clothmen's Hall first. If my memory serves me . . ."

"As it always does . . ." F'nor interjected wryly. He took no advantage of their blood relationship, but he was more at ease with the bronze rider than most of the dragonmen, the other bronze riders included. F'lar was reserved in a close-knit society of easy equality. He flew a tightly disciplined wing, but men maneuvered to serve under him. His wing always excelled in the Games. None ever floundered in *between* to disappear forever, and no beast in his wing sickened, leaving a man in dragonless exile from the Weyr, a part of him numb forever.

"L'tol came this way and settled in one of the High Reaches," F'lar continued.

"L'tol?"

"Yes, a green rider from S'lel's wing. You remember."

An ill-timed swerve during the Spring Games had brought L'tol and his beast into the full blast of a phosphine emission from S'lel's bronze Tuenth. L'tol had been thrown from his beast's neck as the dragon tried to evade the blast. Another wingmate had swooped to catch the rider, but the green dragon, his left wing crisped, his body scorched, had died of shock and phosphine poisoning.

"L'tol would aid our Search," F'nor agreed as the two dragonmen walked up to the bronze doors of the Clothmen's Hall. They paused on the threshold, adjusting their eyes to the dimmer light within. Glows punctuated the wall recesses and hung in clusters above the larger looms where the finer tapestries and fabrics were woven by master craftsmen. The pervading mood was one of quiet, purposeful industry.

Before their eyes had adapted, however, a figure glided to them, muttering a polite if curt request for them to follow him.

They were led to the right of the entrance, to a small office, curtained from the main hall. Their guide turned to them, his face visible in the wallglows. There was that air about him that marked him indefinably as a dragonman. But his face was lined deeply, one side seamed with old burn marks. His eyes, sick with a hungry yearning, dominated his face. He blinked constantly.

"I am now Lytol," he said in harsh voice.

F'lar nodded acknowledgment.

"You would be F'lar," Lytol said, "and you F'nor. You both have the look of your sire."

F'lar nodded again.

Lytol swallowed convulsively, the muscles in his face twitching as the presence of dragonmen revived his awareness of exile. He essayed a smile.

"Dragons in the sky! The news spread faster than Threads."

"Nemorth has laid a female."

"And Jora dead?" Lytol asked concernedly, his face cleared of its nervous movement for a second. "Hath flew her?"

F'lar nodded.

Lytol grimaced bitterly. "R'gul again, huh?" He stared off in the middle distance, his eyelids quiet but the muscles along his jaw taking up the constant movement. "You have the High Reaches? All of them?" Lytol asked, turning back to the dragonman, a slight emphasis on "all."

F'lar gave an affirmative nod again.

"You've seen the women." Lytol's disgust showed through the words. It was a statement, not a question, for he hurried on. "Well, there are no better in all the High Reaches." His tone expressed utmost disdain. He eased himself down to the heavy table that half-filled one corner of the small room. His hands were clenched so tightly around the wide belt that secured the loose tunic to his body that the heavy leather was doubled.

"You would almost expect the opposite, wouldn't you?" Lytol continued. He was talking too much and too fast. It would have been insultingly rude in another, lesser man. It was the terrible loneliness of the man's exile from the Weyr that drove him to garrulity. Lytol skimmed the surfaces with hurried questions he himself answered, rather than dip once into matters too tender to be touched—such as his insatiable need for those of his kind. Yet he was giving the dragonmen exactly the information they needed. "But Fax likes his women comfortably fleshed and docile," Lytol rattled on. "Even the Lady Gemma has learned. It'd be different if he didn't need her family's support. Ah, it would be different indeed. So he keeps her pregnant, hoping to kill her in childbed one day. And he will. He will."

Lytol's laughter grated unpleasantly.

"When Fax came to power, any man with wit sent his daughters down from the High Reaches or drew a brand across their faces." He paused, his countenance dark and bitter memory, his eyes slits of hatred. "I was a fool and thought my position gave me immunity."

Lytol drew himself up, squaring his shoulders, turning full to the two dragonmen. His expression was vindictive, his voice low and tense.

"Kill that tyrant, dragonmen, for the sake and safety of Pern. Of the Weyr. Of the queen. He only bides his time. He spreads discontent among the other Lords. He—" Lytol's laughter had an hysterical edge to it now. "He fancies himself as good as dragonmen."

"There are no candidates then in this Hold?" F'lar said, his voice sharp enough to cut through the man's preoccupation with his curious theory.

Lytol stared at the bronze rider. "Did I not say it? The best either died under Fax or were sent away. What remains is nothing, nothing. Weak-minded, ignorant, foolish, vapid. You had that with Jora.

She—" His jaw snapped shut over his next words. He shook his head, scrubbing his face to ease his anguish and despair.

"In the other Holds?"

Lytol shook his head, frowning darkly. "The same. Either dead or fled."

"What of Ruath Hold?"

Lytol stopped shaking his head and looked sharply at F'lar, his lips curling in a cunning smile. He laughed mirthlessly.

"You think to find a Torene or a Moreta hidden at Ruath Hold in these times? Well, bronze rider, all of Ruathan Blood are dead. Fax's blade was thirsty that day. He knew the truth of those harpers' tales, that Ruathan Lords gave full measure of hospitality to dragonmen and the Ruathan were a breed apart. There were, you know"—Lytol's voice dropped to a confiding whisper—"exiled Weyrmen like myself in that Line."

F'lar nodded gravely, unwilling to deprive the man of such a sop to his self-esteem.

"No, there is little, very little left in Ruatha Valley." Lytol chuckled softly. "Fax gets nothing from that Hold but trouble." This reflection restored Lytol to a semblance of normal behavior, and his face twisted into a better humor. "We of this Hold are now the best clothmen in all Pern. And our smithies turn out a better tempered weapon." His eyes sparkled with pride in his adopted community. "The conscripts from Ruatha tend to die of curious diseases or accidents. And the women Fax used to take . . ." His laugh was nasty. "It is rumored he was impotent for months after."

F'lar's active mind jumped to a curious conclusion. "There are none of the Blood left?"

"None!"

"Any families in the holdings with Weyr blood?"

Lytol frowned, glanced in surprise at F'lar. He rubbed the scarred side of his face thoughtfully.

"There were," he admitted slowly. "There were.

But I doubt if any live on." He thought a moment longer, then shook his head emphatically. "There was such resistance at the invasion and no quarter given. At the Hold Fax beheaded ladies as well as babes. And he imprisoned or executed any known to have carried arms for Ruatha."

F'lar shrugged. The idea had been a probability only. With such severe reprisals, Fax undoubtedly had eliminated the resistance as well as the best crafts-men. That would account for the poor quality of Ruathan products and the emergence of the High Reaches' clothmen as the best in their trade.

"I wish I had better news for you, dragonman," Lytol murmured.

"No matter," F'lar reassured him, one hand poised to part the hanging in the doorway.

Lytol came up to him swiftly, his voice urgent.

"Heed what I say about Fax's ambitions. Force R'gul, or whoever is Weyrleader next, to keep watch on the High Reaches."

"Is Fax aware of your leanings?"

The haunted, hungry yearning crossed Lytol's face. He swallowed nervously, answering with no emotion in his voice.

"That would not signify if it suited the Lord of the High Reaches, but my guild protects me from persecu-tion. I am safe enough in the craft. He is dependent on the proceeds of our industy." He snorted, mocking. "I am the best weaver of battle scenes. To be sure," he added, cocking one eyebrow waggishly, "dragons are no longer woven in the fabric as the comrades of heroes. You noticed, of course, the prevalence of growing greens?"

F'lar grimaced his distaste. "That is not all we have noted, either. But Fax keeps the other traditions. . . ."

Lytol waved this consideration aside. "He does that because it is basic military sense. His neighbors armed after he took Ruatha, for he did it by treachery, let me tell you. And let me warn you also"—Lytol jabbed a finger in the direction of the Hold—"he scoffs openly at tales of the Threads. He taunts the harpers for the stupid nonsense of the old ballads and has banned from their repertoire all dragonlore. The new generation will grow up totally ignorant of duty, tradition, and precaution."

F'lar was not surprised to hear that on top of Lytol's other disclosures, although it disturbed him more than anything else he had heard. Other men, too, denied the verbal transmissions of historic events, accounting them no more than the maunderings of harpers. Yet the Red Star pulsed in the sky, and the time was drawing near when they would hysterically re-avow the old allegiances in fear for their very lives.

"Have you been abroad in the early morning of late?" asked F'nor, grinning maliciously.

"I have," Lytol breathed out in a hushed, choked whisper. "I have. . . ." A groan was wrenched from his guts, and he whirled away from the dragonmen, his head bowed between hunched shoulders. "Go," he said, gritting his teeth. And, as they hesitated, he pleaded, *"Go!"*

F'lar walked quickly from the room, followed by F'nor. The bronze rider crossed the quiet dim Hall with long strides and exploded into the startling sunlight. His momentum took him into the center of the square. There he stopped so abruptly that F'nor, hard on his heels, nearly collided with him.

"We will spend exactly the same time within the other Halls," he announced in a tight voice, his face averted from F'nor's eyes. F'lar's throat was constricted. It was difficult suddenly for him to speak. He swallowed hard, several times.

"To be dragonless . . ." murmured F'nor pityingly. The encounter with Lytol had roiled his depths in a mournful way to which he was unaccustomed. That F'lar appeared equally shaken went far to dispel F'nor's private opinion that his half brother was incapable of emotion.

"There is no other way once First Impression has

been made. You know that," F'lar roused himself to
say curtly. He strode off to the Hall bearing the
leather-men's device.

> Honor those the dragons heed,
> In thought and favor, word and deed.
> Worlds are lost or worlds are saved
> From those dangers dragon-braved.
>
> Dragonman, avoid excess;
> Greed will bring the Weyr distress;
> To the ancient Laws adhere,
> Prospers thus the Dragonweyr.

F'LAR WAS amused . . . and unamused. This was
their fourth day in Fax's company, and only F'lar's
firm control on self and wing was keeping the situation from exploding into violence.

It had been a turn of chance, F'lar mused, as Mnementh held his leisurely glide toward the Breast Pass
into Ruatha, that he, F'lar, had chosen the High
Reaches. Fax's tactics would have been successful
with R'gul, who was very conscious of his honor, or
S'lan or D'nol, who were too young to have developed
much patience or discretion. S'lel would have retreated
in confusion, a course nearly as disastrous for the
Weyr as combat.

He should have correlated the indications long ago.
The decay of the Weyr and its influence did not come
solely from the Holding Lords and their folk. It came
also from within the Weyr, a result of inferior queens
and incompetent Weyrwomen. It came from R'gul's

inexplicable insistence on not "bothering" the Holders, on keeping dragonmen within the Weyr. And yet within the Weyr there had been too much emphasis on preparation for the Games until the internal competition between wings had become the be-all and end-all of Weyr activity.

The encroachment of grass had not come overnight, nor had the Lords awakened one morning recently and decided in a flash not to give all their traditional tithe to the Weyr. It had happened gradually and had been allowed, by the Weyr, to continue, until the purpose and reason of the Weyr and dragonkind had reached this low ebb, where an upstart, collateral heir to an ancient Hold could be so contemptuous of dragonmen and the simple basic precautions that kept Pern free of Threads.

F'lar doubted that Fax would have attempted such a program of aggression against neighboring Holds if the Weyr had maintained its old prominence. Each Hold must have its Lord to protect valley and folk from the Threads. One Hold, one Lord—not one Lord claiming seven Holds. That was against ancient tradition, and evil besides, for how well can one man protect seven valleys at once? Man, except for dragonman, can be in only one place at a time. And unless a man was dragon-mounted, it took hours to get from one Hold to another. No Weyrman of old would have permitted such flagrant disregard of ancient ways.

F'lar saw the gouts of flame along the barren heights of the Pass, and Mnementh obediently altered his glide for a better view. F'lar had sent half the wing ahead of the main cavalcade. It was good training for them to skim irregular terrain. He had issued small pieces of firestone with instructions to sear any growths as practice. It would do to remind Fax, as well as his troops, of the awesome ability of dragonkind, a phenomenon the common folk of Pern appeared to have all but forgotten.

The fiery phosphine emissions as the dragons

belched forth gasses showed the pattern well flown. R'gul could argue against the necessity of firestone drills, he could cite such incidents as that which had exiled Lytol, but F'lar kept the tradition—and so did every man who flew with him, or they left the wing. None failed him.

F'lar knew that the men reveled as much as he did in the fierce joy of riding a flaming dragon; the fumes of phosphine were exhilarating in their own way, and the feeling of power that surged through the man who controlled the might and majesty of a dragon had no parallel in human experience. Dragon-riders were forever men apart once First Impression had been made. And to ride a fighting dragon, blue, green, brown, or bronze, was worth the risks, the unending alertness, the isolation from the rest of mankind.

Mnementh dipped his wings obliquely to slide through the narrow cleft of the Pass that led from Crom to Ruatha. No sooner had they emerged from the cut than the difference between the two Holds was patent.

F'lar was stunned. Through the last four Holds he had been sure that the end of the Search lay within Ruatha.

There had been that little brunette whose father was a clothman in Nabol, but . . . And a tall, willowy girl with enormous eyes, the daughter of a minor Warder in Crom, yet . . . These were possibilities, and had F'lar been S'lel or K'net or D'nol, he might have taken the two in as potential mates, although not likely Weyrwomen.

But throughout he had reassured himself that the real choice would be found to the south. Now he gazed on the ruin that was Ruatha, his hopes dispersed. Below him, he saw Fax's banner dip in the sequence that requested his presence.

Mastering the crushing disappointment he felt, he directed Mnementh to descend. Fax, roughly controlling the terrified plunging of his earthbound mount, waved down into the abandoned-looking valley.

"Behold great Ruatha of which you had such hopes," he enjoined sarcastically.

F'lar smiled coolly back, wondering how Fax had divined that. Had F'lar been so transparent when he had suggested Searching the other Holds? Or was it a lucky guess on Fax's part?

"One sees at a glance why goods from the High Reaches are now preferred," F'lar made himself reply. Mnementh rumbled, and F'lar called him sharply to order. The bronze one had developed a distaste bordering on hatred for Fax. Such antipathy in a dragon was most unusual and of no small concern to F'lar. Not that he would have in the least regretted Fax's demise, but not at Mnementh's breath.

"Little good comes from Ruatha," Fax said in a voice that was close to a snarl. He jerked sharply at the bridle of his beast, and fresh blood colored the foam on its muzzle. The creature threw its head backward to ease the painful bar in its mouth, and Fax savagely smote it a blow between the ears. The blow, F'lar observed, was not intended for the poor, protesting beast but for the sight of unproductive Ruatha. "I am the overlord. My proclamation went unchallenged by any of the Blood. I am in my rights. Ruatha must pay its tribute to its legal overlord. . . ."

"And hunger the rest of the year," F'lar remarked dryly, gazing out over the wide valley. Few of its fields were plowed. Its pastures supported meager herds. Even its orchards looked stunted. Blossoms that had been so profuse on trees in Crom, the next valley over, were sparse, as if reluctant to flower in so dismal a place. Although the sun was well up, there seemed to be no activity in the farmholds or none near enough to be observed. The atmosphere was one of sullen despair.

"There has been resistance to my rule of Ruatha."

F'lar shot a look at Fax, for the man's voice was fierce, his face bleak, auguring further unpleasantness for Ruathan rebels. The vindictiveness that colored Fax's attitude toward Ruatha and its rebels was tinged with another strong emotion which F'lar had been unable to identify but which had been very apparent to him from the first time he had adroitly suggested this tour of the Holds. It could not be fear, for Fax was clearly fearless and obnoxiously self-assured. Revulsion? Dread? Uncertainty? F'lar could not label the nature of Fax's compound reluctance to visit Ruatha, but the man had not relished the prospect and now reacted violently to being within these disturbing boundaries.

"How foolish of the Ruathans," F'lar remarked amiably. Fax swung around on him, one hand poised above his sword hilt, eyes blazing. F'lar anticipated with a feeling close to pleasure that the usurper Fax might actually draw on a dragonman! He was almost disappointed when the man controlled himself, took a firm hold on the reins of his mount, and kicked it forward to a frantic run.

"I shall kill him yet," F'lar said to himself, and Mnementh spread his wings in concord.

F'nor dropped beside his bronze leader.

"Did I see him about to draw on you?" F'nor's eyes were bright, his smile acid.

"Until he remembered I was mounted on a dragon."

"Watch him, bronze rider. He means to kill you soon."

"If he can!"

"He's considered a vicious fighter," F'nor advised, his smile gone.

Mnementh flapped his wings again, and F'lar absently stroked the great, soft-skinned neck.

"I am at some disadvantage?" F'lar asked, stung by F'nor's words.

"To my knowledge, no," F'nor said quickly, startled. "I have not seen him in action, but I don't like what I have heard. He kills often, with and without cause."

"And because we dragonmen do not seek blood, we are not to be feared as fighters?" snapped F'lar. "Are you ashamed of being what you were bred?"

"I, no!" F'nor sucked in his breath at the tone of his leader's voice. "And others of our wing, no! But there is that in the attitude of Fax's men that . . . that makes me wish some excuse to fight."

"As you remarked, we will probably have that fight. There is something here in Ruatha that unnerves our noble overlord."

Mnementh and now Canth, F'nor's brown, extended their wings, flapping to catch their riders' attention.

F'lar stared as the dragon slewed his head back toward his rider, the great eyes gleaming like sunstruck opals.

"There is a subtle strength in this valley," F'lar murmured, gathering the import of the dragon's agitated message.

"A strength, indeed; even my brown feels it," F'nor replied, his face lighting.

"Careful, brown rider," F'lar cautioned. "Careful. Send the entire wing aloft. Search this valley. I should have realized. I should have suspected. It was all there to be evaluated. What fools have dragonmen become!"

The Hold is barred,
The Hall is bare,
        And men vanish.
The soil is barren,
The rock is bald.
        All hope banish.

LESSA WAS shoveling ashes from the hearth when the agitated messenger staggered into the Great Hall. She made herself as inconspicuous as possible so the Warder would not dismiss her. She had contrived to be sent to the Great Hall that morning, knowing that the Warder intended to brutalize the head clothman for the shoddy quality of the goods readied for shipment to Fax.

"Fax is coming! With dragonmen!" the man gasped out as he plunged into the dim Great Hall.

The Warder, who had been about to lash the head clothman, turned, stunned, from his victim. The courier, a farmholder from the edge of Ruatha, stumbled up to the Warder, so excited with his message that he grabbed the Warder's arm.

"How dare you leave your Hold?" The Warder aimed his lash at the astonished Holder. The force of the first blow knocked the man from his feet. Yelping, he scrambled out of reach of a second lashing. "Dragonmen indeed! Fax? Ha! He shuns Ruatha. There!"

The Warder punctuated each denial with another blow, kicking the helpless wretch for good measure, before he turned breathless to glare at the clothman and the two underwarders. "How did he get in here with such a threadbare lie?" The Warder stalked to the Great Hall door. It was flung open just as he reached for the iron handle. The ashen-fased guard officer rushed in, nearly knocking the Warder down.

"Dragonmen! Dragons! All over Ruatha!" the man gibbered, arms flailing wildly. He, too, pulled at the Warder's arm, dragging the stupefied official toward the outer courtyard, to bear out the truth of his statement.

Lessa scooped up the last pile of ashes. Picking up her equipment, she slipped out of the Great Hall. There was a very pleased smile on her face under the screen of matted hair.

A dragonman at Ruatha! An opportunity: she must somehow contrive to get Fax so humiliated or so infuriated that he would renounce his claim to the Hold, in the presence of a dragonman. Then she could claim her birthright.

But she would have to be extraordinarily wary. Dragonriders were men apart. Anger did not cloud their intelligence. Greed did not sully their judgment. Fear did not dull their reactions. Let the dense-witted believe human sacrifice, unnatural lusts, insane revels. She was not so gullible. And those stories went against her grain. Dragonmen were still human, and there was Weyr blood in *her* veins. It was the same color blood as that of anyone else; enough of hers had been spilled to prove that.

She halted for a moment, catching a sudden shallow breath. Was this the danger she had sensed four days ago at dawn? The final encounter in her struggle to regain the Hold? No, Lessa cautioned herself, there was more to that portent than revenge.

The ash bucket banged against her shins as she shuffled down the low-ceilinged corridor to the stable door. Fax would find a cold welcome. She had laid no new fire on the hearth. Her laugh echoed back unpleasantly from the damp walls. She rested her bucket and propped her broom and shovel as she wrestled with the heavy bronze door that gave into the new stables.

They had been built outside the cliff of Ruatha by Fax's first Warder, a subtler man than all eight of his successors. He had achieved more than all the others, and Lessa had honestly regretted the necessity of his death. But he would have made her revenge impossible. He would have found her out before she had learned how to camouflage herself and her little interferences. What had his name been? She could not recall. Well, she regretted his death.

The second man had been properly greedy, and it had been easy to set up a pattern of misunderstanding between Warder and craftsmen. That one had been determined to squeeze all profit from Ruathan goods so that some of it would drop into his pocket before Fax suspected a shortage. The craftsmen who had begun to accept the skillful diplomacy of the first Warder bitterly resented the second's grasping, high-handed ways. They resented the passing of the Old Line and, even more so, the way of its passing. They were unforgiving of the insult to Ruatha, its now secondary position in the High Reaches, and they resented the individual indignities that Holders, craftsmen and farmers alike, suffered under the second Warder. It took little manipulation to arrange for matters at Ruatha to go from bad to worse.

The second was replaced and his successor fared no better. He was caught diverting goods—the best of the goods, at that. Fax had had him executed. His bony head still rolled around in the main firepit above the great Tower.

The present incumbent had not been able to maintain the Holding in even the sorry condition in which he had assumed its management. Seemingly simple matters developed rapidly into disasters. Like the production of cloth. Contrary to his boasts to Fax, the quality had not improved, and the quantity had fallen off.

Now Fax was here. And with dragonmen! Why dragonmen? The import of the question froze Lessa, and the heavy door closing behind her barked her heels painfully. Dragonmen used to be frequent visitors at Ruatha—that she knew and even vaguely remembered. Those memories were like a harper's tale, told of someone else, not something within her own experience. She had limited her fierce attention to Ruatha only. She could not even recall the name of queen, or Weyrwoman from the instructions of her childhood, nor could she recall hearing mention of any queen or Weyrwoman by anyone in the Hold these past ten Turns.

Perhaps the dragonmen were finally going to call the Lords of the Holds to task for the disgraceful show of greenery about the Holds. Well, Lessa was to blame for much of that in Ruatha, but she defied even a dragonman to confront her with her guilt. If all Ruatha fell to the Threads, it would be better than remaining dependent to Fax! The heresy shocked Lessa even as she thought it.

Wishing she could as easily unburden her conscience of such blasphemy, she ditched the ashes on the stable midden. There was a sudden change in air pressure around her. Then a fleeting shadow caused her to glance up.

From behind the cliff above glided a dragon, its enormous wings spread to their fullest as he caught the morning updraft. Turning effortlessly, he descended. A second, a third, a full wing of dragons followed in soundless flight and patterned descent, graceful and awesome. The claxon rang belatedly from the Tower, and from within the kitchen there issued the screams and shrieks of the terrified drudges.

Lessa took cover. She ducked into the kitchen where she was instantly seized by the assistant cook and thrust with a buffet and a kick toward the sinks. There she was put to scrubbing the grease-encrusted serving utensils with cleansing sand.

The yelping canines were already lashed to the spitrun, turning a scrawny herdbeast that had been set to roast. The cook was ladling seasonings on the carcass, swearing at having to offer so poor a meal to so many guests, some of them of high rank. Winter-dried fruits from the last scanty harvest had been set to soak, and two of the oldest drudges were scraping roots to be boiled.

An apprentice cook was kneading bread and another carefully spicing a sauce. Looking fixedly at him, Lessa diverted his hand from one spice box to a less appropriate one as he gave a final shake to the concoction. She innocently added too much wood to the wall oven to insure the ruin of the breads. She controlled the canines deftly, slowing one and speeding the other so that the meat would be underdone on one side, burned on the other. That the feast should result in fast, with the food presented found inedible, was her whole intention.

Above, in the Hold, she had no doubt that certain other measures, undertaken at different times for this exact contingency, were being discovered.

Her fingers bloodied from a beating, one of the Warder's women came shrieking into the kitchen, hopeful of refuge there.

"Insects have eaten the best blankets to shreds! And a canine who had littered on the best linens snarled at me as she gave such. And the rushes are noxious, and the best chambers full of debris driven in by the winter wind. Somebody left the shutters ajar. Just a tiny bit, but it was enough," the woman wailed, clutching her hand to her breast and rocking back and forth.

Lessa bent with great industry to shine the plates.

Watch-wher, watch-wher,
In your lair,
Watch well, watch-wher!
Who goes there?

"THE WATCH-WHER is hiding something," F'lar told F'nor as they consulted in the hastily cleaned great chamber. The room delighted to hold the wintry chill, although a generous fire now burned on the hearth.

"It was but gibbering when Canth spoke to it," F'nor remarked. He was leaning against the mantel, turning slightly from side to side to gather some warmth. He watched his wingleader's impatient pacing.

"Mnementh is calming it down," F'lar replied. "He may be able to sort out the nightmare. The creature may be more senile than sane, but . . ."

"I doubt it," F'nor concurred helpfully. He glanced with apprehension up at the web-hung ceiling. He was certain he'd found most of the crawlers, but he didn't fancy their sting. Not on top of the discomforts already experienced in this forsaken Hold. If the night stayed mild, he intended curling up with Canth on the heights. "That would be a more reasonable suggestion than Fax or his Warder have made."

"Hmmm," F'lar muttered, frowning at the brown rider.

"Well, it's unbelievable that Ruatha could have fallen to such disrepair in ten short Turns. Every dragon caught the feeling of power, and it's obvious the watch-wher has been tampered with. That takes a good deal of control."

"From someone of the Blood," F'lar reminded him.

F'nor shot his wingleader a quick look, wondering if he could possibly be serious in the light of all information to the contrary.

"I grant you there is power here, F'lar," F'nor conceded. "But it could as easily be a hidden male bastard of the old Blood. And we need a female. But Fax made it plain, in his inimitable fashion, that he left none of the old Blood alive in the Hold the day he took it. Ladies, children, all. No, no." The brown rider shook his head, as if he could dispel the lack of faith in his wingleader's curious insistence that the Search would end in Ruath with Ruathan blood.

"That watch-wher is hiding something, and only someone of the Blood of its Hold can arrange that, brown rider," F'lar said emphatically. He gestured around the room and toward the window. "Ruatha has been overcome. But she resists . . . subtly. I say it points to the old Blood *and* power. Not power alone."

The obstinate expression in F'lar's eyes, the set of his jaw, suggested that F'nor seek another topic.

"I'll see what may be seen around fallen Ruatha," he mumbled and left the chamber.

F'lar was heartily bored with the lady Fax had so courteously assigned him. She giggled incessantly and sneezed constantly. She waved about, but did not apply to her nose, a scarf or handkerchief long overdue for a thorough washing. A sour odor, compounded of sweat, sweet oil, and rancid food smells, exuded from her. She was also pregnant by Fax. Not obviously so, but she had confided her condition to F'lar, either oblivious to the insult to the dragonman or directed by her Lord to let drop the information. F'lar deliberately ignored the matter and, except when her company was obligatory on this Search journey, had ignored her, too.

Lady Tela was nervously jabbering away at him about the terrible condition of the rooms to which Lady Gemma and the other ladies of the Lord's procession had been assigned.

"The shutters, both sets, were ajar all winter long, and you should have seen the trash on the floors. We finally got two of the drudges to sweep it all into the fireplace. And then that smoked something fearful till a man was sent up." Lady Tela giggled. "He found the access blocked by a chimney stone fallen aslant. The rest of the chimney, for a wonder, was in good repair."

She waved her handkerchief. F'lar held his breath as the gesture wafted an unappealing odor in his direction.

He glanced up the Hall toward the inner Hold door and saw the Lady Gemma descending, her steps slow and awkward. Some subtle difference about her gait attracted him, and he stared at her, trying to identify it.

"Oh, yes, poor Lady Gemma," Lady Tela babbled, sighing deeply. "We are so concerned. Why my Lord Fax insisted on her coming I do not know. She is not near her time, and yet . . ." The lighthead's concern sounded sincere.

F'lar's incipient hatred for Fax and his brutality matured abruptly. He left his partner chattering to thin air and courteously extended his arm to the Lady Gemma to support her down the steps and to the table. Only the brief tightening of her fingers on his forearm betrayed her gratitude. Her face was very white and drawn, the lines deeply etched around mouth and eyes, showing the effort she was expending.

"Some attempt has been made, I see, to restore order to the Hall," she remarked in a conversational tone.

"Some," F'lar admitted dryly, glancing around the grandly proportioned Hall, its rafters festooned with

the webs of many Turns. The inhabitants of those
gossamer nests dropped from time to time, with ripe
splats, to the floor, onto the table, and into the serving
platters. Nothing replaced the old banners of the
Ruathan Blood, removed from the stark brown stone
walls. Fresh rushes did obscure the greasy flagstones.
The trestle tables appeared recently sanded and
scraped, and the platters gleamed dully in the re-
freshed glows. Those unfortunately, were a mistake,
for brightness was much too unflattering to a scene
that would have been more reassuring in dimmer light.

"This was such a graceful Hall," the Lady Gemma
murmured for F'lar's ears alone.

"You were a friend?" he asked politely.

"Yes, in my youth." Her voice dropped expressively
on the last word, evoking for F'lar a happier girlhood.
"It was a noble line!"

"Think you *one* might have escaped the sword?"

The Lady Gemma flashed him a startled look, then
quickly composed her features, lest the exchange be
noted. She gave a barely perceptible shake of her
head and then shifted her awkward weight to take her
place at the table. Graciously she inclined her head
toward F'lar, both dismissing and thanking him.

He returned to his own partner and placed her at
the table on his left. As the only persons of rank who
would dine that night at Ruatha Hold, Lady Gemma
was seated on his right; Fax would be beyond her.
The dragonmen and Fax's upper soldiery would sit at
the lower tables. No guildmen had been invited to
Ruatha.

Fax arrived just then with his current lady and two
underleaders, the Warder bowing them effusively into
the Hall. The man, F'lar noticed, kept a good distance
from his overlord—as well a Warder might whose responsibility was in this sorry condition. F'lar flicked a
crawler away. Out of the corner of his eye he saw the
Lady Gemma wince and shudder.

Fax stamped up to the raised table, his face black
with suppressed rage. He pulled back his chair

roughly, slamming it into the Lady Gemma's before he seated himself. He pulled the chair to the table with a force that threatened to rock the none too stable trestle-top from its supporting legs. Scowling, he inspected his goblet and plate, fingering the surface, ready to throw them aside if they displeased him.

"A roast, my Lord Fax, and fresh bread, Lord Fax, and such fruits and roots as are left."

"Left? Left? You said there was nothing harvested here."

The Warder's eyes bulged and he gulped, stammering, "Nothing to be sent on. Nothing *good* enough to be sent on. Nothing. Had I but known of your arrival, I could have sent to Crom . . ."

"Sent ot Crom?" roared Fax, slaming the plate he was inspecting onto the table so forcefully that the rim bent under his hands. The Warder winced again as if he himself had been maimed.

"For decent foodstuffs, my Lord," he quavered.

"The day one of my Holds cannot support itself *or* the visit of its rightful overlord, I shall renounce it."

The Lady Gemma gasped. Simultaneously the dragons roared. F'lar felt the unmistakable surge of power. His eyes instinctively sought F'nor at the lower table. The brown rider, all the dragonmen, had experienced that inexplicable shaft of exultation.

"What's wrong, dragonman?" snapped Fax.

F'lar, affecting unconcern, stretched his legs under the table and assumed an indolent posture in the heavy chair.

"Wrong?"

"The dragons!"

"Oh, nothing. They often roar . . . at the sunset, at a flock of passing wherries, at mealtimes," and F'lar smiled amiably at the Lord of the High Reaches. Beside him his tablemate gave a little squeak.

"Mealtimes? Have they not been fed?"

"Oh, yes. Five days ago."

"Oh. Five . . . days ago? And are they hungry . . .

now?" Her voice trailed into a whisper of fear, her eyes grew round.

"In a few days," F'lar assured her. Under cover of his detached amusement, F'lar scanned the Hall. That surge had come from nearby. Either in the Hall or just without it. It must have been from within. It came so soon upon Fax's speech that his words must have triggered it. F'lar saw that F'nor and the other dragonmen were surreptitiously searching every face in the Hall. Fax's soldiers could be disqualified, and the Warder's men. And the power had an indefinably feminine touch to it.

One of Fax's women? F'lar found that hard to credit. Mnementh had been close to all of them, and none had shown a vestige of power, much less—with the exception of Lady Gemma—any intelligence.

One of the Hall women? So far he had seen only the sorry drudges and the aging females the Warder had as housekeepers. The Warder's personal woman? He must discover if that man had one. One of the Hold guards' women? F'lar suppressed an intense desire to rise and search.

"You mount a guard?" he asked Fax casually.

"Double at Ruath Hold!" he was told in a tight, hard voice, ground out from somewhere deep in Fax's chest.

"Here?" F'lar all but laughed out loud, gesturing around the sadly appointed chamber.

"Here!" Fax changed the subject with a roar. "Food!"

Five drudges, two of them women in such grimy brown-gray rags that F'lar hoped they had had nothing to do with the preparation of the meal, staggered in under the emplattered herdbeast. No one with so much as a trace of power would sink to such depths, unless . . .

The aroma that reached him as the platter was placed on the serving table distracted him. It reeked of singed bone and charred meat. Even the pitcher of *klah* being passed smelled bad. The Warder frantically sharpened his tools as if a keen edge could somehow slice acceptable portions from this unlikely carcass.

The Lady Gemma caught her breath again, and F'lar saw her hands curl tightly around the armrests. He saw the convulsive movement of her throat as she swallowed. He, too, did not look forward to this repast.

The drudges reappeared with wooden trays of bread. Burnt crusts had been scraped and cut, in some places, from the loaves before serving. As other trays were borne in, F'lar tried to catch sight of the faces of the servitors. Matted hair obscured the face of the one who presented Lady Gemma with a dish of legumes swimming in greasy liquid. Revolted, F'lar poked through the legumes to find properly cooked portions to offer Lady Gemma. She waved them aside, her face ill concealing her discomfort.

As F'lar was about to turn and serve Lady Tela, he saw Lady Gemma's hand clutch convulsively at the chair arms. He realized then that she was not merely nauseated by the unappetizing food. She was seized with the onslaught of labor contractions.

F'lar glanced in Fax's direction. The overlord was scowling blackly at the attempts of the Warder to find edible portions of meat to serve.

F'lar touched Lady Gemma's arms with light fingers. She turned her face just enough so that she could see F'lar out of the corner of her eye. She managed a socially correct half-smile.

"I dare not leave just now, Lord F'lar. He is always dangerous at Ruatha. And it may only be false pangs . . . at my age."

F'lar was dubious as he saw another shudder pass through her frame. The woman would have been a fine Weyrwoman, he thought ruefully, if she were younger.

The Warder, his hands shaking, presented Fax the sliced meats, slivers of overdone flesh, portions of almost edible meats, but not much of either.

One furious wave of Fax's broad fist and the
Warder had the plate, meats and juice, square in the
face. Despite himself, F'lar sighed, for those undoubtedly constituted the only edible portions of the
entire beast.

"You call this food? *You call this food?*" Fax bellowed. His voice boomed back from the bare vault of
the ceiling, shaking crawlers from their webs as the
sound shattered the fragile strands. *"Slop! Slop!"*

F'lar rapidly brushed crawlers from the Lady
Gemma, who was helpless in the throes of a very
strong contraction.

"It's all we had on such short notice," the
Warder squealed, bloody juices streaking down his
cheeks. Fax threw the goblet at him, and the wine
went streaming down the man's chest. The steaming
dish of roots followed, and the man yelped as the hot
liquid splashed over him.

"My Lord, my Lord, had I but known!"

"Obviously, Ruatha can*not* support the visit of its
Lord. You must renounce it," F'lar heard himself
saying.

His shock at such words issuing from his mouth was
as great as that of everyone else in the Hall. Silence
fell, broken by the splat of crawlers and the drip of
root liquid from the Warder's shoulders to the rushes.
The grating of Fax's boot heel was clearly audible as
he swung slowly around to face the bronze rider.

As F'lar conquered his own amazement and rapidly
tried to predict what to do next to mend matters, he
saw F'nor rise slowly to his feet, hand on dagger hilt.

"I did not hear you correctly?" Fax asked, his face
blank of all expression, his eyes snapping.

Unable to comprehend how he could have uttered
such an arrant challenge, F'lar managed to assume a
languid pose.

"You did mention, my Lord," he drawled, "that if
any of your Holds could not support itself and the
visit of its rightful overlord, you would renounce it."

Fax stared back at F'lar, his face a study of swiftly

suppressed emotions, the glint of triumph dominant. F'lar, his face stiff with the forced expression of indifference, was casting swiftly about in his mind. In the name of the Egg, had he lost all sense of discretion?

Pretending utter unconcern, he stabbed some vegetables onto his knife and began to munch on them. As he did so, he noticed F'nor glancing slowly around the Hall, scrutinizing everyone. Abruptly F'lar realized what had happened. Somehow, in making that statement, he, a dragonman, had responded to a covert use of the power. F'lar, the bronze rider, was being put into a position where he would *have* to fight Fax. Why? For what end? To get Fax to renounce the Hold? Incredible! But there could be only one possible reason for such a turn of events. An exultation as sharp as pain swelled within F'lar. It was all he could do to maintain his pose of bored indifference, all he could do to turn his attention to thwarting Fax, should he press for a duel. A duel would serve no purpose. He, F'lar, had no time to waste on it.

A groan escaped Lady Gemma and broke the eye-locked stance of the two antagonists. Irritated, Fax looked down at her, fist clenched and half-raised to strike her for her temerity at interrupting her lord and master. The contraction that rippled across the swollen belly was as obvious as the woman's pain. F'lar dared not look toward her, but he wondered if she had deliberately groaned aloud to break the tension.

Incredibly, Fax began to laugh. He threw back his head, showing big, stained teeth, and roared.

"Aye, renounce it, in favor of her issue, if it is male . . . and lives!" he crowed, laughing raucously.

"Heard and witnessed!" F'lar snapped, jumping to his feet and pointing to his riders. They were on their feet in an instant. "Heard and witnessed!" they averred in the traditional manner.

With that movement, everyone began to babble at once in nervous relief. The other women, each reacting in her way to the imminence of birth, called orders

to the servants and advice to each other. They converged toward the Lady Gemma, hovering un-
decidedly out of Fax's range like silly wherries
disturbed from their roosts. It was obvious they were
torn between their fear of their Lord and their desire
to reach the laboring woman.

He gathered their intentions as well as their reluctance and, still stridently laughing, knocked back his
chair. He stepped over it, strode down to the meat
stand and stood hacking off pieces with his knife,
stuffing them, juice dripping, into his mouth without
ceasing to guffaw.

As F'lar bent toward the Lady Gemma to assist her
out of her chair, she grabbed his arm urgently. Their
eyes met, hers clouded with pain. She pulled him
closer.

"He means to kill you, bronze rider. He loves to
kill," she whispered.

"Dragonmen are not easily killed, brave lady. I
am grateful to you."

"I do not want you killed," she said softly, biting at
her lip. "We have so few bronze riders."

F'lar stared at her, startled. Did she, Fax's lady,
actually believe in the Old Laws? He beckoned to
two of the Warder's men to carry her up into the
Hold. He caught Lady Tela by the arm as she fluttered past him in their wake.

"What do you need?"

"Oh, oh," she exclaimed, her face twisted with
panic; she was distractedly wringing her hands. "Water, hot, clean. Cloths. And a birthing-woman. Oh,
yes, we must have a birthing-woman."

F'lar looked about for one of the Hold women, his
glance sliding over the first disreputable figure who
had started to mop up the spilled food. He signaled
instead for the Warder and peremptorily ordered him
to send for the birthing-woman. The Warder kicked
at the drudge on the floor.

"You . . . you! Whatever your name is, go get her
from the crafthold. You must know who she is."

With a nimbleness at odds with her appearance of extreme age and decrepitude, the drudge evaded the parting kick the Warder aimed in her direction. She scurried across the Hall and out the kitchen door.

Fax sliced and speared meat, occasionally bursting out with a louder bark of laughter as his thoughts amused him. F'lar sauntered down to the carcass and, without waiting for invitation from his host, began to carve neat slices also, beckoning his men over. Fax's soldiers, however, waited till their Lord had eaten his fill.

Lord of the Hold, your charge is sure
In thick walls, metal doors, and no verdure.

LESSA SPED from the Hall to find the crafthold birthing-woman, her mind seething with frustration. So close! So close! How could she come so close and yet fail? Fax should have challenged the dragonman. And the dragonman was strong and young, his face that of a fighter, stern and controlled. He should not have temporized. Was all honor dead in Pern, smothered by green grass?

And why, oh, why, had the Lady Gemma chosen

that precious moment to go into labor? If her groan hadn't distracted Fax, the fight would have begun, and not even Fax, for all his vaunted prowess as a vicious fighter, would have prevailed against a dragonman who had Lessa's support. The Hold must be secured to its rightful Blood again. Fax would not leave Ruatha alive!

Above her, on the High Tower, the great bronze dragon gave forth a weird croon, his many-faceted eyes sparkling in the gathering darkness.

Unconsciously she silenced him as she would have done the watch-wher. Ah, that watch-wher. He had not come out of his den at her passing. She knew the dragons had been at him. She could hear him gibbering in his panic. They'd drive him to his death.

The slant of the road toward the crafthold lent impetus to her flying feet, and she had to brace herself to a sliding stop at the birthing-woman's stone threshold. She banged on the closed door and heard the frightened exclamation of surprise within.

"A birth. A birth at the Hold," Lessa cried in time to her thumping.

"A birth?" came the muffled cry, and the latches were thrown up on the door. "At the Hold?"

"Fax's lady and, as you love life, hurry, for if it is male, it will be Ruatha's own Lord."

That ought to fetch her, thought Lessa, and in that instant the door was flung open by the man of the house. Lessa could see the birthing-woman gathering up her things in haste, piling them into her shawl. Lessa hurried the woman out, up the steep road to the Hold, under the Tower gate, grabbing the woman as she tried to run at the sight of a dragon peering down at her. Lessa drew her into the Court and pushed her, resisting, into the Hall.

The woman clutched at the inner door, balking at the sight of the gathering there. Lord Fax, his feet up on the trestle table, was paring his fingernails with his knife blade, still chuckling. The dragonmen in their wher-hide tunics, were eating quietly at one table while the soldiers were having their turn at the meat.

The bronze rider noticed their entrance and pointed urgently toward the inner Hold. The birthing-woman seemed frozen to the spot. Lessa tugged futilely at her arm, urging her to cross the Hall. To her surprise, the bronze rider strode to them.

"Go quickly, woman, Lady Gemma is before her time," he said, frowning with concern, gesturing imperatively toward the Hold entrance. He caught her by the shoulder and led her, all unwilling, toward the steps, Lessa tugging away at her other arm.

When they reached the stairs, he relinquished his grip, nodding to Lessa to escort her the rest of the way. Just as they reached the massive inner door, Lessa noticed how sharply the dragonman was looking at them. At her hand on the birthing-woman's arm. Warily, she glanced at her hand and saw it, as if it belonged to a stranger—the long fingers, shapely despite dirt and broken nails, a small hand, delicately boned, gracefully placed despite the urgency of the grip. She blurred it.

The Lady Gemma was indeed in hard labor, and all was not well. When Lessa tried to retire from the room, the birthing-woman shot her such a terrified glance that Lessa reluctantly remained. It was obvious that Fax's other ladies were of no use. They were huddled at one side of the high bed, wringing their hands and talking in shrill, excited tones. It remained to Lessa and the birthing-woman to remove Gemma's clothing, to ease her and hold her hands against the contractions.

There was little left of beauty in the gravid woman's face. She was perspiring heavily, her skin tinged with gray. Her breath was sharp and rasping, and she bit her lips against outcry.

"This is not going well," the birthing-woman muttered under her breath. "You there, stop your sniveling," she ordered, swinging around to point at one of the gaggle. She lost her indecision as the requirements of her calling gave her temporary authority over those of rank. "Bring me hot water. Hand those cloths over. Find something warm for the babe. If it is born alive, it must be kept from drafts and chill."

Reassured by her tyranny, the women stopped their whimpering and did her bidding.

If it survives, the words echoed in Lessa's mind. *Survives to be Lord of Ruatha. One of Fax's get?* That had not been her intention, although . . .

The Lady Gemma grabbed blindly for Lessa's hands, and despite herself, Lessa responded with such comfort as a strong grip would afford the woman.

"She bleeds too much," the birthing-woman muttered. "More cloths."

The women resumed their wailing, uttering little shrieks of fear and protestation.

"She should not have been made to journey so far."

"They will both die."

"Oh, it *is* too much blood."

Too much blood, thought Lessa. *I have no quarrel with her. And the child comes too early. It will die.* She looked down at the contorted face, the bloodied lower lip. *If she does not cry out now, why did she then?* Fury swept through Lessa. This woman had, for some obscure reason, deliberately diverted Fax and F'lar at the crucial moment. She all but crushed Gemma's hands in hers.

Pain from such an unexpected quarter roused Gemma from her brief respite between the shuddering contractions that seized her at shorter and shorter intervals. Blinking sweat from her eyes, she focused desperately on Lessa's face.

"What have I done to you?" she gasped.

"Done? I had Ruatha almost within my grasp again when you uttered your false cry," Lessa said, her head bent so that not even the birthing-woman at the foot of the bed could hear them. She was so angry that she had lost all discretion, but it would not matter, for this woman was close to death.

The Lady Gemma's eyes widened. "But . . . the dragonman . . . Fax cannot kill the dragonman. There

are so few bronze riders. They are all needed. And
the old tales . . . the star . . . star . . ." She could not
continue, for a massive contraction shook her. The
heavy rings on her fingers bit into Lessa's hands as
she clung to the girl.

"What do you mean?" Lessa demanded in a hoarse
whisper.

But the woman's agony was so intense that she
could scarcely breathe. Her eyes seemed to start from
her head. Lessa, hardened though she had become to
all emotion save that of revenge, was shocked to the
deeper feminine instinct of easing a woman's pain in
her extremity. Even so, the Lady Gemma's words
rang through her mind. The woman had not, then,
protected Fax, but the dragonman. The star? Did she
mean the Red Star? Which old tales?

The birthing-woman had both hands on Gemma's
belly, pressing downward, chanting advice to a
woman too far gone in pain to hear. The twisting body
gave a convulsive heave, lifting from the bed. As
Lessa tried to support her, Lady Gemma opened her
eyes wide, her expression one of incredulous relief.
She collapsed into Lessa's arms and lay still.

"She's dead!" shrieked one of the women. She flew,
screaming, from the chamber. Her voice reverberated
down the rock halls. "Dead . . . ead . . . ead . . .
ddddd," echoed back to the dazed women, who stood
motionless in shock.

Lessa laid the woman down on the bed, staring
amazed at the oddly triumphant smile on Gemma's
face. She retreated into the shadows, far more shaken
than anyone else. She who had never hesitated to do
anything that would thwart Fax or beggar Ruatha
further was trembling with remorse. She had forgotten
in her single-mindedness that there might be others
motivated by a hatred of Fax. The Lady Gemma was
one, and one who had suffered far more subjective
brutalities and indignities than Lessa had. Yet Lessa
had hated Gemma, had poured out that hatred on a

woman who had deserved her respect and support rather than her condemnation.

Lessa shook her head to dispel the aura of tragedy and self-revulsion that threatened to overwhelm her. She had no time for regret or contrition. Not now. Not when, by affecting Fax's death, she could avenge not only her own wrongs but Gemma's!

That was it. And she had the lever. The child . . . yes, the child. She'd say it lived. That it was male. The dragonman would have to fight. He had heard and witnessed Fax's oath.

A smile, not unlike the one on the dead woman's face, crossed Lessa's as she hurried down the corridors to the Hall.

She was about to dash into the Hall itself when she realized she had permitted her anticipation of triumph to destroy her self-discipline. Lessa halted at the portal, deliberately took a deep breath. She dropped her shoulders and stepped down, once more the colorless drudge.

The harbinger of death was sobbing in a heap at Fax's feet.

Lessa gritted her teeth against redoubled hatred for the overlord. He was glad the Lady Gemma had died, birthing his seed. Even now he was ordering the hysterical woman to go tell his latest favorite to attend him, doubtless to install her as his first lady.

"The child lives," Lessa cried, her voice distorted with anger and hatred. "It is male."

Fax was on his feet, kicking aside the weeping woman, scowling viciously at Lessa. "What are you saying, woman?"

"The child lives. It is male," she repeated, descending. The incredulity and rage that suffused Fax's face was wonderful to see. The Warder's men stifled their minadvertent cheers.

"Ruatha has a new Lord." The dragons roared.

So intent was she on achieving her purpose that she failed to notice the reactions of others in the hall, failed to hear the roaring of the dragons without.

Fax erupted into action. He leaped across the intervening space, bellowing denials of the news. Before Lessa could dodge, his fist crashed down across her face. She was swept off her feet, off the steps, and fell heavily to the stone floor, where she lay motionless, a bundle of dirty rags.

"Hold, Fax!" F'lar's voice cut across the silence as the Lord of the High Reaches lifted his leg to kick the unconscious body.

Fax whirled, his hand automatically closing on his knife hilt.

"It was heard and witnessed, Fax," F'lar cautioned him, one hand outstretched in warning, "by dragonmen. Stand by your sworn and witnessed oath!"

"Witnessed? By dragonmen?" cried Fax with a derisive laugh. "Dragonwomen, you mean," he sneered, his eyes blazing with contempt, one sweeping gesture of scorn dismissing them all.

He was momentarily taken aback by the speed with which the bronze rider's knife appeared in his hand.

"Dragonwomen?" F'lar queried, his lips curling back over his teeth, his voice dangerously soft. Glowlight flickered off his circling blade as he advanced on Fax.

"Women! Parasites on Pern. The Weyr power is over! Over for good," roared Fax, leaping forward to land in a combat crouch.

The two antagonists were dimly aware of the scurry behind them, of tables pulled roughly aside to give the duelists space. F'lar could spare no glance at the crumpled form of the drudge, yet he was sure, through and beyond instinct sure, that she was the source of power. He had felt it as she entered the room. The dragons' roaring confirmed it. If that fall had killed her . . . He advanced on Fax, leaping away to avoid the slashing blade as Fax unwound from the crouch with a powerful lunge.

F'lar evaded the attack easily, noticing his opponent's reach, deciding he had a slight advantage there. He told himself sternly that wasn't much advantage.

Fax had had much more actual hand-to-hand killing experience than had he whose duels had always ended at first blood on the practice floor. F'lar made due note to avoid closing with the burly Lord. The man was heavy-chested, dangerous from sheer mass. F'lar must use agility as a weapon, not brute strength.

Fax feinted, testing F'lar for weakness or indiscretion. The two crouched, facing each other across six feet of space, knife hands weaving, their free hands, spread-fingered, ready to grab.

Again Fax pressed the attack. F'lar allowed him to close, just close enough to dodge away with a backhanded swipe. He felt fabric tear under the tip of his knife and heard Fax's snarl. The overlord was faster on his feet than his bulk suggested, and F'lar had to dodge a second time, feeling the scoring of Fax's knife across his heavy wher-hide jerkin.

Grimly the two circled, looking for an opening in each other's defense. Fax plowed in, trying to turn his weight and mass to advantage against the lighter, faster man by cornering him between raised platform and wall.

F'lar countered, ducking low under Fax's flailing arm, slashing obliquely across Fax's side. The overlord caught at him, yanking savagely, and F'lar was trapped against the other man's side, straining desperately with his left hand to keep the knife arm up. F'lar brought up his knee, timing a sudden collapse with that blow. He ducked away as Fax gasped and buckled from the pain in his groin. F'lar danced away, sudden fire in his left shoulder witness that he had not escaped unscathed.

Fax's face was red with bloody anger, and he wheezed from pain and shock. But F'lar had no time to follow up the momentary advantage, for the infuriated Lord straightened up and charged. F'lar was forced to sidestep quickly before Fax could close with him. F'lar put the meat table between them, circling warily, flexing his shoulder to assess the extent of his injury. The slash felt as if it had been scored by a brand. Motion was painful, but the arm could be used.

Suddenly Fax seized up a handful of fatty scraps from the meat tray and hurled them at F'lar. The dragonman ducked, and Fax closed the distance around the table with a rush. Instinct prompted F'lar to leap sideways as Fax's flashing blade came within inches of his abdomen. His own knife sliced down the outside of Fax's arm. Instantly the two pivoted to face each other again, but Fax's left arm hung limply at his side.

F'lar darted in, pressing his luck as the Lord of the High Reaches staggered. But F'lar misjudged the man's condition and suffered a terrific kick in the side as he tried to dodge under the feinting knife. Doubled with pain, F'lar rolled frantically away from his charging adversary. Fax was lurching forward, trying to fall on him, to pin the lighter dragonman down for a final thrust. F'lar somehow got to his feet, attempting to straighten up to meet Fax's stumbling charge. His very position saved him. Fax overreached his mark and staggered off balance. F'lar brought his right hand over with as much strength as he could muster, and his knife blade plunged through Fax's unprotected back until he felt the point stick in the chest plate.

The defeated Lord fell flat to the flagstones, the force of his descent dislodging the dagger from his chest bone so that an inch of the bloody blade reemerged from the point of entry.

A thin wailing penetrated the haze of pain and relief. F'lar looked up and saw, through sweat-blurred eyes, women crowding in the Hold doorway. One held a closely swathed object in her arms. F'lar could not immediately grasp the significance of that tableau, but he knew it was very important to clear his thoughts.

He stared down at the dead man. There was no pleasure in killing the man, he realized, only relief that he himself was still alive. He wiped his forehead

on his sleeve and forced himself erect, his side throbbing with the pain of that last kick and his left shoulder burning. He half-stumbled to the drudge, still
sprawled where she had fallen.

He gently turned her over, noting the terrible bruise
spreading across her cheek under the dirty skin. He
heard F'nor take command of the tumult in the Hall.

The dragonman laid a hand, trembling in spite of
an effort to control himself, on the woman's breast to
feel for a heartbeat. . . . It was there, slow but strong.

A deep sigh escaped him, for either blow or fall
could have proved fatal. Fatal, perhaps, for Pern as
well.

Relief was colored with disgust. There was no telling under the filth how old this creature might be.
He raised her to his arms, her light body no burden
even to his battle-weary strength. Knowing F'nor
would handle any trouble efficiently, F'lar carried the
drudge to his own chamber.

He put the body on the high bed, then stirred up
the fire and added more glows to the bedside bracket.
His gorge rose at the thought of touching the filthy
mat of hair, but nonetheless and gently, he pushed it
back from the face, turning the head this way and
that. The features were small, regular. One arm, clear
of rags, was reasonably clean above the elbow but
marred by bruises and old scars. The skin was firm
and unwrinkled. The hands, when he took them in
his, were dirt-encrusted but all the same, well-shaped
and delicately boned.

F'lar began to smile. Yes, she had blurred that
hand so skillfully that he had actually doubted what
he had first seen. And yes, beneath grime and grease,
she was young. Young enough for the Weyr. And no
born drab. She was not young enough, happily, to be
Fax's seed. One of the previous Lords' by-blows? No,
there was no taint of common blood here. It was pure,
no matter whose line, and he rather thought she was
indeed Ruathan. One who had by some unknown
agency escaped the massacre ten Turns ago and bided

her time for revenge. Why else force Fax to renounce the Hold?

Delighted and fascinated by this unexpected luck, F'lar reached out to tear the dress from the unconscious body and found himself constrained not to. The girl had roused. Her great, hungry eyes fastened on his, not fearful or expectant; wary.

A subtle change occurred in her face. F'lar watched, his smile deepening, as she shifted her regular features into an illusion of disagreeable ugliness.

"Trying to confuse a dragonman, girl?" he chuckled. He made no further move to touch her but settled against the great carved post of the bed. He crossed his arms on his chest and then shifted suddenly to ease his sore arm.

"Your name, girl, and rank."

She drew herself upright slowly, her features no longer blurred. Deliberately she slid back against the headboard so they faced each other across the length of the high bed.

"Fax?"

"Dead. Your name!"

A look of exulting triumph flooded her face. She slipped from the bed, standing unexpectedly tall. "Then I reclaim my own. I am of the Ruathan Blood. I claim Ruath," she announced in a ringing voice.

F'lar stared at her a moment, delighted with her proud bearing. Then he threw back his head and laughed.

"This? This crumbling heap?" He could not help but mock the disparity of her manner and her dress. "Oh, no. Besides, fair lady, we dragonmen heard and witnessed Fax's oath renouncing the Hold in favor of his heir. Shall I challenge the babe, too, for you? And choke him with his swaddling clothes?"

Her eyes flashed, her lips parted in a terrible smile.

"There is no heir. Gemma died, the babe unborn. I lied."

"Lied?" F'lar demanded, angry.

"Yes," she taunted him with a toss of her chin. "I lied. There was no babe born. I merely wanted to be sure you challenged Fax."

He grabbed her wrist, stung that he had twice fallen to her prodding.

"You provoked a dragonman to fight? To kill? *When he is on Search?*"

"Search? What should I care for a Search? I have Ruatha as my Hold again. For ten Turns I have worked and waited, schemed and suffered for that. What could your Search mean to me?"

F'lar wanted to strike that look of haughty contempt from her face. He twisted her arm savagely, bringing her to his feet before he released his pressure. She laughed at him and had scuttled to one side and was on her feet and out the door before he could realize what she was about and give chase.

Swearing to himself, he raced down the rocky corridors, knowing she would have to make for the Hall to get out of the Hold. However, when he reached the Hall, there was no sign of her fleeing figure among those still loitering there.

"Has that creature come this way?" he called to F'nor, who was, by chance, standing by the door to the Court.

"No. Is she the source of power, after all?"

"Yes, she is," F'lar answered, galled all the more by her escape. Where had she gone to? "And of the Ruathan Blood, at that!"

"Oh-ho! Does she depose the babe, then?" F'nor asked, gesturing toward the birthing-woman who occupied a seat close to the now blazing hearth.

F'lar paused, about to return to search the Hold's myriad passages. He stared, momentarily confused, at his brown rider.

"Babe? What babe?"

"The male child Lady Gemma bore," F'nor replied, surprised by F'lar's uncomprehending look.

"It lives?"

"Yes. A strong babe, the woman says, for all that

he was premature and taken forcibly from the dead dame's belly."

F'lar threw back his head with a shout of laughter. For all her scheming, she had been outdone by Truth.

At that moment he heard the unmistakable elation in Mnementh's roar, followed by the curious warble of the other dragons.

"Mnementh has caught her," F'lar cried, grinning with jubilation. He strode down the steps, past the body of the former Lord of the High Reaches and out into the main court.

He saw the bronze dragon was gone from his Tower perch and called him. An agitation drew his eyes upward. He saw Mnementh spiraling down into the Court, his front paws clasping something. Mnementh informed F'lar that he had seen her climbing from one of the high windows and had simply plucked her from the ledge, knowing the dragonman sought her. The bronze dragon settled awkwardly onto his hind legs, his wings working to keep him balanced. Carefully he set the girl on her feet and carefully he formed a cage around her with his huge talons. She stood motionless within that circle, her face turned toward the wedge-shaped head that swayed above her.

The watch-wher, shrieking terror, anger, and hatred, was lunging violently to the end of its chain, trying to come to Lessa's aid. It grabbed at F'lar as he strode to the two.

"You've courage enough to fly with, girl," he admitted, resting one hand casually on Mnementh's upper claw. Mnementh was enormously pleased with himself and swiveled his head down for his eye ridges to be scratched.

"You did not lie, you know," F'lar said, unable to resist taunting the girl.

Slowly she turned toward him, her face impassive. She was not afraid of dragons, F'lar realized with approval.

"The babe lives. And it is male."

She could not control her dismay, and her shoulders sagged briefly before she pulled herself erect again.

"Ruatha is mine," she insisted in a tense, low voice.

"Aye, and it would have been had you approached me directly when the wing arrived here."

Her eyes widened. "What do you mean?"

"A dragonman may champion anyone whose grievance is just. By the time we reached Ruath Hold, my lady, I was quite ready to challenge Fax given any reasonable cause, despite the Search." This was not the whole truth, but F'lar must teach this girl the folly of trying to control dragonmen. "Had you paid any attention to your harper's songs, you'd know your rights. And"—F'lar's voice held a vindictive edge that surprised him—"the Lady Gemma might not now lie dead. She, brave soul, suffered far more at that tyrant's hand than you."

Something in her manner told him that she regretted Lady Gemma's death, that it had affected her deeply.

"What good is Ruatha to you now?" he demanded, a broad sweep of his arm taking in the ruined Court yard and the Hold, the entire unproductive valley of Ruatha. "You have indeed accomplished your ends, a profitless conquest and its conqueror's death."

F'lar snorted. "As well, too. Those Holds will all revert to their legitimate Blood, and time they did. One Hold and One Lord. Anything else is against tradition. Of course, you might have to fight others who disbelieve that precept: who have become infected with Fax's greedy madness. Can you hold Ruatha against attack . . . now . . . in her condition?"

"Ruatha is mine!"

"Ruatha?" F'lar's laugh was derisive. "When you could be Weyrwoman?"

"Weyrwoman?" she breathed, staring at him in shocked amazement.

"Yes, little fool. I said I rode in Search . . . it's

about time you attended to more than Ruatha. And the object of my Search is . . . you!"

She stared at the finger he pointed at her, as if it were dangerous.

"By the First Egg, girl, you've power in you to spare when you can turn a dragonman, all unwitting, to do your bidding. Ah, but never again, for I am now on guard against you."

Mnementh crooned approvingly, the sound a soft rumble in his throat. He arched his neck so that one eye was turned directly on the girl, gleaming in the darkness of the Court.

F'lar noticed with detached pride that she neither flinched nor blanched at the proximity of an eye greater than her own head.

"He likes to have his eye ridges scratched," F'lar remarked in a friendly tone, changing tactics.

"I know," she said softly and reached out a hand to do that service.

"Nemorth has laid a golden egg," F'lar continued persuasively. "She is close to death. This time we must have a strong Weyrwoman."

"The Red Star?" the girl gasped, turning frightened eyes to F'lar. That alone surprised him, for she had never once evinced any fear.

"You've seen it? You understand what it means?" He saw her swallow nervously.

"There is danger . . ." she began in a bare whisper, glancing apprehensively eastward.

F'lar did not question by what miracle she appreciated the imminence of danger. He had every intention of taking her to the Weyr by sheer force if necessary. But something within him wanted very much for her to accept the challenge voluntarily. A rebellious Weyrwoman would be even more dangerous than a stupid one. This girl had too much power and was too used to guile and strategy. It would be a calamity to antagonize her with injudicious handling.

"There is danger for all Pern. Not just Ruatha," he said, allowing a note of entreaty to creep into his

voice. "And *you* are needed. Not by Ruatha." A wave
of his hand dismissed that consideration as a negligi-
ble one compared to the total picture. "We are
doomed without a strong Weyrwoman. Without you."

"Gemma said all the bronze riders were needed,"
she murmured in a dazed whisper.

What did she mean by that statement? F'lar
frowned. Had she heard a word he had said? He
pressed his argument, certain only that he had already
struck one responsive chord.

"You've won here. Let the babe"—he saw her
startled rejection of that idea and ruthlessly qualified
it—"Gemma's babe—be reared at Ruatha. You have
command of all the Holds as Weyrwoman, not ruined
Ruatha alone. You've accomplished Fax's death.
Leave off vengeance."

She stared at F'lar with wondering eyes, absorbing
his words.

"I never thought beyond Fax's death," she admitted
slowly. "I never thought what should happen then."

Her confusion was almost childlike and struck F'lar
forcibly. He had had no time or desire to consider her
prodigious accomplishment. Now he realized some
measure of her indomitable character. She could not
have been above ten Turns of age herself when Fax
had murdered her family. Yet somehow, so young,
she had set herself a goal and managed to survive
both brutality and detection long enough to secure the
usurper's death. What a Weyrwoman she would be! In
the tradition of those of Ruathan Blood. The light of
the paler moon made her look young and vulnerable
and almost pretty.

"You can be Weyrwoman," he repeated with gentle
insistence.

"Weyrwoman," she breathed, incredulous, and
gazed around the inner Court bathed in soft moonlight. He thought she wavered.

"Or perhaps you enjoy rags?" he said, making his
voice harsh, mocking. "And matted hair, dirty feet,
and cracked hands? Sleeping in straw, eating rinds?

You are young . . . that is, I assume you are young."
His voice was frankly skeptical. She glared at him
coolly, her lips firmly pressed together. "Is this the
be-all and end-all of your ambition? What are you
that this little corner of the great world is *all* you
want?" He paused, then with utter contempt added,
"The Blood of Ruatha has thinned, I see. You're
afraid!"

"I am Lessa, daughter of the Lord of Ruath," she
countered, stung to responding by the Blood insult.
She drew herself erect, her eyes flashing, her chin
high. "I am afraid of nothing!"

F'lar contented himself with a slight smile.

Mnementh, however, threw up his head and
stretched out his sinuous neck to its whole length. His
full-throated peal rang out down the valley. The
bronze communicated his awareness to F'lar that
Lessa had accepted the challenge. The other
dragons answered back, their warbles shriller than
Mnementh's male bellow. The watch-wher which had
cowered at the end of its chain lifted its voice in a
thin, unnerving screech until the Hold emptied of its
startled occupants.

"F'nor," the bronze rider called, waving his wingleader to him. "Leave half the flight to guard the
Hold. Some nearby Lord might think to emulate Fax's
example, Send one rider to the High Reaches with the
glad news. You go directly to the clothmen's Hall and
speak to L'to . . . Lytol." F'lar grinned. "I think he
would make an exemplary Warder and Lord Surrogate for this Hold in the name of the Weyr and the
baby Lord."

The brown rider's face expressed enthusiasm for
his mission as he began to comprehend his leader's
intentions. With Fax dead and Ruatha under the
protection of dragonmen, particularly that same one
who had dispatched Fax, the Hold would be safe
and flourish under wise management.

"She caused Ruatha's deterioration?" he asked his
leader.

"And nearly ours with her machinations," F'lar replied, but having found the admirable object of his Search, he could now be magnanimous. "Suppress your exultation, brother," he advised quickly as he took note of F'nor's expression. "The new queen must also be Impressed."

"I'll settle arrangements here. Lytol is an excellent choice," F'nor said, although he knew that F'lar needed no one's approval.

"Who is this Lytol?" demanded Lessa pointedly. She had twisted the mass of filthy hair back from her face. In the moonlight the dirt was less noticeable. F'lar caught F'nor looking at her with an all too easily read expression. He signaled F'nor with a peremptory gesture to carry out his orders without delay.

"Lytol is a dragonless man," F'lar told the girl, "no friend to Fax. He will ward the Hold well, and it will prosper." He added persuasively with a quelling stare full on her, "Won't it?"

She regarded him somberly, without answering, until he chuckled softly at her discomfiture.

"We'll return to the Weyr," he announced, proffering a hand to guide her to Mnementh's side.

The bronze one had extended his head toward the watch-wher, who now lay panting on the ground, its chain limp in the dust.

"Oh," Lessa sighed, and dropped beside the grotesque beast. It raised its head slowly, crying piteously.

"Mnementh says it is very old and soon will sleep itself to death."

Lessa cradled the repulsive head in her arms, stroking the eye ridges, scratching behind its ears.

"Come, Lessa of Pern," F'lar said, impatient to be up and away.

She rose slowly but obediently. "It saved me. It knew me."

"It knows it did well," F'lar assured her brusquely, wondering at such an uncharacteristic show of sentiment in her.

He took her hand again, to help her to her feet and lead her back to Mnementh.

In one split second he was knocked off his feet, sprawling across the stones and trying to roll to his feet again, to face his adversary. The force of the initial blow, however, had dazed him, and he lay sprawled on his back, startled to see the watch-wher, its scaly body launched—straight at him.

Simultaneously he heard Lessa's startled exclamation and Mnementh's roar. The bronze's great head was swinging around to knock the watch-wher aside, away from the dragonman. But just as the watch-wher's body was fully extended in its leap, Lessa cried out.

"Don't kill! Don't kill!"

The watch-wher, its snarl turning into an anguished cry of alarm, executed an incredible maneuver in mid-air, turning aside from its trajectory. As it fell to the stone yard at his feet, F'lar heard the dull crack as the force of its landing broke its back.

Before he could get to his feet, Lessa was cradling the hideous head in her arms, her face stricken.

Mnementh lowered his head to tap the dying watch-wher's body gently. He informed F'lar that the beast had guessed Lessa was leaving Ruatha, something one of her Blood should not do. In its senile confusion it could only assume Lessa was in danger. When it heard Lessa's frantic command, it had corrected its error at the expense of its life.

"It was truly only defending me," Lessa added, her voice breaking. She cleared her throat. "It was the only one I could trust. My only friend."

F'lar awkwardly patted the girl's shoulder, appalled that anyone could be reduced to claiming friendship with a watch-wher. He winced because the fall had reopened the knife wound in his shoulder and he hurt.

"In truth a loyal friend," he said, standing patiently until the light in the watch-wher's green-gold eyes dimmed and died out.

All the dragons gave voice to the eerie, hair-raising,

barely audible, high keening note that signified the passing of one of their kind.

"He was only a watch-wher," Lessa murmured, stunned by the tribute, her eyes wide.

"The dragons confer honor where *they* will," F'lar remarked dryly, disclaiming the responsibility.

Lessa looked down for one more long moment at the repulsive head. She laid it down to the stones, caressed the clipped wings. Then, with quick fingers, she undid the heavy buckle that fastened the metal collar around the neck. She threw the collar violently away.

She rose in a fluid movement and walked resolutely to Mnementh without a single backward glance. She stepped calmly to Mnementh's raised leg and seated herself, as F'lar directed her, on the great neck.

F'lar glanced around the Court at the remainder of his wing which had reformed there. The Hold folk had retreated into the safety of the great Hall. When his wingmen were all astride, he vaulted to Mnementh's neck, behind the girl.

"Hold tightly to my arms," he ordered her as he took hold of the smallest neck ridge and gave the command to fly.

Her fingers closed spasmodically around his forearm as the great bronze dragon took off, the enormous wings working to achieve height from the vertical takeoff. Mnementh preferred to fall into flight from a cliff or tower. Dragons tended to indolence. F'lar glanced behind him, saw the other dragonmen form the flight line, spread out to cover the gaps of those still on guard at Ruatha Hold.

When they had reached a sufficient altitude, he told Mnementh to transfer, going *between* to the Weyr.

Only a gasp indicated the girl's astonishment as they hung *between*. Accustomed as he was to the sting of the profound cold, to the awesome utter lack of light and sound, F'lar still found the sensations unnerving. Yet the uncommon transfer spanned no more time than it took to cough thrice.

Mnementh rumbled approval of this candidate's calm reaction as they flicked out of the eerie *between*. She had not been afraid or screamed in panic as other women had. F'lar did feel her heart pounding against his arm that pressed against her ribs, but that was all.

And then they were above the Weyr, Mnementh setting his wings to glide in the bright daylight, half a world away from nighttime Ruatha.

Lessa's hands tightened on his arms, this time in surprise as they circled above the great stony trough of the Weyr. F'lar peered at Lessa's face, pleased with the delight mirrored there; she showed no trace of fear that they hung a thousand lengths above the high Benden mountain range. Then, as the seven dragons roared their incoming cry, an incredulous smile lit her face.

The other wingmen dropped into a wide spiral, down, down, while Mnementh elected to descend in lazy circles. The dragonmen peeled off smartly and dropped, each to his own tier in the caves of the Weyr. Mnementh finally completed his leisurely approach to their quarters, whistling shrilly to himself as he braked his forward speed with a twist of his wings, dropping lightly at last to the ledge. He crouched as F'lar swung the girl to the rough rock, scored from thousands of clawed landings.

"This leads only to our quarters," he told her as they entered the corridor, vaulted and wide for the easy passage of great bronze dragons.

As they reached the huge natural cavern that had been his since Mnementh achieved maturity, F'lar looked about him with eyes fresh from his first prolonged absence from the Weyr. The huge chamber was unquestionably larger than most of the halls he had visited in Fax's procession. Those halls were intended as gathering places for men, not the habitations of dragons. But suddenly he saw his own

quarters were nearly as shabby as all Ruatha. Benden
was, of a certainty, one of the oldest dragonweyrs, as
Ruatha was one of the oldest Holds, but that excused
nothing. How many dragons had bedded in that hollow to make solid rock conform to dragon proportions!
How many feet had worn the path past the dragon's
Weyr into the sleeping chamber, to the bathing room
beyond where the natural warm spring provided ever-
fresh water! But the wall hangings were faded and
unraveling, and there were grease stains on lintel and
floor that could easi y be sanded away.

He noticed the wary expression on Lessa's face as
he paused in the sleeping room.

"I must feed Mnementh immediately. So you may
bathe first," he said, rummaging in a chest and finding
clean clothes for her, discards of former occupants of
his quarters, but far more presentable than her present
covering. He carefully laid back in the chest the white
wool robe that was traditional Impression garb. She
would wear that later. He tossed several garments at
her feet and a bag of sweetsand, gesturing to the hanging that obscured the way to the bath.

He left her then, the clothes in a heap at her feet,
for she made no effort to catch anything.

Mnementh informed him that F'nor was feeding
Canth and that he, Mnementh, was hungry, too. *She*
didn't trust F'lar, but she wasn't afraid of himself.

"Why should she be afraid of you?" F'lar asked.
"You're cousin to the watch-wher who was her only
friend."

Mnementh informed F'lar that he, a fully matured
bronze dragon, was no relation to any scrawny, crawl-
ing, chained, and wing-clipped watch-wher.

"Then why did you accord him a dragon tribute?"
F'lar asked.

Mnementh told him haughtily that it was fitting and
proper to mourn the passing of a loyal and self-
sacrificing personality. Not even a blue dragon could
deny the fact that that Ruathan watch-wher had not
divulged information he had been enjoined to keep,

though the beast had been sorely pressed to do so by himself, Mnementh. Also, in managing, by some physical feat, to turn aside its attack on F'lar, at the cost of its own life, it had elevated itself to dragonlike bravery. Of course, the dragons had uttered a tribute at its passing.

F'lar, pleased at having been able to tease the bronze one, chuckled to himself. With great dignity Mnementh curved down to the feeding ground.

F'lar dropped off as Mnementh hovered near F'nor. The impact with the ground reminded him he had better get the girl to dress his shoulder for him. He watched as the bronze one swooped down on the nearest fat buck in the milling herd.

"The Hatching is due at any hour," F'nor greeted his brother, grinning up at him as he squatted on his haunches. His eyes were bright with excitement.

F'lar nodded thoughtfully. "There will be plenty to choose from for the males," he allowed, knowing F'nor was tauntingly withholding choicer news.

They both watched as F'nor's Canth singled out a doe. The brown dragon neatly grabbed the struggling beast in one claw and rose up, settling on an unoccupied ledge to feast.

Mnementh dispatched his first carcass and glided in again over the herd, to the pens beyond. He singled out a heavy ground bird and lifted with it in his claws. F'lar observed his ascent, experiencing as always the thrill of pride in the effortless sweep of the great pinions, the play of the sun on the bronze hide, the flash of silvery claws, unsheathed for landing. He never tired of watching Mnementh in flight or admiring the unconscious grace and strength.

"Lytol was overwhelmed by the summons," F'nor remarked, "and sends you all honor and respect. He will do well at Ruatha."

"The reason he was chosen," grunted F'lar, nonetheless gratified by Lytol's reaction. Surrogate Lordship was no substitute for loss of one's dragon, but it was an honorable responsibility.

"There was much rejoicing in the High Reaches," F'nor continued, grinning widely, "and honest grief at the passing of Lady Gemma. It will be interesting to see which of the contenders takes title."

"At Ruatha?" F'lar queried, frowning down at his half brother.

"No. At the High Reaches and the other Holds Fax conquered. Lytol will bring his own people to secure Ruatha and to give any soldiery pause before they might attempt that Hold. He knew of many in the High Reaches who would prefer to make a change of Hold, even though Fax no longer dominates the High Reaches. He intended to make all haste to Ruatha so that our men will soon rejoin us."

F'lar nodded approval, turning to salute two more of his wing, blue riders, who dropped with their beasts to the feeding ground. Mnementh went back for another fowl.

"He eats light," F'nor commented. "Canth's still gorging."

"Browns are slow to get full growth," F'lar drawled, watching with satisfaction as F'nor's eyes flashed angrily. That would teach him to withhold news.

"R'gul and S'lel are back," the brown rider finally announced.

The two blues had the herd in a frenzy, stampeding and screaming in fright.

"The others are recalled," F'nor continued. "Nemorth is all but rigid in death." Then he could no longer contain himself. "S'lel brought in two. R'gul has five. Strong-willed, they say, and pretty."

F'lar said nothing. He had expected those two would bring in multiple candidates. Let them bring hundreds if they chose. He, F'lar, the bronze rider, had in his one choice the winner.

Exasperated that his news elicited so little response, F'nor rose.

"We should have backtrailed for that one in Crom and the pretty . . ."

"Pretty?" F'lar retorted, cocking one eyebrow high

in disdain. "Pretty? Jora was pretty," he spat out cynically.

"K'net and T'bor bring contenders from the west," F'nor added urgently, concerned.

The wind-torn roar of homecoming dragons crackled through the air. Both men jerked their heads skyward and saw the double spirals of two returning wings, twenty strong.

Mnementh tossed his head high, crooning. F'lar called him in, pleased the bronze one made no quarrel at recall, although he had eaten very lightly. F'lar, saluting his brother amiably, stepped onto Mnementh's spread foot and was lifted back to his own ledge.

Mnementh hiccuped absently as the two walked the short passage to the vaulted inner chamber. He lumbered over to his hollowed bed and settled himself into the curved stone. When Mnementh had stretched and comfortably laid down his wedge-head, F'lar approached him. Mnementh regarded his friend with the near eye, its many facets glinting and shifting, the inner lids gradually closing as F'lar scratched the eye-ridge soothingly.

Those unfamiliar with it might find such a regard unnerving. But since that moment, twenty Turns before, when the great Mnementh had broken through his shell and stumbled across the Hatching Ground to stand, weaving on weak legs, before the boy F'lar, the dragonman had treasured these quiet moments as the happiest of a long day. No greater tribute could man be paid than the trust and companionship of the winged beasts of Pern. For the loyalty that dragonkind gave their chosen one of mankind was unswerving and complete from the instant of Impression.

Mnementh's inner content was such that the great eye quickly closed. The dragon slept, only the tip of his tail erect, a sure sign that he would be instantly on the alert if the need arose.

By the Golden Egg of Faranth
By the Weyrwoman, wise and true,
Breed a flight of bronze and brown wings,
Breed a flight of green and blue.
Breed riders, strong and daring,
Dragon-loving, born as hatched
Flight of hundreds soaring skyward,
Man and dragon fully matched.

LESSA WAITED until the sound of the dragonman's footsteps proved he had really gone away. She rushed quickly through the big cavern, heard the scrape of claw and the whoosh of the mighty wings. She raced down the short passageway, right to the edge of the yawning entrance. There was the bronze dragon circling down to the wider end of the mile-long barren oval that was Benden Weyr. She had heard of the Weyrs, as any Pernese had, but to be in one was quite a different matter.

She peered up, around, down that sheer rock face. There was no way off but by dragon wing. The nearest cave mouths were an unhandy distance above her, to one side, below her on the other. She was neatly secluded here.

Weyrwoman, he had told her. His woman? In his weyr? Was that what he had meant? No, that was not the impression she got from the dragon. It occurred to her suddenly that it was odd she had understood the dragon. Were common folk able to? Or was it the dragonman Blood in her Line? At all events, Mnementh had implied something greater, some special rank. They must mean her, then, to be Weyrwoman to the unhatched dragon queen. Only how did she, or they, go about it? She remembered vaguely that when dragonmen went on Search, they looked for certain women. Ah, certain women. She was one, then, of several contenders. Yet the bronze rider had offered her the position as if she and she alone qualified. He had his own generous portion of conceit, that one, Lessa decided. Arrogant he was, though not the bully Fax had been.

She could see the bronze dragon swoop down to the running herdbeasts, saw the strike, saw the dragon wheel up to settle on a far ledge to feed. Instinctively she drew back from the opening, back into the dark and relative safety of the corridor.

The feeding dragon evoked scores of horrid tales. Tales at which she had scoffed, but now . . . Was it true, then, that dragons did eat human flesh? Did . . . Lessa halted that trend of thought. Dragonkind was no less cruel than mankind. The dragon, at least, acted from bestial need rather than bestial greed.

Assured that the dragonman would be occupied awhile, she crossed the larger cave into the sleeping room. She scooped up the clothing and the bag of cleansing sand and proceeded to the bathing room. It was small but ample for its purpose. A wide ledge formed a partial lip to the uneven circle of the bathing pool. There was a bench and some shelves for drying cloths. In the glowlight she could see that the near section of the pool had been sanded high so a bather could stand comfortably. Then there was a gradual dip approaching the deeper water that slapped the very rock wall on the farther side.

To be clean! To be completely clean and to be able to stay that way. With a distaste at touching them no less acute than the dragonman's, she stripped off the remains of the rags, kicking them to one side, not knowing where to dispose of them. She shook out a generous handful of the sweetsand and, bending to the pool, wet it.

Quickly she made a soft mud with the sweet soap, and she scoured hands and bruised face. Wetting more sand, she attacked her arms and legs, then her body and feet. She scrubbed hard until she drew blood from half-healed cuts. Then she stepped, or rather jumped, into the pool, gasping as the warm water made the sweetsand foam in her scratches. She ducked under the surface, shaking her head to be sure her hair was thoroughly wetted. Then briskly she rubbed in more sweetsand, rinsing and scrubbing until she felt her hair might possibly be clean. Years, it had been. Great strands floated away in tangles like immense crawlers with attenuated legs, toward the far edge of the pool and then were drawn out of sight. The water, she was glad to note, constantly circulated, the cloudy and dirty replaced with clear. She turned her attention again to her body, scrubbing at ingrained dirt until her skin smarted. It was a ritual cleansing of more than surface soil. She felt a pleasure akin to ecstasy for the luxury of cleanliness.

Finally satisfied her body was as clean as one long soaking could make her, she sanded her hair yet a third time. She left the pool almost reluctantly, wringing out her hair and tucking it up on her head as she dried herself. She shook out the clothing and held one garment against her experimentally. The fabric, a soft green, felt smooth under her water-shrunken fingers, although the nap caught on her roughened hands. She pulled it over her head. It was loose, but the darker-green overtunic had a sash that she pulled in tight at the waist. The unusual sensation of softness against her bare skin made her wriggle with voluptuous pleasure. The skirt, no longer a ragged hem of tatters, swirled heavily around her ankles, making her smile in sheer feminine delight. She took up a fresh drying cloth and began to work on her hair.

A muted sound came to her ears, and she stopped, hands poised, head bent to one side. Straining, she listened. Yes, there were sounds without. The dragonman and his beast must have returned. She grimaced to herself with annoyance at this untimely interruption and rubbed harder at her hair. She ran fingers through the half-dry tangles, the motions arrested as she encountered snarls. She tried patting her hair into place, pushing it defiantly behind her ears. Vexed, she rummaged on the shelves until she found, as she had hoped to, a coarse-toothed metal comb. With this she attacked her unruly hair and, by the dint of much yanking and groaning as she pulled ruthlessly through years of tangles, she was able to groom the mass.

Now dry, her hair suddenly had a life of its own, crackling about her hands and clinging to face and comb and dress. It was difficult to get the silky stuff under control. And her hair was longer than she had thought, for, clean and unmatted, it fell to her waist—when it did not cling to her hands.

She paused, listening, and heard no sound at all. Apprehensively, she stepped to the curtain and glanced warily into the sleeping room. It was empty. She listened and caught the perceptible thoughts of the sleepy dragon. Well, she would rather meet the man in the presence of a sleepy dragon than in a sleeping room. She started across the floor and, out of the corner of her eye, caught sight of a strange woman as she passed a polished piece of metal hanging on the wall.

Amazed, she stopped short, staring, incredulous, at the face the metal reflected. Only when she put her hands to her prominent cheekbones in a gesture of involuntary surprise and the reflection imitated the gesture did she realize she looked at herself.

Why, that girl in the reflector was prettier than the Lady Tela, than the clothman's daughter! But so thin. Her hands of their own volition dropped to her neck, to the protruding collarbones, to her breasts, which did not entirely reflect the gauntness of the rest of her. The dress was too large for her frame, she noted with an unexpected emergence of conceit born in that instant of delighted appraisal. And her hair . . . it stood out around her head like an aureole. It wouldn't lie contained. She smoothed it down with impatient fingers,

automatically bringing locks forward to hang around
her face. As she irritably pushed them back, dismissing a need for disguise, the hair drifted up again.

A slight sound, the scrape of a boot against stone,
caught her back from her bemusement. She waited,
momentarily expecting him to appear. She was suddenly timid. With her face bare to the world, her hair
behind her ears, her body outlined by a clinging fabric,
she was stripped of her accustomed anonymity and was
therefore, in her estimation, vulnerable.

Sternly she controlled the desire to run away, the ir-
rational shock of fearfulness. Observing herself in the
looking metal, she drew her shoulders back, tilted her
head high, chin up; the movement caused her hair to
crackle and cling and shift about her head. She was
Lessa of Ruatha, of a fine old Blood. She no longer
needed to resort to artifice to preserve herself, so she
must stand proudly bare-faced before the world . . .
and that dragonman.

Resolutely she crossed the room, pushing aside the
hanging on the doorway to the great cavern.

He was there, beside the head of the dragon, scratching its eye ridges, a curiously tender expression on his
face. It was a tableau completely at variance with all
she had heard of dragonmen.

She had, of course, heard of the strange affinity between rider and dragon, but this was the first time
she realized that love was part of that bond. Or that
this reserved, cold man was capable of such deep emotion. He had been brusque enough with her over the
old watch-wher. No wonder it had thought he had
meant her harm. The dragons had been more tolerant,
she remembered with an involuntary sniff.

He turned slowly, as if loath to leave the bronze
beast. He caught sight of her and pivoted completely
around, his eyes intense as he took note of her altered
appearance. With quick, light steps he closed the distance between them and ushered her back into the
sleeping room, one strong hand holding her by the elbow.

"Mnementh has fed lightly and will need quiet to rest," he said in a low voice, as if this were the most important consideration. He pulled the heavy hanging into place across the opening.

Then he held her away from him, turning her this way and that, scrutinizing her closely, a curious and slightly surprised expression fleeting across his face.

"You wash up . . . pretty, yes, almost pretty," he allowed with such amused condescension in his voice that she pulled roughly away from him, piqued. His low laugh mocked her. "How could one guess, after all, what was under the grime of . . . ten full Turns, I would say? Yes, you are certainly pretty enough to placate F'nor."

Thoroughly antagonized by his attitude, she asked in icy tones, "And F'nor must be placated at all costs?"

He stood grinning at her till she had to clench her fists at her sides to keep from beating that grin off his face.

At length he said, "No matter, we must eat, and I shall require your services." At her startled exclamation, he turned, grinning maliciously now as his movement revealed the caked blood on his left sleeve. "The least you can do is bathe wounds honorably received in fighting your battle."

He pushed aside a portion of the drapery that curtained the inner wall. "Food for two!" he roared down a black gap in the sheer stone.

She heard a subterranean echo far below as his voice resounded down what must be a long shaft.

"Nemorth is nearly rigid," he was saying as he took supplies from another drapery-hidden shelf, "and the Hatching will soon begin, anyhow."

A coldness settled in Lessa's stomach at the mention of a Hatching. The mildest tales she had heard about that part of dragonlore were chilling, the worst dismayingly macabre. Numbly she took the things he handed her.

"What? Frightened?" the dragonman taunted, pausing as he stripped off his torn and bloodied shirt.

With a shake of her head, Lessa turned her attention to the wide-shouldered, well-muscled back he presented her, the paler skin of his body decorated with random bloody streaks. Fresh blood welled from the point of his shoulder, for the removal of his shirt had broken the tender scabs.

"I will need water," she said and saw she had a flat pan among the items he had given her. She went swiftly to the pool for water, wondering how she had come to agree to venture so far from Ruatha. Ruined though it was, it had been hers and was familiar to her, from Tower to deep cellar. At the moment the idea had been proposed and insidiously prosecuted by the dragonman, she had felt capable of anything, having achieved, at last, Fax's death. Now it was all she could do to keep the water from slopping out of the pan that shook unaccountably in her hands.

She forced herself to deal only with the wound. It was a nasty gash, deep where the point had entered and torn downward in a gradually shallower slice. His skin felt smooth under her fingers as she cleansed the wound. In spite of herself, she noticed the masculine odor of him, compounded not unpleasantly of sweat, leather, and an unusual muskiness that must be from close association with dragons.

Although it must have hurt him when she cleansed away clotted blood, he gave no indication of discomfort, apparently oblivious to the operation. It annoyed her still more that she could not succumb to the temptation of treating him roughly in return for his disregard of her feelings.

She ground her teeth in frustration as she smeared on the healing salve generously. Making a small pad of bandage, she secured the dressing deftly in place with other strips of torn cloth. She stood back when she had finished her ministrations. He flexed his arm experimentally in the constricting bandage, and the motion set the muscles rippling along his side and back.

When he faced her, his eyes were dark and thoughtful.

"Gently done, my lady. My thanks." His smile was ironic.

She backed away as he rose, but he only went to the chest to take out a clean, white shirt.

A muted rumble sounded, growing quickly louder.

Dragons roaring? Lessa wondered, trying to conquer the ridiculous fear that rose within her. Had the Hatching started? There was no watch-wher's lair to secrete herself in here.

As if he understood her confusion, the dragonman laughed good-humoredly and, his eyes on hers, drew aside the wall covering just as some noisy mechanism inside the shaft propelled a tray of food into sight.

Ashamed of her unbased fright and furious that he had witnessed it, Lessa sat rebelliously down on the fur-covered wall seat, heartily wishing him a variety of serious and painful injuries that she could dress with inconsiderate hands. She would not waste future opportunities.

He placed the tray on the low table in front of her, throwing down a heap of furs for his own seat. There were meat, bread, a pitcher of *klah,* a tempting yellow cheese, and even a few pieces of winter fruit. He made no move to eat, nor did she, though the thought of a piece of fruit that was ripe instead of rotten set her mouth to watering. He glanced up at her and frowned.

"Even in the Weyr, the lady breaks bread first," he said and inclined his head politely to her.

Lessa flushed, unused to any courtesy and certainly unused to being first to eat. She broke off a chunk of bread. It was like nothing she remembered having tasted before. For one thing, it was fresh-baked. The flour had been finely sifted, without trace of sand or hull. She took the slice of cheese he proffered her, and it, too, had an uncommonly delicious sharpness. Much emboldened by this indication of her changed status, Lessa reached for the plumpest piece of fruit.

"Now," the dragonman began, his hand touching hers to get her attention.

Guiltily she dropped the fruit, thinking she had erred. She stared at him, wondering at her fault. He retrieved the fruit and placed it back in her hand as he continued to speak. Wide-eyed, she nibbled, disarmed, and gave him her full attention.

"Listen to me. You must not show a moment's fear at whatever happens on the Hatching Ground. And you must not let her overeat." A wry expression crossed his face. "One of our main functions is to keep a dragon from excessive eating."

Lessa lost interest in the taste of the fruit. She placed it carefully back in the bowl and tried to sort out what he had not said but what his tone of voice implied. She looked at the dragonman's face, seeing him as a person, not a symbol, for the first time.

His coldness was caution, she decided, not lack of emotion. His sternness must be assumed to offset his youth, for he couldn't be that much her senior in Turns. There was a blackness about him that was not malevolent; it was a brooding sort of patience. Heavy black hair waved back from a high forehead to brush his shirt collar. Heavy black brows were too often pulled together in a glower or arched haughtily as he looked down a high-bridged nose at his victim; his eyes (an amber, light enough to seem golden) were all too expressive of cynical emotions or cold hauteur. His lips were thin but well-shaped and in repose almost gentle. Why must he always pull his mouth to one side in disapproval or in one of those sardonic smiles? Handsome he must be considered, she supposed candidly, for there was a certain compelling air about him that was magnetic. And at this moment he was completely unaffected.

He meant what he was saying. He did not want her to be afraid. There was no reason for her, Lessa, *to* fear.

He very much wanted her to succeed. In keeping whom from overeating what? Herd animals? A newly hatched dragon certainly wasn't capable of eating a full beast. That seemed a simple enough task to Lessa. The watch-wher had obeyed her and no one else, at Ruath Hold. She had understood the great bronze dragon and had even managed to hush him up as she raced under his Tower perch for the birthing-woman. Main function? *Our* main function?

The dragonman was looking at her expectantly.

"Our main function?" she repeated, an unspoken request for more information inherent in her inflection.

"More of that later. First things first," he said, impatiently waving off other questions.

"But what happens?" she insisted.

"As I was told, so I tell you. No more, no less. Remember those two points. Turn out fear and do not let her overeat."

"But . . ."

"You, however, need to eat. Here." He speared a piece of meat on his knife and thrust it at her, frowning until she managed to choke it down. He was about to force more on her, but she grabbed up her half-eaten fruit and bit down into the firm sweet sphere instead. She had already eaten more at this one meal than she was accustomed to having all day at the Hold.

"We shall soon eat better at the Weyr," he remarked, regarding the tray with a jaundiced eye.

Lessa was surprised, for in her opinion this was a feast.

"More than you're used to? Yes, I forgot you left Ruatha with bare bones indeed."

She stiffened.

"You did well at Ruatha. I mean no criticism," he added, smiling at her reaction. "But look at you," and he gestured at her body, that curious expression crossing his face, half-amused, half-contemplative. "No, I should not have guessed you'd clean up pretty," he remarked. "Nor with such hair." This time his expression was frankly admiring.

Involuntarily she put one hand to her head, the hair crackling over her fingers. But what reply she might have made him, indignant as she was, died a-borning. An unearthly keening filled the chamber.

The sounds set up a vibration that ran down the bones behind her ear to her spine. She clapped both hands to her ears. The noise rang through her skull, despite her defending hands. As abruptly as it started, it ceased.

Before she knew what he was about, the dragonman had grabbed her by the wrist and pulled her over to the chest.

"Take those off," he ordered, indicating dress and tunic. While she stared at him stupidly, he held up a loose white robe, sleeveless and beltless, a matter of two lengths of fine cloth fastened at shoulder and side seams. "Take it off, or do I assist you?" he asked with no patience at all.

The wild sound was repeated, and its unnerving tone made her fingers fly faster. She had no sooner loosened the garments she wore, letting them slide to her feet, than he had thrown the other over her head. She managed to get her arms in the proper places before he grabbed her wrist again and was speeding with her out of the room, her hair whipping out behind her, alive with static.

As they reached the outer chamber, the bronze dragon was standing in the center of the cavern, his head turned to watch the sleeping room door. He seemed impatient to Lessa; his great eyes, which fascinated her so, sparkled iridescently. His manner breathed an inner excitement of great proportions, and from his throat a high-pitched croon issued, several octaves below the unnerving cry that had roused them all.

Rushed and impatient as they both were, the dragon and dragonman paused. Suddenly Lessa realized they were conferring about her. The great dragon's head was suddenly directly in front of her, his nose blotting out everything else. She felt the warm exhalation of his breath, slightly phosphorus-laden. She heard him inform the dragonman that he approved more and more of this woman from Ruatha.

With a yank that rocked her head on her neck, the dragonman pulled her along the passage. The dragon padded beside them at such speed that Lessa fully expected they would all catapult off the ledge. Somehow, at the crucial stride, she was perched on the bronze neck, the dragonman holding her firmly about the waist. In the same fluid movement they were gliding across the great bowl of the Weyr to the higher wall opposite. The air was full of wings and dragon tails, rent with a chorus of sounds, echoing and reechoing across the stony valley.

Mnementh set what Lessa was certain would be a collision course with other dragons, straight for a huge round blackness in the cliff-face, high up. Magically, the beasts filed in, the greater wingspread of Mnementh just clearing the sides of the entrance.

The passageway reverberated with the thunder of wings. The air compressed around her thickly. Then they broke out into a gigantic cavern.

Why, the entire mountain must be hollow, thought Lessa, incredulous. Around the enormous cavern dragons perched in serried ranks, blues, greens, browns, and only two great bronze beasts like Mnementh, on ledges meant to accommodate hundreds. Lessa gripped the bronze neck scales before her, instinctively aware of the imminence of a great event.

Mnementh wheeled downward, disregarding the ledge of the bronze ones. Then all Lessa could see was what lay on the sandy floor of the great cavern: dragon eggs. A clutch of ten monstrous, mottled eggs, their shells moving spasmodically as the fledglings within tapped their way out. To one side, on a raised portion of the floor, was a golden egg, larger by half again the size of the mottled ones. Just beyond the golden egg lay the motionless ocher hulk of the old queen.

Just as she realized Mnementh was hovering over the floor in the vicinity of that egg, Lessa felt the dragonman's hands on her, lifting her from Mnementh's neck.

Apprehensively she grabbed at him. His hands tightened and inexorably swung her down. His eyes, fierce with amber fire locked with hers.

"Remember, Lessa!"

Mnementh added an encouraging note, one great compound eye turned on her. Then he rose from the floor. Lessa half-raised one hand in entreaty, bereft of all support, even that of the sure inner compulsion that had sustained her in her struggle for revenge on Fax. She saw the bronze dragon settle on the first ledge, at some distance from the other two bronze beasts. The dragonman dismounted, and Mnementh curved his sinuous neck until his head was beside his rider. The man reached up and absently, it seemed to Lessa, caressed his mount.

Loud screams and wailings diverted Lessa, and she saw more dragons descend to hover just above the cavern floor, each rider depositing a young woman until there were twelve girls, including Lessa. She remained a little apart from them as they clung to one another. She regarded them curiously, contemptuous of their tears, although her heart was probably beating no less rapidly than theirs. It did not occur to her that tears were any help. The girls were not injured in any way that she could see, so why such weeping? Her contempt of their bleating made her aware of her own temerity, and she took a deep breath against the coldness within her. Let *them* be afraid. She was Lessa of Ruatha and did not need to be afraid.

Just then, the golden egg moved convulsively. Gasping as one, the girls edged away from it, back against the rocky wall. One, a lovely blonde, her heavy plait of golden hair swinging just above the ground, started to step off the raised floor and stopped, shrieking, backing fearfully toward the scant comfort of her peers.

Lessa wheeled to see what cause there might be for the look of horror on the girl's face. She stepped back involuntarily herself.

In the main section of the sandy arena, several of the handful of eggs had already cracked wide open. The fledglings, crowing weakly, were moving toward— and Lessa gulped—the young boys standing stolidly in a semicircle. Some of them were no older than she had been when Fax's army had swooped down on Ruath Hold.

The shrieking of the women subsided to muffled gasps and sobs as one fledgling reached out with claw and beak to grab a boy.

Lessa forced herself to watch as the young dragon mauled the boy, throwing him roughly aside as if unsatisfied in some way. The boy did not move, and Lessa could see blood seeping onto the sand from dragon-inflicted wounds.

A second fledgling lurched against another boy and halted, flapping its damp wings impotently, raising its scrawny neck and croaking a parody of the encouraging croon Mnementh often gave. The boy uncertainly lifted a hand and began to scratch the eye ridge. Incredulous, Lessa watched as the fledgling, its crooning increasingly more mellow, ducked its head, pushing at the boy. The child's face broke into an unbelieving smile of elation.

Tearing her eyes from this astounding sight, Lessa saw that another fledgling was beginning the same performance with another boy. Two more dragons had emerged in the interim. One had knocked a boy down and was walking over him, oblivious of the fact that its claws were raking great gashes. The fledgling who followed its hatch-mate stopped by the wounded child, ducking its head to the boy's face, crooning anxiously. As Lessa watched, the boy managed to struggle to his feet, tears of pain streaming down his cheeks. She could hear him pleading with the dragon not to worry, that he was only scratched a little.

It was over very soon. The young dragons paired off with boys. Green riders dropped down to carry off the unacceptable. Blue riders settled to the floor with their beasts and led the couples out of the cavern, the

young dragons squealing, crooning, flapping wet wings
as they staggered off, encouraged by their newly ac-
quired Weyrmates.

Lessa turned resolutely back to the rocking golden
egg, knowing what to expect and trying to divine what
the successful boys had or had not done that caused
the baby dragons to single them out.

A crack appeared in the golden shell and was
greeted by the terrified screams of the girls. Some had
fallen into little heaps of white fabric, others embraced
tightly in their mutual fear. The crack widened and the
wedge head broke through, followed quickly by the
neck, gleaming gold. Lessa wondered with unexpected
detachment how long it would take the beast to mature, considering its by no means small size at birth.
For the head was larger than that of the male dragons,
and they had been large enough to overwhelm sturdy
boys of ten full Turns.

Lessa was aware of a loud hum within the Hall.
Glancing up at the audience, she realized it emanated
from the watching bronze dragons, for this was the
birth of their mate, their queen. The hum increased in
volume as the shell shattered into fragments and the
golden, glistening body of the new female emerged.
It staggered out, dipping its sharp beak into the soft
sand, momentarily trapped. Flapping its wet wings, it
righted itself, ludicrous in its weak awkwardness. With
sudden and unexpected swiftness, it dashed toward the
terror-stricken girls. Before Lessa could blink, it shook
the first girl with such violence that her head snapped
audibly and she fell limply to the sand. Disregarding
her, the dragon leaped toward the second girl but misjudged the distance and fell, grabbing out with one
claw for support and raking the girl's body from shoulder to thigh. Screaming, the mortally injured girl distracted the dragon and released the others from their
horrified trance. They scattered in panicky confusion,
racing, running, tripping, stumbling, falling across the
sand toward the exit the boys had used.

As the golden beast, crying piteously, lurched down

from the raised arena toward the scattered women, Lessa moved. Why hadn't that silly clunk-headed girl stepped aside, Lessa thought, grabbing for the wedge-head, at birth not much larger than her own torso. The dragon was so clumsy and weak she was her own worst enemy.

Lessa swung the head around so that the many-faceted eyes were forced to look at her . . . and found herself lost in that rainbow regard.

A feeling of joy suffused Lessa; a feeling of warmth, tenderness, unalloyed affection, and instant respect and admiration flooded mind and heart and soul. Never again would Lessa lack an advocate, a defender, an intimate, aware instantly of the temper of her mind and heart, of her desires. How wonderful was Lessa, the thought intruded into Lessa's reflections, how pretty, how kind, how thoughtful, how brave and clever!

Mechanically Lessa reached out to scratch the exact spot on the soft eye ridge.

The dragon blinked at her wistfully, extremely sad that she had distressed Lessa. Lessa reassuringly patted the slightly damp, soft neck that curved trustingly toward her. The dragon reeled to one side and one wing fouled on the hind claw. It hurt. Carefully Lessa lifted the erring foot, freed the wing, folding it back across the dorsal ridge with a pat.

The dragon began to croon in her throat, her eyes following Lessa's every move. She nudged at Lessa, and Lessa obediently attended the other eye ridge.

The dragon let it be known she was hungry.

"We'll get you something to eat directly," Lessa assured her briskly and blinked back at the dragon in amazement. How could she be so callous? It was a fact that this little menace had just seriously injured, if not killed, two women.

She couldn't believe her sympathies could swing so alarmingly toward the beast. Yet it was the most natural thing in the world for her to wish to protect this fledgling.

The dragon arched her neck to look Lessa squarely in the eyes. Ramoth repeated wistfully how exceedingly hungry she was, so long confined in that shell without nourishment.

Lessa wondered how she knew the golden dragon's name, and Ramoth replied: Why shouldn't she know her own name since it was hers and no one else's? And then Lessa was lost in the wonder of those magnificently expressive eyes.

Oblivious to the descending bronze dragons, oblivious to the presence of their riders, Lessa stood caressing the head of the most wonderful creature of all Pern, fully prescient of troubles and glories, but most immediately aware that Lessa of Pern was Weyrwoman to Ramoth the Golden for now and forever.

PART II

Dragonflight

Seas boil and mountains move,
Sands heat, dragons prove
Red Star passes.
Stones pile and fires burn,
Green withers, arm Pern.
Guard all passes.
Star Stone watch, scan sky.
Ready the Weyrs, all riders fly;
Red Star passes.

"IF A QUEEN isn't meant to fly, why does she have wings?" asked Lessa. She was genuinely trying to maintain a tone of sweet reason.

She had had to learn that, although it was her nature to seethe, she must seethe discreetly. Unlike the average Pernese, dragonriders were apt to perceive strong emotional auras.

R'gul's heavy eyebrows drew together in a startled frown. He snapped his jaws together with exasperation. Lessa knew his answer before he uttered it.

"Queens don't fly," he said flatly.

"Except to mate," S'lel amended. He had been dozing, a state he achieved effortlessly and frequently, although he was younger than the vigorous R'gul.

They are going to quarrel again, Lessa thought with an inward groan. She could stand about half an hour of that, and then her stomach would begin to churn. Their notion of instructing the new Weyrwoman in "Duties to Dragon, Weyr, and Pern" too often deteriorated into extended arguments over minor details in the lessons she had to memorize and recite word-perfect. Sometimes, as now, she entertained the fragile hope that she might wind them up so tightly in their own inconsistencies that they would inadvertently reveal a truth or two.

"A queen flies only to mate," R'gul allowed the correction.

"Surely," Lessa said with persistent patience, "if she can fly to mate, she can fly at other times."

"Queens don't fly," R'gul's expression was stubborn.

"Jora never did fly a dragon at all," S'lel mumbled, blinking rapidly in his bemusement with the past. His expression was vaguely troubled. "Jora never left these apartments."

"She took Nemorth to the feeding grounds," R'gul snapped irritably.

Bile rose in Lessa's throat. She swallowed. She would simply have to force them to leave. Would they realize that Ramoth woke all too conveniently at times? Maybe she'd better rouse R'gul's Hath. Inwardly she permitted herself a smug smile as her secret ability to hear and talk to any dragon in the Weyr, green, blue, brown, or bronze, momentarily soothed her.

"When Jora could get Nemorth to stir at all," S'lel muttered, picking at his underlip worriedly.

R'gut glared at S'lel to silence him and, succeeding, tapped pointedly on Lessa's slate.

Stifling her sigh, she picked up the stylus. She had already written this ballad out nine times, letter-perfect. Ten was apparently R'gul's magic number. For she had written every single one of the traditional Teaching Ballads, the Disaster Sagas, and the Laws, letter-perfect, ten times each. True, she had not understood half of them, but she knew them by heart.

"Seas boil, and mountains move," she wrote.

Possibly. If there is a major inner upheaval of the land. One of Fax's guards at Ruath Hold had once regaled the Watch with a tale from his great-grandsire's days. A whole coastal village in East Fort had slid into the sea. There had been monumental tides that year and, beyond Ista, a mountain had allegedly emerged at the same time, its top afire. It had subsided years later. That might be to what the line referred. Might be.

"Sands heat . . ." True, in summer it was said that Igen Plain could be unendurable. No shade, no trees, no caves, just bleak sand desert. Even dragonmen eschewed that region in deep summer. Come to think of it, the sands of the Hatching Ground were always warm underfoot. Did those sands ever get hot enough to burn? And what warmed them, anyway? The same unseen internal fires that heated the water in the bathing pools throughout Benden Weyr?

"Dragons prove . . ." Ambiguous for half a dozen interpretations, and R'gul won't even suggest one as official. Does it mean that dragons prove the Red Star passes? How? Coming out with a special keen, similar to the one they utter when one of their own kind passes to die *between?* Or did the dragons prove themselves in some other way *as* the Red Star passes? Besides, of course, their traditional function of burning the Threads out of the skies? Oh, all the things these ballads don't say, and no one ever explains. Yet there must originally have been a reason.

"Stone pile and fires burn/Green withers, arm Pern." More enigma. Is someone piling the stones on the fires? Do they mean firestone? Or do the stones pile themselves as in an avalanche? The balladeer might at least have suggested the season involved—or did he, with *"green withers"?* Yet vegetation purportedly attracted Threads, which was the reason, traditionally, that greenery was not permitted around human habitations. But stones couldn't stop a Thread from burrowing underground and multiplying. Only the phosphine emissions of a firestone-eating dragon stopped a

Thread. And nowadays, Lessa smiled thinly, no one not even dragonmen—with the notable exceptions of F'lar and his wingmen—bothered to drill with fire-stone, much less uproot grass near houses. Lately hilltops, scoured barren for centuries, were allowed to burgeon with green in the spring.

"Guard all passes."

She dug the phrase out with the stylus, thinking to herself: So no dragonrider can leave the Weyr unde-tected.

R'gul's current course of inaction as Weyrleader was based on the idea that if no one, Lord or holder, saw a dragonrider, no one could be offended. Even tradi-tional patrols were flown now over uninhabited areas, to allow the current agitation about the "parasitical" Weyr to die down. Fax, whose open dissension had sparked that movement, had not taken the cause to his grave. Larad, the young Lord of Telgar, was said to be the new leader.

R'gul as Weyrleader. That rankled Lessa deeply. He was so patently inadequate. But his Hath had taken Nemorth on her last flight. Traditionally (and that word was beginning to nauseate Lessa for the sins of omission ascribable to its name) the Weyrleader was the rider of the queen's mate. Oh, R'gul looked the part—a big, husky man, physically vigorous and domi-neering, his heavy face suggesting a sternly disciplined personality. Only, to Lessa's thinking, the discipline was misdirected.

Now F'lar . . . he had disciplined himself and his wingriders in what Lessa considered the proper direc-tion. For he, unlike the Weyrleader, not only sincerely believed in the Laws and Traditions he followed, he understood them. Time and again she had managed to make sense of a puzzling lesson from a phrase or two F'lar tossed in her direction. But, traditionally, only the Weyrleader instructed the Weyrwoman.

Why, in the name of the Egg, hadn't Mnementh, F'lar's bronze giant, flown Nemorth? Hath was a noble beast, in full prime, but he could not compare with

Mnementh in size, wingspread, or strength. There would have been more than ten eggs in that last clutch of Nemorth's if Mnementh had flown her.

Jora, the late and unlamented Weyrwoman, had been obese, stupid, and incompetent. On this everyone agreed. Supposedly the dragon reflected its rider as much as the rider the dragon. Lessa's thoughts turned critical. Undoubtedly Mnementh had been as repelled by the dragon, as a man like F'lar would be by the rider—unrider, Lessa corrected herself, sardonically glancing at the drowsing S'lel.

But if F'lar had gone to the trouble of that desperate duel with Fax to save Lessa's life back in Ruath Hold to bring her to the Weyr as a candidate at the Impression, why had he not taken over the Weyr when she proved successful, and ousted R'gul? What was he waiting for? He had been vehement and persuasive enough in making Lessa relinquish Ruatha and come to Benden Weyr. Why, now, did he adopt such an aloof pose of detachment as the Weyr tumbled further and further into disfavor?

"To save Pern," F'lar's words had been. From what if not R'gul? F'lar had better start salvation procedures. Or was he biding his time until R'gul blundered fatally? R'gul won't blunder, Lessa thought sourly, because he won't *do* anything. Most particularly he wouldn't explain what she wanted to know.

"Star Stone watch, scan sky." From her ledge, Lessa could see the gigantic rectangle of the Star Stone outlined against the sky. A watch-rider always stood by it. One day she'd get up there. It gave a magnificent view of the Benden Range and the high plateau that came right up to the foot of the Weyr. Last Turn there had been quite a ceremony at Star Stone, when the rising sun seemed to settle briefly on Finger Rock, marking the winter solstice. However, that only explained the significance of the Finger Rock, not the Star Stone. Add one more unexplained mystery.

"Ready the Weyrs," Lessa wrote morosely. Plural. Not Weyr but Weyr*s*. R'gul couldn't deny there were

five empty Weyrs around Pern, deserted for who knows
how many Turns. She'd had to learn the names, the
order of their establishment, too. Fort was the first and
mightiest, then Benden, High Reaches, Hot Igen, Ocean
Ista and plainland Telgar. Yet no explanation as to
why five had been abandoned. Nor why great Benden,
capable of housing five hundred beasts in its myriad
weyr-caverns, maintained a scant two hundred. Of
course, R'gul had fobbed their new Weyrwoman off
with the convenient excuse that Jora had been an incompetent and neurotic Weyrwoman, allowing her
dragon queen to gorge unrestrained. (No one told
Lessa why this was so undesirable, nor why, contradic-
torily, they were so pleased when Ramoth stuffed herself.) Of course, Ramoth was growing, growing so
rapidly that the changes were apparent overnight.

Lessa smiled, a tender smile that not even the presence of R'gul and S'lel could embarrass. She glanced
up from her writing to the passageway that led from
the Council Room up to the great cavern that was
Ramoth's weyr. She could sense that Ramoth was still
deeply asleep. She longed for the dragon to wake,
longed for the reassuring regard of those rainbow eyes,
for the comforting companionship that made life in the
Weyr endurable. Sometimes Lessa felt she was two
people: gay and fulfilled when she was attending
Ramoth, gray and frustrated when the dragon slept.
Abruptly Lessa cut off this depressing reflection and
bent diligently to her lesson. It did pass time.

"Red Star passes."

That benighted, begreened Red Star, and Lessa
jammed her stylus into the soft wax with the symbol for
a completed score.

There had been that unforgettable dawn, over two
full Turns ago, when she had been roused by an ominous presentiment from the damp straw of the cheeseroom at Ruatha. And the Red Star had gleamed at her.

Yet here she was. And that bright, active future F'lar
had so glowingly painted had not materialized. Instead
of using her subtle power to manipulate events and

people for Pern's good, she was forced into a round of inconclusive, uninstructive, tedious days, bored to active nausea by R'gul and S'lel, restricted to the Weyr-woman's apartments (however much of an improvement that was over her square foot of the cheeseroom floor) and the feeding grounds and the bathing lake. The only time she used her ability was to terminate these sessions with her so-called tutors. Grinding her teeth, Lessa thought that if it weren't for Ramoth, she would just leave. Oust Gemma's son and take Hold at Ruatha as she ought to have done once Fax was dead.

She caught her lip under her teeth, smiling in self-derision. If it weren't for Ramoth, she wouldn't have stayed here a moment past Impression anyway. But, from the second in which her eyes had met those of the young queen on the Hatching Ground, nothing but Ramoth mattered. Lessa was Ramoth's and Ramoth was hers, mind and heart, irrevocably attuned. Only death could dissolve that incredible bond.

Occasionally a dragonless man remained living, such as Lytol, Ruatha's Warder, but he was half shadow and that indistinct self lived in torment. When his rider died, a dragon winked into *between,* that frozen noth-ingness through which a dragon somehow moved himself and his rider, instantly, from one geographical posi-tion on Pern to another. To enter *between* held dan-ger to the uniniated, Lessa knew, the danger of being trapped *between* for longer than it took a man to cough three times.

Yet Lessa's one dragonflight on Mnementh's neck had filled her with an insatiable compulsion to repeat the experience. Naïvely she had thought she would be taught, as the young riders and dragonets were. But she, supposedly the most important inhabitant of the Weyr next to Ramoth, remained earthbound while the youngsters winked in and out of *between* above the Weyr in endless practice. She chafed at the intolerable restriction.

Female or not, Ramoth must have the same innate ability to pass *between* as the males did. This theory

was supported—unequivocally in Lessa's mind—by
"The Ballad of Moreta's Ride." Were not ballads con-
structed to inform? To teach those who could not read
and write? So that the young Pernese, whether he be
dragonman, Lord, or holder, might learn his duty toward Pern and rehearse Pern's bright history? These
two arrant idiots might deny the existence of that
Ballad, but how had Lessa learned it if it did not exist?
No doubt, Lessa thought acidly, for the same reason
queens had wings!

When R'gul consented—and she would wear him
down till he did—to allow her to take up her "traditional" responsibility as Keeper of the Records, she
would find that Ballad. One day it was going to have
to be R'gul's much delayed "right time."

Right time! she fumed. *Right time! I have too much
of the wrong time on my hands. When will this particular right time of theirs occur? When the moons turn
green? What are they waiting for? And what might the
superior F'lar be waiting for? The passing of the Red
Star he alone believes in?* She paused, for even the
most casual reference to that phenomenon evoked
a cold, mocking sense of menace within her.

She shook her head to dispel it. Her movement was
injudicious. It caught R'gul's attention. He looked up
from the Records he was laboriously reading. As he
drew her slate across the stone Council table, the clatter roused S'lel. He jerked his head up, uncertain of
his surroundings.

"Humph? Eh? Yes?" he mumbled, blinking to focus
sleep-blurred eyes.

It was too much. Lessa quickly made contact with
S'lel's Tuenth, himself just rousing from a nap. Tuenth
was quite agreeable.

"Tuenth is restless, must go," S'lel promptly muttered. He hastened up the passageway, his relief at
leaving no less than Lessa's at seeing him go. She was
startled to hear him greet someone in the corridor and
hoped the new arrival would provide an excuse to rid
herself of R'gul.

It was Manora who entered. Lessa greeted the head-woman of the Lower Caverns with thinly disguised relief. R'gul, always nervous in Manora's presence, immediately departed.

Manora, a stately woman of middle years, exuded an aura of quiet strength and purpose, having come to a difficult compromise with life which she maintained with serene dignity. Her patience tacitly chided Lessa for her fretfulness and petty grievances. Of all the women she had met in the Weyr, (when she was permitted by the dragonmen to meet any) Lessa admired and respected Manora most. Some instinct in Lessa made her bitterly aware that she would never be on easy or intimate terms with any of the women in the Weyr. Her carefully formal relationship with Manora, however, was both satisfying and satisfactory.

Manora had brought the tally slates of the Supply Caves. It was her responsibility as headwoman to keep the Weyrwoman informed of the domestic management of the Weyr. (One duty R'gul insisted she perform.)

"Bitra, Benden, and Lemos have sent in their tithes, but that won't be enough to see us through the deep cold this Turn."

"We had only those three last Turn and seemed to eat well enough."

Manor smiled amiably, but it was obvious she did not consider the Weyr generously supplied.

"True, but that was because we had stores of preserved and dried foods from more bountiful Turns to sustain us. That reserve is now gone. Except for those barrels and barrels of fish from Tillek . . ." Her voice trailed off expressively.

Lessa shuddered. Dried fish, salted fish, fish, had been served all too frequently of late.

"Our supplies of grain and flour in the Dry Caves are very low, for Benden, Bitra, and Lemos are not grain producers."

"Our biggest needs are grains and meat?"

"We could use more fruits and root vegetables for variety," Manora said thoughtfully. "Particularly if we have the long cold season the weather-wise predict. Now we did go to Igen Plain for the spring and fall nuts, berries . . ."

"We? to Igen Plain?" Lessa interrupted her, stunned.

"Yes," Manora answered, surprised at Lessa's reaction. "We always pick there. And we beat out the water grains from the low swamplands."

"How do you get there?" asked Lessa sharply. There could be only one answer.

"Why, the old ones fly us. They don't mind, and it gives the beasts something to do that isn't tiring. You knew that, didn't you?"

"That the women in the Lower Caverns fly with dragonriders?" Lessa pursed her lips angrily. "No. I wasn't told." Nor did it help Lessa's mood to see the pity and regret in Manora's eyes.

"As Weyrwoman," she said gently, "your obligations restrict you where . . ."

"If I should ask to be flown to . . . Ruatha, for instance," Lessa cut in, ruthlessly pursuing a subject she sensed Manora wanted to drop, "would it be refused me?"

Manora regarded Lessa closely, her eyes dark with concern. Lessa waited. Deliberately she had put Manora into a position where the woman must either lie outright, which would be distasteful to a person of her integrity, or prevaricate, which could prove more instructive.

"An absence for any reason these days might be disastrous. Absolutely disastrous," Manora said firmly and, unaccountably, flushed. "Not with the queen growing so quickly. You *must* be here." Her unexpectedly urgent entreaty, delivered with a mounting anxiety, impressed Lessa far more than all R'gul's pompous exhortations about constant attendance on Ramoth.

"You must be here," Manora repeated, her fear naked.

"Queens do not fly," Lessa reminded her acidly. She suspected Manora was about to echo S'lel's reply to that statement, but the older woman suddenly shifted to a safer subject.

"We cannot, even with half-rations," Manora blurted out breathlessly, with a nervous shuffling of her slates, "last the full Cold."

"Hasn't there ever been such a shortage before . . . in all Tradition?" Lessa demanded with caustic sweetness.

Manora raised questioning eyes to Lessa, who flushed, ashamed of herself for venting her frustrations with the dragonmen on the headwoman. She was doubly contrite when Manora gravely accepted her mute apology. In that moment Lessa's determination to end R'gul's domination over herself and the Weyr crystallized.

"No," Manora went on calmly, "traditionally," and she accorded Lessa a wry smile, "the Weyr is supplied from the first fruits of the soil and hunt. True, in recent Turns we have been chronically shorted, but it didn't signify. We had no young dragons to feed. They do eat, as you know." The glances of the two women locked in a timeless feminine amusement over the vagaries of the young under their care. Then Manora shrugged. "The riders used to hunt their beasts in the High Reaches or on the Keroon plateau. Now, however . . ."

She made a helpless grimace to indicate that R'gul's restrictions deprived them of that victual relief.

"Time was," she went on, her voice soft with nostalgia, "we would pass the coldest part of the Turn in one of the southern Holds. Or, if we wished and could, return to our birthplaces. Families used to take pride in daughters with dragonfolk sons." Her face settled into sad lines. "The world turns and times change."

"Yes," Lessa heard herself say in a grating voice, "the world does turn, and times . . . times will change."

Manora looked at Lessa, startled.

"Even R'gul will see we have no alternative," Manora continued hastily, trying to stick to her problem.

"To what? Letting the mature dragons hunt?"

"Oh, no. He's so adamant about that. No. We'll have to barter at Fort or Telgar."

Righteous indignation flared up in Lessa.

"The day the Weyr has to buy what should be given . . ." and she halted in midsentence, stunned as much by such a necessity as by the ominous echo of other words. "The day one of my Holds cannot support itself *or* the visit of its rightful overlord . . ." Fax's words rang in her head. Did those words again foreshadow disaster? For whom? For what?

"I know, I know," Manora was saying worriedly, unaware of Lessa's shock. "It goes against the grain. But if R'gul will not permit judicious hunting, there is no other choice. He will not like the pinch of hunger in his belly."

Lessa was struggling to control her inner terror. She took a deep breath.

"He'd probably then cut his throat to isolate his stomach," she snapped, her acid comment restoring her wits. She ignored Manora's startled look of dismay and went on. "It is traditional for you as headwoman of the Lower Cavern to bring such matters to the attention of the Weyrwoman, correct?"

Manora nodded, unsettled by Lessa's rapid switches of mood.

"I, then, as Weyrwoman, presumably bring this to the attention of the Weyrleader who, presumably,"— she made no attempt to moderate her derision—"acts upon it?"

Manora nodded, her eyes perplexed.

"Well," Lessa said in a pleasant, light voice, "you have dutifully discharged your traditional obligation. It is up to me now to discharge mine. Right?"

Manora regarded Lessa warily. Lessa smiled at her reassuringly.

"You may leave it in my hands, then."

Manora rose slowly. Without taking her eyes from Lessa, she began to gather up her records.

"It is said that Fort and Telgar had unusually good harvests," she suggested, her light tone not quite masking her anxiety. "Keroon, too, in spite of that coastal flooding."

"Is that so?" Lessa murmured politely.

"Yes," Manora continued helpfully, "and the herds at Keroon and Tillek had good increase."

"I'm happy for them."

Manora shot her a measuring look, not at all assured by Lessa's sudden affability. She finished gathering up her Records, then set them down again in a careful pile.

"Have you noticed how K'net and his wingriders chafe at R'gul's restrictions?" she asked, watching Lessa closely.

"K'net?"

"Yes. And old C'gan. Oh, his leg is still stiff, and Tagath may be more gray with age than blue, but he was of Lidith's hatching. Her last clutch had fine beasts in it," she remarked. "C'gan remembers other days . . ."

"Before the world turned and times changed?"

Lessa's sweet voice did not mislead Manora now.

"It is not just as Weyrwoman that you are attractive to the dragonmen, Lessa of Pern," Manora said sharply, her face stern. "There are several of the brown riders, for instance . . ."

"F'nor?" Lessa asked pointedly.

Manora drew herself up proudly. "He is a man grown, Weyrwoman, and we of the Lower Caverns have learned to disregard the ties of blood and affection. It is as a brown rider, not the son I bore, that I recommend him. Yes, I'd recommend F'nor, as I would also recommend T'sum and L'rad."

"Do you suggest them because they are of F'lar's wing and bred in the true traditions? Less apt to be swayed by my blandishments . . ."

"I suggest them because they believe in the tradition that the Weyr must be supplied from the Holds."

"All right." Lessa grinned at Manora, seeing the woman could not be baited about F'nor. "I shall take your recommendations to heart, for I do not intend . . ." She broke off her sentence. "Thank you for apprising me of our supply problems. We need fresh meat most of all?" she asked, rising to her feet.

"Grains, too, and some of the southern root vegetables would be very welcome," Manora replied formally.

"Very well," Lessa agreed.

Manora left, her expression thoughtful.

Lessa reflected for long moments on that interview, sitting like a slim statuette in the capacious stony chair, her legs curled up under her on the padding.

Foremost was the disturbing knowledge that Manora was deeply afraid of the mere prospect of Lessa absent from the Weyr, from Ramoth's side, for any reason, for any length of time. Her instinctive fear reaction was a far more effective argument than any of R'gul's sententious mouthings. However, Manora had given no hint of the reason for that necessity. Very well, Lessa would not try to fly one of the other dragons, with or without the rider, as she had been beginning to think she could.

As for this matter of short supplies, on that Lessa would act. Especially since R'gul would not. And, since R'gul could not protest what he did not know, she would contrive, with the help of K'net or F'nor or however many she needed, to keep the Weyr decently supplied. Eating regularly had become a pleasant habit she did not wish to curtail. She did not intend being greedy, but a little judicious pilfering of a bountiful harvest would go unnoticed by the Hold Lords.

K'net, though, was young; he might be rash and indiscreet. Perhaps F'nor would be the wiser choice. But was he as free to maneuver as K'net, who was, after all, a bronze rider? Maybe C'gan. The absence of a retired blue rider, time heavy on his hands, might not be noticed at all.

Lessa smiled to herself, but her smile faded quickly.

"The day the Weyr has to barter for what should be given . . ." She thrust back the premonitory shudder, concentrated on the ignominy of that situation. It certainly emphasized the measure of her self-delusion.

Why had she thought being at the Weyr would be so different from Ruath Hold? Had her early childhood training instilled such a questionless reverence for the Weyr that life must alter its pattern because Lessa of Ruatha had been Impressed by Ramoth? How could she have been such a romantic little fool?

Look around you, Lessa of Pern, look around the Weyr with unveiled eyes. Old and hallowed is the Weyr? Yes, but shabby and worn—and disregarded. Yes, you were elated to sit in the Weyrwoman's great chair at the Council Table, but the padding is thin and the fabric dusty. Humbled to think your hands rest where Moreta's and Torene's had rested? Well, the stone is ingrained with dirt and needs a good scrubbing. And your rump may rest where theirs did—but that's not where you have your brains.

The shabby Weyr reflected the deterioration of its purpose in the scheme of life on Pern. Those handsome dragonriders, too, so brave in their wher-hide accouterments, proud on the necks of their great beasts—they did not submit kindly to close examination without a few disappointing revelations. They were only men, with manlike lusts and ambitions, full of very human faults and frustrations, unwilling to disrupt their easy existence for the harsh exigencies that would reestablish the Weyr. They had settled too deeply in their isolation from the rest of their race; they did not realize they were little thought of. There was no real leader at their head . . .

F'lar! What was he waiting for? For Lessa to see through R'gul's ineffectiveness? No, Lessa decided slowly, for Ramoth to grow up. For Mnementh to fly her when he can . . . traditionalist that F'lar is, and Lessa thought this excuse to be specious . . . when the mating dragon's rider became, traditionally, the Weyrleader. That rider!

Well, F'lar might just find events not turning out as *he* planned.

My eyes were dazzled by Ramoth's, but I can see

around the rainbow now, Lessa thought, steeling herself against the tenderness that always accompanied any thought of the golden beast. Yes, I can see into the black and gray shadows now, where my apprenticeship at Ruatha should stand me in good stead. True, there's more to control than one small Hold and far more perceptive minds to influence. Perceptive but dense in their own way. A greater hazard if I lose. But how can I? Lessa's smile broadened. She rubbed her palms against her thighs in anticipation of the challenge. They can do nothing with Ramoth without me, and they must have Ramoth. No one can coerce Lessa of Ruatha, and they're as stuck with me as they were with Jora. Only, I'm no Jora!

Elated, Lessa jumped from the chair. She felt alive again. And more powerful in herself than she felt when Ramoth was awake.

Time, time, time. R'gul's time. Well, Lessa had done with marking his time. She'd been a silly fool. Now she'd be the Weyrwoman F'lar had beguiled her to think she could be.

F'lar . . . her thoughts returned to him constantly. She'd have to watch out for him. Particularly when she started "arranging" things to suit herself. But she had an advantage he couldn't know—that she could speak to all the dragons, not just Ramoth. Even to his precious Mnementh.

Lessa threw back her hand and laughed, the sound echoing hollowly in the large, empty Council Room. She laughed again, delighted with an exercise she had had rare occasion to use. Her mirth roused Ramoth. The exultation of her decision was replaced by that of knowing the golden dragon was waking.

Ramoth stirred again and stretched restlessly as hunger pierced slumber. Lessa ran up the passage on light feet, eager as a child for the first sight of the glorious eyes and the sweetness that characterized the dragon's personality.

Ramoth's huge golden wedge-shaped head swiveled around as the sleepy dragon instinctively sought her

Weyrmate. Lessa quickly touched her blunt chin, and the searching head was still, comforted. The several protecting lids parted over the many-faceted eyes, and Ramoth and Lessa renewed the pledge of their mutual devotion.

Ramoth had had those dreams again, she told Lessa, shuddering slightly. It was so cold *there!* Lessa caressed the soft down above her eye-ridge, soothing the dragon. Linked firmly to Ramoth as she had become, she was acutely aware of the dismay those curious sequences produced.

Ramoth complained of an itch by the left dorsal ridge.

"The skin is flaking again," Lessa told her, quickly spreading sweet oil on the affected area. "You're growing so fast," she added with mock and tender dismay.

Ramoth repeated that she itched abominably.

"Either eat less so you'll sleep less or stop outgrowing your hide overnight."

She chanted dutifully as she rubbed in the oil, "The dragonet must be oiled daily as the rapid growth in early development can overstretch fragile skin tissues, rendering them tender and sensitive."

They itch, Ramoth corrected petulantly, squirming.

"Hush. I'm only repeating what I was taught."

Ramoth issued a dragon-sized snort that blew Lessa's robe tightly around her legs.

"Hush. Daily bathing is compulsory, and thorough oiling must accompany these ablutions. Patchy skin becomes imperfect hide in the adult dragon. Imperfect hide results in skin ruptures that may prove fatal to a flying beast."

Don't stop rubbing, Ramoth entreated.

"Flying beast indeed!"

Ramoth informed Lessa she was so hungry. Couldn't she bathe and oil later?

"The moment that cavern you call a belly is full, you're so sleepy you can barely crawl. You've gotten too big to be carried."

Ramoth's tart rejoinder was interrupted by a low

chuckle. Lessa whirled, hastily controlling the annoyance she felt at seeing F'lar lounging indolently against the archway to the ledge-corridor.

He had obviously been flying a patrol, for he still wore the heavy wher-hide gear. The stiff tunic clung to the flat chest, outlined the long, muscular legs. His bony but handsome face was still reddened by the ultra-cold of *between*. His curiously amber eyes glinted with amusement and, Lessa added, conceit.

"She grows sleek," he commented, approaching Ramoth's couch with a courteous bow to the young queen.

Lessa heard Mnementh give a greeting to Ramoth from his perch on the ledge.

Ramoth rolled her eyes coquettishly at the wing-leader. His smile of almost possessive pride in her doubled Lessa's irritation.

"The escort arrives in good time to bid the queen good day."

"Good day, Ramoth," F'lar said obediently. He straightened, slapping his heavy gloves against his thigh.

"We interrupted your patrol pattern?" asked Lessa, sweetly apologetic.

"No matter. A routine flight," F'lar replied, undaunted. He sauntered to one side of Lessa for an unimpeded view of the queen. "She's bigger than most of the browns. There have been high seas and flooding at Telgar. And the tidal swamps at Igen are dragon-deep." His grin flashed as if this minor disaster pleased him.

As F'lar said nothing without purpose, Lessa filed that statement away for future reference. However irritating F'lar might be, she preferred his company to that of the other bronze riders.

Ramoth interrupted Lessa's reflections with a tart reminder: If she had to bathe before eating, could they get on with it before she expired from hunger?

Lessa heard Mnementh's amused rumble without the cavern.

"Mnementh says we'd better humor her," F'lar remarked indulgently.

Lessa suppressed the desire to retort that she could perfectly well hear what Mnementh said. One day it was going to be most salutary to witness F'lar's stunned reaction to the knowledge that she could hear and speak to every dragon in the Weyr.

"I neglect her shockingly," Lessa said, as if contritely.

She saw F'lar about to answer her. He paused, his amber eyes narrowing briefly. Smiling affably, he gestured for her to lead the way.

An inner perversity prompted Lessa to bait F'lar whenever possible. One day she would pierce that pose and flay him to the quick. It would take doing. He was sharp-witted.

The three joined Mnementh on the ledge. He hovered protectingly over Ramoth as she glided awkwardly down to the far end of the long oval Weyr Bowl. Mist, rising from the warmed water of the small lake, parted in the sweep of Ramoth's ungainly wings. Her growth had been so rapid that she had had no time to coordinate muscle and bulk. As F'lar set Lessa on Mnementh's neck for the short drop, she looked anxiously after the gawky, blundering queen.

Queens don't fly because they can't, Lessa told herself with bitter candor, contrasting Ramoth's grotesque descent with Mnementh's effortless drift.

"Mnementh says to assure you she'll be more graceful when she gets her full growth," F'lar's amused voice said in her ear.

"But the young males are growing just as fast, and they're not a bit . . ." She broke off. She wouldn't admit anything to that F'lar.

"They don't grow as large, and they constantly practice . . ."

"Flying! . . ." Lessa leaped on the word, and then, catching a glimpse of the bronze rider's face, said no more. He was just as quick with a casual taunt.

Ramoth had immersed herself and was irritably

waiting to be sanded. The left dorsal ridge itched abominably. Lessa dutifully attacked the affected area with a sandy hand.

No, her life at the Weyr was no different from that at Ruatha. She was still scrubbing. And there was more of Ramoth to scrub each day, she thought as she finally sent the golden beast into the deeper water to rinse. Ramoth wallowed, submerging to the tip of her nose. Her eyes, covered by the thin inner lid, glowed just below the surface—watery jewels. Ramoth languidly turned over, and the water lapped around Lessa's ankles.

All occupations were suspended when Ramoth was abroad. Lessa noticed the women clustered at the entrance to the Lower Caverns, their eyes wide with fascination. Dragons perched on their ledges or idly circled overhead. Even the weyrlings, boy and dragonet, wandered forth curiously from the fledgling barracks of the training fields.

A dragon trumpeted unexpectedly on the heights by the Star Stone. He and his rider spiraled down.

"Tithings, F'lar, a train in the pass," the blue rider announced, grinning broadly until he became disappointed by the calm way his unexpected good news was received by the bronze rider.

"F'nor will see to it," F'lar told him indifferently. The blue dragon obediently lifted his rider to the wing-second's ledge.

"Who could it be?" Lessa asked F'lar. "The loyal three are in."

F'lar waited until he saw F'nor on brown Canth wheel up and over the protecting lip of the Weyr, followed by several green riders of the wing.

"We'll know soon enough," he remarked. He turned his head thoughtfully eastward, an unpleasant smile touching the corner of his mouth briefly. Lessa, too, glanced eastward where, to the knowing eye, the faint spark of the Red Star could be seen, even though the sun was full up.

"The loyal ones will be protected," F'lar muttered under his breath, "when the Red Star passes."

How and why they two were in accord in their unpopular belief in the significance of the Red Star Lessa did not know. She only knew that she, too, recognized it as Menace. It had actually been the foremost consideration in all F'lar's arguments that she leave Ruatha and come to the Weyr. Why *he* had not succumbed to the pernicious indifference that had emasculated the other dragonmen she did not know. She had never asked him—not out of spite, but because it was so obvious that his belief was beyond question. He *knew*. And she *knew*.

And occasionally that knowledge must stir in the dragons. At dawn, as one, they stirred restlessly in their sleep—if they slept—or lashed their tails and spread their wings in protest if they were awake. Manora, too, seemed to believe. F'nor must. And perhaps some of F'lar's surety had infected his wingriders. He certainly demanded implicit obedience to tradition in his riders and received it, to the point of open devotion.

Ramoth emerged from the lake and half-flapped, half-floundered her way to the feeding grounds. Mnementh arranged himself at the edge and permitted Lessa to seat herself on his foreleg. The ground away from the Bowl rim was cold underfoot.

Ramoth ate, complaining bitterly over the stringy bucks that made her meal and resenting it when Lessa restricted her to six.

"Others have to eat, too, you know."

Ramoth informed Lessa that she was queen and had priority.

"You'll itch tomorrow."

Mnementh said she could have his share. He had eaten well of a fat buck in Keroon two days ago. Lessa regarded Mnementh with considerable interest. Was that why all the dragons in F'lar's wing looked so smug? She must pay more attention as to who frequented the feeding grounds and how often.

Ramoth had settled into her weyr again and was

already drowsing when F'lar brought the train-captain into the quarters.

"Weyrwoman," F'lar said, "this messenger is from Lytol with duty to you."

The man, reluctantly tearing his eyes from the glowing golden queen, bowed to Lessa.

"Tilarek, Weyrwoman, from Lytol, Warder of Ruath Hold," he said respectfully, but his eyes, as he looked at Lessa, were so admiring as to be just short of impudence. He withdrew a message from his belt and hesitated, torn between the knowledge that women did not read and his instructions to give it to the Weyrwoman. Just as he caught F'lar's amused reassurance, Lessa extended her hand imperiously.

"The queen sleeps," F'lar remarked, indicating the passageway to the Council Room.

Adroit of F'lar, Lessa thought, to be sure the messenger had a long look at Ramoth. Tilarek would spread the word on his return journey, properly elaborated with each retelling, of the queen's unusual size and fine health. Let Tilarek also broadcast his opinion of the new Weyrwoman.

Lessa waited until she saw F'lar offer the courier wine before she opened the skin. As she deciphered Lytol's inscription, Lessa realized how glad she was to receive news of Ruatha. But why did Lytol's first words have to be:

The babe grows strong and is healthy . . .

She cared little for that infant's prosperity. Ah . . .

Ruatha is green-free, from hill crown to craft-hold verge. The harvest has been very good, and the beasts multiply from the new studs. Herewith is the due and proper tithe of Ruath Hold. May it prosper the Weyr which protects us.

Lessa snorted under her breath. Ruatha knew its duty, true, but not even the other three tithing holds had sent proper greetings. Lytol's message contained ominously:

> A word to the wise. With Fax's death, Telgar has come to the fore in the growing sedition. Meron, so-called Lord of Nabol, is strong and seeks, I feel, to be first: Telgar is too cautious for him. The dissension strengthens and is more widespread than when I last spoke with Bronze Rider F'lar. The Weyr must be doubly on its guard. If Ruatha may serve, send word.

Lessa scowled at the last sentence. It only emphasized the fact that too few Holds served in any way.

". . . laughed at we were, good F'lar," Tilarek was saying, moistening his throat with a generous gulp of Weyr-made wine, "for doing as men ought.

"Funny thing, that, for the nearer we got to Benden Range the less laughing we heard. Sometimes it's hard to make sense of some things, being as how you don't do 'em much. Like if I were not to keep my sword arm strong and used to the weight of a blade," and he made vigorous slashes and thrusts with his right arm, "I'd be put to it to defend myself come a long-drawn fight. Some folk, too, believe what the loudest talker says. And some folk because it frightens them not to. However," he went on briskly, "I'm soldier-bred and it goes hard to take the gibes of mere crafters and holders. But we'd orders to keep our swords sheathed, and we did. Just as well," he said with a wry grimace, "to talk soft. The Lords have kept full guard since . . . since the Search . . ."

Lessa wondered what he had been about to say, but he went on soberly.

"There are those that'll be sorry when the Threads fall again on all that green around their doors."

F'lar refilled the man's cup, asking casually about the harvests seen on the road here.

"Fine, fat and heavy," the courier assured him. "They do say this Turn has been the best in memory of living man. Why, the vines in Crom had bunches this big!" He made a wide circle with his two huge hands, and his listeners made proper response. "And I've never seen the Telgar grain so full and heavy. Never."

"Pern prospers," F'lar remarked dryly.

"Begging your pardon"—Tilarek picked up a wizened piece of fruit from the tray—"I've scooped better than this dropped on the road behind a harvest wagon." He ate the fruit in two bites, wiping his hands on the tunic. Then, realizing what he had said, he added in hasty apology, "Ruatha Hold sent you its best. First fruits as man ought. No ground pickings from us. You may be sure."

"It is reassuring to know we have Ruatha's loyalty as well as its full measure," F'lar assured him. "Roads were clear?"

"Aye, and there's a funny thing this time of year. Cold, then suddenly warm like the weather couldn't remember the season. No snow and little rain. But winds! Like you'd never believe. They do say as how the coasts have been hit hard with high water." He rolled his eyes expressively and then, hunching his shoulders, confidentially added, "They do say Ista's smoking mountain that does appear and then . . . *phffst* . . . disappears . . . has appeared again."

F'lar looked properly skeptical, although Lessa did not miss the gleam of excitement in his eyes. The man sounded like one of R'gul's ambiguous verses.

"You must stay a few days for a good rest," F'lar invited Tilarek genially, guiding him out past sleeping Ramoth.

"Aye and grateful. Man gets to the Weyr maybe once or twice in his life," Tilarek was saying absently, craning his neck to keep Ramoth in sight as F'lar led him out. "Never knew queens grew so big."

"Ramoth is already much larger and stronger than Nemorth," F'lar assured him as he turned the messenger over to the weyrling waiting to escort him to quarters.

"Read this," Lessa said, impatiently shoving the

skin at the bronze rider as soon as they were again in the Council Room.

"I expected little else," F'lar remarked, unconcerned, perching on the edge of the great stone table.

"And . . .?" Lessa demanded fiercely.

"Time will tell," F'lar replied serenely, examining a fruit for spots.

"Tilarek implied that not all the holders echo their Lords' seditious sentiments," Lessa commented, trying to reassure herself.

F'lar snorted. "Tilarek says 'as will please his listeners,' " he said in a passable imitation of the man's speech.

"You'd better know, too," F'nor said from the doorway, "he doesn't speak for all his men. There was a good deal of grumbling in the escort." F'nor accorded Lessa a courteous if absentminded salute. "It was felt that Ruatha has been too long poor to give such a share to the Weyr its first profitable Turn. And I'll say that Lytol was more generous than he ought to be. We'll eat well . . . for a while."

F'lar tossed the messageskin to the brown rider.

"As if we didn't know that," F'nor grunted after he had quickly scanned the contents.

"If you know that, what will you do about it?" Lessa spoke up. "The Weyr is in such disrepute that the day is coming when it can't feed its own."

She used the phrase deliberately, noticing with satisfaction that it stung the memories of both dragonmen. The look they turned on her was almost savage. Then F'lar chuckled so that F'nor relaxed with a sour laugh.

"Well?" she demanded.

"R'gul and S'lel will undoubtedly get hungry," F'nor said, shrugging.

"And you two?"

F'lar shrugged, too, and, rising, bowed formally to Lessa. "As Ramoth is deep asleep, Weyrwoman, your permission to withdraw."

"Get out!" Lessa shouted at them.

They had turned, grinning at each other, when R'gul came storming into the chamber, S'lel, D'nol, T'bor, and K'net close on his heels.

"What is this I hear? That Ruatha alone of the High Reaches sends tithes?"

"True, all too true," F'lar conceded calmly, tossing the messageskin at R'gul.

The Weyrleader scanned it, mumbling the words under his breath, frowning at its content. He passed it distastefully to S'lel, who held it for all to read.

"We fed the Weyr last year on the tithings of three Holds," R'gul announced disdainfully.

"*Last* year," Lessa put in, "but only because there were reserves in the supply caves. Manora has just reported that those reserves are exhausted. . . ."

"Ruatha has been very generous," F'lar put in quickly. "It should make the difference."

Lessa hesitated a moment, thinking she hadn't heard him right.

"Not that generous." She rushed on, ignoring the remanding glare F'lar shot her way.

"The dragonets require more this year, anyway. So there's only one solution. The Weyr must barter with Telgar and Fort to survive the Cold."

Her words touched off instant rebellion.

"Barter? Never!"

"The Weyr reduced to bartering? Raid!"

"R'gul, we'll raid first. Barter never!"

That had stung all the bronze riders to the quick. Even S'lel reacted with indignation. K'net was all but dancing, his eyes sparkling with anticipation of action.

Only F'lar remained aloof, his arms folded across his chest, glaring at her coldly.

"Raid?" R'gul's voice rose authoritatively above the noise. "There can be no raid!"

Out of conditioned reflex to his commanding tone, they quieted momentarily.

"No raids?" T'bor and D'nol demanded in chorus.

"Why not?" D'nol went on, the veins in his neck standing out.

He was not the one, groaned Lessa to herself, trying to spot S'lar, only to remember that he was out on the training field. Occasionally he and D'nol acted together against R'gul in Council, but D'nol was not strong enough to stand alone.

Lessa glanced hopefully toward F'lar. Why didn't he speak up now?

"I'm sick of stringy old flesh, of bad bread, of wood-tasting roots," D'nol was shouting, thoroughly incensed. "Pern prospered this Turn. Let some spill over into the Weyr as it ought!"

T'bor, standing belligerently beside him, growled agreement, his eyes fixing on first one, then another of the silent bronze riders. Lessa caught at the hope that T'bor might act as substitute for S'lan.

"One move from the Weyr at this moment," R'gul interrupted, his arm raised warningly, "and all the Lords will move—against us." His arm dropped dramatically.

He stood, squarely facing the two rebels, feet slightly apart, head high, eyes flashing. He towered a head and a half above the stocky, short D'nol and the slender T'bor. The contrast was unfortunate: the tableau was of the stern patriarch reprimanding errant children.

"The roads are clear," R'gul went on portentously, "with neither rain nor snow to stay an advancing army. The Lords have kept full guards under arms since Fax was killed." R'gul's head turned just slightly in F'lar's direction. "Surely you all remember the scant hospitality we got on Search?" Now R'gul pinned each bronze rider in turn with a significant stare. "You know the temper of the Holds, you saw their strength." He jerked his chin up. "Are you fools to antagonize them?"

"A good firestoning . . ." D'nol blurted out angrily and stopped. His rash words shocked himself as much as anyone else in the room.

Even Lessa gasped at the idea of deliberately using firestone against man.

"Something has to be done . . ." D'nol blundered on desperately, turning first to F'lar, then, less hopefully, to T'bor.

If R'gul wins, it will be the end, Lessa thought, coldly furious, and reacted, turning her thoughts toward T'bor. At Ruatha it had been easiest to sway angry men. If she could just . . . A dragon trumpeted outside.

An excruciatingly sharp pain lanced from her instep up her leg. Stunned, she staggered backward, unexpectedly falling into F'lar. He caught her arm with fingers like iron bands.

"You dare control . . ." he whispered savagely in her ear and, with false solicitude, all but slammed her down into her chair. His hand grasped her arm with vise-fingered coercion.

Swallowing convulsively against the double assault, she sat rigidly. When she could take in what had happened, she realized the moment of crisis had passed.

"Nothing can be done at this time," R'gul was saying forcefully.

"At this time . . ." The words ricocheted in Lessa's ringing ears.

"The Weyr has young dragons to train. Young men to bring up in the proper Traditions."

Empty Traditions, Lessa thought numbly, her mind seething with bitterness. And they will empty the very Weyr itself.

She glared with impotent fury at F'lar. His hand tightened warningly on her arm until his fingers pressed tendon to bone and she gasped again with pain. Through the tears that sprang to her eyes, she saw defeat and shame written on K'net's young face. Hope flared up, renewed.

With an effort she forced herself to relax. Slowly, as if F'lar had really frightened her. Slowly enough for him to believe in her capitulation.

As soon as she could, she would get K'net aside. He was ripe for the idea she had just conceived. He was young, malleable, attracted to her anyway. He would serve her purpose admirably.

"Dragonman, avoid excess," R'gul was intoning. "Greed will cause the Weyr distress."

Lessa stared at the man, honestly appalled that he could clothe the Weyr's moral defeat with hypocritical homily.

> Honor those the dragons heed
> In thought and favor, word and deed.
> Worlds are lost or worlds are saved
> From the dangers dragon-braved.

"WHAT'S THE matter? Noble F'lar going against tradition?" Lessa demanded of F'nor as the brown rider appeared with a courteous explanation of the wingleader's absence.

Lessa no longer bothered to leash her tongue in F'nor's presence. The brown rider knew it was not directed at himself, so he rarely took offense. Some of his half brother's reserve had rubbed off on him.

His expression today, however, was not tolerant; it was sternly disapproving.

"He's tracing K'net," F'nor said bluntly, his dark eyes troubled. He pushed his heavy hair back from his forehead, another habit picked up from F'lar, which added fuel to Lessa's grievance with the absent weyrman.

"Oh, is he? He'd do well to imitate him instead," she snapped.

F'nor's eyes flashed angrily.

Good, thought Lessa. I'm getting to him, too.

"What you do not realize, Weyrwoman, is that K'net takes your instructions too liberally. A judicious pilfering would raise no protest, but K'net is too young to be circumspect."

"My instructions?" Lessa repeated innocently. Surely F'nor and F'lar hadn't a shred of evidence to go on. Not that she cared. "He's just too fed up with the whole cowardly mess!"

F'nor clamped his teeth down tightly against an angry rebuttal. He shifted his stance, clamped his hands around the wide rider's belt until his knuckles whitened. He returned Lessa's gaze coldly.

In that pause Lessa regretted antagonizing F'nor. He had tried to be friendly, pleasant, and had often amused her with anecdotes as she became more and more embittered. As the world turned colder, rations had gotten slimmer at the Weyr in spite of the systematic additions of K'net. Despair drifted through the Weyr on the icy winds.

Since D'nol's abortive rebellion, all spirit had drained out of the dragonmen. Even the beasts reflected it. Diet alone would not account for the dullness of their hide and their deadened attunement. Apathy could—and did. Lessa wondered that R'gul did not rue the result of his spineless decision.

"Ramoth is not awake," she told F'nor calmly, "so you do not need to dance attendance on *me*."

F'nor said nothing, and his continued silence began to discomfit Lessa. She rose, rubbing her palms on her thighs as if she could erase her last hasty words. She paced back and forth, glancing from her sleeping chamber into Ramoth's, where the golden queen, now larger than any of the bronze dragons, lay in deep slumber.

If only she would wake, Lessa thought. When she's awake, everything's all right. As right as it can be, that is. But she's like a rock.

"So . . ." she began, trying to keep her nervousness out of her voice, "F'lar is at last doing something, even if it is cutting off our one source of supply."

"Lytol sent in a message this morning," F'nor said curtly. His anger had subsided, but not his disapproval.

Lessa turned to face him, expectantly.

"Telgar and Fort have conferred with Keroon," F'nor went on heavily. "They've decided the Weyr is behind their losses. Why," and his anger flared hot again, "if you picked K'net, didn't you keep a close check on him? He's too green. C'gan, T'sum, *I* would have . . ."

"You? You don't sneeze without F'lar's consent," she retorted.

F'nor laughed outright at her.

"F'lar did give you more credit than you deserve," he replied, contemptuous of his own turn. "Haven't you realized why he must wait?"

"No," Lessa shouted at him. "I haven't! Is this something I must divine, by instinct, like the dragons? By the shell of the first Egg, F'nor, no one *explains* anything to me!

"But it is nice to know that he has a reason for waiting. I just hope it's valid. That it is not too late already. Because I think it is."

It was too late when he stopped me from reinforcing T'bor, she thought, but refrained from saying. Instead, she added, "It was too late when R'gul was too cowardly to feel the shame of . . ."

F'nor swung on her, his face white with anger. "It took more courage than you'll ever have to watch that moment slide by."

"Why?"

F'nor took a half step forward, so menacingly that Lessa steeled herself for a blow. He mastered the impulse, shaking his head violently to control himself.

"It is not R'gul's fault," he said finally, his face old

and drawn, his eyes troubled and hurt. "It has been hard, hard to watch and to know you *had* to wait."

"*Why?*" Lessa all but shrieked.

F'nor would no longer be goaded. He continued in a quiet voice.

"*I* thought you ought to know, but it goes against F'lar's grain to apologize for one of his own."

Lessa bit back the sarcastic remark that rose to her lips, lest she interrupt this long-awaited enlightenment.

"R'gul is Weyrleader only by default. He'd be well enough, I suppose, if there hadn't been such a long Interval. The Records warn of the dangers . . ."

"Records? Dangers? What do you mean by Interval?"

"An Interval occurs when the Red Star does not pass close enough to excite the Threads. The Records indicate it takes about two hundred Turns before the Red Star swings back again. F'lar figures nearly twice that time has elapsed since the last Threads fell."

Lessa glanced apprehensively eastward. F'nor nodded solemnly.

"Yes, and it'd be rather easy to forget fear and caution in four hundred years. R'gul's a good fighter and a good wingleader, but he has to see and touch and smell danger before he admits it exists. Oh, he learned the Laws and all the Traditions, but he never understood them in his bones. Not the way F'lar does or the way I have come to," he added defiantly, seeing the skeptical expression on Lessa's face. His eyes narrowed, and he pointed an accusing finger at her. "Nor the way you do, only you don't know why."

She backed away, not from him but from the menace she *knew* existed, even if she didn't know why she believed.

"The moment F'lar Impressed Mnementh, F'lon began training him to take over. Then F'lon got himself killed in that ridiculous brawl." An expression comprised of anger, regret, and irritation passed over F'nor's face. Belatedly Lessa realized the man was speaking of his father. "F'lar was too young to take over, and before anyone could intervene, R'gul got Hath to fly Nemorth and *we* had to wait. But R'gul couldn't control Jora's grief over F'lon, and she deteriorated rapidly. And he misinterpreted F'lon's plan for carrying us over the last of the Interval to mean isolation. Consequently"—F'nor shrugged expressively—"the Weyr lost prestige faster all the time."

"Time, time, time," Lessa railed. "It's always the wrong time. When is *now* the time?"

"Listen to me." F'nor's stern words interrupted her tirade as effectively as if he had grabbed and shaken her. She had not suspected F'nor of such forcefulness. She looked at him with increased respect.

"Ramoth is full-grown, ready for her first mating flight. When she flies, all the bronzes rise to catch her. The strongest does not always get the queen. Sometimes it is the one everyone in the Weyr wants to have win her." He enunciated his words slowly and clearly. "That was how R'gul got Hath to fly Nemorth. The older riders wanted R'gul. They couldn't stomach a nineteen-year-old over them as Weyrleader, son though he was to F'lon. So Hath got Nemorth. And they got R'gul. They got what they wanted. And look what they've got!" His scornful gesture took in the threadbare weyr.

"It is too late, it is too late," Lessa moaned, understanding a great deal, too well, too late.

"It may be, thanks to your prodding K'net into uncontrolled raiding," F'nor assured her cynically. "You didn't need him, you know. Our wing was handling it quietly. But when so much kept coming in, we cut our operations down. It's a case of too much too soon, since the Hold Lords are getting imprudent enough to retaliate. Think, Lessa of Pern," and F'nor leaned toward her, his smile bitter, "what R'gul's reaction will be. You didn't stop to think of that, did you? Think, now, what he will do when the well-armed Lords of the Hold appear, to demand satisfaction?"

Lessa closed her eyes, appalled at the scene she could picture all too clearly. She caught at her chair arm, limply sat down, undone by the knowledge she had miscalculated. Overconfident because she had been able to bring haughty Fax to his death, she was about to bring the Weyr to its ruin through that same arrogance.

There was suddenly noise enough for half the Weyr to be storming up the passageway from the ledge. She could hear the dragons calling excitedly to each other, the first outburst she had heard from them in two months.

Startled, she jumped up. Had F'lar failed to intercept K'net? Had K'net, by some horrible chance, been caught by the Lords? Together she and F'nor rushed out into the queen's weyr.

It was not F'lar and K'net and an angry Lord—or several—in tow who entered. It was R'gul, his cautious face distorted, his eyes wide with excitement. From the outside ledge Lessa could hear Hath generating the same intense agitation. R'gul shot a quick glance at Ramoth, who slumbered on obliviously. His eyes as he approached Lessa were coldly calculating. D'nol came rushing into the weyr at a dead run, hastily buckling on his tunic. Close on his heels came S'lan, S'lel, T'bor. They all converged in a loose semicircle around Lessa.

R'gul stepped forward, arm outstretched as if to embrace her. Before Lessa could step back, for there was something in R'gul's expression that revolted her, F'nor moved adroitly to her side, and R'gul, angry, lowered his arm.

"Hath is blooding his kill?" the brown rider asked ominously.

"Binth and Orth, too," T'bor blurted out, his eyes bright with the curious fever that seemed to be affecting all the bronze riders.

Ramoth stirred restlessly, and everyone paused to watch her intently.

"Blood their kill?" Lessa exclaimed, perplexed but knowing that this was strangely significant.

"Call in K'net and F'lar," F'nor ordered with more

authority than a brown rider should use in the presence of bronzes.

R'gul's laugh was unpleasant.

"No one knows where they went."

D'nol started to protest, but R'gul cut him off with a savage gesture.

"You wouldn't dare, R'gul," F'nor said with cold menace.

Well, Lessa would dare. Her frantic appeal to Mnementh and Piyanth produced a faint reply. Then there was absolute blankness where Mnementh had been.

"She will wake," R'gul was saying, his eyes piercing Lessa's. "She will wake and rise ill-tempered. You must allow her only to blood her kill. I warn you she will resist. If you do not restrain her, she will gorge and cannot fly."

"She rises to mate," F'nor snapped, his voice edged with cold and desperate fury.

"She rises to mate with whichever bronze can catch her," R'gul continued, his voice exultant.

And he means for F'lar not to be here, Lessa realized.

"The longer the flight, the better the clutch. And she cannot fly well or high if she is stuffed with heavy meat. She must not gorge. She must be permitted only to blood her kill. Do you understand?"

"Yes, R'gul," Lessa said, "I understand. For once I do understand you, all too well. F'lar and K'net are not here." Her voice grew shrill. "But Ramoth will never be flown by Hath if I have to take her *between*."

She saw naked fear and shock wipe R'gul's face clear of triumph, and she watched as he got himself under control. A malevolent sneer replaced surprise at her threat. Did he think her defiance was empty?

"Good afternoon," said F'lar pleasantly from the entrance. K'net grinned broadly at his side. "Mnementh informs me that the bronzes blood their kill. How kind of you to call us in for the spectacle."

Relief temporarily swept her recent antagonism for

F'lar out of Lessa's mind. The sight of him, calm, arrogant, mocking, buoyed her.

R'gul's eyes darted around the semicircle of bronze riders, trying to pick out who had called in these two. And Lessa knew R'gul hated as well as feared F'lar. She could sense, too, that F'lar had changed. There was nothing passive or indifferent or detached about him now. Instead, there was tense anticipation. F'lar was done with waiting!

Ramoth roused, suddenly and completely awake. Her mind was in such a state that Lessa candidly realized F'lar and K'net had arrived none too soon. So intense were Ramoth's hunger pangs that Lessa hastened to her head to soothe her. But Ramoth was in no mood for placation.

With unexpected agility she rose, making for the ledge. Lessa ran after her, followed by the dragonmen. Ramoth hissed in agitation at the bronzes who hovered near the ledge. They scattered quickly out of her way. Their riders made for the broad stairs that led from the queen's weyr to the Bowl.

In a daze Lessa felt F'nor place her on Canth's neck and urge his dragon quickly after the others to the feeding grounds. Lessa watched, amazed, as Ramoth glided effortlessly and gracefully in over the alarmed, stampeding herd. She struck quickly, seizing her kill by the neck and furling her wings suddenly, dropping down on it, too ravenous to carry it aloft.

"Control her!" F'nor gasped, depositing Lessa unceremoniously to the ground.

Ramoth screamed defiance of her Weyrwoman's order. She sloughed her head around, rustling her wings angrily, her eyes blazing opalescent pools of fire. She extended her neck skyward to its full reach, shrilling her insubordination. The harsh echoes reverberated against the walls of the Weyr. All around, the dragons, blue, green, brown, and bronze, extended their wings in mighty sweeps, their answering calls brass thunder in the air.

Now indeed must Lessa call on the strength of will

she had developed through hungry, vengeful years. Ramoth's wedge-shaped head whipped back and forth; her eyes glowed with incandescent rebellion. This was no amiable, trusting dragon child. This was a violent demon.

Across the bloody field Lessa matched wills with the transformed Ramoth. With no hint of weakness, no vestige of fear or thought of defeat. Lessa forced Ramoth to obey. Screeching protest, the golden dragon dropped her head to her kill, her tongue lashing at the inert body, her great jaws opening. Her head wavered over the steaming entrails her claws had ripped out. With a final snarl of reproach, Ramoth fastened her teeth on the thick throat of the buck and sucked the carcass dry of blood.

"Hold her," F'nor murmured. Lessa had forgotten him.

Ramoth rose, screaming, and with incredible speed landed on a second squealing buck. She made a second attempt to eat from the soft belly of her kill. Again Lessa exerted her authority and won. Shrilling defiance, Ramoth reluctantly blooded again.

She did not resist Lessa's orders the third time. The dragon had begun to realize now that irresistible instinct was upon her. She had not known anything but fury until she got the taste of hot blood. Now she knew what she needed: to fly fast, far, and long, away from the Weyr, away from these puny, wingless ones, far in advance of those rutting bronzes.

Dragon instinct was limited to here-and-now, with no ability to control or anticipate. Mankind existed in partnership with them to supply wisdom and order, Lessa found herself chanting silently.

Without hesitation, Ramoth struck for the fourth time, hissing with greed as she sucked at the beast's throat.

A tense silence had fallen over the Weyr Bowl, broken only by the sound of Ramoth's feeding and the high keening of the wind.

Ramoth's skin began to glow. She seemed to enlarge, not with gorging but with luminescence. She raised her bloody head, her tongue forking out to lick her muzzle. She straightened, and simultaneously a hum arose from the bronzes ringing the feeding ground in silent anticipation.

With a sudden golden movement Ramoth arched her great back. She sprang into the sky, wings wide. With unbelievable speed she was airborne. After her, in the blink of an eye, seven bronze shapes followed, their mighty wings churning buffets of sand-laden air into the faces of the watching weyrfolk.

Her heart in her mouth at the prodigious flight, Lessa felt her soul lifting with Ramoth.

"Stay with her," F'nor whispered urgently. "Stay with her. She must not escape your control now."

He stepped away from Lessa, back among the folk of the Weyr, who, as one, turned their eyes skyward to the disappearing shining motes of the dragons.

Lessa, her mind curiously suspended, retained only enough physical consciousness to realize that she was in fact earthbound.

All other sense and feeling were aloft with Ramoth. And she, Ramoth-Lessa, was alive with limitless power, her wings beating effortlessly to the thin heights, elation surging through her frame, elation and—desire.

She sensed rather than saw the great bronze males pursuing her. She was contemptuous of their ineffectual efforts. For she was wingfree and unconquerable.

She snaked her head under one wing and mocked their puny efforts with shrill taunts. High above them she soared. Suddenly, folding her wings, she plummeted down, delighting to see them veer off in wing-crowding haste to avoid collision.

She soared quickly above them again as they labored to make up their lost speed and altitude.

So Ramoth flirted leisurely with her lovers, splendid in her newfound freedom, daring the bronze ones to outfly her.

One dropped, spent. She crowed her superiority. Soon a second abandoned the chase as she played with them, diving and darting in intricate patterns. Sometimes she was oblivious of their existence, so lost was she in the thrill of flight.

When, at last, a little bored, she condescended to glance at her followers, she was vaguely amused to see only three great beasts still pursuing. She recognized Mnementh, Orth, and Hath. All in their prime; worthy, perhaps, of her.

She glided down, tantalizing them, amused at their now labored flights. Hath she couldn't bear. Orth? Now Orth was a fine young beast. She dropped her wings to slide between him and Mnementh.

As she swung past Mnementh, he suddenly closed his wings and dropped beside her. Startled, she tried to hover and found her wings fouled with his, his neck winding tightly about hers.

Entwined, they fell. Mnementh, calling on hidden reserves of strength, spread his wings to check their downward fall. Outmaneuvered and startled by the terrific speed of their descent, Ramoth, too, extended her great wings. And then . . .

Lessa reeled, her hands wildly grabbing out for any support. She seemed to be exploding back into her body, every nerve throbbing.

"Don't faint, you fool. Stay with her." F'lar's voice grated in her ear. His arms roughly sustained her.

She tried to focus her eyes. She caught a startled glimpse of the walls of her own weyr. She clutched at F'lar, touching bare skin, shaking her head, confused.

"Bring her back."

"How?" she cried, panting, unable to comprehend what could possibly entice Ramoth from such glory.

The pain of stinging blows on her face made her angrily aware of F'lar's disturbing proximity. His eyes were wild, his mouth distorted.

"Think with her. She cannot go *between*. Stay with her."

Trembling at the thought of losing Ramoth *between*, Lessa sought the dragon, still locked wing to wing with Mnementh.

The mating passion of the two dragons at that moment spiraled wide to include Lessa. A tidal wave rising relentlessly from the sea of her soul flooded Lessa. With a longing cry she clung to F'lar. She felt his body rock-firm against hers, his hard arms lifting her up, his mouth fastening mercilessly on hers as she drowned deep in another unexpected flood of desire.

"Now! *We* bring them safely home," he murmured.

> Dragonman, dragonman,
> Between thee and thine,
> Share me that glimpse of love
> Greater than mine.

F'LAR CAME suddenly awake. He listened attentively, heard and was reassured by Mnementh's gratified rumble. The bronze was perched on the ledge outside the queen's weyr. All was peacefully in order in the Bowl below.

Peaceful but different. F'lar, through Mnementh's eyes and senses, perceived this instantly. There was an overnight change in the Weyr. F'lar permitted himself a satisfied grin at the previous day's tumultuous events. Something might have gone wrong.

Something nearly did, Mnementh reminded him. Who had called K'net and himself back? F'lar mused again. Mnementh only repeated that he had been called back. Why wouldn't he identify the informer?

A nagging worry intruded on F'lar's waking ruminations.

"Did F'nor remember to . . ." he began aloud.

F'nor never forgets your orders, Mnementh reassured him testily. *Canth told me that the sighting at dawn today puts the Red Star at the top of the Eye Rock. The sun is still off, too.*

F'lar ran impatient fingers through his hair. "At the top of the Eye Rock. Closer, and closer the Red Star came," just as the Old Records predicted. And that dawn when the Star gleamed scarlet at the watcher *through* the Eye Rock heralded a dangerous passing and . . . the Threads.

There was certainly no other explanation for that careful arrangement of gigantic stones and special rocks on Benden Peak. Nor for its counterpart on the eastern walls of each of the five abandoned Weyrs.

First, the Finger Rock on which the rising sun balanced briefly at dawn at the winter solstice. Then, two dragon lengths behind it, the rectangular, enormous Star Stone, chest-high to a tall man, its polished surface incised by two arrows, one pointing due east toward the Finger Rock, the other slightly north of due east, aimed directly at the Eye Rock, so ingeniously and immovably set into the Star Stone.

One dawn, in the not too distant future, he would look through the Eye Rock and meet the baleful blink of the Red Star. And then . . .

Sounds of vigorous splashing interrupted F'lar's reflections. He grinned again as he realized it was the girl bathing. She certainly cleaned up pretty, and undressed . . . He stretched with leisurely recollection, reviewing what his reception from that quarter might be. She ought to have no complaints at all. What a flight! He chuckled softly.

Mnementh commented from the safety of his ledge that F'lar had better watch his step with Lessa.

Lessa, is it? thought F'lar back to his dragon.

Mnementh enigmatically repeated his caution. F'lar chuckled his self-confidence.

Suddenly Mnementh was alert to an alarm.

Watchers were sending out a rider to identify the unusually persistent dust clouds on the plateau below Benden Lake, Mnementh informed his wingleader crisply.

F'lar rose hastily, gathered up his scattered clothes, and dressed. He was buckling the wide rider's belt when the curtain to the bathing room was flipped aside. Lessa confronted him, fully clothed.

He was always surprised to see how slight she was, an incongruous physical vessel for such strength of mind. Her newly washed hair framed her narrow face with a dark cloud. There was no hint in her composed eyes of the dragon-roused passion they had experienced together yesterday. There was no friendliness about her at all. No warmth. Was this what Mnementh meant? What was the matter with the girl?

Mnementh gave an additional alarming report, and F'lar set his jaw. He would have to postpone the understanding they must reach intellectually until after this emergency. To himself he damned R'gul's green handling of her. The man had all but ruined the Weyrwoman, as he had all but destroyed the Weyr.

Well, F'lar, bronze Mnementh's rider, was now Weyrleader, and changes were long overdue.

Long overdue, Mnementh confirmed dryly. *The Lords of the Holds gather in force on the lake plateau.*

"There's trouble," F'lar announced to Lessa by way of greeting. His announcement did not appear to alarm her.

"The Lords of the Hold come to protest?" she asked coolly.

He admired her composure even as he decried her part in this development.

"You'd have done better to let me handle the raiding. K'net's still boy enough to be carried away with the joy of it all."

Her slight smile was secretive. F'lar wondered fleetingly if that wasn't what she had intended in the first place. Had Ramoth not risen yesterday, it would be a different story altogether today. Had she thought of that?

Mnementh forewarned him that R'gul was at the ledge. R'gul was all chest and indignant eye, the dragon commented, which meant he was feeling his authority.

"He has none," F'lar snapped out loud, thoroughly awake and pleased with events, despite their precipitation.

"R'gul?"

She was quick-witted all right, F'lar admitted.

"Come, girl." He gestured her toward the queen's weyr. The scene he was about to play with R'gul ought to redeem that shameful day in the Council Room two months back. He knew it had rankled in her as in him.

They had no sooner entered the queen's weyr than R'gul, followed by an excited K'net, stormed in from the opposite side.

"The watch informs me," R'gul began, "that there is a large body of armed men, with banners of many Holds, approaching the Tunnel. K'net here"—R'gul was furious with the youngster—"confesses he has been raiding systematically—against all reason and most certainly against my distinct orders. Of course, we'll deal with him later," he informed the errant rider ominously, "that is, if there is a Weyr left after the Lords are through with us."

He turned back to F'lar, his frown deepening as he realized F'lar was grinning at him.

"Don't stand there," R'gul growled. "There's nothing to grin about. We've got to think how to placate them."

"No, R'gul," F'lar contradicted the older man, still grinning, "the days of placating the Lords are over."

"What? Are you out of your mind?"

"No. But *you* are out of order," F'lar said, his grin gone, his face stern.

R'gul's eyes widened as he stared at F'lar as if he had never seen him before.

"You've forgotten a very important fact," F'lar went on ruthlessly. "Policy changes when the leader of the Weyr is replaced. *I*, F'lar, Mnementh's rider, am Weyrleader now."

On that ringing phrase, S'lel, D'nol, T'bor, and S'lan came striding into the room. They stopped, shock-still, staring at the motionless tableau.

F'lar waited, giving them a chance to absorb the fact that the dissension in the room meant that authority had indeed passed to him.

"Mnementh," he said aloud, "call in all wingseconds and brown riders. We've some arrangements to make before our . . . guests arrive. As the queen is asleep, dragonmen, into the Council Room, please. After you, Weyrwoman."

He stepped aside to permit Lessa to pass, noticing the slight flush on her cheeks. She was not completely in command of her emotions, after all.

No sooner had they taken places at the Council Table than the brown riders began to stream in. F'lar took careful note of the subtle difference in their attitudes. They walked taller, he decided. And—yes, the air of defeat and frustration was replaced by tense excitement. All else being equal, today's events ought to revive the pride and purpose of the Weyr.

F'nor and T'sum, his own seconds, strode in. There was no doubt of their high, proud good humor. Their eyes flashed around daring anyone to defy their promotion as T'sum stood by the archway and F'nor marched smartly around to his position behind F'lar's chair. F'nor paused to make a deeply respectful bow to the girl. F'lar saw her flush and drop her eyes.

"Who's at our gate, F'nor?" the new Weyrleader asked affably.

"The Lords of Telgar, Nabol, Fort, and Keroon, to name the principal banners," F'nor answered in a similar vein.

R'gul rose from his chair; the half-formed protest died on his lips as he caught the expression in the faces of the bronze riders. S'lel, beside him, started to mumble, picking at his lower lip.

"Estimated strength?"

"In excess of a thousand. In good order and well-armed," F'nor reported indifferently.

F'lar shot his second a remonstrating look. Confidence was one thing, indifference preferable to defeat, but there was no wisdom in denying the situation was very tight.

"Against the Weyr?" S'lel gasped.

"Are we dragonmen or cowards?" D'nol snapped, jumping up, his fist pounding the table. "This is the final insult."

"Indeed it is," F'lar concurred heartily.

"It has to be put down. We'll swallow no more," D'nol continued vehemently, encouraged by F'lar's attitude. "A few flaming . . ."

"That's enough," F'lar said in a hard voice. "We are dragonmen! Remember that, and remember also —never forget it—this fellowship is sworn to *protect*." He enunciated that word distinctly, pinning each man with a fierce stare. "Is that point clear?" He glared questioningly at D'nol. There were to be no private heroics today.

"We do not need firestone," he continued, certain that D'nol had taken his meaning, "to disperse these foolish Lords." He leaned back and went on more calmly, "I noticed on Search, as I'm sure you all did, that the common holder has not lost one jot of his . . . let us say . . . respect for dragonkind."

T'bor grinned, and someone chuckled reminiscently.

"Oh, they follow their Lords quickly enough, incited with indignation and lots of new wine. But it's quite another matter to face a dragon, hot, tired, and cold sober. Not to mention on foot without a wall or Hold in sight." He could sense their concurrence. "The mounted men, too, will be too much occupied with their beasts to do any serious fighting," he added with a chuckle, echoed by most of the men in the room.

"However consoling these reflections are, there are more powerful factors in our favor. I doubt the good Lords of the Hold have bothered to review them. I suspect"—he glanced around sardonically at his riders —"they have probably forgotten them . . . as they have conveniently forgotten so much dragonlore . . . and tradition.

"It is now time to reeducate them." His voice was steel. An affirming mutter answered him. Good, he had them.

"For instance, they are here at our gates. They've traveled long and hard to reach this remote Weyr. Undoubtedly some units have been marching for weeks. F'nor," he said in a calculated aside, "remind me to discuss patrol schedules later today. Ask yourselves this, dragonmen, if the Lords of the Holds are here, who is holding the Holds for the Lords? Who keeps guard on the Inner Hold, over all the Lords hold dear?"

He heard Lessa chuckling wickedly. She was quicker than any of the bronze riders. He had chosen well that day in Ruatha, even if it had meant killing while on Search.

"Our Weyrwoman perceives my plan. T'sum, implement it." He snapped that order out crisply. T'sum, grinning broadly, departed.

"I don't understand," S'lel complained, blinking in confusion.

"Oh, let me explain," Lessa put in quickly, her words couched in the sweet, reasonable tone F'lar was learning to identify as Lessa at her worst. He couldn't

blame her for wanting to get some of her own back
from S'lel, but this taste of hers for vengeance could
become pernicious.

"Someone ought to explain something," S'lel said
querulously. "I don't like what's going on. Holders at
the Tunnel Road. Dragons permitted firestone. I don't
understand."

"It's so simple," Lessa assured him sweetly, not
waiting for F'lar's permission. "I'm embarrassed to
have to explain."

"Weyrwoman!" F'lar called her sharply to order.

She didn't look at him, but she did stop needling
S'lel.

"The Lords have left their Holds unprotected," she
said. "They appear not to have considered that dragons can move *between* in seconds. T'sum, if I am not
mistaken, has gone to assemble sufficient hostages
from the unguarded Holds to insure that the Lords
respect the sanctity of the Weyr." F'lar nodded con-
firmation. Lessa's eyes flashed angrily as she continued. "It is not the fault of the Lords that they have
lost respect for the Weyr. The Weyr has . . ."

"The Weyr," F'lar cut in sharply. Yes, he would
have to watch this slim girl very carefully and very
respectfully. ". . . the Weyr is about to insist on its
traditional rights and prerogatives. Before I outline
exactly how, Weyrwoman, would you greet our newest
guests? A few words might be in order to reinforce the
object lesson we will impress on all Pernese today."

The girl's eyes sparkled with anticipation. She
grinned with such intense pleasure that F'lar wondered if he was wise to let her instruct the defenseless
hostages.

"I rely on your discretion," he said emphatically,
"and intelligence to handle the assignment adroitly."
He caught her glance, held it until she briefly inclined
her head in acknowledgement of his admonition. As
she left, he sent a word ahead to Mnementh to keep
an eye on her.

Mnementh informed him that that would be wasted

effort. Hadn't Lessa shown more wit than anyone else in the Weyr? She was circumspect by instinct.

Circumspect enough to have precipitated today's invasion, F'lar reminded his dragon.

"But . . . the . . . Lords," R'gul was sputtering.

"Oh, freeze up," K'net suggested. "If we hadn't listened to you for so long, we wouldn't be in this position at all. Shove *between* if you don't like it, but F'lar is Weyrleader now. And I say about time!"

"K'net! R'gul!" F'lar called them to order, shouting over the cheers K'net's impudent words produced. "These are my orders," he went on when he had their complete attention. "I expect them to be followed exactly." He glanced at each man to be sure there was no further question of his authority. Then he outlined his intentions concisely and quickly, watching with satisfaction as uncertainty was replaced with admiring respect.

Assured that every bronze and brown rider understood the plan perfectly, he asked Mnementh for the latest report.

The advancing army was streaming out across the lake plateau, the foremost units on the Tunnel road, the one ground entrance to the Weyr. Mnementh added that the Holders' women were profiting from their stay in the Weyr.

"In what way?" F'lar demanded immediately.

Mnementh rumbled with the dragon equivalent of laughter. Two of the young greens were feeding, that was all. But for some reason such a normal occupation appeared to upset the women.

The woman was diabolically clever, F'lar thought privately, careful not to let Mnementh sense his concern. That bronze clown was as besotted with the rider as he was with the queen. What kind of fascination did the Weyrwoman have for a bronze dragon?

"Our guests are at the lake plateau," he told the dragonmen. "You have your positions. Order your wings out." Without a backward look, he marched out, conquering an intense urge to hurry to the ledge.

He absolutely did not want those hostages scared witless.

Down the valley by the lake, the women were lightly attended by four of the smallest greens—big enough for the uninitiated—and the women were probably too scared at having been seized to notice that all four riders were barely out of adolescence. He spotted the slight figure of the Weyrwoman, seated to one side of the main group. A sound of muffled weeping drifted up to his ears. He looked beyond them, to the feeding grounds, and saw a green dragon single out a buck and run it down. Another green was perched on a ledge above, eating with typical messy, dragon greed. F'lar shrugged and mounted Mnementh, clearing the ledge for the hovering dragons who waited to pick up their own riders.

As Mnementh circled above the confusion of wings and gleaming bodies, F'lar nodded approvingly. A high, fast mating flight coupled with the promise of action improved everyone's morale.

Mnementh snorted.

F'lar paid him no attention, watching R'gul as he assembled his wing. The man had taken a psychological defeat. He would bear watching and careful handling. Once the Threads started to fall and R'gul's faith was restored, he'd come around.

Mnementh asked him if they should pick up the Weyrwoman.

"She doesn't belong in this," F'lar said sharply, wondering why under the double moons the bronze had made such a suggestion. Mnementh replied that he thought Lessa would like to be there.

D'nol's wing and T'bor's rose in good formation. Those two were making good leaders. K'net took up a double wing to the Bowl lip and winked out neatly, bound to reappear behind the approaching army. C'gan, the old blue rider, had the youngsters organized.

F'lar told Mnementh to have Canth tell F'nor to

proceed. With a final look to be sure the stones to the Lower Caverns were in place, F'lar gave Mnementh the signal to go *between*.

From the Weyr and from the Bowl,
Bronze and brown and blue and green,
Rise the dragonmen of Pern,
Aloft, on wing; seen, then unseen.

LARAD, LORD of Telgar, eyed the monolithic heights of Benden Weyr. The striated stone looked like frozen waterfalls at sunset. And about as hospitable. A long moribund awe squirmed at the back of his mind for the blasphemy he and the army he led were about to commit. He stifled that thought firmly.

The Weyr had outlived its usefulness. That was obvious. There was no longer any need for the Holders to give up the profits of their sweat and labor to the lazy weyrfolk. The Holders had been patient. They had supported the Weyr in good part out of gratitude for past services. But the dragonmen had overstepped the borders of grateful generosity.

First, this archaic Search foolishness. So a queen-egg was laid. Why did the dragonmen need to steal away the prettiest women among the Holders when they had women of their own in the Weyr proper? No need to appropriate Larad's sister, Kylora, eagerly awaiting a far different alliance with Brant of Igen one evening and gone on that ridiculous Search the next. Never heard from since, either.

And killing Fax! Albeit the man had been dangerously ambitious, he was of the Blood. And the Weyr had not been asked to meddle in the affairs of the High Reaches.

But this steady pilfering. That was beyond enough. Oh, a holder might excuse a few bucks now and again. But when a dragon appeared out of nowhere (a talent that disturbed Larad deeply) and snatched the best stud bucks from a herd carefully protected and nurtured, that tore it!

The Weyr must be made to understand its subordinate position in Pern. It would have to make other provisions to victual its people, for no further tithes would come from anyone. Benden, Bitra, and Lemos would come around soon. They ought to be pleased to end this superstitious domination by the Weyr.

Nevertheless, the closer they came to the gigantic mountain, the more doubts Larad experienced as to just how in the world the Lords would penetrate that massif. He signaled Meron, so-called Lord of Nabol (he didn't really trust this sharp-faced ex-Warder with no Blood at all) to draw his riding beast closer.

Meron whipped his mount abreast of Larad.

"There is no other way into the Weyr proper but the Tunnel?"

Meron shook his head. "Even the locals are agreed."

This did not dismay Meron, but he caught Larad's doubtful expression.

"I have sent a party on ahead, to the southern lip of the Peak," and he indicated the area. "There might be a low, scalable cliff there where the brow dips."

"You sent a party without consulting us? *I* was named leader . . ."

"True," Meron agreed, with an amiable show of teeth. "A mere notion of mine."

"A distinct possibility, I agree, but you'd have done better . . ." Larad glanced up at the Peak.

"They have seen us, have no doubt of that, Larad," Meron assured him, contemptuously regarding the silent Weyr. "That will be sufficient. Deliver our ultimatum and they will surrender before such a force as ours. They've proved themselves cowards over and over. I gave insult twice to the bronze rider they call F'lar, and he ignored it. What *man* would?"

A sudden rustling roar and a blast of the coldest air in the world interrupted their conference. As he mastered his plunging beast, Larad caught a confused panorama of dragons, all colors, sizes, and everywhere. The air was filled with the panic-stricken shrieks of plunging beasts, the cries of startled, terrified men.

Larad managed, with great effort, to drag his beast around to face the dragonmen.

By the Void that spawned us, he thought, struggling to control his own fear, I'd forgotten dragons are so big.

Foremost in that frightening array was a triangular formation of four great bronze beasts, their wings overlapping in a tremendous criss-cross pattern as they hovered just above the ground. A dragon's length above and beyond them, there ranged a second line, longer, wider, of brown beasts. Curving beyond them and higher up were blue and green and more brown beasts, all with their huge wings fanning cold air in great drafts on the terrified mob that had been an army moments before.

Where did that piercing cold come from, Larad wondered. He yanked down on his beast's mouth as it began to plunge again.

The dragonmen just sat there on their beasts' necks, watching, waiting.

"Get them off their beasts and the things away so we can talk," Meron shouted to Larad as his mount cavorted and screamed in terror.

Larad signaled foot soldiers forward, but it took

four men per mount to quiet them enough so the
Lords could dismount.

Miscalculation number two, Larad thought with
grim humor. We forgot the effect of dragons on the
beasts of Pern. Man included. Settling his sword,
pulling his gloves up onto his wrists, he jerked his
head at the other Lords, and they all moved forward.

As he saw the Lords dismount, F'lar told Mnementh to pass the word to land the first three ranks.
Like a great wave, the dragons obediently settled to
the ground, furling their wings with an enormous
rustling sigh.

Mnementh told F'lar that the dragons were excited
and pleased. This was much more fun than Games.

F'lar told Mnementh sternly that this was not fun
at all.

"Larad of Telgar," the foremost man introduced
himself, his voice crisp, his manner soldierly and confident for one relatively young.

"Meron of Nabol."

F'lar immediately recognized the swarthy face with
the sharp features and restless eyes. A mean and pro-
vocative fighter.

Mnementh relayed F'lar an unusual message from
the Weyr. F'lar nodded imperceptibly and continued
to acknowledge introductions.

"I have been appointed spokesman," Larad of Telgar began. "The Holder Lords unanimously agree
that the Weyr has outlived its function. Consequently
demands from the Weyr are out of order. There are to
be no more Searches among our Holds. No more
raiding on the herds and barns of any Hold by any
dragonfolk."

F'lar gave him courteous attention. Larad was
well-spoken and succinct. F'lar nodded. He looked at
each of the Lords before him carefully, getting their
measure. Their stern faces expressed their conviction
and righteous indignation.

"As Weyrleader, I, F'lar, Mnementh's rider, answer
you. Your complaint is heard. Now listen to what the

Weyrleader commands." His casual pose was gone.
Mnementh rumbled a menacing counterpoint to his
rider's voice as it rang harshly metallic across the
plateau, the words carried clearly back so that even
the mob heard him.

"You will turn and go back to your Holds. You will
then go into your barns and among your herds. You
will make a just and equable tithe. This will be on its
way to the Weyr within three days of your return."

"The Weyrleader is ordering the Lords to tithe?"
Meron of Nabol's derisive laugh rang out.

F'lar signaled, and two more wings of dragonmen
appeared to hover over the Nabolese contingent.

"The Weyrleader gives orders to the Lords to
tithe," F'lar affirmed. "And until such time as the
Lords do send their tithings, we regret that the ladies
of Nabol, Telgar, Fort, Igen, Keroon must make their
homes with us. Also, the ladies of Hold Balan, Hold
Gar, Hold . . ."

He paused, for the Lords were muttering angrily
and excitedly among themselves as they heard this
list of hostages. F'lar gave Mnementh a quick message to relay.

"Your bluff won't work," Meron sneered, stepping
forward, his hand on his sword hilt. Raiding among
the herds could be credited; it had happened. But the
Holds were sacrosanct! They'd not dare—

F'lar asked Mnementh to pass the signal, and
T'sum's wing appeared. Each rider held a Lady on
the neck of his dragon. T'sum held his group aloft but
close enough so the Lords could identify each scared
or hysterical woman.

Meron's face contorted with shock and new hatred.

Larad stepped forward, tearing his eyes from his
own Lady. She was a new wife to him and much be-
loved. It was small consolation that she neither wept
nor fainted, being a quiet and brave little person.

"You have the advantage of us," Larad admitted
bleakly. "We will retire and send the tithe." He was

about to wheel when Meron pushed forward, his face wild.

"We tamely submit to their demands? Who is a dragonman to order us?"

"Shut up," Larad ordered, grabbing the Nabolese's arm.

F'lar raised his arm in an imperious signal. A wing of blues appeared, carrying Meron's would-be mountaineers, some bearing evidence of their struggle with the southern face of Benden Peak.

"Dragonmen do order. And nothing escapes their notice." F'lar's voice rang out coldly.

"You will retire to your Holds. You will send proper tithing because we shall know if you do not. You will then proceed, under pain of firestone, to clear your habitations of green, croft and Hold alike. Good Telgar, look to that southern outer Hold of yours. The exposure is acutely vulnerable. Clear all firepits on ridge defenses. You've let them become fouled. The mines are to be reopened and firestone stockpiled."

"Tithes, yes, but the rest . . ." Larad interrupted.

F'lar's arm shot skyward.

"Look up, Lord. Look well. The Red Star pulses by day as well as night. The mountains beyond Ista steam and spout flaming rock. The seas rage in high tides and flood the coast. Have you all forgotten the Sagas and Ballads? As you've forgotten the abilities of dragons? Can you dismiss these portents that always presage the coming of Threads?"

Meron would never believe until he saw the silver Threads streaking across the skies. But Larad and many of the others, F'lar knew, now did.

"And the queen," he continued, "has risen to mate in her second year. Risen to mate and flown high and far."

The heads of all before him jerked upward. Their eyes were wide. Meron, too, looked startled. F'lar heard R'gul gasp behind him, yet he dared not look, himself, lest it be a trick.

Suddenly, on the periphery of his vision, he caught the glint of gold in the sky.

Mnementh, he snapped, and Mnementh merely rumbled happily. The queen wheeled into view just then, a brave and glowing sight, F'lar grudgingly admitted.

Dressed in flowing white, Lessa was distinctly visible on the curved golden neck. Ramoth hovered, her wing-span greater than even Mnementh's as she vaned idly. From the way she arched her neck, it was obvious that Ramoth was in good and playful spirits, but F'lar was furious.

The spectacle of the queen aloft had quite an effect on all beholders. F'lar was aware of its impact on himself and saw it reflected in the faces of the incredulous Holders, knew it from the way the dragons hummed, heard it from Mnementh.

"And, of course, our greatest Weyrwomen— Moreta, Torene, to name only a few—have all come from Ruath Hold, as does Lessa of Pern."

"Ruatha . . ." Meron grated out the name, clenched his jaw sullenly, his face bleak.

"Threads are coming?" asked Larad.

F'lar nodded slowly. "Your harper can reinstruct you on the signs. Good Lords, the tithe is required. Your women will be returned. The Holds are to be put in order. The Weyr prepares Pern, as the Weyr is pledged to protect Pern. Your cooperation is expected—" he paused significantly—"and will be enforced."

With that, he vaulted to Mnementh's neck, keeping the queen always in sight. He saw her golden wings beat as the dragon turned and soared upward.

It was infuriating of Lessa to take this moment, when all his energy and attention ought to go to settling the Holders' grievance for a show of rebellion. Why did she have to flaunt her independence so, in full sight of the entire Weyr and all the Lords? He longed to chase immediately after her and could not. Not until he had seen the army in actual retreat, not until he had signaled for the final show of Weyr strength for the Holders' elucidation.

Gritting his teeth, he signaled Mnementh aloft. The wings rose behind him with spectacular trumpetings and dartings so that there appeared to be thousands of dragons in the air instead of the scant two hundred Benden Weyr boasted.

Assured that that part of his strategy was proceeding in order, he bade Mnementh fly after the Weyrwoman, who was now dipping and gliding high above the Weyr.

When he got his hands on that girl, he would tell her a thing or two. . . .

Mnementh informed him caustically that telling her a thing or two might be a very good idea. Much better than flying so vengefully after a pair who were only trying their wings out. Mnementh reminded his irate rider that, after all, the golden dragon had flown far and wide yesterday, having blooded four, but had not eaten since. She'd be neither capable of nor interested in any protracted flying until she had eaten fully. However, if F'lar insisted on this ill-considered and completely unnecessary pursuit, he might just antagonize Ramoth into jumping *between* to escape him.

The very thought of that untutored pair going *between* cooled F'lar instantly. Controlling himself, he realized that Mnementh's judgment was more reliable than his at the moment. He'd let anger and anxiety influence his decisions, but . . .

Mnementh circled in to land at the Star Stone, the tip of Benden Peak being a fine vantage point from which F'lar could observe both the decamping army and the queen.

Mnementh's great eyes gave the appearance of whirling as the dragon adjusted his vision to its farthest reach.

He reported to F'lar that Piyanth's rider felt the dragons' supervision of the retreat was causing hys-

teria among the men and beasts. Injuries were occur-
ring in the resultant stampedes.

F'lar immediately ordered K'net to assume surveil-
lance altitude until the army camped for the night. He
was to keep close watch on the Nabolese contingent
at all times, however.

Even as F'lar had Mnementh relay these orders, he
realized his mind had dismissed the matter. All his
attention was really on that high-flying pair.

You had better teach her to fly between, Mnementh
remarked, one great eye shining directly over F'lar's
shoulder. *She's quick enough to figure it out for herself, and then where are we?*

F'lar let the sharp retort die on his lips as he
watched, breathless. Ramoth suddenly folded her
wings, a golden streak diving through the sky. Effortlessly she pulled out at the critical point and soared
upward again.

Mnementh deliberately called to mind their first
wildly aerobatic flight. A tender smile crossed F'lar's
face, and suddenly he knew how much Lessa must
have longed to fly, how bitter it must have been for
her to watch the dragonets practice when she was
forbidden to try.

Well, he was no R'gul, torn by indecision and
doubt.

And she is no Jora, Mnementh reminded him pun-
gently. *I'm calling them in,* the dragon added.
Ramoth has turned a dull orange.

F'lar watched as the flyers obediently began a
downward glide, the queen's wings arching and curving as she slowed her tremendous forward speed. Un-
fed or not, she could fly!

He mounted Mnementh, waving them on, down
toward the feeding grounds. He caught a fleeting
glimpse of Lessa, her face vivid with elation and rebellion.

Ramoth landed, and Lessa dropped to the ground,
gesturing the dragon on to eat.

The girl turned then, watching Mnementh glide in

and hover to let F'lar dismount. She straightened her shoulders, her chin lifted belligerently as her slender body gathered itself to face his censure. Her behavior was like that of any weyrling, anticipating punishment and determined to endure it, soundless. She was not the least bit repentant!

Admiration for this indomitable personality replaced the last trace of F'lar's anger. He smiled as he closed the distance between them.

Startled by his completely unexpected behavior, she took a half-step backward.

"Queens can, too, fly," she blurted out, daring him.

His grin broadening to suffuse his face, he put his hands on her shoulders and gave her an affectionate shake.

"Of course they can fly," he assured her, his voice full of pride and respect. "That's why they have wings!"

PART III

Dust Fall

The Finger points
At an Eye blood-red.
Alert the Weyrs
To sear the Thread.

"YOU STILL doubt, R'gul?" F'lar asked, appearing
slightly amused by the older bronze rider's perversity.

R'gul, his handsome features stubbornly set, made
no reply to the Weyrleader's taunt. He ground his
teeth together as if he could grind away F'lar's authority over him.

"There have been no Threads in Pern's skies for
over four hundred Turns. There are no more!"

"There is always that possibility," F'lar conceded
amiably. There was not, however, the slightest trace
of tolerance in his amber eyes. Nor the slightest hint
of compromise in his manner.

He was more like F'lon, his sire, R'gul decided,
than a son had any right to be. Always so sure of himself, always slightly contemptuous of what others did
and thought. Arrogant, that's what F'lar was. Imperti-
nent, too, and underhanded in the matter of that
young Weyrwoman. Why, R'gul had trained her up to
be one of the finest Weyrwomen in many Turns. Before he'd finished her instruction, she'd known all the
Teaching Ballads and Sagas letter-perfect. And then

the silly child had turned to F'lar. Didn't have sense
enough to appreciate the merits of an older, more
experienced man. Undoubtedly she felt a first obligation to F'lar for discovering her on Search.

"You do, however," F'lar was saying, "admit that
when the sun hits the Finger Rock at the moment of
dawn, winter solstice has been reached?"

"Any fool knows that's what the Finger Rock is
for," R'gul grunted.

"Then why don't you, you old fool, admit that the
Eye Rock was placed on Star Stone to bracket the
Red Star when it's about to make a Pass?" burst out
K'net.

R'gul flushed, half-starting out of his chair, ready to
take the young sprout to task for such insolence.

"K'net!" F'lar's voice cracked authoritatively. "Do
you really like flying the Igen patrol so much you
want another few weeks at it?"

K'net hurriedly seated himself, flushing at the reprimand and the threat.

"There is, you know, R'gul, incontrovertible evidence to support my conclusions," F'lar went on with
deceptive mildness. 'The Finger points/At an Eye
blood-red. . .' "

"Don't quote me verses I taught you as a weyrling,"
R'gul exclaimed heatedly.

"Then have faith in what you taught," F'lar
snapped back, his amber eyes flashing dangerously.

R'gul, stunned by the unexpected forcefulness,
sank back into his chair.

"You cannot deny, R'gul," F'lar continued quietly,
"that no less than half an hour ago the sun balanced
on the Finger's tip at dawn and the Red Star was
squarely framed by the Eye Rock."

The other dragonriders, bronze as well as brown,
murmured and nodded their agreement to that phenomenon. There was also an undercurrent of resentment for R'gul's continual contest of F'lar's policies as
the new Weyrleader. Even old S'lel, once R'gul's
avowed supporter, was following the majority.

"There have been no Threads in four hundred Turns. There are no Threads," R'gul muttered.

"Then, my fellow dragonman," F'lar said cheerfully, "all you have taught is falsehood. The dragons are, as the Lords of the Holds wish to believe, parasites on the economy of Pern, anachronisms. And so are we.

"Therefore, far be it from me to hold you here against the dictates of your conscience. You have my permission to leave the Weyr and take up residence where you will."

Someone laughed.

R'gul was too stunned by F'lar's ultimatum to take offense at the ridicule. Leave the Weyr? Was the man mad? Where would he go? The Weyr had been his life. He had been bred up to it for generations. All his male ancestors had been dragonriders. Not all bronze, true, but a decent percentage. His own dam's sire had been a Weyrleader just as he, R'gul, had been until F'lar's Mnementh had flown the new queen.

But dragonmen never left the Weyr. Well, they did if they were negligent enough to lose their dragons, like that Lytol fellow at Ruath Hold. And how could he leave the Weyr *with* a dragon?

What did F'lar want of him? Was it not enough that he was Weyrleader now in R'gul's stead? Wasn't F'lar's pride sufficiently swollen by having bluffed the Lords of Pern into disbanding their army when they were all set to coerce the Weyr and dragonmen? Must F'lar dominate *every* dragonman, body and will, too? He stared a long moment, incredulous.

"I do not believe we are parasites," F'lar said, breaking the silence with a soft, persuasive voice. "Nor anachronistic. There have been long Intervals before. The Red Star does not always pass close enough to drop Threads on Pern. Which is why our ingenious ancestors thought to position the Eye Rock and the Finger Rock as they did . . . to confirm *when* a Pass will be made. And another thing"—his face turned grave—"there have been other times when dragonkind has all but died out . . . and Pern with it because of skeptics like you." F'lar smiled and relaxed indolently in his chair. "I prefer not to be recorded as a skeptic. How shall we record you, R'gul?"

The Council Room was tense. R'gul was aware of someone breathing harshly and realized it was himself. He looked at the adamant face of the young Weyrleader and knew that the threat was not empty. He would either concede to F'lar's authority completely, though concession rankled deeply, or leave the Weyr.

And where could he go, unless to one of the other Weyrs, deserted for hundreds of Turns? And—R'gul's thoughts were savage—wasn't that indication enough of the cessation of Threads? Five empty Weyrs? No, by the Egg of Faranth, he would practice some of F'lar's own brand of deceit and bide his time. When all Pern turned on the arrogant fool, he, R'gul, would be there to salvage something from the ruins.

"A dragonman stays in his Weyr," R'gul said with what dignity he could muster.

"And accepts the policies of the current Weyrleader?" The tone of F'lar's voice made it less of a question and more of an order.

So as not to perjure himself, R'gul gave a curt nod of his head. F'lar continued to stare at him and R'gul wondered if the man could read his thoughts as his dragon might. He managed to return the gaze calmly. His turn would come. He'd wait.

Apparently accepting the capitulation, F'lar stood up and crisply delegated patrol assignments for the day.

"T'bor, you're weather-watch. Keep an eye on those tithing trains as you do. Have you the morning's report?"

"Weather is fair at dawning . . . all across Telgar and Keroon . . . if all too cold," T'bor said with a wry grin. "Tithing trains have good hard roads, though, so they ought to be here soon." His eyes twinkled with anticipation of the feasting that would follow the supplies' arrival—a mood shared by all, to judge by the expressions around the table.

F'lar nodded. "S'lan and D'nol, you are to continue an adroit Search for likely boys. They should be striplings, if possible, but do not pass over anyone suspected of talent. It's all well and good to present, for Impression, boys reared up in the Weyr traditions." F'lar gave a one-sided smile. "But there are not enough in the Lower Caverns. We, too, have been behind in begetting. Anyway, dragons reach full growth faster than their riders. We must have more young *men* to Impress when Ramoth hatches. Take the southern holds, Ista, Nerat, Fort, and South Boll where maturity comes earlier. You can use the guise of inspecting Holds for greenery to talk to the boys. And take along firestone and run a few flaming passes on those heights that haven't been scoured in—oh—dragon's years. A flaming beast impresses the young and arouses envy."

F'lar deliberately looked at R'gul to see the ex-Weyrleader's reaction to the order. R'gul had been dead set against going outside the Weyr for more candidates. In the first place, R'gul had argued that there were eighteen youngsters in the Lower Caverns, some quite young, to be sure, but R'gul would not admit that Ramoth would lay more than the dozen Nemorth had always dropped. In the second place, R'gul persisted in wanting to avoid any action that might antagonize the Lords.

R'gul made no overt protest, and F'lar went on. "K'net, back to the mines. I want the dispositions of each firestone-dump checked and quantities available. R'gul, continue drilling recognition points with the weyrlings. They must be positive about their references. If they're used as messengers and suppliers, they may be sent out quickly and with no time to ask questions.

"F'nor, T'sum"—F'lar turned to his own brown riders—"you're clean-up squad today." He allowed himself a grin at their dismay. "Try Ista Weyr. Clear the Hatching Cavern and enough Weyrs for a double wing. And, F'nor, don't leave a single Record behind. They're worth preserving.

"That will be all, dragonmen. Good flying." And with that, F'lar rose and strode from the Council Room up to the queen's weyr.

Ramoth still slept, her hide gleaming with health, its color deepening to a shade of gold closer to bronze, indicating her pregnancy. As he passed her, the tip of her long tail twitched slightly.

All the dragons were restless these days, F'lar reflected. Yet when he asked Mnementh, the bronze dragon could give no reason. He woke, he went back to sleep. That was all. F'lar couldn't ask a leading question for that would defeat his purpose. He had to remain discontented with the vague fact that the restlessness was some kind of instinctive reaction.

Lessa was not in the sleeping room, nor was she still bathing. F'lar snorted. That girl was going to scrub her hide off with this constant bathing. She'd had to live grimy to protect herself in Ruath Hold, but bathing twice a day? He was beginning to wonder if this might be a subtle Lessa-variety insult to him personally. F'lar sighed. That girl. Would she never turn to him of her own accord? Would he ever touch that elusive inner core of Lessa? She had more warmth for his half brother, F'nor, and for K'net, the youngest of the bronze riders than she had for F'lar who shared her bed.

He pulled the curtain back into place, irritated. Where had she gone to today when, for the first time in weeks, he had been able to get all the wings out of the Weyr just so he could teach her to fly *between?*

Ramoth would soon be too egg-heavy for such activity. He had promised the Weyrwoman, and he meant to keep that promise. She had taken to wearing the wherhide riding gear as a flagrant reminder of his unfulfilled pledge. From certain remarks she had dropped, he knew she would not wait much longer for his aid. That she should try it on her own didn't suit him at all.

He crossed the queen's weyr again and peered down the passage that led to the Records Room. She was often to be found there, poring over the musty skins. And that was one more matter that needed urgent consideration. Those Records were deteriorating past legibility. Curiously enough, earlier ones were still in good condition and readable. Another technique forgotten.

That girl! He brushed his thick forelock of hair back from his brow in a gesture habitual to him when he was annoyed or worried. The passage was dark, which meant she could not be below in the Records Room.

"Mnementh," he called silently to his bronze dragon, sunning on the ledge outside the queen's weyr. "What is that girl doing?"

Lessa, the dragon replied, stressing the Weyrwoman's name with pointed courtesy, *is talking to Manora. She's dressed for riding,* he added after a slight pause.

F'lar thanked the bronze sarcastically and strode down the passage to the entrance. As he turned the last bend, he all but ran Lessa down.

You hadn't asked me where *she was,* Mnementh plaintively answered F'lar's blistering reprimand.

Lessa rocked back on her heels from the force of their encounter. She glared up at him, her lips thin with displeasure, her eyes flashing.

"Why didn't I have the opportunity of seeing the Red Star through the Eye Rock?" she demanded in a hard, angry voice.

F'lar pulled at his hair. Lessa at her most difficult would complete the list of this morning's trials.

"Too many to accommodate as it was on the Peak," he muttered, determined not to let her irritate him today. "And you already believe."

"I'd've liked to see it," she snapped and pushed

past him toward the weyr. "If only in my capacity as Weyrwoman and Recorder."

He caught her arm and felt her body tense. He set his teeth, wishing, as he had a hundred times since Ramoth rose in her first mating flight, that Lessa had not been virgin, too. He had not thought to control his dragon-incited emotions, and Lessa's first sexual experience had been violent. It had surprised him to be first, considering that her adolescent years had been spent drudging for lascivious warders and soldier-types. Evidently no one had bothered to penetrate the curtain of rags and the coat of filth she had carefully maintained as a disguise. He had been a considerate and gentle bedmate ever since, but, unless Ramoth and Mnementh were involved, he might as well call it rape.

Yet he knew someday, somehow, he would coax her into responding wholeheartedly to his lovemaking. He had a certain pride in his skill, and he was in a position to persevere.

Now he took a deep breath and released her arm slowly.

"How fortunate you're wearing riding gear. As soon as the wings have cleared out and Ramoth wakes, I shall teach you to fly *between*."

The gleam of excitement in her eyes was evident even in the dimly lit passageway. He heard her inhale sharply.

"Can't put it off too much longer or Ramoth'll be in no shape to fly at all," he continued amiably.

"You mean it?" Her voice was low and breathless, its usual acid edge missing. "You will teach us today?" He wished he could see her face clearly.

Once or twice he had caught an unguarded expression on her face, loving and tender. He would give much to have that look turned on him. However, he admitted wryly to himself, he ought to be glad that melting regard was directed only at Ramoth and not at another human.

"Yes, my dear Weyrwoman, I mean it. I will teach

you to fly *between* today. If only," and he bowed to her with a flourish, "to keep you from trying it yourself."

Her low chuckle informed him his taunt was well-aimed.

"Right now, however," he said, indicating for her to lead the way back to the weyr, "I could do with some food. We were up before the kitchen."

They had entered the well-lighted weyr, so he did not miss the trenchant look she shot him over her shoulder. She would not so easily forgive being left out of the group at the Star Stone this morning, certainly not with the bribe of flying *between*.

How different this inner room was now that Lessa was Weyrwoman, F'lar mused as Lessa called down the service shaft for food. During Jora's incompetent tenure as Weyrwoman, the sleeping quarters had been crowded with junk, unwashed apparel, uncleared dishes. The state of the Weyr and the reduced number of dragons were as much Jora's fault as R'gul's, for she had indirectly encouraged sloth, negligence, and gluttony.

If he, F'lar, had been just a few years older when F'lon, his father, had died . . . Jora had been disgusting, but when dragons rose in mating flight, the condition of your partner counted for nothing.

Lessa took a tray of bread and cheese, and mugs of the stimulating *klah* from the platform. She served him deftly.

"You'd not eaten, either?" he asked.

She shook her head vigorously, the braid into which she had plaited her thick, fine dark hair bobbing across her shoulders. The hairdressing was too severe for her narrow face, but it did not, if that was her intention, disguise her femininity or the curious beauty of her delicate features. Again F'lar wondered that such a slight body contained so much shrewd intelligence and resourceful . . . cunning—yes, that was the word, cunning. F'lar did not make the mistake, as others had, of underestimating her abilities.

"Manora called me to witness the birth of Kylara's child."

F'lar maintained an expression of polite interest. He knew perfectly well that Lessa suspected the child was his, and it could have been, he admitted privately, but he doubted it. Kylara had been one of the ten candidates from the same Search three years ago which had discovered Lessa. Like others who survived Impression, Kylara had found certain aspects of Weyr life exactly suited to her temperament. She had gone from one rider's weyr to another's. She had even seduced F'lar—not at all against his will, to be sure. Now that he was Weyrleader, he found it wiser to ignore her efforts to continue the relationship. T'bor had taken her in hand and had had his hands full until he retired her to the Lower Caverns, well advanced in pregnancy.

Aside from having the amorous tendencies of a green dragon, Kylara was quick and ambitious. She would make a strong Weyrwoman, so F'lar had charged Manora and Lessa with the job of planting the notion in Kylara's mind. In the capacity of Weyrwoman . . . of another Weyr . . . her intense drives would be used to Pern's advantage. She had not learned the severe lessons of restraint and patience that Lessa had, and she didn't have Lessa's devious mind. Fortunately she was in considerable awe of Lessa, and F'lar suspected that Lessa was subtly influencing this attitude. In Kylara's case, F'lar preferred not to object to Lessa's meddling.

"A fine son," Lessa was saying.

F'lar sipped his *klah*. She was not going to get him to admit any responsibility.

After a long pause Lessa added, "She has named him T'kil."

F'lar suppressed a grin at Lessa's failure to get a rise from him.

"Discreet of her."

"Oh?"

"Yes," F'lar replied blandly. "T'lar might be confusing if she took the second half of her name as is customary. 'T'kil,' however, still indicates sire as well as dam."

"While I was waiting for Council to end," Lessa said after clearing her throat, "Manora and I checked the supply caverns. The tithing trains, which the Holds have been so gracious as to send us"—her voice was sharp—"are due within the week. There will shortly be bread fit to eat," she added, wrinkling her nose at the crumbling gray pastry she was attempting to spread with cheese.

"A nice change," F'lar agreed.

She paused.

"The Red Star performed its scheduled antic?"

He nodded.

"And R'gul's doubts have been wiped away in the enlightening red glow?"

"Not at all." F'lar grinned back at her, ignoring her sarcasm. "Not at all, but he will not be so vocal in his criticism."

She swallowed quickly so she could speak. "You'd do well to cut out his criticism," she said ruthlessly, gesturing with her knife as if plunging it into a man's heart. "He is never going to accept your authority with good grace."

"We need every bronze rider . . . there are only seven, you know," he reminded her pointedly. "R'gul's a good wingleader. He'll settle down when the Threads fall. He needs proof to lay his doubts aside."

"And the Red Star in the Eye Rock is not proof?" Lessa's expressive eyes were wide.

F'lar was privately of Lessa's opinion—that it might be wiser to remove R'gul's stubborn contentiousness. But he could not sacrifice a wingleader, needing every dragon and rider as badly as he did.

"I don't trust him," she added darkly. She sipped at her hot drink, her gray eyes dark over the rim of her mug. As if, F'lar mused, she didn't trust him, either.

And she didn't, past a certain point. She had made that plain, and, in honesty, he couldn't blame her. She

did recognize that every action F'lar took was toward
one end . . . the safety and preservation of dragonkind
and weyrfolk and consequently the safety and preservation of Pern. To effect that end, he needed her full
cooperation. When Weyr business or dragonlore were
discussed, she suspended the antipathy he knew she
felt for him. In conferences she supported him wholeheartedly and persuasively, but always he suspected
the double edge to her comments and saw a specula-
tive, suspicious look in her eyes. He needed not only
her tolerance but her empathy.

"Tell me," she said after a long silence, "did the sun
touch the Finger Rock before the Red Star was
bracketed in the Eye Rock or after?"

"Matter of fact, I'm not sure, as I did not see it
myself . . . the concurrence lasts only a few moments
. . . but the two are supposed to be simultaneous."

She frowned at him sourly. "Whom did you waste it
on? R'gul?" She was provoked, her angry eyes looked
everywhere but at him.

"I am Weyrleader," he informed her curtly. She
was unreasonable.

She awarded him one long, hard look before she
bent to finish her meal. She ate very little, quickly and
neatly. Compared to Jora, she didn't eat enough in
the course of an entire day to nourish a sick child. But
then, there was no point in ever comparing Lessa to
Jora.

He finished his own breakfast, absently piling the
mugs together on the empty tray. She rose silently
and removed the dishes.

"As soon as the Weyr is free, we'll go," he told her.

"So you said." She nodded toward the sleeping
queen, visible through the open arch. "We still must
wait upon Ramoth."

"Isn't she rousing? Her tail's been twitching for an
hour."

"She always does that about this time of day."

F'lar leaned across the table, his brows drawn together thoughtfully as he watched the golden-forked

tip of the queen's tail jerk spasmodically from side to side.

"Mnementh, too. And always at dawn and early morning. As if somehow they associate that time of day with trouble . . ."

"Or the Red Star's rising?" Lessa interjected.

Some subtle difference in her tone caused F'lar to glance quickly at her. It wasn't anger now over having missed the morning's phenomenon. Her eyes were fixed on nothing; her face, smooth at first, was soon wrinkled with a vaguely anxious frown as tiny lines formed between her arching, well-defined brows.

"Dawn . . . that's when all warnings come," she murmured.

"What kind of warnings?" he asked with quiet encouragement.

"There was that morning . . . a few days before . . . before you and Fax descended on Ruath Hold. Something woke me . . . a feeling, like a very heavy pressure . . . the sensation of some terrible danger threatening." She was silent. "The Red Star was just rising." The fingers of her left hand opened and closed. She gave a convulsive shudder. Her eyes refocused on him.

"You and Fax did come out of the northeast from Crom," she said sharply, ignoring the fact, F'lar noticed, that the Red Star also rises north of true east.

"Indeed we did," he grinned at her, remembering that morning vividly. "Although," he added, gesturing around the great cavern to emphasize, "I prefer to believe I served you well that day . . . you remember it with displeasure?"

The look she gave him was coldly inscrutable.

"Danger comes in many guises."

"I agree," he replied amiably, determined not to rise to her bait. "Had any other rude awakenings?" he inquired conversationally.

The absolute stillness in the room brought his attention back to her. Her face had drained of all color.

"The day Fax invaded Ruath Hold." Her voice was a barely articulated whisper. Her eyes were wide and staring. Her hands clenched the edge of the table. She said nothing for such a long interval that F'lar became concerned. This was an unexpectedly violent reaction to a casual question.

"Tell me," he suggested softly.

She spoke in unemotional, impersonal tones, as if she were reciting a Traditional Ballad or something that had happened to an entirely different person.

"I was a child. Just eleven. I woke at dawn . . ." Her voice trailed off. Her eyes remained focused on nothing, staring at a scene that had happened long ago.

F'lar was stirred by an irresistible desire to comfort her. It struck him forcibly, even as he was stirred by this unusual compassion, that he had never thought that Lessa, of all people, would be troubled by so old a terror.

Mnementh sharply informed his rider that Lessa was obviously bothered a good deal. Enough so that her mental anguish was rousing Ramoth from sleep. In less accusing tones Mnementh informed F'lar that R'gul had finally taken off with his weyrling pupils. His dragon, Hath, however, was in a fine state of disorientation due to R'gul's state of mind. Must F'lar unsettle everyone in the Weyr . . .

"Oh, be quiet," F'lar retorted under his breath.

"Why?" Lessa demanded in her normal voice.

"I didn't mean you, my dear Weyrwoman," he assured her, smiling pleasantly, as if the entranced interlude had never occurred. "Mnementh is full of advice these days."

"Like rider, like dragon," she replied tartly.

Ramoth yawned mightily. Lessa was instantly on her feet, running to her dragon's side, her slight figure dwarfed by the six-foot dragon head.

A tender, adoring expression flooded her face as she gazed into Ramoth's gleaming opalescent eyes. F'lar clenched his teeth, envious, by the Egg, of a rider's affection for her dragon.

In his mind he heard Mnementh's dragon equivalent of laughter.

"She's hungry," Lessa informed F'lar, an echo of her love for Ramoth lingering in the soft line of her mouth, in the kindness in her gray eyes.

"She's always hungry," he observed and followed them out of the weyr.

Mnementh hovered courteously just beyond the ledge until Lessa and Ramoth had taken off. They glided down the Weyr Bowl, over the misty bathing lake, toward the feeding ground at the opposite end of the long oval that comprised the floor of Benden Weyr. The striated, precipitous walls were pierced with the black mouths of single weyr entrances, deserted at this time of day by the few dragons who might otherwise doze on their ledges in the wintry sun.

As F'lar vaulted to Mnementh's smooth bronze neck, he hoped that Ramoth's clutch would be spectacular, erasing the ignominy of the paltry dozen Nemorth had laid in each of her last few clutches.

He had no serious doubts of the improvement after Ramoth's remarkable mating flight with his Mnementh. The bronze dragon smugly echoed his rider's certainty, and both looked on the queen possessively as she curved her wings to land. She was twice Nemorth's size, for one thing; her wings were half-a-wing again longer than Mnementh's, who was the biggest of the seven male bronzes. F'lar looked to Ramoth to repopulate the five empty Weyrs, even as he looked to himself and Lessa to rejuvenate the pride and faith of dragonriders and of Pern itself. He only hoped time enough remained to him to do what was necessary. The Red Star had been bracketed by the Eye Rock. The Threads would soon be falling. Somewhere, in one of the other Weyrs' Records, must be the information he needed to ascertain *when*, exactly, Threads would fall.

Mnementh landed. F'lar jumped down from the curving neck to stand beside Lessa. The three watched as Ramoth, a buck grasped in each of her forefeet, rose to a feeding ledge.

"Will her appetite never taper off?" Lessa asked with affectionate dismay.

As a dragonet, Ramoth had been eating to grow. Her full stature attained, she was, of course, now eating for her young, and she applied herself conscientiously.

F'lar chuckled and squatted, hunter fashion. He picked up shale-flakes, skating them across the flat dry ground, counting the dust puffs boyishly.

"The time will come when she won't eat everything in sight," he assured Lessa. "But she's young . . ."

". . . and needs her strength," Lessa interrupted, her voice a fair imitation of R'gul's pedantic tones.

F'lar looked up at her, squinting against the wintry sun that slanted down at them.

"She's a finely grown beast, especially compared to Nemorth." He gave a contemptuous snort. "In fact, there *is* no comparison. However, look here," he ordered peremptorily.

He tapped the smoothed sand in front of him, and she saw that his apparently idle gestures had been to a purpose. With a sliver of stone, he drew a design in quick strokes.

"In order to fly a dragon *between,* he has to know where to go. And so do you." He grinned at the astonished and infuriated look of comprehension on her face. "Ah, but there are certain consequences to an ill-considered jump. Badly visualized reference points often result in staying *between.*" His voice dropped ominously. Her face cleared of its resentment. "So there are certain reference or recognition points arbitrarily taught all weyrlings. That,"—he pointed first to his facsimile and then to the actual Star Stone with its Finger and Eye Rock companions, on Benden Peak—"is the first recognition point a weyrling learns. When I take you aloft, you will reach an altitude just above the Star Stone, near enough for you to be able to see the hole in the Eye Rock clearly. Fix that picture sharply in your mind's eye, relay it to Ramoth. That will always get you home."

"Understood. But how do I learn recognition points of places I've never seen?"

He grinned up at her. "You're drilled in them. First by your instructor," and he pointed the sliver at his chest, "and then by going there, having directed your dragon to get the visualization from her instructor," and he indicated Mnementh. The bronze dragon lowered his wedge-shaped head until one eye was focused on his rider and his mate's rider. He made a pleased noise deep in his chest.

Lessa laughed up at the gleaming eye and, with unexpected affection, patted the soft nose.

F'lar cleared his throat in surprise. He had been aware that Mnementh showed an unusual affection for the Weyrwoman, but he had had no idea Lessa was fond of the bronze. Perversely, he was irritated.

"However," he said, and his voice sounded unnatural to himself, "we take the young riders constantly to and from the main reference points all across Pern, to all the Holds so that they have eyewitness impressions on which to rely. As a rider becomes adept in picking out landmarks, he gets additional references from other riders. Therefore, to go *between*, there is actually only one requirement: a clear picture of where you want to go. *And* a dragon!" He grinned at her. "Also, you should always plan to arrive above your reference point in clear air."

Lessa frowned.

"It is better to arrive in open air"—F'lar waved a hand above his head—"rather than underground," and he slapped his open hand onto the dirt. A puff of dust rose warningly.

"But the wings took off within the Bowl itself the day the Lords of the Hold arrived," Lessa reminded him.

F'lar chuckled at her uptake. "True, but only the most seasoned riders. Once we came across a dragon and a rider entombed together in solid rock. They . . . were . . . very young." His eyes were bleak.

"I take the point," she assured him gravely. "That's her fifth," she added, pointing toward Ramoth, who was carrying her latest kill up to the bloody ledge.

"She'll work them off today, I assure you," F'lar remarked. He rose, brushing off his knees with sharp slaps of his riding gloves. "Test her temper."

Lessa did so with a silent, *Had enough?* She grimaced at Ramoth's indignant rejection of the thought.

The queen went swooping down for a huge fowl, rising in a flurry of gray, brown and white feathers.

"She's not as hungry as she's making you think, the deceitful creature," F'lar chuckled and saw that Lessa had reached the same conclusion. Her eyes were snapping with vexation.

"When you've finished the bird, Ramoth, do let us learn how to fly *between*," Lessa said aloud for F'lar's benefit, "before our good Weyrleader changes his mind."

Ramoth looked up from her gorging, turned her head toward the two riders at the edge of the feeding ground. Her eyes gleamed. She bent her head again to her kill, but Lessa could sense the dragon would obey.

It was cold aloft. Lessa was glad of the fur lining in her riding gear, and the warmth of the great golden neck which she bestrode. She decided not to think of the absolute cold of *between* which she had experienced only once. She glanced below on her right where bronze Mnementh hovered, and she caught his amused thought.

F'lar tells me to tell Ramoth to tell you to fix the alignment of the Star Stone firmly in your mind as a homing. Then, Mnementh went on amiably, *we shall fly down to the lake. You will return from* between *to this exact point. Do you understand?*

Lessa found herself grinning foolishly with anticipation and nodded vigorously. How much time was saved because she could speak directly to the dragons!

Ramoth made a disgruntled noise deep in her throat. Lessa patted her reassuringly.

"Have you got the picture in your mind, dear one?" she asked, and Ramoth again rumbled, less annoyed, because she was catching Lessa's excitement.

Mnementh stroked the cold air with his wings, greenish-brown in the sunlight, and curved down gracefully toward the lake on the plateau below Benden Weyr. His flight line took him very low over the rim of the Weyr. From Lessa's angle, it looked like a collision course. Ramoth followed closely in his wake. Lessa caught her breath at the sight of the jagged boulders just below Ramoth's wing tips.

It was exhilarating, Lessa crowed to herself, doubly stimulated by the elation that flowed back to her from Ramoth.

Mnementh halted above the farthest shore of the lake, and there, too, Ramoth came to hover.

Mnementh flashed the thought to Lessa that she was to place the picture of where she wished to go firmly in her mind and direct Ramoth to get there.

Lessa complied. The next instant the awesome, bone-penetrating cold of black *between* enveloped them. Before either she or Ramoth was aware of more than that biting touch of cold and impregnable darkness, they were above the Star Stone.

Lessa let out a cry of pure triumph.

It is extremely simple. Ramoth seemed disappointed.

Mnementh reappeared beside and slightly below them.

You are to return by the same route to the Lake, he ordered, and before the thought had finished, Ramoth took off.

Mnementh was beside them above the lake, fuming with his own and F'lar's anger. *You did not visualize before transferring. Don't think a first successful trip makes you perfect. You have no conception of the dangers inherent in* between. *Never fail to picture your arrival point again.*

Lessa glanced down at F'lar. Even two wingspans apart, she could see the vivid anger on his face, almost feel the fury flashing from his eyes. And laced through the wrath, a terrible sinking fearfulness for her safety that was a more effective reprimand than his wrath. Lessa's safety, she wondered bitterly, or Ramoth's?

You are to follow us, Mnementh was saying in a calmer tone, *rehearsing in your mind the two reference points you have already learned. We shall jump to and from them this morning, gradually learning other points around Benden.*

They did. Flying as far away as Benden Hold itself, nestled against the foothills above Benden Valley, the Weyr Peak a far point against the noonday sky, Lessa did not neglect to visualize a clearly detailed impression each time.

This was as marvelously exciting as she had hoped it would be, Lessa confided to Ramoth. Ramoth replied: yes, it was certainly preferable to the time-consuming methods others had to use, but she didn't think it was exciting at all to jump *between* from Benden Weyr to Benden Hold and back to Benden Weyr again. It was dull.

They had met with Mnementh above the Star Stone again. The bronze dragon sent Lessa the message that this was a very satisfactory initial session. They would practice some distant jumping tomorrow.

Tomorrow, thought Lessa glumly, some emergency will occur or our hard-working Weyrleader will decide today's session constitutes keeping his promise and that will be that.

There was one jump she could make *between,* from anywhere on Pern, and not miss her mark.

She visualized Ruatha for Ramoth as seen from the heights above the Hold . . . to satisfy that requirement. To be scrupulously clear, Lessa projected the pattern of the firepits. Before Fax invaded and she had had to manipulate its decline, Ruatha had been such a lovely, prosperous valley. She told Ramoth to jump *between.*

The cold was intense and seemed to last for many heartbeats. Just as Lessa began to fear that she had somehow lost them *between,* they exploded into the air above the Hold. Elation filled her. That for F'lar and his excessive caution! With Ramoth she could jump anywhere! For there was the distinctive pattern of Ruatha's fire-guttered heights. It was just before dawn, the Breast Pass between Crom and Ruatha, black cones against the lightening gray sky. Fleetingly she noticed the absence of the Red Star that now blazed in the dawn sky. And fleetingly she noticed a difference in the air. Chill, yes, but not wintry . . . the air held that moist coolness of early spring.

Startled, she glanced downward, wondering if she could have, for all her assurance, erred in some fashion. But no, this was Ruath Hold. The Tower, the inner Court, the aspect of the broad avenue leading down to the crafthold were just as they should be. Wisps of smoke from distant chimneys indicated people were making ready for the day.

Ramoth caught the tenor of her insecurity and began to press for an explanation.

This is Ruatha, Lessa replied stoutly. *It can be no other. Circle the heights. See, there are the firepit lines I gave you. . . .*

Lessa gasped, the coldness in her stomach freezing her muscles.

Below her in the slowly lifting predawn gloom, she saw the figures of many men toiling over the breast of the cliff from the hills beyond Ruatha, men moving with quiet stealth like criminals.

She ordered Ramoth to keep as still as possible in the air so as not to direct their attention upward. The dragon was curious but obedient.

Who would be attacking Ruatha? It seemed incredible. Lytol was, after all, a former dragonman and had savagely repelled one attack already. Could there possibly be a thought of aggression among the Holds now that F'lar was Weyrleader? And what

Hold Lord would be foolish enough to mount a territorial war in the winter?

No, not winter. The air was definitely springlike.

The men crept on, over the firepits to the edge of the heights. Suddenly Lessa realized they were lowering rope ladders over the face of the cliff, down toward the open shutters of the Inner Hold.

Wildly she clutched at Ramoth's neck, certain of what she saw.

This was the invader Fax, now dead nearly three Turns—Fax and his men as they began their attack on Ruatha nearly thirteen Turns ago.

Yes, there was the Tower guard, his face a white blot turned toward the Cliff itself, watching. He had been paid his bribe to stand silent this morning.

But the watch-wher, trained to give alarm for any intrusion—why was it not trumpeting its warning? Why was it silent?

Because, Ramoth informed her rider with calm logic, *it senses your presence as well as mine, so how could the Hold be in danger?*

No, No! Lessa moaned. *What can I do now? How can I wake them? Where is the girl I was? I was asleep, and then I woke. I remember. I dashed from my room. I was so scared. I went down the steps and nearly fell. I knew I had to get to the watch-wher's kennel. . . . I knew. . . .*

Lessa clutched at Ramoth's neck for support as past acts and mysteries became devastatingly clear.

She herself had warned herself, just as it was her presence on the queen dragon that had kept the watch-wher from giving alarm. For as she watched, stunned and speechless, she saw the small, gray-robed figure that could only be herself as a youngster, burst from the Hold Hall door, race uncertainly down the cold stone steps into the Court, and disappear into the watch-wher's stinking den. Faintly she heard it crying in piteous confusion.

Just as Lessa-the-girl reached that doubtful sanctuary, Fax's invaders swooped into the open window embrasures and began the slaughter of her sleeping family.

"Back—back to the Star Stone!" Lessa cried. In her wide and staring eyes she held the image of the guiding rocks like a rudder for her sanity as well as Ramoth's direction.

The intense cold acted as a restorative. And then they were above the quiet, peaceful wintry Weyr as if they had never paradoxically visited Ruatha.

F'lar and Mnementh were nowhere to be seen.

Ramoth, however, was unshaken by the experience. She had only gone where she had been told to go and had not quite understood that going where she had been told to go had shocked Lessa. She suggested to her rider that Mnementh had probably followed them to Ruatha so if Lessa would give her the *proper* references, she'd take her there. Ramoth's sensible attitude was comforting.

Lessa carefully drew for Ramoth not the child's memory of a long-vanished, idyllic Ruatha but her more recent recollection of the Hold, gray, sullen, at dawning, with a Red Star pulsing on the horizon.

And there they were again, hovering over the Valley, the Hold below them on the right. The grasses grew untended on the heights, clogging firepit and brickwork; the scene showed all the deterioration she had encouraged in her effort to thwart Fax of any profit from conquering Ruath Hold

But, as she watched, vaguely disturbed, she saw a figure emerge from the kitchen, saw the watch-wher creep from its lair and follow the raggedly dressed figure as far across the Court as the chain permitted. She saw the figure ascend the Tower, gaze first eastward, then northeastward. This was still not Ruatha of today and now! Lessa's mind reeled, disoriented. This time she had come back to visit herself of three Turns ago, to see the filthy drudge plotting revenge on Fax.

She felt the absolute cold of *between* as Ramoth snatched them back, emerging once more above the Star Stone. Lessa was shuddering, her eyes frantically taking in the reassuring sight of the Weyr Bowl, hoping she had not somehow shifted backward in time yet again. Mnementh suddenly erupted into the air a few lengths below and beyond Ramoth. Lessa greeted him with a cry of intense relief.

Back to your weyr! There was no disguising the white fury in Mnementh's tone. Lessa was too unnerved to respond in any way other than instant compliance. Ramoth glided swiftly to their ledge, quickly clearing the perch for Mnementh to land.

The rage on F'lar's face as he leaped from Mnementh and advanced on Lessa brought her wits back abruptly. She made no move to evade him as he grabbed her shoulders and shook her violently.

"How dare you risk yourself and Ramoth? Why must you defy me at every opportunity? Do you realize what would happen to all Pern if we lost Ramoth? Where did you go?" He was spitting with anger, punctuating each question that tumbled from his lips by giving her a head-wrenching shake.

"Ruatha," she managed to say, trying to keep herself erect. She reached out to catch at his arms, but he shook her again.

"Ruatha? We were there. You weren't. Where did you go?"

"Ruatha!" Lessa cried louder, clutching at him distractedly because he kept jerking her off balance. She couldn't organize her thoughts with him jolting her around.

She was *at Ruatha,* Mnementh said firmly.

We were there twice, Ramoth added.

As the dragons' calmer words penetrated F'lar's fury, he stopped shaking Lessa. She hung limply in his grasp, her hands weakly plucking at his arms, her eyes closed, her face gray. He picked her up and strode rapidly into the queen's Weyr, the dragons following. He placed her upon the couch, wrapping her tightly in the fur cover. He called down the service shaft for the duty cook to send up hot *klah*.

"All right, what happened?" he demanded.

She didn't look at him, but he got a glimpse of her haunted eyes. She blinked constantly as if she longed to erase what she had just seen.

Finally she got herself somewhat under control and said in a low, tired voice, "I did go to Ruatha. Only . . . I went *back* to Ruatha."

"Back to Ruatha?" F'lar repeated the words stupidly; the significance momentarily eluded him.

It certainly does, Mnementh agreed and flashed to F'lar's mind the two scenes he had picked out of Ramoth's memory.

Staggered by the import of the visualization, F'lar found himself slowly sinking to the edge of the bed.

"You went *between* times?"

She nodded slowly. The terror was beginning to leave her eyes.

"Between times," F'lar murmured. "I wonder . . ."

His mind raced through the possibilities. It might well tip the scales of survival in the Weyr's favor. He couldn't think exactly how to use this extraordinary ability, but there *must* be an advantage in it for dragonfolk.

The service shaft rumbled. He took the pitcher from the platform and poured two mugs.

Lessa's hands were shaking so much that she couldn't get hers to her lips. He steadied it for her, wondering if going *between* times would regularly cause this kind of shock. If so, it wouldn't be any advantage at all. If she'd had enough of a scare this day, she might not be so contemptuous of his orders the next time; which would be to his benefit.

Outside in the weyr, Mnementh snorted his opinion on that. F'lar ignored him.

Lessa was trembling violently now. He put an arm around her, pressing the fur against her slender body. He held the mug to her lips, forcing her to drink. He could feel the tremors ease off. She took long, slow, deep breaths between swallows, equally determined to get herself under control. The moment he felt her stiffen under his arm, he released her. He wondered if Lessa had ever had someone to turn to. Certainly not after Fax invaded her family Hold. She had been only eleven, a child. Had hate and revenge been the only emotions the growing girl had practiced?

She lowered the mug, cradling it in her hands carefully as if it had assumed some undefinable importance to her.

"Now. Tell me," he ordered evenly.

She took a long deep breath and began to speak, her hands tightening around the mug. Her inner turmoil had not lessened; it was merely under control now.

"Ramoth and I were bored with the weyrling exercises," she admitted candidly.

Grimly F'lar recognized that, while the adventure might have taught her to be more circumspect, it had not scared her into obedience. He doubted that anything would.

"I gave her the picture of Ruatha so we could go *between* there." She did not look at him, but her profile was outlined against the dark fur of the rug. "The Ruatha I knew so well—I accidentally sent myself backward in time to the day Fax invaded."

Her shock was now comprehensible to him.

"And . . ." he prompted her, his voice carefully neutral.

"And I saw myself—" Her voice broke off. With an effort she continued. "I had visualized for Ramoth the designs of the firepits and the angle of the Hold if one looked down from the pits into the Inner Court. That was where we emerged. It was just dawn"—she lifted her chin with a nervous jerk—"and there was no Red Star in the sky." She gave him a quick, defensive look as if she expected him to contest this detail. "And I saw men creeping over the firepits, lowering rope ladders to the top windows of the Hold. I saw the Tower guard watching. Just watching." She clenched her teeth at such treachery, and her eyes gleamed malevolently. "And I saw myself run from the Hall into the watch-wher's lair. And do you know why"—her voice lowered to a bitter whisper—"the watch-wher did not alarm the Hold?"

"Why?"

"Because there was a dragon in the sky, and *I,* Lessa of Ruatha, was on her." She flung the mug from her as if she wished she could reject the knowledge, too. "Because *I* was there, the watch-wher did not alarm the Hold, thinking the intrusion legitimate, with one of the Blood on a dragon in the sky. So I" —her body grew rigid, her hands clasped so tightly that the knuckles were white—"*I* was the cause of my family's massacre. Not Fax! If I had not acted the captious fool today, I would not have been there with Ramoth and the watch-wher would—"

Her voice had risen to an hysterical pitch of re-crimination. He slapped her sharply across the cheeks, grabbing her, robe and all, to shake her.

The stunned look in her eyes and the tragedy in her face alarmed him. His indignation over her willful-ness disappeared. Her unruly independence of mind and spirit attracted him as much as her curious dark beauty. Infuriating as her fractious ways might be, they were too vital a part of her integrity to be exor-cised. Her indomitable will had taken a grievous shock today, and her self-confidence had better be restored quickly.

"On the contrary, Lessa," he said sternly, "Fax would still have murdered your family. He had planned it very carefully, even to scheduling his attack on the morning when the Tower guard was one who could be bribed. Remember, too, it was dawn and the watch-wher, being a nocturnal beast, blind by day-light, is relieved of responsibility at dawn and knows it. Your presence, damnable as it may appear to you, was not the deciding factor by any means. It did, and I draw your attention to this very important fact, cause you to save yourself, by warning Lessa-the-child. Don't you see that?"

"I could have called out," she murmured, but the

frantic look had left her eyes and there was a faint
hint of normal color in her lips.

"If you wish to flail around in guilt, go right
ahead," he said with deliberate callousness.

Ramoth interjected a thought that, since the two of
them had been there that previous time as Fax's men
had prepared to invade, it had already happened, so
how could it be changed? The act was inevitable both
that day and today. For how else could Lessa have
lived to come to the Weyr and impress Ramoth at
the hatching?

Mnementh relayed Ramoth's message scrupulously,
even to imitating Ramoth's egocentric nuances. F'lar
looked sharply at Lessa to see the effect of Ramoth's
astringent observation.

"Just like Ramoth to have the final word," she said
with a hint of her former droll humor.

F'lar felt the muscles along his neck and shoulders
begin to relax. She'd be all right, he decided, but it
might be wiser to make her talk it all out now, to put
the whole experience into proper perspective.

"You said you were there twice?" He leaned back
on the couch, watching her closely. "When was the
second time?"

"Can't you guess?" she asked sarcastically.

"No," he lied.

"When else but the dawn I was awakened, feeling
the Red Star was a menace to me? . . . Three days
before you and Fax came out of the northeast."

"It would seem," he remarked dryly, "that you
were your own premonition both times."

She nodded.

"Have you had any more of these presenti-
ments . . . or should I say reinforced warnings?"

She shuddered but answered him with more of her
old spirit.

"No, but if I should, *you* go. I don't want to."

F'lar grinned maliciously.

"I would, however," she added, "like to know why
and how it could happen."

"I've never run across a mention of it anywhere," he told her candidly. "Of course, if you have done it —and you undeniably have," he assured her hastily at her indignant protest, "it obviously can be done. You say you thought of Ruatha, but you thought of it as it was on that particular day. Certainly a day to be remembered. You thought of spring, before dawn, no Red Star—yes, I remember your mentioning that—so one would have to remember references peculiar to a significant day to return *between* times to the past."

She nodded slowly, thoughtfully.

"You used the same method the second time, to get to the Ruatha of three Turns ago. Again, of course, it was spring."

He rubbed his palms together, then brought his hands down on his knees with an emphatic slap and rose to his feet.

"I'll be back," he said and strode from the room, ignoring her half-articulated cry of warning.

Ramoth was curling up in the Weyr as he passed her. He noticed that her color remained good in spite of the drain on her energies by the morning's exercises. She glanced at him, her many-faceted eye already covered by the inner, protective lid.

Mnementh awaited his rider on the ledge, and the moment F'lar leaped to his neck, took off. He circled upward, hovering above the Star Stone.

You wish to try Lessa's trick, Mnementh said, unperturbed by the prospective experiment.

F'lar stroked the great curved neck affectionately. *You understand how it worked for Ramoth and Lessa?*

As well as anyone can, Mnementh replied with the approximation of a shrug. *When did you have in mind?*

Before that moment F'lar had had no idea. Now, unerringly, his thoughts drew him backward to the summer day R'gul's bronze Hath had flown to mate the grotesque Nemorth, and R'gul had become Weyrleader in place of his dead father, F'lon.

Only the cold of *between* gave them any indication
that they had transferred; they were still hovering
above the Star Stone. F'lar wondered if they had
missed some essential part of the transfer. Then he
realized that the sun was in another quarter of the sky
and the air was warm and sweet with summer. The
Weyr below was empty; there were no dragons sunning themselves on the ledges, no women busy at
tasks in the Bowl. Noises impinged on his senses: rau-
cous laughter, yells, shrieks, and a soft crooning noise
that dominated the bedlam.

Then, from the direction of the weyrling barracks
in the Lower Caverns, two figures emerged—a strip-
ling and a young bronze dragon. The boy's arm lay
limply along the beast's neck. The impression that
reached the hovering observers was one of utter de-
jection. The two halted by the lake, the boy peering
into the unruffled blue waters, then glancing upward
toward the queen's weyr.

F'lar knew the boy for himself, and compassion
for that younger self filled him. If only he could reassure that boy, so torn by grief, so filled with resentment, that he would one day become Weyrleader. . . .

Abruptly, startled by his own thoughts, he ordered
Mnementh to transfer back. The utter cold of *between* was like a slap in his face, replaced almost
instantly as they broke out of *between* into the cold of
normal winter.

Slowly, Mnementh flew back down to the queen's
weyr, as sobered as F'lar by what they had seen.

Rise high in glory,   Count three months and more,
Bronze and gold.   And five heated weeks,
Dive entwined,   A day of glory and
Enhance the Hold.   In a month, who seeks?

         A strand of silver
         In the sky . . .
         With heat, all quickens
         And all times fly.

"I DON'T KNOW why you insisted that F'nor unearth these ridiculous things from Ista Weyr," Lessa exclaimed in a tone of exasperation. "They consist of nothing but trivial notes on how many measures of grain were used to bake daily bread."

F'lar glanced up at her from the Records he was studying. He sighed, leaned back in his chair in a bone-popping stretch.

"And I used to think," Lessa said with a rueful expression on her vivid, narrow face, "that those venerable Records would hold the total sum of all dragonlore and human wisdom. Or so I was led to believe," she added pointedly.

F'lar chuckled. "They do, but you have to disinter it."

Lessa wrinkled her nose. "Phew. They smell as if we had . . . and the only decent thing to do would be to rebury them."

"Which is another item I'm hoping to find . . . the

old preservative technique that kept the skins from hardening and smelling."

"It's stupid, anyhow, to use skins for recording. There ought to be something better. We have become, dear Weyrleader, entirely too hidebound."

While F'lar roared with appreciation of her pun, she regarded him impatiently. Suddenly she jumped up, fired by another of her mercurial moods.

"Well, you won't find it. You won't find the facts you're looking for. Because I know what you're really after, and it isn't recorded!"

"Explain yourself."

"It's time we stopped hiding a rather brutal truth from ourselves."

"Which is?"

"Our mutual feeling that the Red Star is a menace and that the Threads *will* come! *We* decided that out of pure conceit and then went back *between* times to particularly crucial points in our lives and strengthened that notion, in our earlier selves. And for you, it was when you decided you were destined"—her voice made the word mocking—"to become Weyrleader one day."

"Could it be," she went on scornfully, "that our ultraconservative R'gul has the right of it? That there have been no Threads for four hundred Turns because there are no more? And that the reason we have so few dragons is because the dragons sense they are no longer essential to Pern? That we *are* anachronisms as well as parasites?"

F'lar did not know how long he sat looking up at her bitter face or how long it took him to find answers to her probing questions.

"Anything is possible, Weyrwoman," he heard his voice replying calmly. "Including the unlikely fact that an eleven-year-old child, scared stiff, could plot revenge on her family's murderer and—against all odds—succeed."

She took an involuntary step forward, struck by his unexpected rebuttal. She listened intently.

"I prefer to believe," he went on inexorably, "that there is more to life than raising dragons and playing spring games. That is not enough for me. And I have made others look further, beyond self-interest and comfort. I have given them a purpose, a discipline. Everyone, dragonfolk and Holder alike, profits.

"I am not looking in these Records for reassurance. I'm looking for solid facts.

"I can prove, Weyrwoman, that there have been Threads. I can prove that there have been Intervals during which the Weyrs have declined. I can prove that if you sight the Red Star directly bracketed by the Eye Rock at the moment of winter solstice, the Red Star will pass close enough to Pern to throw off Threads. Since I can prove those facts, I believe Pern is in danger. *I* believe . . . not the youngster of fifteen Turns ago. F'lar, the bronze rider, the Weyrleader, believes it!"

He saw her eyes reflecting shadowy doubts, but he sensed his arguments were beginning to reassure her.

"You felt constrained to believe in me once before," he went on in a milder voice, "when I suggested that you could be Weyrwoman. You believed me and . . ." He made a gesture around the weyr as substantiation.

She gave him a weak, humorless smile.

"That was because I had never planned what to do with my life once I did have Fax lying dead at my feet. Of course, being Ramoth's Weyrmate is wonderful, but"—she frowned slightly— "it isn't enough anymore, either. That's why I wanted so to learn to fly and . . ."

". . . that's how this argument started in the first place," F'lar finished for her with a sardonic smile.

He leaned across the table urgently.

"Believe with me, Lessa, until you have cause not to. I respect your doubts. There's nothing wrong in doubting. It sometimes leads to greater faith. But believe with me until spring. If the Threads have not fallen by then . . ." He shrugged fatalistically.

She looked at him for a long moment and then inclined her head slowly in agreement.

He tried to suppress the relief he felt at her decision. Lessa, as Fax had discovered, was a ruthless adversary and a canny advocate. Besides these, she was Weyrwoman: essential to his plans.

"Now, let's get back to the contemplation of trivia. They do tell me, you know, time, place, and duration of Thread incursions," he grinned up at her reassuringly. "And those facts I must have to make up my timetable."

"Timetable? But you said you didn't know the time."

"Now the day to the second when the Threads may spin down. For one thing, while the weather holds so unusually cold for this time of year, the Threads simply turn brittle and blow away like dust. They're harmless. However, when the air is warm, they are viable and . . . deadly." He made fists of both hands, placing one above and to one side of the other. "The Red Star is my right hand, my left is Pern. The Red Star turns very fast and in the opposite direction from us. It also wobbles erratically."

"How do you know that?"

"Diagram on the walls of the Fort Weyr Hatching Ground. That was the very first Weyr, you know."

Lessa smiled sourly. "I know."

"So, when the Star makes a pass, the Threads spin off, down toward us, in attacks that last six hours and occur approximately fourteen hours apart."

"Attacks last six hours?"

He nodded gravely.

"When the Red Star is closest to us. Right now it is just beginning its Pass."

She frowned.

He rummaged among the skin sheets on the table, and an object dropped to the stone floor with a metallic clatter.

Curious, Lessa bent to pick it up, turning the thin sheet over in her hands.

"What's this?" She ran an exploratory finger lightly across the irregular design on one side.

"I don't know. F'nor brought it back from Fort Weyr. It was nailed to one of the chests in which the Records had been stored. He brought it along, thinking it might be important. Said there was a plate like it just under the Red Star diagram on the wall of the Hatching Ground."

"This first part is plain enough: 'Mother's father's father, who departed for all time *between,* said this was the key to the mystery, and it came to him while doodling: he said that he said: ARRHENIUS? EUREKA! MYCORRHIZA. . . .' Of course, that part doesn't make any sense at all," Lessa snorted. "It isn't even Pernese—just babbling, those last three words."

"I've studied it, Lessa," F'lar replied, glancing at it again and tipping it toward him to reaffirm his conclusions. "The only way to depart for all time *between* is to die, right? People just don't fly away on their own, obviously. So it is a death vision, dutifully recorded by a grandchild, who couldn't spell very well either. 'Doodling' as the present tense of dying!" He smiled indulgently. "And as for the rest of it, after the nonsense—like most death visions, it 'explains' what everyone has always known. Read on."

" 'Flamethrowing fire lizards to wipe out the spores. Q.E.D.'?"

"No help there, either. Obviously just a primitive rejoicing that he is a dragonman, who didn't even know the right word for Threads." F'lar's shrug was expressive.

Lessa wet one fingertip to see if the patterns were inked on. The metal was shiny enough for a good mirror if she could get rid of the designs. However, the patterns remained smooth and precise.

"Primitive or no, they had a more permanent way of recording their visions that is superior to even the well-preserved skins," she murmured.

"Well-preserved babblings," F'lar said, turning

back to the skins he was checking for understandable data.

"A badly scored ballad?" Lessa wondered and then dismissed the whole thing. "The design isn't even pretty."

F'lar pulled forward a chart that showed overlapping horizontal bands imposed on the projection of Pern's continental mass.

"Here," he said, "this represents waves of attack, and this one"—he pulled forward the second map with vertical bandings—"shows time zones. So you can see that with a fourteen-hour break only certain parts of Pern are affected in each attack. One reason for spacing of the Weyrs."

"Six full Weyrs," she murmured, "close to three thousand dragons."

"I'm aware of the statistics," he replied in a voice devoid of expression. "It meant no one Weyr was overburdened during the height of the attacks, not that three thousand beasts must be available. However, with these timetables, we can manage until Ramoth's first clutches have matured."

She turned a cynical look on him. "You've a lot of faith in one queen's capacity."

He waved that remark aside impatiently. "I've more faith, no matter what your opinion is, in the startling repetitions of events in these Records."

"Ha!"

"I don't mean how many measures for daily bread, Lessa," he retorted, his voice rising. "I mean such things as the time such and such a wing was sent out on patrol, how long the patrol lasted, how many riders were hurt. The brooding capacities of queens, during the fifty years a Pass lasts and the Intervals between such Passes. Yes, it tells that. By all I've studied here," and he pounded emphatically on the nearest stack of dusty, smelly skins, "Nemorth should have been mating twice a Turn for the last ten. Had she even kept to her paltry twelve a clutch, we'd have two hundred and forty more beasts. . . . Don't interrupt. But we had Jora as Weyrwoman and R'gul as Weyrleader, and we had fallen into planet-wide disfavor during a four hundred Turn Interval. Well, Ramoth will brood over no measly dozen, and she'll lay a queen egg, mark my words. She will rise often to mate and lay generously. By the time the Red Star is passing closest to us and the attacks become frequent, we'll be ready."

She stared at him, her eyes wide with incredulity. "Out of Ramoth?"

"Out of Ramoth and out of the queens she'll lay. Remember, there are Records of Faranth laying sixty eggs at a time, including several queen eggs."

Lessa could only shake her head slowly in wonder.

" 'A strand of silver/In the sky. . . . With heat, all quickens/And all times fly,' " F'lar quoted to her.

"She's got weeks more to go before laying, and then the eggs must hatch . . ."

"Been on the Hatching Ground recently? Wear your boots. You'll be burned through sandals."

She dismissed that with a guttural noise. He sat back, outwardly amused by her disbelief.

"And then you have to make Impression and wait till the riders—" she went on.

"Why do you think I've insisted on older boys? The dragons are mature long before their riders."

"Then the system is faulty."

He narrowed his eyes slightly, shaking the stylus at her.

"Dragon tradition started out as a guide . . . but there comes a time when man becomes too traditional, too—what was it you said?—too hidebound? Yes, it's traditional to use the weyrbred, because it's been convenient. And because this sensitivity to dragons strengthens where both sire and dam are weyrbred. That doesn't mean weyrbred is best. You, for example . . ."

"There's Weyrblood in the Ruathan line," she said proudly.

"Granted. Take young Naton; he's craftbred from Nabol, yet F'nor tells me he can make Canth understand him."

"Oh, that's not hard to do," she interjected.

"What do you mean?" F'lar jumped on her statement.

They were both interrupted by a high-pitched, penetrating whine. F'lar listened intently for a moment and then shrugged, grinning.

"Some green's getting herself chased again."

"And that's another item these so-called all-knowing Records of yours never mention. Why is it that only the gold dragon can reproduce?"

F'lar did not suppress a lascivious chuckle.

"Well, for one thing, firestone inhibits reproduction. If they never chewed stone, a green could lay, but at best they produce small beasts, and we need big ones. And, for another thing"—his chuckle rolled out as he went on deliberately, grinning mischievously—"if the greens could reproduce, considering their amorousness and the numbers we have of them, we'd be up to our ears in dragons in next to no time."

The first whine was joined by another, and then a low hum throbbed as if carried by the stones of the Weyr itself.

F'lar, his face changing rapidly from surprise to triumphant astonishment, dashed up the passage.

"What's the matter?" Lessa demanded, picking up her skirts to run after him. "What does that mean?"

The hum, resonating everywhere, was deafening in the echo-chamber of the queen's weyr. Lessa registered the fact that Ramoth was gone. She heard F'lar's boots pounding down the passage to the ledge, a sharp *ta-ta-tat* over the kettledrum booming hum. The whine was so high-pitched now that it was inaudible, but still nerve-racking. Disturbed, frightened, Lessa followed F'lar out.

By the time she reached the ledge, the Bowl was a-whir with dragons on the wing, making for the high entrance to the Hatching Ground. Weyrfolk, riders, women, children, all screaming with excitement, were pouring across the Bowl to the lower entrance to the Ground.

She caught sight of F'lar, charging across to the entrance, and she shrieked at him to wait. He couldn't have heard her across the bedlam.

Fuming because she had the long stairs to descend, then must double back as the stairs faced the feeding grounds at the opposite end of the Bowl from the Hatching Ground, Lessa realized that she, the Weyrwoman, would be the last one there.

Why had Ramoth decided to be secretive about laying? Wasn't she close enough to her own weyrmate to want her with her?

A dragon knows what to do, Ramoth calmly informed Lessa.

You could have told me, Lessa wailed, feeling much abused.

Why, at the time F'lar had been going on largely about huge clutches and three thousand beasts, that infuriating dragon-child had been doing it!

It didn't improve Lessa's temper to have to recall another remark of F'lar's—on the state of the Hatching Grounds. The moment she stepped into the mountain-high cavern, she felt the heat through the soles of her sandals. Everyone was crowded in a loose circle around the far end of the cavern. And everyone was swaying from foot to foot. As Lessa was short to begin with, this only decreased the likelihood of her ever seeing what Ramoth had done.

"Let me through!" she demanded imperiously, pounding on the wide backs of two tall riders.

An aisle was reluctantly opened for her, and she went through, looking neither to her right or left at the excited weyrfolk. She was furious, confused, hurt, and knew she looked ridiculous because the hot sand made her walk with a curious mincing quickstep.

She halted, stunned and wide-eyed at the mass of eggs, and forgot such trivial things as hot feet.

Ramoth was curled around the clutch, looking

enormously pleased with herself. She, too, kept shifting, closing and opening a protective wing over her eggs, so that it was difficult to count them.

No one will steal them, silly, so stop fluttering, Lessa advised as she tried to make a tally.

Obediently Ramoth folded her wings. To relieve her maternal anxiety, however, she snaked her head out across the circle of mottled, glowing eggs, looking all around the cavern, flicking her forked tongue in and out.

An immense sigh, like a gust of wind, swept through the cavern. For there, now that Ramoth's wings were furled, gleamed an egg of glowing gold among the mottled ones. A queen egg!

"A queen egg!" The cry went up simultaneously from half a hundred throats. The Hatching Ground rang with cheers, yells, screams, and howls of exultation.

Someone seized Lessa and swung her around in an excess of feeling. A kiss landed in the vicinity of her mouth. No sooner did she recover her footing than she was hugged by someone else—she thought it was Manora—and then pounded and buffeted around in congratulation until she was reeling in a kind of dance between avoiding the celebrants and easing the growing discomfort of her feet.

She broke from the milling revelers and ran across the Ground to Ramoth. Lessa came to a sudden stop before the eggs. They seemed to be pulsing. The shells looked flaccid. She could have sworn they were hard the day she Impressed Ramoth. She wanted to touch one, just to make sure, but dared not.

You may, Ramoth assured her condescendingly. She touched Lessa's shoulder gently with her tongue.

The egg was soft to touch and Lessa drew her hand back quickly, afraid of doing injury.

The heat will harden it, Ramoth said.

"Ramoth, I'm so proud of you," Lessa sighed, looking adoringly up at the great eyes that shone in rainbows of pride. "You are the most marvelous queen ever. I do believe you will redragon all the Weyrs. I do believe you will."

Ramoth inclined her head regally, then began to sway it from side to side over the eggs, protectingly. She began to hiss suddenly, raising from her crouch, beating the air with her wings, before settling back into the sands to lay yet another egg.

The weyrfolk, uncomfortable on the hot sands, were beginning to leave the Hatching Ground now that they had paid tribute to the arrival of the golden egg. A queen took several days to complete her clutch so there was no point to waiting. Seven eggs already lay beside the important golden one, and if there were seven already, this augured well for the eventual total. Wagers were being made and taken even as Ramoth produced her ninth mottled egg.

"Just as I predicted, a queen egg, by the mother of us all," F'lar's voice said in Lessa's ear. "And I'll wager there'll be ten bronzes at least."

She looked up at him, completely in harmony with the Weyrleader at this moment. She was conscious now of Mnementh, crouching proudly on a ledge, gazing fondly at his mate. Impulsively Lessa laid her hand on F'lar's arm.

"F'lar, I do believe you."

"Only now?" F'lar teased her, but his smile was wide and his eyes proud.

Weyrman, watch; Weyrman, learn
Something new in every Turn.
Oldest may be coldest, too.
Sense the right; find the true!

IF F'LAR'S orders over the next months caused no
end of discussion and muttering among the weyrfolk, they seemed to Lessa to be only the logical out-
comes of their discussion after Ramoth had finished
laying her gratifying total of forty-one eggs.

F'lar discarded tradition right and left, treading on
more than R'gul's conservative toes.

Out of perverse distaste for outworn doctrines
against which she herself had chafed during R'gul's
leadership, and out of respect for F'lar's intelligence,
Lessa backed him completely. She might not have
respected her earlier promise to him that she would
believe with him until spring if she had not seen his
predictions come true, one after another. These were
based, however, not on the premonitions she no
longer trusted after her experience *between* times,
but on recorded facts.

As soon as the eggshells hardened and Ramoth had
rolled her special queen egg to one side of the mottled
clutch for attentive brooding, F'lar brought the prospective riders into the Hatching Ground. Tradition-

ally the candidates saw the eggs for the first time on the day of Impression. To this precedent F'lar added others: very few of the sixty-odd were weyrbred, and most of them were in their late teens. The candidates were to get used to the eggs, touch them, caress them, be comfortable with the notion that out of these eggs young dragons would hatch, eager and waiting to be Impressed. F'lar felt that such a practice might cut down on casualties during Impression when the boys were simply too scared to move out of the way of the awkward dragonets.

F'lar also had Lessa persuade Ramoth to let Kylara near her precious golden egg. Kylara readily enough weaned her son and spent hours, with Lessa acting as her tutor, beside the golden egg. Despite Kylara's loose attachment to T'bor, she showed an open preference for F'lar's company. Therefore, Lessa took great pains to foster F'lar's plan for Kylara since it meant her removal, with the new-hatched queen, to Fort Weyr.

F'lar's use of the Hold-born as riders served an additional purpose. Shortly before the actual Hatching and Impression, Lytol, the Warder appointed at Ruath Hold, sent another message.

"The man positively delights in sending bad news," Lessa remarked as F'lar passed the message skin to her.

"He's gloomy," F'nor agreed. He had brought the message. "I feel sorry for that youngster cooped up with such a pessimist."

Lessa frowned at the brown rider. She still found distasteful any mention of Gemma's son, now Lord of her ancestral Hold. Yet . . . as she had inadvertently caused his mother's death and she could not be Weyrwoman and Lady Holder at the same time, it was fitting that Gemma's Jaxom be Lord at Ruatha.

"I, however," F'lar said, "am grateful for his warnings. I suspected Meron would cause trouble again."

"He has shifty eyes, like Fax's," Lessa remarked.

"Shifty-eyed or not, he's dangerous," F'lar an-

swered. "And I cannot have him spreading rumors
that we are deliberately choosing men of the Blood to
weaken Family Lines."

"There are more craftsmen's sons than Holders'
boys, in any case," F'nor snorted.

"I don't like him questioning that the Threads
have not appeared," Lessa said gloomily.

F'lar shrugged. "They'll appear in due time. Be
thankful the weather has continued cold. When the
weather warms up and still no Threads appear, then
I will worry." He grinned at Lessa in an intimate reminder of her promise.

F'nor cleared his throat hastily and looked away.

"However," the Weyrleader went on briskly, "I
can do something about the other accusation."

So, when it was apparent that the eggs were about
to hatch, he broke another long-standing tradition and
sent riders to fetch the fathers of the young candidates
from craft and Hold.

The great Hatching Cavern gave the appearance
of being almost full as Holder and Weyrfolk watched
from the tiers above the heated Ground. This time,
Lessa observed, there was no aura of fear. The youth-
ful candidates were tense, yes, but not frightened out
of their wits by the rocking, shattering eggs. When the
ill-coordinated dragonets awkwardly stumbled—it
seemed to Lessa that they deliberately looked around
at the eager faces as though pre-Impressed—the
youths either stepped to one side or eagerly advanced
as a crooning dragonet made his choice. The Impressions were made quickly and with no accidents. All
too soon, Lessa thought, the triumphant procession of
stumbling dragons and proud new riders moved erratically out of the Hatching Ground to the barracks.

The young queen burst from her shell and moved
unerringly for Kylara, standing confidently on the hot
sands. The watching beasts hummed their approval.

"It was over too soon," Lessa said in a disappointed voice that evening to F'lar.

He laughed indulgently, allowing himself a rare

evening of relaxation now that another step had gone as planned. The Holder folk had been ridden home, stunned, dazed, and themselves impressed by the Weyr and the Weyrleader.

"That's because you were watching this time," he remarked, brushing a lock of her hair back. It obscured his view of her profile. He chuckled again. "You'll notice Naton . . ."

"N'ton," she corrected him.

"All right, N'ton—Impressed a bronze."

"Just as you predicted," she said with some asperity.

"And Kylara is Weyrwoman for Pridith."

Lessa did not comment on that, and she did her best to ignore his laughter.

"I wonder which bronze will fly her," he murmured softly.

"It had better be T'bor's Orth," Lessa said, bridling.

He answered her the only way a wise man could.

Crack dust, blackdust,
Turn in freezing air.
Waste dust, spacedust,
From Red Star bare.

LESSA WOKE abruptly, her head aching, her eyes
blurred, her mouth dry. She had the immediate memory of a terrible nightmare that, just as quickly, escaped recall. She brushed her hair out of her face and
was surprised to find that she had been sweating
heavily.

"F'lar?" she called in an uncertain voice. He had
evidently risen early. "F'lar," she called again, louder.

He's coming, Mnementh informed her. Lessa sensed
that the dragon was just landing on the ledge. She
touched Ramoth and found that the queen, too, had
been bothered by formless, frightening dreams. The
dragon roused briefly and then fell back into deeper
sleep.

Disturbed by her vague fears, Lessa rose and
dressed, forgoing a bath for the first time since she had
arrived at the Weyr.

She called down the shaft for breakfast, then plaited
her hair with deft fingers as she waited.

The tray appeared on the shaft platform just as F'lar entered. He kept looking back over his shoulder at Ramoth.

"What's gotten into her?"

"Echoing my nightmare. I woke in a cold sweat."

"You were sleeping quietly enough when I left to assign patrols. You know, at the rate those dragonets are growing, they're already capable of limited flight. All they do is eat and sleep, and that's . . ."

". . . what makes a dragon grow," Lessa finished for him and sipped thoughtfully at her steaming hot *klah*. "You are going to be extra-careful about their drill procedures, aren't you?"

"You mean to prevent an inadvertent flight *between* times? I certainly am," he assured her. "I don't want bored dragonriders irresponsibly popping in and out." He gave her a long, stern look.

"Well, it wasn't my fault no one taught me to fly early enough," she replied in the sweet tone she used when she was being especially malicious. "If I'd been drilled from the day of Impression to the day of my first flight, I'd never have discovered that trick."

"True enough," he said solemnly.

"You know, F'lar, if I discovered it, someone else must have, and someone else may. If they haven't already."

F'lar drank, making a face as the *klah* scalded his tongue. "I don't know how to find out discreetly. We would be foolish to think we were the first. It is, after all, an inherent ability in dragons, or you would never have been able to do it."

She frowned, took a quick breath, and then let it go, shrugging.

"Go on," he encouraged her.

"Well, isn't it possible that our conviction about the imminence of the Threads could stem from one of us coming back when the Threads are actually falling? I mean . . ."

"My dear girl, we have both analyzed every stray thought and action—even your dream this morning upset you, although it was no doubt due to all the wine you drank last night—until we wouldn't know an honest presentiment if it walked up and slapped us in the face."

"I can't dismiss the thought that this *between* times ability is of crucial value," she said emphatically.

"That, my dear Weyrwoman, *is* an honest presentiment."

"But why?"

"Not why," he corrected her cryptically. *"When."* An idea stirred vaguely in the back of his mind. He tried to nudge it out where he could mull it over. Mnementh announced that F'nor was entering the weyr.

"What's the matter with you?" F'lar demanded of his half brother, for F'nor was choking and sputtering, his face red with the paroxysm.

"Dust . . ." he coughed, slapping at his sleeves and chest with his riding gloves. "Plenty of dust, but no Threads," he said, describing a wide arc with one arm as he fluttered his fingers suggestively. He brushed his tight wher-hide pants, scowling as a fine black dust drifted off.

F'lar felt every muscle in his body tense as he watched the dust float to the floor.

"Where did you get so dusty?" he demanded.

F'nor regarded him with mild surprise. "Weather patrol in Tillek. Entire north has been plagued with dust storms lately. But what I came in for . . ." He broke off, alarmed by F'lar's taut immobility. "What's the matter with dust?" he asked in a baffled voice.

F'lar pivoted on his heel and raced for the stairs to the Record Room. Lessa was right behind him, F'nor belatedly trailing after.

"Tillek, you said?" F'lar barked at his wingsecond. He was clearing the table of stacks for the four charts he then laid out. "How long have these storms been going on? Why didn't you report them?"

"Report dust storms? You wanted to know about warm air masses."

"How long have these storms been going on?" F'lar's voice crackled.

"Close to a week."

"How close?"

"Six days ago the first storm was noticed in upper Tillek. They have been reported in Bitra, Upper Telgar, Crom, and the High Reaches," F'nor reported tersely.

He glanced hopefully at Lessa but saw she, too, was staring at the four unusual charts. He tried to see why the horizontal and vertical strips had been superimposed on Pern's land mass, but the reason was beyond him.

F'lar was making hurried notations, pushing first one map and then another away from him.

"Too involved to think straight, to see clearly, to understand," the Weyrleader snarled to himself, throwing down the stylus angrily.

"You did say only warm air masses," F'nor heard himself saying humbly, aware that he had somehow failed his Weyrleader.

F'lar shook his head impatiently.

"Not your fault, F'nor. Mine. I should have asked. I knew it was good luck that the weather held so cold." He put both hands on F'nor's shoulders, looking directly into his eyes. "The Threads have been falling," he announced gravely. "Falling into cold air, freezing into bits to drift on the wind"—F'lar imitated F'nor's finger-fluttering—"as specks of black dust."

" 'Crack dust, blackdust,' " Lessa quoted. "In 'The Ballad of Moreta's Ride,' the chorus is all about black dust."

"I don't need to be reminded of Moreta right now," F'lar growled, bending to the maps. "She could talk to any dragon in the Weyrs."

"But I can do that!" Lessa protested.

Slowly, as if he didn't quite credit his ears, F'lar turned back to Lessa. "What did you just say?"

"I said I can talk to any dragon in the Weyr."

Still staring at her, blinking in utter astonishment, F'lar sank down to the table top.

"How long," he managed to say, "have you had *this* particular skill?"

Something in his tone, in his manner, caused Lessa to flush and stammer like an erring weyrling.

"I . . . I always could. Beginning with the watchwher at Ruatha." She gestured indecisively in Ruatha's westerly direction. "And I talked to Mnementh at Ruatha. And . . . when I got here, I could . . ." Her voice faltered at the accusing look in F'lar's cold, hard eyes. Accusing and, worse, contemptuous.

"I thought you had agreed to help me, to believe in me."

"I'm truly sorry, F'lar. It never occurred to me it was of any use to anyone, but . . ."

F'lar exploded onto both feet, his eyes blazing with aggravation.

"The one thing I could not figure out was how to direct the wings and keep in contact with the Weyr during an attack, how I was going to get reinforcements and firestone in time. And you . . . you have been sitting there, spitefully hiding the . . ."

"I am NOT spiteful," she screamed at him. "I said I was sorry. I am. But you've a nasty, smug habit of keeping your own counsel. How was I to know you didn't have the same trick? You're F'lar, the Weyrleader, you can do *any*thing. Only you're just as bad as R'gul because you never *tell* me half the things I ought to know . . ."

F'lar reached out and shook her until her angry voice was stopped.

"Enough We can't waste time arguing like children." Then his eyes widened, his jaw dropped. "Waste time? That's it."

"Go *between* times?" Lessa gasped.

"*Between* times!"

F'nor was totally confused. "What are you two talking about?"

"The Threads started falling at dawn in Nerat," F'lar said, his eyes bright, his manner decisive.

F'nor could feel his guts congealing with apprehension. At dawn in Nerat? Why, the rainforests would be demolished. He could feel a surge of adrenalin charging through his body at the thought of danger.

"So we're going *back* there, *between* times, and be there when the Threads started falling, two hours ago. F'nor, the dragons can go not only where we direct them but *when*."

"Where? When?" F'nor repeated, bewildered. "That could be dangerous."

"Yes, but today it will save Nerat. Now, Lessa," and F'lar gave her another shake, compounded of pride and affection, "order out all the dragons, young, old, any that can fly. Tell them to load themselves down with firestone sacks. I don't know if you can talk across time . . ."

"My dream this morning . . ."

"Perhaps. But right now rouse the Weyr." He pivoted to F'nor. "If Threads are falling . . . were falling . . . at Nerat at dawn, they'll be falling on Keroon and Ista right now, because they are in that time pattern. Take two wings to Keroon. Arouse the plains. Get them to start the firepits blazing. Take some weyrlings with you and send them on to Igen and Ista. Those Holds are not in as immediate danger as Keroon. I'll reinforce you as soon as I can. And . . . keep Canth in touch with Lessa."

F'lar clapped his brother on the shoulder and sent him off. The brown rider was too used to taking orders to argue.

"Mnementh says R'gul is duty officer and R'gul wants to know . . ." Lessa began.

"C'mon, girl," F'lar said, his eyes brilliant with excitement. He grabbed up his maps and propelled her up the stairs.

They arrived in the weyr just as R'gul entered with

T'sum. R'gul was muttering about this unusual summons.

"Hath told me to report," he complained. "Fine thing when your own dragon . . ."

"R'gul, T'sum, mount your wings. Arm them with all the firestone they can carry, and assemble above Star Stone. I'll join you in a few minutes. We go to Nerat at dawn."

"Nerat? I'm watch officer, not patrol . . ."

"This is no patrol," F'lar cut him off.

"But, sir," T'sum interrupted, his eyes wide, "Nerat's dawn was two hours ago, the same as ours."

"And that is *when* we are going to, brown riders." The dragons, we have discovered, can go *between* places temporally as well as geographically. At dawn Threads fell at Nerat. We're going back, *between* time, to sear them from the sky."

F'lar paid no attention to R'gul's stammered demand for explanation. T'sum, however, grabbed up firestone sacks and raced back to the ledge and his waiting Munth.

"Go on, you old fool," Lessa told R'gul irascibly. "The Threads are here. You were wrong. Now be a dragonman! Or go *between* and stay there!"

Ramoth, awakened by the alarms, poked at R'gul with her man-sized head, and the ex-Weyrleader came out of his momentary shock. Without a word he followed T'sum down the passageway.

F'lar had thrown on his heavy wher-hide tunic and shoved on his riding boots.

"Lessa, be sure to send messages to all the Holds. Now, this attack will stop about four hours from now. So the farthest west it can reach will be Ista. But I want every Hold and craft warned."

She nodded, her eyes intent on his face lest she miss a word.

"Fortunately, the Star is just beginning its Pass, so we won't have to worry about another attack for a few days. I'll figure out the next one when I get back.

"Now, get Manora to organize her women. We'll

need pails of ointment. The dragons are going to be laced, and that hurts. Most important, if something goes wrong, you'll have to wait till a bronze is at least a year old to fly Ramoth . . ."

"No one's flying Ramoth but Mnementh," she cried, her eyes sparkling fiercely.

F'lar crushed her against him, his mouth bruising hers as if all her sweetness and strength must come with him. He released her so abruptly that she staggered back against Ramoth's lowered head. She clung for a moment to her dragon, as much for support as for reassurance.

That is, if Mnementh can catch me, Ramoth amended smugly.

> Wheel and turn
> Or bleed and burn.
> Fly *between,*
> Blue and green.
> Soar, dive down,
> Bronze and brown
> Dragonmen must fly
> When Threads are in the sky.

As F'LAR raced down the passageway to the ledge, firesacks bumping against his thighs, he was suddenly grateful for the tedious sweeping patrols over every Hold and hollow of Pern. He could see Nerat clearly in his mind's eye. He could see the many-petaled vineflowers which were the distinguished feature of the rainforest at this time of the year. Their ivory blossoms would be glowing in the first beams of sunlight like dragon eyes among the tall, wide-leaved plants.

Mnementh, his eyes flashing with excitement, hovered skittishly over the ledge. F'lar vaulted to the bronze neck.

The Weyr was seething with wings of all colors, noisy with shouts and countercommands. The atmosphere was electric, but F'lar could sense no panic in that ordered confusion. Dragon and human bodies oozed out of openings around the Bowl walls. Women scurried across the floor from one Lower Cavern to another. The children playing by the lake were sent to gather wood for a fire. The weyrlings, supervised by old C'gan, were forming outside their barracks. F'lar looked up to the Peak and approved the tight formation of the wings assembled there in close flying order. Another wing formed up as he watched. He recognized brown Canth, F'nor on his neck, just as the entire wing vanished.

He ordered Mnementh aloft. The wind was cold and carried a hint of moisture. A late snow? This was the time for it, if ever.

R'gul's wing and T'bor's fanned out on his left, T'sum and D'nol on his right. He noted each dragon was well-laden with sacks. Then he gave Mnementh the visualization of the early spring rainforest in Nerat, just before dawn, the vineflowers gleaming, the sea breaking against the rocks of the High Shoal. . . .

He felt the searing cold of *between*. And he felt a stab of doubt. Was he injudicious, sending them all possibly to their deaths *between* times in this effort to outtime the Threads at Nerat?

Then they were all there, in the crepuscular light that promises day. The lush, fruity smells of the rainforest drifted up to them. Warm, too, and that was frightening. He looked up and slightly to the north. Pulsing with menace, the Red Star shone down.

The men had realized what had happened, their voices raised in astonishment. Mnementh told F'lar that the dragons were mildly surprised at their riders' fuss.

"Listen to me, dragonriders," F'lar called, his voice harsh and distorted in an effort to be heard by all. He waited till the men had moved as close as possible. He told Mnementh to pass the information on to each dragon. Then he explained what they had done and why. No one spoke, but there were many nervous looks exchanged across bright wings.

Crisply he ordered the dragonriders to fan out in a staggered formation, keeping a distance of five wings' spread up or down.

The sun came up.

Slanting across the sea, like an ever-thickening mist, Threads were falling, silent, beautiful, treacherous. Silvery gray were those space-traversing spores, spinning from hard frozen ovals into coarse filaments as they penetrated the warm atmospheric envelope of Pern. Less than mindless, they had been ejected from their barren planet toward Pern, a hideous rain that sought organic matter to nourish it into growth. One Thread, sinking into fertile soil, would burrow deep, propagating thousands in the warm earth, rendering it into a black-dusted wasteland. The southern continent of Pern had already been sucked dry. The true parasites of Pern were Threads.

A stifled roar from the throats of eighty men and dragons broke the dawn air above Nerat's green heights—as if the Threads might hear this challenge, F'lar mused.

As one, dragons swiveled their wedge-shaped heads to their riders for firestone. Great jaws macerated the hunks. The fragments were swallowed and more firestone was demanded. Inside the beasts, acids churned and the poisonous phosphines were readied. When the dragons belched forth the gas, it would ignite in the air into ravening flame to sear the Threads from the sky. And burn them from the soil.

Dragon instinct took over the moment the Threads began to fall above Nerat's shores.

As much admiration as F'lar had always held for his bronze companion, it achieved newer heights in the next hours. Beating the air in great strokes, Mnementh soared with flaming breath to meet the down-rushing menace. The fumes, swept back by the wind, choked F'lar until he thought to crouch low on the lea side of the bronze neck. The dragon squealed as a Thread flicked the tip of one wing. Instantly F'lar and he ducked into *between,* cold, calm, black. The frozen Thread cracked off. In the flicker of an eye, they were back to face the reality of Threads.

Around him F'lar saw dragons winking in and out of *between,* flaming as they returned, diving, soaring. As the attack continued and they drifted across Nerat, F'lar began to recognize the pattern in the dragons' instinctive evasion-attack movements. And in the Threads. For, contrary to what he had gathered from his study of the Records, the Threads fell in patches. Not as rain will, in steady unbroken sheets, but like flurries of snow, here, above, there, whipped to one side suddenly. Never fluidly, despite the continuity their name implied.

You could see a patch above you. Flaming, your dragon would rise. You'd have the intense joy of seeing the clump shrivel from bottom to top. Sometimes, a patch would fall between riders. One dragon would signal he would follow and, spouting flame, would dive and sear.

Gradually the dragonriders worked their way over the rainforests, so densely, so invitingly green. F'lar refused to dwell on what just one live Thread burrow would do to that lush land. He would send back a low-flying patrol to quarter every foot. One Thread, just one Thread, could put out the ivory eyes of every luminous vineflower.

A dragon screamed somewhere to his left. Before he could identify the beast, it had ducked *between.* F'lar heard other cries of pain, from men as well as dragons. He shut his ears and concentrated, as dragons did, on the here-and-now. Would Mnementh re-

member those piercing cries later? F'lar wished he
could forget them now.

He, F'lar, the bronze rider, felt suddenly superflu-
ous. It was the dragons who were fighting this en-
gagement. You encouraged your beast, comforted
him when the Threads burned, but you depended on
his instinct and speed.

Hot fire dripped across F'lar's cheek, burrowing
like acid into his shoulder . . . a cry of surprised
agony burst from F'lar's lips. Mnementh took them
to merciful *between*. The dragonman battled with
frantic hands at the Threads, felt them crumble in the
intense cold of *between* and break off. Revolted, he
slapped at injuries still afire. Back in Nerat's humid
air, the sting seemed to ease. Mnementh crooned comfortingly and then dove at a patch, breathing fire.

Shocked at self-consideration, F'lar hurriedly exam-
ined his mount's shoulder for telltale score marks.

I duck very quickly, Mnementh told him and
veered away from a dangerously close clump of
Threads. A brown dragon followed them down and
burned them to ash.

It might have been moments, it might have been a
hundred hours later when F'lar looked down in surprise at the sunlit sea. Threads now dropped harmlessly into the salty waters. Nerat was to the east of
him on his right, the rocky tip curling westward.

F'lar felt weariness in every muscle. In the excitement of frenzied battle, he had forgotten the bloody
scores on cheek and shoulder. Now, as he and Mnementh glided slowly, the injuries ached and stung.

He flew Mnementh high and when they had
achieved sufficient altitude, they hovered. He could
see no Threads falling landward. Below him, the
dragons ranged, high and low, searching for any
sign of a burrow, alert for any suddenly toppling trees
or disturbed vegetation.

"Back to the Weyr," he ordered Mnementh with a
heavy sigh. He heard the bronze relay the command
even as he himself was taken *between*. He was

so tired he did not even visualize where—much less, when—relying on Mnementh's instinct to bring him safely home through time and space.

> Honor those the dragons heed,
> In thought and favor, word and deed.
> Worlds are lost or worlds are saved
> From those dangers dragon-braved.

CRANING HER neck toward the Star Stone at Benden Peak, Lessa watched from the ledge until she saw the four wings disappear from view.

Sighing deeply to quiet her inner fears, Lessa raced down the stairs to the floor of Benden Weyr. She noticed that someone was building a fire by the lake and that Manora was already ordering her women around, her voice clear but calm.

Old C'gan had the weyrlings lined up. She caught the envious eyes of the newest dragonriders at the barracks windows. They'd have time enough to fly a flaming dragon. From what F'lar had intimated, they'd have Turns.

She shuddered as she stepped up to the weyrlings but managed to smile at them. She gave them their orders and sent them off to warn the Holds, checking quickly with each dragon to be sure the rider had given clear references. The Holds would shortly be stirred up to a froth.

Canth told her that there were Threads at Keroon, falling on the Keroon side of Nerat Bay. He told her that F'nor did not think two wings were enough to protect the meadowlands.

Lessa stopped in her tracks, trying to think how many wings were already out.

K'net's wing is still here, Ramoth informed her. *On the Peak.*

Lessa glanced up and saw bronze Piyanth spread his wings in answer. She told him to get *between* to Keroon, close to Nerat Bay. Obediently the entire wing rose and then disappeared.

She turned with a sigh to say something to Manora when a rush of wind and a vile stench almost overpowered her. The air above the Weyr was full of dragons. She was about to demand of Piyanth why he hadn't gone to Keroon when she realized there were far more beasts a-wing than K'net's twenty.

But you just left, she cried as she recognized the unmistakable bulk of bronze Mnementh.

That was two hours ago for us, Mnementh said with such weariness in his tone that Lessa closed her eyes in sympathy.

Some dragons were gliding in fast. From their awkwardness it was evident that they were hurt.

As one, the women grabbed salve pots and clean rags and beckoned the injured down. The numbing ointment was smeared on score marks where wings resembled black and red lace.

No matter how badly injured he might be, every rider tended his beast first.

Lessa kept one eye on Mnementh, sure that F'lar would not keep the huge bronze hovering like that if he'd been hurt. She was helping T'sum with Munth's cruelly pierced right wing when she realized the sky above the Star Stone was empty.

She forced herself to finish with Munth before she

went to find the bronze and his rider. When she did locate them, she also saw Kylara smearing salve on F'lar's cheek and shoulder. She was advancing purposefully across the sands toward the pair when Canth's urgent plea reached her. She saw Mnementh's head swing upward as he, too, caught the brown's thought.

"F'lar, Canth says they need help," Lessa cried. She didn't notice then that Kylara slipped away into the busy crowd.

F'lar wasn't badly hurt. She reassured herself about that. Kylara had treated the wicked burns that seemed to be shallow. Someone had found him another fur to replace the tatters of the Thread-bared one. He frowned—winced because the frown creased his burned cheek. He gulped hurriedly at his *klah*.

Mnementh, what's the tally of able-bodied? Oh, never mind, just get 'em aloft with a full load of firestone.

"You're all right?" Lessa asked, a detaining hand on his arm. He couldn't just go off like this, could he?

He smiled tiredly down at her, pressed his empty mug into her hands, giving them a quick squeeze. Then he vaulted to Mnementh's neck. Someone handed him a heavy load of sacks.

Blue, green, brown, and bronze dragons lifted from the Weyr Bowl in quick order. A trifle more than sixty dragons hovered briefly above the Weyr where eighty had lingered so few minutes before.

So few dragons. So few riders. How long could they take such toll?

Canth said F'nor needed more firestone.

She looked about anxiously. None of the weyrlings were back yet from their messenger rounds. A dragon was crooning plaintively, and she wheeled, but it was only young Pridith, stumbling across the Weyr to the feeding grounds, butting playfully at Kylara as they walked. The only other dragons were injured or —her eye fell on C'gan, emerging from the weyrling barracks.

"C'gan, can you and Tagath get more firestone to F'nor at Keroon?"

"Of course," the old blue rider assured her, his chest lifting with pride, his eyes flashing. She hadn't thought to send him anywhere, yet he had lived his life in training for this emergency. He shouldn't be deprived of a chance at it.

She smiled her approval at his eagerness as they piled heavy sacks on Tagath's neck. The old blue dragon snorted and danced as if he were young and strong again. She gave them the references Canth had visualized to her.

She watched as the two blinked out above the Star Stone.

It isn't fair. They have all the fun, said Ramoth peevishly. Lessa saw her sunning herself on the Weyr ledge, preening her enormous wings.

"You chew firestone and you're reduced to a silly green," Lessa told her Weyrmate sharply. She was inwardly amused by the queen's disgruntled complaint.

Lessa passed among the injured then. B'fol's dainty green beauty moaned and tossed her head, unable to bend one wing that had been threaded to bare cartilage. She'd be out for weeks, but she had the worst injury among the dragons. Lessa looked quickly away from the misery in B'fol's worried eyes.

As she did the rounds, she realized that more men were injured than beasts. Two in R'gul's wing had sustained serious head damages. One man might lose an eye completely. Manora had dosed him unconscious with numb-weed. Another man's arm had been burned clear to the bone. Minor though most of the wounds were, the tally dismayed Lessa. How many more would be disabled at Keroon?

Out of one hundred and seventy-two dragons, fifteen already were out of action, some only for a day or two, however.

A thought struck Lessa. If N'ton had actually ridden Canth, maybe he could ride out on the next dragonade on an injured man's beast, since there were more injured riders than dragons. F'lar broke traditions as he chose. Here was another one to set aside—if the dragon was agreeable.

Presuming N'ton was not the only new rider able to transfer to another beast, what good would such flexibility do in the long run? F'lar had definitely said the incursions would not be so frequent at first, when the Red Star was just beginning its fifty-Turn-long circling pass of Pern. How frequent was frequent? He would know, but he wasn't here.

Well, he *had* been right this morning about the appearance of Threads at Nerat, so his exhaustive study of those old Records had proved worthwhile.

No, that wasn't quite accurate. He had forgotten to have the men alert for signs of black dust as well as warming weather. As he had put the matter right by going *between* times, she would graciously allow him that minor error. But he did have an infuriating habit of guessing correctly. Lessa corrected herself again. He didn't guess. He studied. He planned. He thought and then he used common good sense. Like figuring out where and when Threads would strike according to entries in those smelly Records. Lessa began to feel better about their future.

Now, if he would just make the riders learn to trust their dragons' sure instinct in battle, they would keep casualties down, too.

A shriek pierced air and ear as a blue dragon emerged above the Star Stone.

Ramoth! Lessa screamed in an instinctive reaction, hardly knowing why. The queen was a-wing before the echo of her command had died. For the careening blue was obviously in grave trouble. He was trying to brake his forward speed, yet one wing would not function. His rider had slipped forward over the great shoulder, precariously clinging to his dragon's neck with one hand.

Lessa, her hands clapped over her mouth, watched fearfully. There wasn't a sound in the Bowl but the flapping of Ramoth's immense wings. The queen rose swiftly to position herself against the desperate blue, lending him wing support on the crippled side.

The watchers gasped as the rider slipped, lost his hold, and fell—landing on Ramoth's wide shoulders.

The blue dropped like a stone. Ramoth came to a gentle stop near him, crouching low to allow the weyrfolk to remove her passenger.

It was C'gan.

Lessa felt her stomach heave as she saw the ruin the Threads had made of the old harper's face. She dropped beside him, pillowing his head in her lap. The weyrfolk gathered in a respectful, silent circle.

Manora, her face, as always, serene, had tears in her eyes. She knelt and placed her hand on the old rider's heart. Concern flickered in her eyes as she looked up at Lessa. Slowly she shook her head. Then, setting her lips in a thin line, she began to apply the numbing salve.

"Too toothless old to flame and too slow to get *between*," C'gan mumbled, rolling his head from side to side. "Too old. But 'Dragonmen must fly/ when Threads are in the sky. . . .' " His voice trailed off into a sigh. His eyes closed.

Lessa and Manora looked at each other in anguish. A terrible, ear-shattering note cut the silence. Tagath sprang aloft in a tremendous leap. C'gan's eyes rolled slowly open, sightless. Lessa, breath suspended, watched the blue dragon, trying to deny the inevitable as Tagath disappeared in mid-air.

A low moan sprang up around the Weyr, like the torn, lonely cry of a keening wind. The dragons uttered tribute.

"Is he . . . gone?" Lessa asked, although she knew.

Manora nodded slowly, tears streaming down her cheeks as she reached over to close C'gan's dead eyes.

Lessa rose slowly to her feet, motioning to some of the women to remove the old rider's body. Absently she rubbed her bloody hands dry on her skirts, trying to concentrate on what might be needed next.

Yet her mind turned back to what had just happened. A dragonrider had died. His dragon, too. The Threads had claimed one pair already. How many more would die this cruel Turn? How long could the Weyr survive? Even after Ramoth's forty matured, and the ones she soon would conceive, and her queen-daughters, too?

Lessa walked apart to quiet her uncertainties and ease her grief. She saw Ramoth wheel and glide aloft, to land on the Peak. One day soon would Lessa see those golden wings laced red and black from Thread marks? Would Ramoth . . . disappear?

No, Ramoth would not. Not while Lessa lived.

F'lar had told her long ago that she must learn to look beyond the narrow confines of Hold Ruatha and mere revenge. He was, as usual, right. As Weyr-woman under his tutelage, she had further learned that living *was* more than raising dragons and Spring Games. Living was struggling to do something impossible—to succeed, or die, knowing you had tried!

Lessa realized that she had, at last, fully accepted her role: as Weyrwoman and as mate, to help F'lar shape men and events for many Turns to come—to secure Pern against the Threads.

Lessa threw back her shoulders and lifted her chin high.

Old C'gan had had the right of it.

Dragonmen *must* fly
When Threads are in the sky!

Worlds are lost or worlds are saved
By those dangers dragon-braved.

As F'LAR had predicted, the attack ended by high noon, and weary dragons and riders were welcomed by Ramoth's high-pitched trumpeting from the Peak.

Once Lessa assured herself that F'lar had taken no additional injury, that F'nor's were superficial and that Manora was keeping Kylara busy in the kitchens, she applied herself to organizing the care of the injured and the comfort of the worried.

As dusk fell, an uneasy peace settled on the Weyr —the quiet of minds and bodies too tired or too hurtful to talk. Lessa's own words mocked her as she made out the list of wounded men and beasts. Twenty-eight men or dragons were out of the air for the next Thread battle. C'gan was the only fatality, but there had been four more seriously injured dragons at Keroon and seven badly scored men, out of action entirely for months to come.

Lessa crossed the Bowl to her Weyr, reluctant but resigned to giving F'lar this unsettling news.

She expected to find him in the sleeping room, but

it was vacant. Ramoth was asleep already as Lessa passed her on the way to the Council Room—also empty. Puzzled and a little alarmed, Lessa half-ran down the steps to the Records Room, to find F'lar, haggard of face, poring over musty skins.

"What are you doing here?" she demanded angrily. "You ought to be asleep."

"So should you," he drawled, amused.

"I was helping Manora settle the wounded . . ."

"Each to his own craft." But he did lean back from the table, rubbing his neck and rotating the uninjured shoulder to ease stiffened muscles.

"I couldn't sleep," he admitted, "so I thought I'd see what answers I might turn up in the Records."

"More answers? To what?" Lessa cried, exasperated with him. As if the Records ever answered anything. Obviously the tremendous responsibilities of Pern's defense against the Threads were beginning to tell on the Weyrleader. After all, there had been the stress of the first battle, not to mention the drain of the traveling *between* time itself to get to Nerat to forestall the Threads.

F'lar grinned and beckoned Lessa to sit beside him on the wall bench.

"I need the answer to the very pressing question of how one understrength Weyr can do the fighting of six."

Lessa fought the panic that rose, a cold flood, from her guts.

"Oh, your time schedules will take care of that," she replied gallantly. "You'll be able to conserve the dragon-power until the new forty can join the ranks."

F'lar raised a mocking eyebrow.

"Let us be honest between ourselves, Lessa."

"But there have been Long Intervals before," she argued, "and since Pern survived them, Pern can again."

"Before there were always six Weyrs. And twenty or so Turns before the Red Star was due to begin its Pass, the queens would start to produce enormous clutches. All the queens, not just one faithful golden Ramoth. Oh, how I curse Jora!" He slammed to his feet and started pacing, irritably brushing the lock of black hair that fell across his eyes.

Lessa was torn with the desire to comfort him and the sinking, choking fear in her belly that made it difficult to think at all.

"You were not so doubtful . . ."

He whirled back to her. "Not until I had actually had an encounter with the Threads and reckoned up the numbers of injuries. That sets the odds against us. Even supposing we can mount other riders to uninjured dragons, we will be hard put to keep a continuously effective force in the air and still maintain a ground guard." He caught her puzzled frown. "There's Nerat to be gone over on foot tomorrow. I'd be a fool indeed if I thought we'd caught and seared every Thread in mid-air."

"Get the Holders to do that. They can't just immure themselves safely in their Inner Holds and let us do all. If they hadn't been so miserly and stupid . . ."

He cut off her complaint with an abrupt gesture. "They'll do their part all right," he assured her. "I'm sending for a full Council tomorrow, all Hold Lords and all Craftmasters. But there's more to it than just marking where Threads fall. How do you destroy a burrow that's gone deep under the surface? A dragon's breath is fine for the air and surface work but no good three feet down."

"Oh, I hadn't thought of that aspect. But the firepits . . ."

". . . are only on the heights and around human habitations, not on the meadowlands of Keroon or on Nerat's so green rainforests."

This consideration was daunting indeed. She gave a rueful little laugh.

"Shortsighted of me to suppose our dragons are all poor Pern needs to dispatch the Threads. Yet . . ." She shrugged expressively.

"There are other methods," F'lar said, "or there

were. There must have been. I have run across
frequent mention that the Holds were organizing
ground groups and that they were armed with fire.
What kind is never mentioned because it was so well-
known." He threw up his hands in disgust and sagged
back down on the bench. "Not even five hundred
dragons could have seared all the Threads that fell
today. Yet *they* managed to keep Pern Thread-free."

"Pern, yes, but wasn't the Southern Continent lost?
Or did they just have their hands too full with Pern
itself?"

"No one's bothered with the Southern Continent in
a hundred thousand Turns," F'lar snorted.

"It's on the maps," Lessa reminded him.

He scowled disgustedly at the Records, piled in un-
communicative stacks on the long table.

"The answer must be there. Somewhere."

There was an edge of desperation in his voice, the
hint that he held himself to blame for not having discovered those elusive facts.

"Half those things couldn't be read by the man who
wrote them," Lessa said tartly. "Besides that, it's been
your *own* ideas that have helped us most so far. You
compiled the time maps, and look how valuable they
have been already."

"I'm getting too hidebound again, huh?" he asked,
a half smile tugging at one corner of his mouth.

"Undoubtedly," she assured him with more confidence than she felt. "We both know the Records are
guilty of the most ridiculous omissions."

"Well said, Lessa. So let us forget these misguiding
and antiquated precepts and think up our own
guides. First, we need more dragons. Second, we need
them now. Third, we need something as effective as a
flaming dragon to destroy Threads which have burrowed."

"Fourth, we need sleep, or we won't be able
to think of anything," she added with a touch of her
usual asperity.

F'lar laughed outright, hugging her.

"You've got your mind on one thing, haven't you?" he teased, his hands caressing her eagerly.

She pushed ineffectually at him, trying to escape. For a wounded, tired man, he was remarkably amorous. One with that Kylara. Imagine that woman's presumption, dressing his wounds.

"My responsibility as Weyrwoman includes care of you, the Weyrleader."

"But you spend hours with blue dragonriders and leave me to Kylara's tender ministrations."

"You didn't look as if you objected."

F'lar threw back his head and roared. "Should I open Fort Weyr and send Kylara on?" he taunted her.

"I'd as soon Kylara were Turns as well as miles away from here," Lessa snapped, thoroughly irritated.

F'lar's jaw dropped, his eyes widened. He leaped to his feet with an astonished cry.

"You've said it!"

"Said what?"

"Turns away! That's it. We'll send Kylara back, *between* times, with her queen and the new dragonets." F'lar excitedly paced the room while Lessa tried to follow his reasoning. "No, I'd better send at least one of the older bronzes. F'nor, too . . . I'd rather have F'nor in charge. . . . Discreetly, of course—"

"Send Kylara back . . . where to? When to?" Lessa interrupted him.

"Good point." F'lar dragged out the ubiquitous charts. "Very good point. Where can we send them around here without causing anomalies by being present at one of the other Weyrs? The High Reaches are remote. No, we've found remains of fires there, you know, still warm, and no inkling as to who built them or why. And if we had already sent them back, they'd've been ready for today, and they weren't. So they can't have been in two places already. . . ." *He* shook his head, dazed by the paradoxes.

Lessa's eyes were drawn to the blank outline of the neglected Southern Continent.

"Send them there," she suggested sweetly, pointing.

"There's nothing there."

"They bring in what they need. There must be water, for Threads can't devour that. We fly in whatever else is needed, fodder for the herdbeasts, grain. . . ."

F'lar drew his brows together in concentration, his eyes sparkling with thought, the depression and defeat of a few moments ago forgotten.

"Threads wouldn't be there ten Turns ago. And haven't been there for close to four hundred. Ten Turns would give Pridith time to mature and have several clutches. Maybe more queens."

Then he frowned and shook his head dubiously. "No, there's no Weyr there. No Hatching Ground, no . . ."

"How do we know that?" Lessa caught him up sharply, too delighted with many aspects of this project to give it up easily. "The Records don't mention the Southern Continent, true, but they omit a great deal. How do we know it isn't green again in the four hundred Turns since the Threads last spun? We do know that Threads can't last long unless there is something organic on which to feed and that once they've devoured all, they dry up and blow away."

F'lar looked at her admiringly. "Now, why hasn't someone wondered about that before?"

"Too hidebound." Lessa wagged her finger at him. "Besides, there's been no need to bother with it."

"Necessity—or is it jealousy?—hatches many a tough shell." There was a smile of pure malice on his face, and Lessa whirled away as he reached for her.

"The good of the Weyr," she retorted.

"Furthermore, I'll send you along with F'nor tomorrow to look. Only fair, since it is your idea."

Lessa stood still. "You're not going?"

"I feel confident I can leave this project in your very capable, interested hands." He laughed and caught her against his uninjured side, smiling down at her, his eyes glowing. "I must play ruthless Weyr-leader and keep the Hold Lords from slamming shut their Inner Doors. And I'm hoping"—he raised his head, frowning slightly—"one of the Craftmasters may know the solution to the third problem—getting rid of Thread burrows."

"But . . ."

"The trip will give Ramoth something to stop her fuming." He pressed the girl's slender body more closely to him, his full attention at last on her odd, delicate face. "Lessa, you are my fourth problem." He bent to kiss her.

At the sound of hurried steps in the passageway, F'lar scowled irritably, releasing her.

"At this hour?" he muttered, ready to reprove the intruder scathingly. "Who goes there?"

"F'lar?" It was F'nor's voice, anxious, hoarse.

The look on F'lar's face told Lessa that not even his half brother would be spared a reprimand, and it pleased her irrationally. But the moment F'nor burst into the room, both Weyrleader and Weyrwoman were stunned silent. There was something subtly wrong with the brown rider. And as the man blurted out his inco-herent message, the difference suddenly registered in Lessa's mind. He was tanned! He wore no bandages and hadn't the slightest trace of the Thread-mark along his cheek that she had tended this evening!

"F'lar, it's not working out! You can't be alive in two times at once!" F'nor was exclaiming distractedly. He staggered against the wall, grabbing the sheer rock to hold himself upright. There were deep circles under his eyes, visible despite the tan. "I don't know how much longer we can last like this. We're all affected. Some days not as badly as others."

"I don't understand."

"Your dragons are all right," F'nor assured the Weyrleader with a bitter laugh. "It doesn't bother them. They keep all their wits about them. But their riders . . . all the weyrfolk . . . we're shadows, half alive, like dragonless men, part of us gone forever.

Except Kylara." His face contorted with intense dislike. "All she wants to do is go back and watch herself. The woman's egomania will destroy us all, I'm afraid."

His eyes suddenly lost focus, and he swayed wildly. His eyes widened, and his mouth fell open. "I can't stay. I'm here already. Too close. Makes it twice as bad. But I had to warn you. I promise, F'lar, we'll stay as long as we can, but it won't be much longer . . . so it won't be long enough, but we tried. We tried!"

Before F'lar could move, the brown rider whirled and ran, half-crouched, from the room.

"But he hasn't gone yet!" Lessa gasped. "He hasn't even gone yet!"

PART IV

The Cold Between

F'LAR stared after his half brother, his brows contracting with the keen anxiety he felt.

"What can have happened?" Lessa demanded of the Weyrleader. "We haven't even told F'nor. We ourselves just finished considering the idea." Her hand flew to her own cheek. "And the Thread-mark—I dressed it myself tonight—it's gone. Gone. So he's been gone a long while." She sank down to the bench.

"However, he has come back. So he did go," F'lar remarked slowly in a reflective tone of voice. "Yet we now know the venture is not entirely successful even before it begins. And knowing this, we have sent him back ten Turns for whatever good it is doing." F'lar paused thoughtfully. "Consequently we have no alternative but to continue with the experiment."

"But what could be going wrong?"

"I think I know and there is no remedy." He sat down beside her, his eyes intent on hers. "Lessa, you were very upset when you got back from going *between* to Ruatha that first time. But I think now it was more than just the shock of seeing Fax's men invading your own Hold or in thinking your return might have been responsible for that disaster. I think it has to do with being in two times at once." He hesitated again, trying to understand this immense new concept even as he voiced it.

Lessa regarded him with such awe that he found himself laughing with embarrassment.

"It's unnerving under any conditions," he went on, "to think of returning and seeing a younger self."

"That must be what he meant about Kylara," Lessa gasped, "about her wanting to go back and watch herself . . . as a child. Oh, that wretched girl!" Lessa was filled with anger for Kylara's self-absorption. "Wretched, selfish creature. She'll ruin everything."

"Not yet," F'lar reminded her. "Look, although F'nor warned us that the situation in his time is getting desperate, he didn't tell us how much he was able to accomplish. But you noticed that his scar had healed to invisibility—consequently some Turns must have elapsed. Even if Pridith lays only one good-sized clutch, even if just the forty of Ramoth's are mature enough to fight in three days' time, we have accomplished something. Therefore, Weyrwoman," and he noticed how she straightened up at the sound of her title, "we must disregard F'nor's return. When you fly to the Southern Continent tomorrow, make no allusion to it. Do you understand?"

Lessa nodded gravely and then gave a little sigh. "I don't know if I'm happy or disappointed to realize, even before we get there tomorrow, that the Southern Continent obviously will support a Weyr," she said with dismay. "It was kind of exciting to wonder."

"Either way," F'lar told her with a sardonic smile, "we have found only part of the answers to problems one and two."

"Well, you'd better answer number four right now!" Lessa suggested. "Decisively!"

Weaver, Miner, Harper, Smith,
Tanner, Farmer, Herdsman, Lord,
Gather, wingsped, listen well
To the Weyrman's urgent word.

THEY BOTH managed to guard against any reference to his premature return when they spoke to F'nor the next morning. F'lar asked brown Canth to send his rider to the queen's weyr as soon as he awoke and was pleased to see F'nor almost immediately. If the brown rider noticed the curiously intent stare Lessa gave his bandaged face, he gave no sign of it. As a matter of fact, the moment F'lar outlined the bold venture of scouting the Southern Continent with the possibility of starting a Weyr ten Turns back in time, F'nor forgot all about his wounds.

"I'll go willingly only if you send T'bor along with Kylara. I'm not waiting till N'ton and his bronze are big enough to take her on. T'bor and she are as—" F'nor broke off with a grimace in Lessa's direction. "Well, they're as near a pair as can be. I don't object to being . . . importuned, but there are limits to what a man is willing to do out of loyalty to dragonkind."

F'lar barely managed to restrain the amusement he felt over F'nor's reluctance. Kylara tried her wiles on every rider, and, because F'nor had not been amenable, she was determined to succeed with him.

"I hope two bronzes are enough. Pridith may have a mind of her own, come matingtime."

"You can't turn a brown into a bronze!" F'nor exclaimed with such dismay that F'lar could no longer restrain himself.

"Oh, stop it!" And that touched off Lessa's laughter. "You're as bad a pair," F'nor snapped, getting to his feet. "If we're going south, Weyrwoman, we'd better get started. Particularly if we're going to give this laughing maniac a chance to compose himself before the solemn Lords descend. I'll get provisions from Manora. Well, Lessa? *Are* you coming with me?"

Muffling her laughter, Lessa grabbed up her furred flying cloak and followed him. At least the adventure was starting off well.

Carrying the pitcher of *klah* and his cup, F'lar adjourned to the Council Room, debating whether to tell the Lords and Craftmasters of this southern venture or not. The dragons' ability to fly *between* times as well as places was not yet well-known. The Lords might not realize it had been used the previous day to forestall the Threads. If F'lar could be sure that project was going to be successful—well, it would add an optimistic note to the meeting.

Let the charts, with the waves and times of the Thread attacks clearly visible, reassure the Lords.

The visitors were not long in assembling. Nor were they all successful in hiding their apprehension and the shock they had received now that Threads had again spun down from the Red Star to menace all life on Pern. This was going to be a difficult session, F'lar decided grimly. He had a fleeting wish, which he quickly suppressed, that he had gone with F'nor and Lessa to the Southern Continent. Instead, he bent with apparent industry to the charts before him.

Soon there were but two more to come, Meron of Nabol (whom he would have liked not to include, for the man was a troublemaker) and Lytol of Ruatha.

F'lar had sent for Lytol last because he did not wish Lessa to encounter the man. She was still overly—and, to his mind, foolishly—sensitive at having had to resign her claim to Ruatha Hold for the Lady Gemma's posthumous son. Lytol, as Warder of Ruatha, had a place in this conference. The man was also an ex-dragonman, and his return to the Weyr was painful enough without Lessa's compounding it with her resentment. Lytol was, with the exception of young Larad of Telgar, the Weyr's most valuable ally.

S'lel came in with Meron a step behind him. The Holder was furious at this summons; it showed in his walk, in his eyes, in his haughty bearing. But he was also as inquisitive as he was devious. He nodded only to Larad among the Lords and took the seat left vacant for him by Larad's side. Meron's manner made it obvious that that place was too close to F'lar by half a room.

The Weyrleader acknowledged S'lel's salute and indicated the bronze rider should be seated. F'lar had given thought to the seating arrangements in the Council Room, carefully interspersing brown and bronze dragonriders with Holders and Craftsmen. There was now barely room to move in the generously proportioned cavern, but there was also no room in which to draw daggers if tempers got hot.

A hush fell on the gathering, and F'lar looked up to see that the stocky, glowering ex-dragonman from Ruatha had stopped on the threshold of the Council. He slowly brought his hand up in a respectful salute to the Weyrleader. As F'lar returned the salute, he noticed that the tic in Lytol's left cheek jumped almost continuously.

Lytol's eyes, dark with pain and inner unquiet, ranged the room. He nodded to the members of his former wing, to Larad and Zurg, head of his own weavers' craft. Stiff-legged, he walked to the remaining seat, murmuring a greeting to T'sum on his left.

F'lar rose.

"I appreciate your coming, good Lords and Craft-

masters. The Threads spin once again. The first attack
has been met and seared from the sky. Lord Vincet,"
and the worried Holder of Nerat looked up in alarm,
"we have dispatched a patrol to the rainforest to do a
low-flight sweep to make certain there are no burrows."

Vincet swallowed nervously, his face paling at the
thought of what Threads could do to his fertile, lush
holdings.

"We shall need your best junglemen to help—"

"Help? But you said . . . the Threads were seared
in the sky?"

"There is no point in taking the slightest chance,"
F'lar replied, implying that the patrol was only a
precaution instead of the necessity he knew it would
be.

Vincet gulped, glancing anxiously around the room
for sympathy, and found none. Everyone would soon
be in his position.

"There is a patrol due at Keroon and at Igen."
F'lar looked first at Lord Corman, then at Lord
Banger, who gravely nodded. "Let me say by way of
reassurance that there will be no further attacks for
three days and four hours." F'lar tapped the appropriate chart. "The Threads will begin approximately
here on Telgar, drift westward through the southern-
most portion of Crom, which is mountainous, and on,
through Ruatha and the southern end of Nabol."

"How can you be so certain of that?"

F'lar recognized the contemptuous voice of Meron
of Nabol.

"The Threads do not fall like a child's jackstraws,
Lord Meron," F'lar replied. "They fall in a definitely
predictable pattern; the attacks last exactly six hours.
The intervals between attacks will gradually shorten
over the next few Turns as the Red Star draws closer.
Then, for about forty full Turns, as the Red Star
swings past and around us, the attacks occur every
fourteen hours, marching across our world in a time-
able fashion."

"So *you* say," Meron sneered, and there was a low mumble of support.

"So the Teaching Ballads say," Larad put in firmly.

Meron glared at Telgar's Lord and went on, "I recall another of your predictions about how the Threads were supposed to begin falling right after Solstice."

"Which they did," F'lar interrupted him. "As black dust in the Northern Holds. For the reprieve we've had, we can thank our lucky stars that we have had an unusually hard and long Cold Turn."

"Dust?" demanded Nessel of Crom. "That dust was Threads?" The man was one of Fax's blood connections and under Meron's influence: an older man who had learned lessons from his conquering relative's bloody ways and had not the wit to improve on or alter the original. "My Hold is still blowing with them. They're dangerous?"

F'lar shook his head emphatically. "How long has the black dust been blowing in your Hold? Weeks? Done any harm yet?"

Nessel frowned.

"I'm interested in your charts, Weyrleader," Larad of Telgar said smoothly. "Will they give us an accurate idea of how often we may expect Threads to fall in our own Holds?"

"Yes. You may also anticipate that the dragonmen will arrive shortly before the invasion is due," F'lar went on. "However, additional measures of your own are necessary, and it is for this that I called the Council."

"Wait a minute," Corman of Keroon growled. "I want a copy of those fancy charts of yours for my own. I want to know what those bands and wavy lines really mean. I want . . ."

"Naturally you'll have a timetable of your own. I mean to impose on Masterharper Robinton"—F'lar nodded respectfully toward that Craftmaster—"to oversee the copying and make sure everyone understands the timing involved."

Robinton, a tall, gaunt man with a lined, saturnine face, bowed deeply. A slight smile curved his wide lips at the now hopeful glances favored him by the Hold Lords. His craft, like that of the dragonmen, had been much mocked, and this new respect amused him. He was a man with a keen eye for the ridiculous, and an active imagination. The circumstances in which doubting Pern found itself were too ironic not to appeal to his innate sense of justice. He now contented himself with a deep bow and a mild phrase.

"Truly all shall pay heed to the master." His voice was deep, his words enunciated with no provincial cial slurring.

F'lar, about to speak, looked sharply at Robinton as he caught the double barb of that single line. Larad, too, looked around at the Masterharper, clearing his throat hastily.

"We shall have our charts," Larad said, forestalling Meron, who had opened his mouth to speak. "We shall have the dragonmen when the Threads spin. What are these additional measures? And why are they necessary?"

All eyes were on F'lar again.

"We have one Weyr where six once flew."

"But word is that Ramoth has hatched over forty more," someone in the back of the room declared. "And why did you Search out still more of our young men?"

"Forty-one as yet unmatured dragons," F'lar said. Privately, he hoped that this southern venture would still work out. There was real fear in that man's voice. "They grow well and quickly. Just at present, while the Threads do not strike with great frequency as the Red Star begins its Pass, our Weyr is sufficient . . . if we have your cooperation on the ground. Tradition is that"—he nodded tactfully toward Robinton, the dispenser of Traditional usage—"you Holders are responsible for only your dwellings, which, of course, are adequately protected by firepits and raw stone. However, it is spring and our heights have been allowed to grow wild with vegetation. Arable land is blossoming with crops. This presents vast acreage vulnerable to the Threads which one Weyr, at this time, is not able to patrol without severely draining the vitality of our dragons and riders."

At this candid admission, a frightened and angry mutter spread rapidly throughout the room.

"Ramoth rises to mate again soon," F'lar continued in a matter-of-fact way. "Of course, in other times, the queens started producing heavy clutches many Turns before the critical solstice as well as more queens. Unfortunately, Jora was ill and old, and Nemorth intractable. The matter—" He was interrupted.

"You dragonmen with your high and mighty airs will bring destruction on us all!"

"You have yourselves to blame," Robinton's voice stabbed across the ensuing shouts. "Admit it, one and all. You've paid less honor to the Weyr than you would your watch-wher's kennel—and that not much! But now the thieves are on the heights, and you are screaming because the poor reptile is nigh to death from neglect. Beat him, will you? When you exiled him to his kennel because he tried to warn you? Tried to get you to prepare against the invaders? It's on *your* conscience, not the Weyrleader's or the dragonriders', who have honestly done their duty these hundreds of Turns in keeping dragonkind alive . . . against your protests. How many of you"—his tone was scathing—"have been generous in thought and favor toward dragonkind? Even since I became master of my craft, how often have my harpers told me of being beaten for singing the old songs as is their duty? You earn only the right, good Lords and Craftsmen, to squirm inside your stony Holds and writhe as your crops die a-borning."

He rose.

" 'No Threads will fall. It's a harper's winter tale,' " he whined, in faultless imitation of Nessel. " 'These dragonmen leech us of heir and harvest,' " and his voice took on the constricted, insinuating tenor that could only be Meron's. "And now the truth is as bitter as a brave man's fears and as difficult as mockweed to swallow. For all the honor you've done them, the dragonmen should leave you to be spun on the Threads' distaff."

"Bitra, Lemos, and I," spoke up Raid, the wiry Lord of Benden, his blunt chin lifted belligerently, "have always done our duty to the Weyr."

Robinton swung around to him, his eyes flashing as he gave that speaker a long, slow look.

"Aye, and you have. Of all the Great Holds, you three have been loyal. But you others," and his voice rose indignantly, "as spokesmen for my craft, I know, to the last full stop in the score, your opinion of dragonkind. I heard the first whisper of your attempt to ride out against the Weyr." He laughed harshly and pointed a long finger at Vincet. "Where would you be today, good Lord Vincet, if the Weyr had *not* sent you packing back, hoping your ladies would be returned you? All of you," and his accusing finger marked each of the Lords of that abortive effort, "actually rode against the Weyr because . . . 'there . . . were . . . no . . . more . . . Threads!'"

He planted his fists on either hip and glared at the assembly. F'lar wanted to cheer. It was easy to see why the man was Masterharper, and he thanked circumstance that such a man was the Weyr's partisan.

"And now, at this critical moment, you have the incredible presumption to protest against any measure the Weyr suggests?" Robinton's supple voice oozed derision and amazement. "Attend what the Weyrleader says and spare him your petty carpings!" He snapped those words out as a father might enjoin an erring child. "You were," and he switched to the mildest of polite conversational tones as he addressed F'lar, "I believe, asking our cooperation, good F'lar? In what capacities?"

F'lar hastily cleared his throat.

"I shall require that the Holds police their own

fields and woods, during the attacks if possible, definitely once the Threads have passed. All burrows which might land must be found, marked, and destroyed. The sooner they are located, the easier it is to be rid of them."

"There's no time to dig firepits through all the lands . . . we'll lose half our growing space," Nessel exclaimed.

"There were other ways, used in olden times, which I believe our Mastersmith might know." F'lar gestured politely toward Fandarel, the archetype of his profession if ever such existed.

The Smith Craftmaster was by several inches the tallest man in the Council Room, his massive shoulders and heavily muscled arms pressed against his nearest neighbors, although he had made an effort not to crowd against anyone. He rose, a giant tree-stump of a man, hooking thumbs like beast-horns in the thick belt that spanned his waistless midsection. His voice, by no means sweet after Turns of bellowing above roaring hearths and hammers, was, by comparison to Robinton's superb delivery, a diluted, unsupported light baritone.

"There were machines, that much is true," he allowed in deliberate, thoughtful tones. "My father, it was he, told me of them as a curiosity of the Craft. There may be sketches in the Hall. There may not. Such things do not keep on skins for long." He cast an oblique look under beetled brows at the Tanner Craftmaster.

"It is our own hides we must worry about preserving," F'lar remarked to forestall any intercraft disputes.

Fandarel grumbled in his throat in such a way that F'lar was not certain whether the sound was the man's laughter or a guttural agreement.

"I shall consider the matter. So shall all my fellow craftsmen," Fandarel assured the Weyrleader. "To sear Threads from the ground without damaging the soil may not be so easy. There are, it is true, fluids which burn and sear. We use an acid to etch design on daggers and ornamental metals. We of the Craft call it agenothree. There is also the black heavy-water that lies on the surface of pools in Igen and Boll. It burns hot and long. And if, as you say, the Cold Turn made the Threads break into dust, perhaps ice from the coldest northlands might freeze and break grounded Threads. However, the problem is to bring such to the Threads where they fall since they will not oblige us by falling where we want them. . . ." He screwed up his face in a grimace.

F'lar stared at him, surprised. Did the man realize how humorous he was? No, he was speaking with sincere concern. Now the Mastersmith scratched his head, his tough fingers making audible grating sounds along his coarse hair and heat-toughened scalp.

"A nice problem. A nice problem," he mused, undaunted. "I shall give it every attention." He sat down, the heavy bench creaking under his weight.

The Masterfarmer raised his hand tentatively.

"When I became Craftmaster, I recall coming across a reference to the sandworms of Igen. They were once cultivated as a protective—"

"Never heard Igen produced anything useful except heat and sand," quipped someone.

"We need every suggestion," F'lar said sharply, trying to identify that heckler. "Please find that reference, Craftmaster. Lord Banger of Igen, find me some of those sandworms!"

Banger, equally surprised that his arid Hold had a hidden asset, nodded vigorously.

"Until we have more efficient ways of killing Threads, all Holders must be organized on the ground during attacks, to spot and mark burrows, to set firestone to burn in them. I do not wish any man to be scored, but we know how quickly Threads burrow deep, and no burrow can be left to multiply. You stand to lose more," and he gestured emphatically at the Holder Lords, "than any others. Guard not just yourselves, for a burrow on one man's border may grow across to his neighbor's. Mobilize every man, woman, and child, farm and crafthold. Do it now."

The Council Room was fraught with tension and stunned reflection until Zurg, the Masterweaver, rose to speak.

"My craft, too, has something to offer . . . which is only fair since we deal with thread every day of our lives . . . in regard to the ancient methods." Zurg's voice was light and dry, and his eyes, in their creases of spare, lined flesh, were busy, darting from one face in his audience to another. "In Ruath Hold I once saw upon the wall . . . where the tapestry now resides, who knows?" He slyly glanced at Meron of Nabol and then at Bargen of the High Reaches who had succeeded to Fax's title there. "The work was as old as dragonkind and showed, among other things, a man on foot, carrying upon his back a curious contraption. He held within his hand a rounded, sword-long object from which tongues of flame . . . magnificently woven in the orange-red dyes now lost to us . . . spouted toward the ground. Above, of course, were dragons in close formation, bronzes predominating . . . again we've lost that true dragon-bronze shade. Consequently I remember the work as much for what we now lack as for its subject matter."

"A flamethrower?" the Smith rumbled. "A flame-thrower," he repeated with a falling inflection. "A flame-thrower," he murmured thoughtfully, his heavy brows drawn into a titanic scowl. "A thrower of what sort of flame? It requires thought." He lowered his head and didn't speak, so engrossed in the required thought that he lost interest in the rest of the discussion.

"Yes, good Zurg, there have been many tricks of every trade lost in recent Turns," F'lar commented sardonically. "If we wish to continue living, such knowledge must be revived . . . fast. I would particularly like to recover the tapestry of which Master Zurg speaks."

F'lar looked significantly at those Lords who had quarreled over Fax's seven Holds after his death.

"It may save all of you much loss. I suggest that it appear at Ruatha. Or at Zurg's or Fandarel's crafthall. Whichever is most convenient."

There was some shuffling of feet, but no one admitted ownership.

"It might then be returned to Fax's son, who is now Ruatha's Lord," F'lar added, wryly amused at such magnanimous justice.

Lytol snorted softly and glowered around the room. F'lar supposed Lytol to be amused and experienced a fleeting regret for the orphaned Jaxom, reared by such a cheerless if honest guardian.

"If I may, Lord Weyrleader," Robinton broke in, "we might all benefit, as your maps prove to us, from research in our own Records." He smiled suddenly, an unexpectedly embarrassed smile. "I own I find myself in some disgrace for we Harpers have let slip unpopular ballads and skimped on some of the longer Teaching Ballads and Sagas . . . for lack of listeners and, occasionally, in the interest of preserving our skins."

F'lar stifled a laugh with a cough. Robinton was a genius.

"I must see that Ruathan tapestry," Fandarel suddenly boomed out.

"I'm sure it will be in your hands very soon," F'lar assured him with more confidence than he dared feel. "My Lords, there is much to be done. Now that you understand what we all face, I leave it in your hands as leaders in your separate Holds and crafts how best to organize your own people. Craftsmen, turn your best minds to our special problems: review all Records that might turn up something to our purpose. Lords Telgar, Crom, Ruatha, and Nabol, I shall be with you in three days. Nerat, Keroon, and Igen, I am at your disposal to help destroy any burrow on your lands. While we have the Masterminer here, tell him your needs. How stands your craft?"

"Happy to be so busy at our trade, Weyrleader," piped up the Masterminer.

Just then F'lar caught sight of F'nor, hovering about in the shadows of the hallway, trying to catch his eye. The brown rider wore an exultant grin, and it was obvious he was bursting with news.

F'lar wondered how they could have returned so swiftly from the Southern Continent, and then he realized that F'nor—again—was tanned. He gave a jerk of his head, indicating that F'nor take himself off to the sleeping quarters and wait.

"Lords and Craftmasters, a dragonet will be at the disposal of each of you for messages and transportation. Now, good morning."

He strode out of the Council Room, up the passageway into the queen's weyr, and parted the still swinging curtains into the sleeping room just as F'nor was pouring himself a cup of wine.

"Success!" F'nor cried as the Weyrleader entered. "Though how you knew to send just thirty-two candidates I'll never understand. I thought you were insulting our noble Pridith. But thirty-two eggs she laid in four days. It was all I could do to keep from riding out when the first appeared."

F'lar responded with hearty congratulations, relieved that there would be at least that much benefit from this apparently ill-fated venture. Now all he had to figure out was how much longer F'nor had stayed south until his frantic visit the night before. For there were no worry lines or strain in F'nor's grinning, well-tanned face.

"No queen egg?" asked F'lar hopefully. With thirty-two in the one experiment, perhaps they could send a second queen back and try again.

F'nor's face lengthened. "No, and I was sure there would be. But there are fourteen bronzes. Pridith outmatched Ramoth there," he added proudly.

"Indeed she did. How goes the Weyr otherwise?"

F'nor frowned, shaking his head against an inner

bewilderment. "Kylara's . . . well, she's a problem.
Stirs up trouble constantly. T'bor leads a sad time with
her, and he's so touchy everyone keeps a distance
from him." F'nor brightened a little. "Young N'ton is
shaping up into a fine wingleader, and his bronze may
outfly T'bor's Orth when Pridith flies to mate the next
time. Not that I'd wish Kylara on N'ton . . . or anyone."

"No trouble then with supplies?"

F'nor laughed outright. "If you hadn't made it so
plain we must not communicate with you here, we
could supply you with fruits and fresh greens that
are superior to anything in the north. We eat the way
dragonmen should! F'lar, we must consider a supply
Weyr down there. Then we shall never have to worry
about tithing trains and . . ."

"In good time. Get back now. You know you
must keep these visits short."

F'nor grimaced. "Oh, it's not so bad. I'm not here
in this time, anyway."

"True," F'lar agreed, "but don't mistake the time
and come while you're still here."

"Hmmm? Oh, yes, that's right. I forget time is
creeping for us and speeding for you. Well, I shan't be
back again till Pridith lays the second clutch."

With a cheerful good-bye, F'nor strode out of the
weyr. F'lar watched him thoughtfully as he slowly retraced his steps to the Council Room. Thirty-two new
dragons, fourteen of them bronzes, was no small gain
and seemed worth the hazard. Or would the hazard
wax greater?

Someone cleared his throat deliberately. F'lar
looked up to see Robinton standing in the archway
that led to the Council Room.

"Before I can copy and instruct others about those
maps, Weyrleader, I must myself understand them
completely. I took the liberty of remaining behind."

"You make a good champion, Masterharper."

"You have a noble cause, Weyrleader," and then

Robinton's eyes glinted maliciously. "I've been begging the Egg for an opportunity to speak out to so noble an audience."

"A cup of wine first?"

"Benden grapes are the envy of Pern."

"If one has the palate for such a delicate bouquet."

"It is carefully cultivated by the knowledgeable."

F'lar wondered when the man would stop playing with words. He had more on his mind than studying the time-charts.

"I have in mind a ballad which, for lack of explanation, I had set aside when I became the Master of my crafthall," he said judiciously after an appreciative savoring of his wine. "It is an uneasy song, both the tune and the words. One develops, as a harper must, a certain sensitivity for what will be received and what will be rejected . . . forcefully," and he winced in retrospect. "I found that this ballad unsettled singer as well as audience and retired it from use. Now, like that tapestry, it bears rediscovery."

After his death C'gan's instrument had been hung on the Council Room wall till a new Weyrsinger could be chosen. The guitar was very old, its wood thin. Old C'gan had kept it well-tuned and covered. The Masterharper handled it now with reverence, lightly stroking the strings to hear the tone, raising his eyebrows at the fine voice of the instrument.

He plucked a chord, a dissonance. F'lar wondered if the instrument was out of tune or if the harper had, by some chance, struck the wrong string. But Robinton repeated the odd discord, then modulating into a weird minor that was somehow more disturbing than the first notes.

"I told you it was an uneasy song. And I wonder if you know the answers to the questions it asks. For I've turned the puzzle over in my mind many times of late."

Then abruptly he shifted from the spoken to the sung tone.

Gone away, gone ahead,
Echoes away, gone unansweréd.
Empty, open, dusty, dead,
Why have all the Weyrfolk fled?

Where have dragons gone together?
Leaving Weyrs to wind and weather?
Setting herdbeasts free of tether?
Gone, our safeguards, gone, but whither?

Have they flown to some new Weyr
Where cruel Threads some others fear?
Are they worlds away from here?
Why, oh, why, the empty Weyr?

The last plaintive chord reverberated.

"Of course, you realize that the song was first recorded in the craft annals some four hundred Turns
ago," Robinton said lightly, cradling the guitar in
both arms. "The Red Star had just passed beyond attack-proximity. The people had ample reason
to be stunned and worried over the sudden loss of the
populations of five Weyrs. Oh, I imagine at the time
they had any one of a number of explanations, but
none . . . not one explanation . . . is recorded." Robinton paused significantly.

"I have found none recorded, either," F'lar replied.
"As a matter of fact, I had all the Records brought
here from the other Weyrs . . . in order to compile
accurate attack timetables. And those other Weyr Records simply end—" F'lar made a chopping gesture
with one hand. "In Benden's Records there is no
mention of sickness, death, fire, disaster—not one
word of explanation for the sudden lapse of the usual
intercourse between the Weyrs. Benden's Records
continue blithely, but only for Benden. There is one
entry that pertains to the mass disappearance . . . the
initiation of a Pern-wide patrol routing, not just
Benden's immediate responsibility. And that is all."

"Strange," Robinton mused. "Once the danger from
the Red Star was past, the dragons and riders may

have gone *between* to ease the drain on the Holds. But I simply cannot believe that. Our craft Records do mention that harvests were bad and that there had been several natural catastrophes . . . other than the Threads. Men may be gallant and your breed the most gallant of all, but mass suicide? I simply do not accept that explanation . . . not for dragonmen."

"My thanks," F'lar said with mild irony.

"Don't mention it," Robinton replied with a gracious nod.

F'lar chucked appreciatively. "I see we have been too weyrbound as well as too hidebound."

Robinton drained his cup and looked at it mournfully until F'lar refilled it.

"Well, your isolation served some purpose, you know, and you handled that uprising of the Lords magnificently. I nearly choked to death laughing," Robinton remarked, grinning broadly. "Stealing their women in the flash of a dragon's breath!" He chuckled again, then suddenly sobered, looking F'lar straight in the eye. "Accustomed as I am to hearing what a man does *not* say aloud, I suspect there is much you glossed over in that Council meeting. You may be sure of my discretion . . . and . . . you may be sure of my wholehearted support and that of my not ineffectual craft. To be blunt, how may my harpers aid you?" and he strummed a vigorous marching air. "Stir men's pulses with ballads of past glories and success?" The tune, under his flashing fingers, changed abruptly to a stern but determined rhythm. "Strengthen their mental and physical sinews for hardship?"

"If all your harpers could stir men as you yourself do, I should have no worries that five hundred or so additional dragons would not immediately end."

"Oh, then despite your brave words and marked charts, the situation is"—a dissonant twang on the guitar accented his final words—"more desperate than you carefully did not say."

"It may be."

"The flamethrowers old Zurg remembered and Fandarel must reconstruct—will they tip the scales?"

F'lar regarded this clever man thoughtfully and made a quick decision.

"Even Igen's sandworms will help, but as the world turns and the Red Star nears, the interval between daily attacks shortens and we have only seventy-two new dragons to add to those we had yesterday. One is now dead and several will not fly for several weeks."

"Seventy-two?" Robinton caught him up sharply. "Ramoth hatched but forty, and they are still too young to eat firestone."

F'lar outlined F'nor and Lessa's expedition, taking place at that moment. He went on to F'nor's reappearance and warning, as well as the fact that the experiment had been successful in part with the hatching of thirty-two new dragons from Pridith's first clutch. Robinton caught him up.

"How can F'nor already have returned when you haven't heard from Lessa and him that there is a breeding place on the Southern Continent?"

"Dragons can go *between* times as well as places. They go as easily to a *when* as to a *where*."

Robinton's eyes widened as he digested this astonishing news.

"That is how we forestalled the attack on Nerat yesterday morning. We jumped back two hours *between* time to meet the Threads as they fell."

"You can actually jump backward? How far back?"

"I don't know. Lessa, when I was teaching her to fly Ramoth, inadvertently returned to Ruath Hold, to the dawn thirteen Turns ago when Fax's men invaded from the heights. When she returned to the present, I attempted a *between* times jump of some ten Turns. To the dragons it is a simple matter to go *between* times or spaces, but there appears to be a terrific drain on the rider. Yesterday, by the time we returned from Nerat and had to go on to Keroon, I felt as though I had been pounded flat and left to dry for a summer on Igen Plain." F'lar shook his head. "We have obviously succeeded in sending Kylara, Pridith, and the others ten Turns *between,* because F'nor has already reported to me that he has been there several Turns. The drain on humans, however, is becoming more and more marked. But even seventy-two more mature dragons will be a help."

"Send a rider ahead in time to see if it is sufficient," Robinton suggested helpfully. "Save you a few days' worrying."

"I don't know how to get to a *when* that has not yet happened. You must give your dragon reference points, you know. How can you refer him to times that have not yet occurred?"

"You've got an imagination. Project it."

"And perhaps lose a dragon when I have none to spare? No, I must continue . . . because obviously I have, judging by F'nor's returns . . . as I decided to start. Which reminds me, I must give orders to start packing. Then I shall go over the time-charts with you."

It wasn't until after the noon meal, which Robinton took with the Weyrleader, that the Masterharper was confident that he understood the charts and left to begin their copying.

Across a waste of lonely tossing sea,
Where no dragonwings had lately spread,
Flew a gold and a sturdy brown in spring,
Searching if a land be dead.

As RAMOTH and Canth bore Lessa and F'nor up to
the Star Stone, they saw the first of the Hold Lords
and Craftmasters arriving for the Council.

In order to get back to the Southern Continent of
ten Turns ago, Lessa and F'nor had decided it was
easiest to transfer first *between* times to the Weyr of
ten Turns back which F'nor remembered. Then they
would go *between* places to a seapoint just off the
coast of the neglected Southern Continent which was
as close to it as the Records gave any references.

F'nor put Canth in mind of a particular day he remembered ten Turns back, and Ramoth picked up
the references from the brown's mind. The awesome
cold of *between* times took Lessa's breath away, and
it was with intense relief that she caught a glimpse of
the normal weyr activity before the dragons took them
between places to hover over the turgid sea.

Beyond them, smudged purple on this overcast and
gloomy day, lurked the Southern Continent. Lessa felt

a new anxiety replace the uncertainty of the temporal displacement. Ramoth beat forward with great sweeps of her wings, making for the distant coast. Canth gallantly tried to maintain a matching speed.

He's only a brown, Lessa scolded her golden queen.

If he is flying with me, Ramoth replied coolly, *he must stretch his wings a little.*

Lessa grinned, thinking very privately that Ramoth was still piqued that she had not been able to fight with her weyrmates. All the males would have a hard time with her for a while.

They saw the flock of wherries first and realized that there would have to be some vegetation on the Continent. Wherries needed greens to live, although they could subsist on little else besides occasional grubs if necessary.

Lessa had Canth relay questions to his rider. *If the Southern Continent was rendered barren by the Threads, how did new growth start? Where did the wherries come from?*

Ever notice the seed pods split open and the flakes carried away by the winds? Ever notice that wherries fly south after the autumn solstice?

Yes, but . . .

Yes, but!

But the land was Thread-bared!

In less than four hundred Turns even the scorched hilltops of our Continent begin to sprout in the springtime, F'nor replied by way of Canth, *so it is easy to assume the Southern Continent could revive, too.*

Even at the pace Ramoth set, it took time to reach the jagged shoreline with its forbidding cliffs, stark stone in the sullen light. Lessa groaned inwardly but urged Ramoth higher to see over the masking highlands. All seemed gray and desolate from that altitude.

Suddenly the sun broke through the cloud cover and the gray dissolved into dense greens and browns, living colors, the live greens of lush tropical growth, the browns of vigorous trees and vines. Lessa's cry of triumph was echoed by F'nor's hurrah and the brass voices of the dragons. Wherries, startled by the unusual sound, rose in squeaking alarm from their perches.

Beyond the headland, the land sloped away to jungle and grassy plateau, similar to mid-Boll. Though they searched all morning, they found no hospitable cliffs wherein to found a new Weyr. Was that a contributing factor in the southern venture's failure, Lessa wondered.

Discouraged, they landed on a high plateau by a small lake. The weather was warm but not oppressive, and while F'nor and Lessa ate their noonday meal, the two dragons wallowed in the water, refreshing themselves.

Lessa felt uneasy and had little appetite for the meat and bread. She noticed that F'nor was restless, too, shooting surreptitious glances around the lake and the jungle verge.

"What under the sun are we expecting? Wherries don't charge, and wild whers would come nowhere near a dragon. We're ten Turns before the Red Star, so there can't be any Threads."

F'nor shrugged, grimacing sheepishly as he tossed his unfinished bread back into the food pouch.

"Place feels so empty, I guess," he tendered, glancing around. He spotted ripe fruit hanging from a moonflower vine. "Now that looks familiar and good enough to eat, without tasting like dust in the mouth."

He climbed nimbly and snagged the orange-red fruit.

"Smells right, feels ripe, looks ripe," he announced and deftly sliced the fruit open. Grinning, he handed Lessa the first slice, carving another for himself. He lifted it challengingly. "Let us eat and die together!"

She couldn't help but laugh and saluted him back. They bit into the succulent flesh simultaneously. Sweet juices dribbled from the corners of her mouth, and Lessa hurriedly licked her lips to capture the least drop of the delicious liquid.

"Die happy—I will," F'nor cried, cutting more fruit.

Both were subtly reassured by the experiment and were able to discuss their discomposure.

"I think," F'nor suggested, "it is the lack of cliff and cavern and the still, still quality of the place, the knowing that there are no other men or beasts about but us."

Lessa nodded her head in agreement. "Ramoth, Canth, would having no Weyr upset you?"

We didn't always live in caves, Ramoth replied, somewhat haughtily as she rolled over in the lake. Sizable waves rushed up the shore almost to where Lessa and F'nor were seated on a fallen tree trunk. *The sun here is warm and pleasant, the water cooling. I would enjoy it here, but I am not to come.*

"She is out of sorts," Lessa whispered to F'nor. "Let Pridith have it, dear one," she called soothingly to the golden queen. "You've the Weyr and all!"

Ramoth ducked under the water, blowing up a froth in disgruntled reply.

Canth admitted that he had no reservations at all about living Weyrless. The dry earth would be warmer than stone to sleep on, once a suitably comfortable hollow had been achieved. No, he couldn't object to the lack of the cave as long as there was enough to eat.

"We'll have to bring herdbeasts in," F'nor mused. "Enough to start a good-sized herd. Of course, the wherries here are huge. Come to think of it, I believe this plateau has no exits. We wouldn't need to pasture it off. I'd better check. Otherwise, this plateau with the lake and enough clear space for Holds seems ideal. Walk out and pick breakfast from the tree."

"It might be wise to choose those who were not Hold-reared," Lessa added. "They would not feel so uneasy away from protecting heights and stone-security." She gave a short laugh. "I'm more a creature of habit than I suspected. All these open spaces, untenanted and quiet, seem . . . indecent." She gave a delicate shudder, scanning the broad and open plain beyond the lake.

"Fruitful and lovely," F'nor amended, leaping up to secure more of the orange-red succulents. "This tastes uncommonly good to me. Can't remember anything this sweet and juicy from Nerat, and yet it's the same variety."

"Undeniably superior to what the Weyr gets. I suspect Nerat serves home first, Weyr last."

They both stuffed themselves greedily.

Further investigation proved that the plateau was isolated, and ample to pasture a huge herd of food-beasts for the dragons. It ended in a sheer drop of several dragonlengths into denser jungle on one side, the sea-side escarpment on the other. The timber stands would provide raw material from which dwellings could be made for the Weyrfolk. Ramoth and Canth stoutly agreed dragonkind would be comfortable enough under the heavy foliage of the dense jungle. As this part of the continent was similar, weatherwise, to Upper Nerat, there would be neither intense heat nor cold to give distress.

However, if Lessa was glad enough to leave, F'nor seemed reluctant to start back.

"We can go *between* time and place on the way back," Lessa insisted finally, "and be in the Weyr by late afternoon. The Lords will surely be gone by then."

F'nor concurred, and Lessa steeled herself for the trip *between*. She wondered why the *when between* bothered her more than the *where,* for it had no effect on the dragons at all. Ramoth, sensing Lessa's depression, crooned encouragingly. The long, long black suspension of the utter cold of *between* where and when ended suddenly in sunlight above the Weyr.

Somewhat startled, Lessa saw bundles and sacks spread out before the Lower Caverns as dragonriders supervised the loading of their beasts.

"What has been happening?" F'nor exclaimed.

"Oh, F'lar's been anticipating success," she assured him glibly.

Mnementh, who was watching the bustle from the ledge of the queen's weyr, sent a greeting to the travelers and the information that F'lar wished them to join him in the weyr as soon as they returned.

They found F'lar, as usual, bent over some of the oldest and least legible Record skins that he had had brought to the Council Room.

"And?" he asked, grinning a broad welcome at them.

"Green, lush, and livable," Lessa declared, watching him intently. He knew something else, too. Well, she hoped he'd watch his words. F'nor was no fool, and this foreknowledge was dangerous.

"That is what I had so hoped to hear you say," F'lar went on smoothly. "Come. tell me in detail what you observed and discovered. It'll be good to fill in the blank spaces on the chart."

Lessa let F'nor give most of the account, to which F'lar listened with sincere attention, making notes.

"On the chance that it would be practical, I started packing supplies and alerting the riders to go with you," he told F'nor when the account was finished. "Remember, we've only three days in this time in which to start you back ten Turns ago. *We* have no moments to spare. And we must have many more mature dragons ready to fight at Telgar in three days' time. So, though ten Turns will have passed for you, three days only will elapse here. Lessa, your thought that the farm-bred might do better is well-taken. We're lucky that our recent Search for rider candidates for the dragons Pridith will have come mainly from the crafts and farms. No problem there. And most of the thirty-two are in their early teens."

"Thirty-two?" F'nor exclaimed. "We should have fifty. The dragonets must have some choice, even if we get the candidates used to the dragonets before they're hatched."

F'lar shrugged negligently. "Send back for more. *You'll* have time, remember," and F'lar chuckled as though he had started to add something and decided against it.

F'nor had no time to debate with the Weyrleader, for F'lar immediately launched on other rapid instructions.

F'nor was to take his own wingriders to help train the weyrlings. They would also take the forty young dragons of Ramoth's first clutch: Kylara with her queen Pridith, T'bor and his bronze Piyanth. N'ton's young bronze might also be ready to fly and mate by the time Pridith was, so that gave the young queen two bronzes at least.

"Suppose we'd found the continent barren?" F'nor asked, still puzzled by F'lar's assurance. "What then?"

"Oh, we'd've sent them back to, say, the High Reaches," F'lar replied far too glibly, but quickly went on. "I should send on other bronzes, but I'll need everyone else here to ride burrow-search on Keroon and Nerat. They've already unearthed several at Nerat. Vincet, I'm told, is close to heart attack from fright."

Lessa made a short comment on that Hold Lord.

"What of the meeting this morning?" F'nor asked, remembering.

"Never mind that now. You've got to start shifting *between* by evening, F'nor."

Lessa gave the Weyrleader a long hard look and decided she would have to find out what had happened in detail very soon.

"Sketch me some references, will you, Lessa?" F'lar asked.

There was a definite plea in his eyes as he drew clean hide and a stylus to her. He wanted no questions from her now that would alarm F'nor. She sighed and picked up the drawing tool.

She sketched quickly, with one or two details added by F'nor until she had rendered a reasonable map of the plateau they had chosen. Then, abruptly, she had trouble focusing her eyes. She felt light-headed.

"Lessa?" F'lar bent to her.

"Everything's . . . moving . . . circling . . ." and she collapsed backward into his arms.

As F'lar raised her slight body into his arms, he exchanged an alarmed look with his half brother.

"How do you feel?" the Weyrleader called after his brother.

"Tired but no more than that," F'nor assured him as he shouted down the service shaft to the kitchens for Manora to come and for hot *klah*. He needed that, and no doubt of it.

F'lar laid the Weyrwoman on the sleeping couch, covering her gently.

"I don't like this," he muttered, rapidly recalling what F'nor had said of Kylara's decline, which F'nor could not know was yet to come in his future. Why should it start so swiftly with Lessa?

"Time-jumping makes one feel slightly—" F'nor paused, groping for the exact wording. "Not entirely . . . whole. You fought *between* times at Nerat yesterday. . . ."

"I fought," F'lar reminded him, "but neither you nor Lessa battled anything today. There may be some inner . . . mental . . . stress simply to going *between* times. Look, F'nor, I'd rather only you came back once you reach the southern Weyr. I'll make it an order and get Ramoth to inhibit the dragons. That way no rider can take it into his head to come back even if he wants to. There is some factor that may be more serious than we can guess. Let's take no unnecessary risks."

"Agreed."

"One other detail, F'nor. Be very careful which times you pick to come back to see me. I wouldn't jump *between* too close to any time you were actually here. I can't imagine what would happen if you walked into your own self in the passageway, and I can't lose you."

With a rare demonstration of affection, F'lar gripped his half brother's shoulder tightly.

"Remember, F'nor. I was here all morning and you did not arrive back from the first trip till midafternoon. And remember, too, *we* have only three days. You have ten Turns."

F'nor left, passing Manora in the hall.

The woman could find nothing obviously the matter with Lessa, and they finally decided it might be simple fatigue; yesterday's strain when Lessa had to relay messages between dragons and fighters followed by the disjointing *between* times trip today.

When F'lar went to wish the southern venturers a good trip, Lessa was in a normal sleep, her face pale, but her breathing easy.

F'lar had Mnementh relay to Ramoth the prohibition he wished the queen to instill in all dragonkind assigned to the venture. Ramoth obliged, but added in an aside to bronze Mnementh, which he passed on to F'lar, that everyone else had adventures while she, the Weyr queen, was forced to stay behind.

No sooner had the laden dragons, one by one, winked out of the sky above the Star Stone than the young weyrling assigned to Nerat Hold as messenger came gliding down, his face white with fear.

"Weyrleader, many more burrows have been found, and they cannot be burned out with fire alone. Lord Vincet wants you."

F'lar could well imagine that Vincet did.

"Get yourself some dinner, boy, before you start back. I'll go shortly."

As he passed through to the sleeping quarters, he heard Ramoth rumbling in her throat. She had settled herself down to rest.

Lessa still slept, one hand curled under her cheek, her dark hair trailing over the edge of the bed. She looked fragile, childlike, and very precious to him. F'lar smiled to himself. So she was jealous of Kylara's attentions yesterday. He was pleased and flattered. Never would Lessa learn from him that Kylara, for all her bold beauty and sensuous nature, did not have one tenth the attraction for him that the unpredictable, dark, and delicate Lessa held. Even her stubborn intractableness, her keen and malicious humor, added zest to their relationship. With a tenderness he would never show her awake, F'lar bent and kissed her lips. She stirred and smiled, sighing lightly in her sleep.

Reluctantly returning to what must be done, F'lar left her so. As he paused by the queen, Ramoth raised her great, wedge-shaped head; her many-faceted eyes gleamed with bright luminescence as she regarded the Weyrleader.

"Mnementh, please ask Ramoth to get in touch with the dragonet at Fandarel's crafthall. I'd like the Mastersmith to come with me to Nerat. I want to see what his agenothree does to Threads."

Ramoth nodded her head as the bronze dragon relayed the message to her.

She has done so, and the green dragon comes as soon as he can. Mnementh reported to his rider. *It is easier to do, this talking about, when Lessa is awake,* he grumbled.

F'lar agreed heartily. It had been quite an advantage yesterday in the battle and would be more and more of an asset.

Maybe it would be better if she tried to speak, across time, to F'nor . . . but no, F'nor had come back.

F'lar strode into the Council Room, still hopeful that somewhere within the illegible portions of the old Records was the one clue he so desperately needed. There must be a way out of this impasse. If not the southern venture, then something else. Something!

Fandarel showed himself a man of iron will as well as sinew; he looked calmly at the exposed tangle of perceptibly growing Threads that writhed and intertwined obscenely.

"Hundreds and thousands in this one burrow," Lord Vincet of Nerat was exclaiming in a frantic tone of voice. He waved his hands distractedly around the plantation of young trees in which the burrow had been discovered. "These stalks are already withering even as you hesitate. Do something! How many more young trees will die in this one field alone? How many more burrows escaped dragon's breath yesterday? Where is a dragon to sear them? Why are you just standing there?"

F'lar and Fandarel paid no attention to the man's raving, both fascinated as well as revolted by their first sight of the burrowing stage of their ancient foe. Despite Vincet's panicky accusations, it was the only burrow on this particular slope. F'lar did not like to contemplate how many more might have slipped through the dragons' efforts and had reached Nerat's warm and fertile soil. If they had only had time enough to set out watchmen to track the fall of stray clumps. They could, at least, remedy that error in Telgar, Crom, and Ruatha in three days. But it was not enough. Not enough.

Fandarel motioned forward the two craftsmen who had accompanied him. They were burdened with an odd contraption: a large cylinder of metal to which was attached a wand with a wide nozzle. At the other end of the cylinder was another short pipe-length and then a short cylinder with an inner plunger. One craftsman worked the plunger vigorously, while the second, barely keeping his hands steady, pointed the nozzle end toward the Thread burrow. At a nod from this pumper, the man released a small knob on the nozzle, extending it carefully away from him and over the burrow. A thin spray danced from the nozzle and drifted down into the burrow. No sooner had the spray motes contacted the Thread tangles than steam hissed out of the burrow. Before long, all that remained of the pallid writhing tendrils was a smoking mass of blackened strands. Long after Fandarel had waved the craftsmen back, he stared at the grave. Finally he grunted and found himself a long stick with which he poked and prodded the remains. Not one Thread wriggled.

"Humph," he grunted with evident satisfaction. "However, we can scarcely go around digging up every burrow. I need another."

With Lord Vincet a hand-wringing moaner in their wake, they were escorted by the junglemen to another undisturbed burrow on the sea-side of the rainforest. The Threads had entered the earth by the side of a huge tree that was already drooping.

With his prodding stick Fandarel made a tiny hole at the top of the burrow and then waved his craftsmen forward. The pumper made vigorous motions at his end, while the nozzle-holder adjusted his pipe before inserting it in the hole. Fandarel gave the sign to start and counted slowly before he waved a cutoff. Smoke oozed out of the tiny hole.

After a suitable lapse of time, Fandarel ordered the junglemen to dig, reminding them to be careful not to come in contact with the agenothree liquid. When the burrow was uncovered, the acid had done its work, leaving nothing but a thoroughly charred mass of tangles.

Fandarel grimaced but this time scratched his head in dissatisfaction.

"Takes too much time, either way. Best to get them still at the surface," the Mastersmith grumbled.

"Best to get them in the air," Lord Vincet chattered. "And what will that stuff do to my young orchards? What will it do?"

Fandarel swung around, apparently noticing the distressed Holder for the first time.

"Little man, agenothree in diluted form is what you use to fertilize your plants in the spring. True, this field has been burned out for a few years, but it is *not* Thread-full. It *would* be better if we could get the spray up high in the air. Then it would float down and dissipate harmlessly—fertilizing very evenly, too." He paused, scratched his heaed gratingly. "Young dragons could carry a team aloft. . . . Hmmm. A possibility, but the apparatus is bulky yet." He turned his back on the surprised Hold Lord then and asked F'lar if the tapestry had been returned. "I cannot yet discover how to make a tube throw flame. I got this mechanism from what we make for the orchard farmers."

"I'm still waiting for word on the tapestry," F'lar

replied, "but this spray of yours is effective. The Thread burrow is dead."

"The sandworms are effective too, but not really efficient," Fandarel grunted in dissatisfaction. He beckoned abruptly to his assistants and stalked off into the increasing twilight to the dragons.

Robinton awaited their return at the Weyr, his outward calm barely masking his inner excitement. He inquired politely, however, of Fandarel's efforts. The Mastersmith grunted and shrugged.

"I have all my craft at work."

"The Mastersmith is entirely too modest," F'lar put in. "He has already put together an ingenious device that sprays agenothree into Thread burrows and sears them into a black pulp."

"Not efficient. *I* like the idea of flamethrowers," the smith said, his eyes gleaming in his expressionless face. "A thrower of flame," he repeated, his eyes unfocusing. He shook his heavy head with a bone-popping crack. "I go," and with a curt nod to the harper and the Weyrleader, he left.

"I like that man's dedication to an idea," Robinton observed. Despite his amusement with the man's eccentric behavior, there was a strong undercurrent of respect for the smith. "I must set my apprentices a task for an appropriate Saga on the Mastersmith. I understand," he said, turning to F'lar, "that the southern venture has been inaugurated."

F'lar nodded unhappily.

"Your doubts increase?"

"This *between* times travel takes its own toll," he admitted, glancing anxiously toward the sleeping room.

"The Weyrwoman is ill?"

"Sleeping, but today's journey affected her. We need another, less dangerous answer!" and F'lar slammed one fist into the other palm.

"I came with no real answer," Robinton said then, briskly, "but with what I believe to be another part of the puzzle. I have found an entry. Four hundred Turns ago the then Masterharper was called to Fort Weyr not long after the Red Star retreated away from Pern in the evening sky."

"An entry? What is it?"

"Mind you, the Thread attacks had just lifted and the Masterharper was called one late evening to Fort Weyr. An unusual summons. However," and Robinton emphasized the distinction by pointing a long, callous-tipped finger at F'lar, "no further mention is ever made of that visit. There ought to have been, for all such summonses have a purpose. All such meetings are recorded, yet no explanation of this one is given. The record is taken up several weeks later by the Masterharper as though he had not left his crafthall at all. Some ten months afterward, the Question Song was added to compulsory Teaching Ballads."

"You believe the two are connected with the abandonment of the five Weyrs?"

"I do, but I could not say why. I only feel that the events, the visit, the disappearances, the Question Song, are connected."

F'lar poured them both cups of wine.

"I have checked back, too, seeking some indications." He shrugged. "All must have been normal right up to the point they disappeared. There are Records of tithing trains received, supplies stored, the list of injured dragons and men returning to active patrols. And then the Records cease at full Cold, leaving only Benden Weyr occupied."

"And why that one Weyr of the six to choose from?" Robinton demanded. "Island Ista would be a better choice if only one Weyr was to be left. Benden so far north is not a likely place to pass four hundred Turns."

"Benden is high and isolated. A disease that struck the others and was prevented from reaching Benden?"

"And no explanation of it? They can't all—dragons, riders, weyrfolk—have dropped dead on the same instant and left no carcasses rotting in the sun."

"Then let us ask ourselves, why was the harper

called? Was he told to construct a Teaching Ballad covering this disappearance?"

"Well," Robinton snorted, "it certainly wasn't meant to reassure us, not with that tune—if one cares to call it a tune at all, and I don't—nor does it answer any questions! It poses them."

"For us to answer?" suggested F'lar softly.

"Aye." Robinton's eyes shone. "For us to answer, indeed, for it is a difficult song to forget. Which means it was meant to be remembered. Those questions are important, F'lar!"

"Which questions are important?" demanded Lessa, who had entered quietly.

Both men were on their feet. F'lar, with unusual attentiveness, held a chair for Lessa and poured her wine.

"I'm not going to break apart," she said tartly, almost annoyed at the excess of courtesy. Then she smiled up at F'lar to take the sting out of her words. "I slept and I feel much better. What were you two getting so intense about?"

F'lar quickly outlined what he and the Masterharper had been discussing. When he mentioned the Question Song, Lessa shuddered.

"That's one I can't forget, either. Which, I've always been told," and she grimaced, remembering the hateful lessons with R'gul, "means it's important. But why? It only asked questions." Then she blinked, her eyes went wide with amazement.

" 'Gone away, gone . . . *ahead!*' " she cried, on her feet. "That's it! All five Weyrs went . . . *ahead*. But to when?"

F'lar turned to her, speechless.

"They came ahead to our time! Five Weyrs full of dragons," she repeated in an awed voice.

"No, that's impossible," F'lar contradicted.

"Why?" Robinton demanded excitedly. "Doesn't that solve the problem we're facing? The need for fighting dragons? Doesn't it explain why they left so suddenly with no explanation except that Question Song?"

F'lar brushed back the heavy lock of hair that overhung his eyes.

"It would explain their actions in leaving," he admitted, "because they couldn't leave any clues saying where they went, or it would cancel the whole thing. Just as I couldn't tell F'nor I knew the southern venture would have problems. But how do they get here —if here is *when* they came? They aren't here now. How would they have known they were needed—or *when* they were needed? And this is the real problem —how can you conceivably give a dragon references to a *when* that has not yet occurred?"

"Someone here must go back to give them the proper references," Lessa replied in a very quiet voice.

"You're mad, Lessa," F'lar shouted at her, alarm written on his face. "You know what happened to you today. How can you consider going back to a *when* you can't remotely imagine? To a *when* four hundred Turns ago? Going back ten Turns left you fainting and half-ill."

"Wouldn't it be worth it?" she asked him, her eyes grave. "Isn't Pern worth it?"

F'lar grabbed her by the shoulders, shaking her, his eyes wild with fear.

"Not even Pern is worth losing you, or Ramoth. Lessa, Lessa, don't you dare disobey me in this." His voice dropped to an intense, icy whisper, shaking with anger.

"Ah, there may be a way of effecting that solution, momentarily beyond us, Weyrwoman," Robinton put in adroitly. "Who knows what tomorrow holds? It certainly is not something one does without considering every angle."

Lessa did not shrug off F'lar's viselike grip on her shoulders as she gazed at Robinton.

"Wine?" the Masterharper suggested, pouring a mug for her. His diversionary action broke the tableau of Lessa and F'lar.

"Ramoth is not afraid to try," Lessa said, her mouth set in a determined line.

F'lar glared at the golden dragon who was regarding the humans, her neck curled around almost to the shoulder joint of her great wing.

"Ramoth is young," F'lar snapped and then caught Mnementh's wry thought even as Lessa did.

She threw her head back, her peal of laughter echoing in the vaulting chamber.

"I'm badly in need of a good joke myself," Robinton remarked pointedly.

"Mnementh told F'lar that he was neither young nor afraid to try, either. It was just a long step," Lessa explained, wiping tears from her eyes.

F'lar glanced dourly at the passageway, at the end of which Mnementh lounged on his customary ledge.

A laden dragon comes, the bronze warned those in the Weyr. *It is Lytol behind young B'rant on brown Fanth.*

"Now he brings his own bad news?" Lessa asked sourly.

"It is hard enough for Lytol to ride another's dragon or come here at all, Lessa of Ruatha. Do not increase his torment one jot with your childishness," F'lar said sternly.

Lessa dropped her eyes, furious with F'lar for speaking so to her in front of Robinton.

Lytol stumped into the queen's weyr, carrying one end of a large rolled rug. Young B'rant, struggling to uphold the other end, was sweating with the effort. Lytol bowed respectfully toward Ramoth and gestured the young brown rider to help him unroll their burden. As the immense tapestry uncoiled, F'lar could understand why Masterweaver Zurg had remembered it. The colors, ancient though they undoubtedly were, remained vibrant and undimmed. The subject matter was even more interesting.

"Mnementh, send for Fandarel. Here's the model he needs for his flamethrower," F'lar said.

"That tapestry is Ruatha's," Lessa cried indignantly. "I remember it from my childhood. It hung in the Great Hall and was the most cherished of my Blood

Line's possessions. Where has it been?" Her eyes were flashing.

"Lady, it is being returned to where it belongs," Lytol said stolidly, avoiding her gaze. "A masterweaver's work, this," he went on, touching the heavy fabric with reverent fingers. "Such colors, such patterning. It took a man's life to set up the loom, a craft's whole effort to complete, or I am no judge of true craftsmanship."

F'lar walked along the edge of the immense arras, wishing it could be hung to afford the proper perspective of the heroic scene. A flying formation of three wings of dragons dominated the upper portion of half the hanging. They were breathing flame as they dove upon gray, falling clumps of Threads in the brilliant sky. A sky just that perfect autumnal blue, F'lar decided, that cannot occur in warmer weather. Upon the lower slopes of the hills, foliage was depicted as turning yellow from chilly nights. The slatey rocks suggested Ruathan country. Was that why the tapestry had hung in Ruatha Hall? Below, men had left the protecting Hold, cut into the cliff itself. The men were burdened with the curious cylinders of which Zurg had spoken. The tubes in their hands belched brilliant tongues of flame in long streams, aimed at the writhing Threads that attempted to burrow in the ground.

Lessa gave a startled exclamation, walking right onto the tapestry, staring down at the woven outline of the Hold, its massive door ajar, the details of its bronze ornamentation painstakingly rendered in fine yarns.

"I believe that's the design on the Ruatha Hold door," F'lar remarked.

"It is . . . and it isn't," Lessa replied in a puzzled voice.

Lytol glowered at her and then at the woven door. "True. It isn't and yet it is, and I went through that door a scant hour ago." He scowled down at the door before his toes.

"Well, here are the designs Fandarel wants to study," F'lar said with relief, as he peered at the flame-throwers.

Whether or not the smith could produce a working model from this woven one in time to help them three days hence F'lar couldn't guess. But if Fandarel could not, no man could.

The Mastersmith was, for him, jubilant over the presence of the tapestry. He lay upon the rug, his nose tickled by the nap as he studied the details. He grumbled, moaned, and muttered as he sat cross-legged to sketch and peer.

"Has been done. Can be done. Must be done," he was heard to rumble.

Lessa called for *klah,* bread, and meat when she learned from young B'rant that neither he nor Lytol had eaten yet. She served all the men, her manner gay and teasing. F'lar was relieved for Lytol's sake. Lessa even pressed food and *klah* on Fandarel, a tiny figure beside the mammoth man, insisting that he come away from the tapestry and eat and drink before he could return to his mumbling and drawing.

Fandarel finally decided that he had enough sketches and disappeared, to be flown back to his crafthold.

"No point in asking him when he'll be back. He's too deep in thought to hear," F'lar remarked, amused.

"If you don't mind, I shall excuse myself as well," Lessa said, smiling graciously to the four remaining around the table. "Good Warder Lytol, young B'rant should soon be excused, too. He's half asleep."

"I most certainly am not, Weyrlady," B'rant assured her hastily, widening his eyes with stimulated alertness.

Lessa merely laughed as she retreated into the sleeping chamber. F'lar stared thoughtfully after her.

"I mistrust the Weyrwoman when she uses that particularly docile tone of voice," he said slowly.

"Well, we must all depart," Robinton suggested, rising.

"Ramoth is young but not that foolish," F'lar murmured after the others had left.

Ramoth slept, oblivious of his scrutiny. He reached for the consolation Mnementh could give him, without response. The big bronze was dozing on his ledge.

Black, blacker, blackest,
And cold beyond frozen things.
Where is *between* when there is naught
To Life but fragile dragon wings?

"I JUST want to see that tapestry back on the wall
at Ruatha," Lessa insisted to F'lar the next day. "I
want it where it belongs."

They had gone to check on the injured and had
had one argument already over F'lar's having sent
N'ton along with the southern venture. Lessa had
wanted him to try riding another's dragon. F'lar had
preferred for him to learn to lead a wing of his own in
the south, given the Turns to mature in. He had
reminded Lessa, in the hope that it might prove inhibit-
ing to any ideas she had about going four hundred
Turns back, about F'nor's return trips, and he had
borne down hard on the difficulties she had already
experienced.

She had become very thoughtful, although she had
said nothing.

Therefore, when Fandarel sent word that he would
like to show F'lar a new mechanism, the Weyrleader
felt reasonably safe in allowing Lessa the triumph of
returning the purloined tapestry to Ruatha. She went

to have the arras rolled and strapped to Ramoth's back.

He watched Ramoth rise with great sweeps of her wide wings, up to the Star Stone before going *between* to Ruatha. R'gul appeared on the ledge just then, reporting that a huge train of firestone was entering the Tunnel. Consequently, busy with such details, it was midmorning before he could get to see Fandarel's crude and not yet effective flamethrower . . . the fire did not "throw" from the nozzle of the tube with any force at all. It was late afternoon before he reached the Weyr again.

R'gul announced sourly that F'nor had been looking for him—twice, in fact.

"Twice?"

"Twice, as I said. He would not leave a message with me for you." R'gul was clearly insulted by F'nor's refusal.

By the evening meal, when there was still no sign of Lessa, F'lar sent to Ruatha to learn that she had indeed brought the tapestry. She had badgered and bothered the entire Hold until the thing was properly hung. For upward of several hours she had sat and looked at it, pacing its length occasionally.

She and Ramoth had then taken to the sky above the Great Tower and disappeared. Lytol had assumed, as had everyone at Ruatha, that she had returned to Benden Weyr.

"Mnementh," F'lar bellowed when the messenger had finished. "Mnementh, where are they?"

Mnementh's answer was a long time in coming.

I cannot hear them, he said finally, his mental voice soft and as full of worry as a dragon's could be.

F'lar gripped the table with both hands, staring at the queen's empty weyr. He knew, in the anguished privacy of his mind, where Lessa had tried to go.

Cold as death, death-bearing,
Stay and die, unguided.
Brave and braving, linger.
This way was twice decided.

BELOW THEM was Ruatha's Great Tower. Lessa coaxed Ramoth slightly to the left, ignoring the dragon's acid comments, knowing that she was excited, too.

That's right, dear, this is exactly the angle at which the tapestry illustrates the Hold door. Only when that tapestry was designed, no one had carved the lintels or capped the door. And there was no Tower, no inner Court, no gate. She stroked the surprisingly soft skin of the curving neck, laughing to hide her own tense nervousness and apprehension at what she was about to attempt.

She told herself there were good reasons prompting her action in this matter. The ballad's opening phrase, "Gone away, gone ahead," was clearly a reference to *between* times. And the tapestry gave the required reference points for the jump *between* whens. Oh, how she thanked the Masterweaver who had woven that doorway. She must remember to tell him how well he had wrought. She hoped she'd be able to. Enough of that. Of course, she'd be able to. For hadn't the Weyrs

259

disappeared? Knowing they had gone ahead, knowing
how to go back to bring them ahead, it was she, obviously, who must go back and lead them. It was
very simple, and only she and Ramoth could do it.
Because they already had.

She laughed again, nervously, and took several
deep, shuddering breaths.

"All right, my golden love," she murmured. "You
have the reference. You know when I want to go.
Take me *between*, Ramoth, *between* four hundred
Turns."

The cold was intense, even more penetrating than
she had imagined. Yet it was not a physical cold. It
was the awareness of the absence of *everything*. No
light. No sound. No touch. As they hovered, longer,
and longer, in this nothingness, Lessa recognized
full-blown panic of a kind that threatened to overwhelm her reason. She knew she sat on Ramoth's
neck, yet she could not feel the great beast under her
thighs, under her hands. She tried to cry out inadvertently and opened her mouth to . . . nothing . . .
no sound in her own ears. She could not even feel the
hands that she knew she had raised to her own cheeks.

I am here, she heard Ramoth say in her mind.
We are together, and this reassurance was all that kept
her from losing her grasp on sanity in that terrifying
aeon of unpassing, timeless nothingness.

Someone had sense enough to call for Robinton.
The Masterharper found F'lar sitting at the table, his
face deathly pale, his eyes staring at the empty weyr.
The craftmaster's entrance, his calm voice, reached
F'lar in his shocked numbness. He sent the others out
with a peremptory wave.

"She's gone. She tried to go back four hundred
Turns," F'lar said in a tight, hard voice.

The Masterharper sank into the chair opposite the
Weyrleader.

"She took the tapestry back to Ruatha," F'lar continued in that same choked voice. "I'd told her about F'nor's returns. I told her how dangerous this was. She didn't argue very much, and I know going *between* times had frightened her, if anything could frighten Lessa." He banged the table with an important fist. "I should have suspected her. When she thinks she's right, she doesn't stop to analyze, to consider. She just does it!"

"But she's not a foolish woman," Robinton reminded him slowly. "Not even she would jump *between* times without a reference point. Would she?"

" 'Gone away, gone ahead'—that's the only clue we have!"

"Now wait a moment," Robinton cautioned him, then snapped his fingers. "Last night, when she walked upon the tapestry, she was uncommonly interested in the Hall door. Remember, she discussed it with Lytol."

F'lar was on his feet and halfway down the passageway.

"Come on, man, we've got to get to Ruatha."

Lytol lit every glow in the Hold for F'lar and Robinton to examine the tapestry clearly.

"She spent the afternoon just looking at it," the Warder said, shaking his head. "You're sure she has tried this incredible jump?"

"She must have. Mnementh can't hear either her or Ramoth anywhere. Yet he says he can get an echo from Canth many Turns away and in the Southern Continent." F'lar stalked past the tapestry. "What is it about the door, Lytol? Think, man!"

"It is much as it is now, save that there are no carved lintels, there is no outer Court or Tower . . ."

"That's it. Oh, by the first Egg, it is so simple. Zurg said this tapestry is old. Lessa must have decided it was four hundred Turns, and she has used it as the reference point to go back *between* times."

"Why, then, she's there and safe," Robinton cried, sinking with relief in a chair.

"Oh, no, harper. It is not as easy as that," F'lar murmured, and Robinton caught his stricken look and the despair echoed in Lytol's face.

"What's the matter?"

"There is nothing *between*," F'lar said in a dead voice. "To go *between* places takes only as much time as for a man to cough three times. *Between* four hundred Turns. . . ." His voice trailed off.

Who wills,
Can.
Who tries,
Does.
Who loves,
Lives.

THERE WERE voices that first were roars in her aching ears and then hushed beyond the threshold of sound. She gasped as the whirling, nauseating sensation apparently spun her, and the bed which she felt beneath her, around and around. She clung to the sides of the bed as pain jabbed through her head, from somewhere directly in the middle of her skull. She screamed, as much in protest at the pain as from the terrifying, rolling, whirling, dropping lack of a solid ground.

Yet some frightening necessity kept her trying to

gabble out the message she had come to give. Sometimes she felt Ramoth trying to reach her in that vast swooping darkness that enveloped her. She would try to cling to Ramoth's mind, hoping the golden queen could lead her out of this torturing nowhere. Exhausted, she would sink down, down, only to be torn from oblivion by the desperate need to communicate.

She was finally aware of a soft, smooth hand upon her arm, of a liquid, warm and savory, in her mouth. She rolled it around her tongue, and it trickled down her sore throat. A fit of coughing left her gasping and weak. Then she experimentally opened her eyes, and the images before her did not lurch and spin.

"Who . . . are . . . you?" she managed to croak.

"Oh, my dear Lessa . . ."

"Is that who I am?" she asked, confused.

"So your Ramoth tells us," she was assured. "I am Mardra of Fort Weyr."

"Oh, F'lar will be so angry with me," Lessa moaned as her memory came rushing back. "He will shake me and shake me. He always shakes me when I disobey him. But I was right. I was right. Mardra? . . . Oh, that . . . awful . . . nothingness," and she felt herself drifting off into sleep, unable to resist that overwhelming urge. Comfortingly, her bed no longer rocked beneath her.

The room, dimly lit by wallglows, was both like her own at Benden Weyr and subtly different. Lessa lay still, trying to isolate that difference. Ah, the weyrwalls were very smooth here. The room was larger, too, the ceiling higher and curving. The furnishings, now that her eyes were used to the dim light and she could distinguish details, were more finely crafted. She stirred restlessly.

"Ah, you're awake again, mystery lady," a man said. Light beyond the parted curtain flooded in from the outer weyr. Lessa sensed rather than saw the presence of others in the room beyond.

A woman passed under the man's arm, moving swiftly to the bedside.

"I remember you. You're Mardra," Lessa said with surprise.

"Indeed I am, and here is T'ton, Weyrleader at Fort."

T'ton was tossing more glows into the wallbasket, peering over his shoulder at Lessa to see if the light bothered her.

"Ramoth!" Lessa exclaimed, sitting upright, aware for the first time that it was not Ramoth's mind she touched in the outer weyr.

"Oh, that one," Mardra laughed with amused dismay. "She'll eat us out of the weyr, and even my Loranth has had to call the other queens to restrain her."

"She perches on the Star Stones as if she owned them and keens constantly," T'ton added, less charitably. He cocked an ear. "Ha. She's stopped."

"You can come, can't you?" Lessa blurted out.

"Come? Come where, my dear?" Mardra asked, confused. "You've been going on and on about our 'coming,' and Threads approaching, and the Red Star bracketed in the Eye Rock, and . . . my dear, don't you realize the Red Star has been past Pern these two months?"

"No, no, they've started. That's why I came back *between* times . . ."

"Back? *Between* times?" T'ton exclaimed, striding over to the bed, eyeing Lessa intently.

"Could I have some *klah*? I know I'm not making much sense, and I'm not really awake yet. But I'm not mad or still sick, and this is rather complicated."

"Yes, it is," T'ton remarked with deceptive mildness. But he did call down the service shaft for *klah*. And he did drag a chair over to her bedside, settling himself to listen to her.

"Of course you're not mad," Mardra soothed her, glaring at her weyrmate. "Or she wouldn't ride a queen."

T'ton had to agree to that. Lessa waited for the *klah*

to come; when it did, she sipped gratefully at its stimulating warmth.

Then she took a deep breath and began, telling them of the Long Interval between the dangerous passes of the Red Star: how the sole Weyr had fallen into disfavor and contempt, how Jora had deteriorated and lost control over her queen, Nemorth, so that, as the Red Star neared, there was no sudden increase in the size of clutches. How she had Impressed Ramoth to become Benden's Weyrwoman. How F'lar had outwitted the dissenting Hold Lords the day after Ramoth's first mating flight and taken firm command of Weyr and Pern, preparing for the Threads he knew were coming. She told her by now rapt audience of her own first attempts to fly Ramoth and how she had inadvertently gone back *between* time to the day Fax had invaded Ruath Hold.

"Invade . . . my family's Hold?" Mardra cried, aghast.

"Ruatha has given the Weyrs many famous Weyrwomen," Lessa said with a sly smile at which T'ton burst out laughing.

"She's Ruathan, no question," he assured Mardra.

She told them of the situation in which Dragonmen now found themselves, with an insufficient force to meet the Thread attacks. Of the Question Song and the great tapestry.

"A tapestry?" Mardra cried, her hand going to her cheek in alarm. "Describe it to me!"

And when Lessa did, she saw—at last—belief in both their faces.

"My father has just commissioned a tapestry with such a scene. He told me of it the other day because the last battle with the Threads was held over Ruatha." Incredulous, Mardra turned to T'ton, who no longer looked amused. "She must have done what she has said she'd done. How could she possibly know about the tapestry?"

"You might also ask your queen dragon, and mine," Lessa suggested.

"My dear, we do not doubt you now," Mardra said sincerely, "but it is a most incredible feat."

"I don't think," Lessa said, "that I would ever try it again, knowing what I do know."

"Yes, this shock makes a forward jump *between* times quite a problem if your F'lar must have an effective fighting force," T'ton remarked.

"You will come? You will?"

"There is a distinct possibility we will," T'ton said gravely, and his face broke into a lopsided grin. "You said we left the Weyrs . . . abandoned them, in fact, and left no explanation. We went somewhere . . . somewhen, that is, for we are still here now. . . ."

They were all silent, for the same alternative occurred to them simultaneously. The Weyrs had been left vacant, but Lessa had no way of proving that the five Weyrs reappeared in her time.

"There must be a way. There must be a way," Lessa cried distractedly. "And there's no time to waste. No time at all!"

T'ton gave a bark of laughter. "There's plenty of time at this end of history, my dear."

They made her rest then, more concerned than she was that she had been ill some weeks, deliriously screaming that she was falling and could not see, could not hear, could not touch. Ramoth, too, they told her, had suffered from the appalling nothingness of a protracted stay *between,* emerging above ancient Ruatha a pale yellow wraith of her former robust self.

The Lord of Ruatha Hold, Mardra's father, had been surprised out of his wits by the appearance of a staggering rider and a pallid queen on his stone verge. Naturally and luckily he had sent to his daughter at Fort Weyr for help. Lessa and Ramoth had been transported to the Weyr, and the Ruathan Lord kept silence on the matter.

When Lessa was strong enough, T'ton called a Council of Weyrleaders. Curiously, there was no opposition to going . . . provided they could solve the problem of time-shock and find reference points along the way. It did not take Lessa long to comprehend why the dragonriders were so eager to attempt the journey. Most of them had been born during the present Thread incursions. They had now had close to four months of unexciting routine patrols and were bored with monotony. Training Games were pallid substitutes for the real battles they had all fought. The Holds, which once could not do dragonmen favors enough, were beginning to be indifferent. The Weyrleaders could see these incidents increasing as Thread-generated fears receded. It was a morale decay as insidious as a wasting disease in Weyr and Hold. The alternative which Lessa's appeal offered was better than a slow decline in their own time.

Of Benden, only the Weyrleader himself was privy to these meetings. Because Benden was the only Weyr in Lessa's time, it must remain ignorant, and intact, until her time. Nor could any mention be made of Lessa's presence, for that, too, was unknown in her Turn.

She insisted that they call in the Masterharper because her Records said he had been called. But when he asked her to tell him the Question Song, she smiled and demurred.

"You'll write it, or your successor will, when the Weyrs are found to be abandoned," she told him. "But it must be your doing, not my repeating."

"A difficult assignment to know one must write a song that four hundred Turns later gives a valuable clue."

"Only be sure," she cautioned him, "that it is a Teaching tune. It must *not* be forgotten, for it poses questions that I have to answer."

As he started to chuckle, she realized she had already given him a pointer.

The discussions—how to go so far safely with no sustained sense deprivations—grew heated. There were more constructive notions, however impractical, on how to find reference points along the way. The five Weyrs had not been ahead in time, and Lessa, in her

one gigantic backward leap, had not stopped for inter-
mediate time marks.

"You did say that a *between* times jump of ten years
caused no hardship?" T'ton asked of Lessa as all the
Weyrleaders and the Masterharper met to discuss this
impasse.

"None. It takes . . . oh, twice as long as a *between*
places jump."

"It is the four hundred Turn leap that left you im-
balanced. Hmmm. Maybe twenty or twenty-five Turn
segments would be safe enough."

That suggestion found merit until Ista's cautious
leader, D'ram, spoke up.

"I don't mean to be a Hold-hider, but there is
one possibility we haven't mentioned. How do we
know we made the jump *between* to Lessa's time? Going *between* is a chancy business. Men go missing
often. And Lessa barely made it here alive."

"A good point, D'ram," T'ton concurred briskly,
"but I feel there is more to prove that we do—did
—will—go forward. The clues, for one thing—they
were aimed at Lessa. The very emergency that left
five Weyrs empty sent her back to appeal for our
help—"

"Agreed, agreed," D'ram interrupted earnestly, "but
what I mean is can you be sure we reached Lessa's
time? It hadn't happened yet. Do we know it can?"

T'ton was not the only one who searched his mind
for an answer to that. All of a sudden he slammed
both hands, palms down, on the table.

"By the Egg, it's die slow, doing nothing, or die
quick, trying. I've had a surfeit of the quiet life we
dragonmen must lead after the Red Star passes till we
go *between* in old age. I confess I'm almost sorry to see
the Red Star dwindle farther from us in the evening sky. I say, grab the risk with both hands and shake
it till it's gone. We're dragonmen, aren't we, bred to
fight the Threads? Let's go hunting . . . four hundred
Turns ahead!"

Lessa's drawn face relaxed. She had recognized the

validity of D'ram's alternate possibility, and it had touched off bitter fear in her heart. To risk herself was her own responsibility, but to risk these hundreds of men and dragons, the weyrfolk who would accompany their men. . . ?

T'ton's ringing words for once and all dispensed with that consideration.

"And I believe," the Masterharper's exultant voice cut through the answering shouts of agreement, "I have your reference points." A smile of surprised wonder illuminated his face. "Twenty Turns or twenty hundred, you have a guide! And T'ton said it. As the Red Star dwindles in the evening sky . . ."

Later, as they plotted the orbit of the Red Star, they found how easy that solution actually was and chuckled that their ancient foe should be their guide.

Atop Fort Weyr, as on all the Weyrs, were great stones. They were so placed that at certain times of the year they marked the approach and retreat of the Red Star, as it orbited in its erratic two hundred Turn-long course around their sun. By consulting the Records which, among other morsels of information, included the Red Star's wanderings, it was not hard to plan jumps *between* of twenty-five Turns for each Weyr. It had been decided that the complement of each separate Weyr would jump *between* above its own base, for there would unquestionably be accidents if close to eighteen hundred laden beasts tried it at one point.

Each moment now was one too long away from her own time for Lessa. She had been a month away from F'lar and missed him more than she had thought possible. Also, she was worried that Ramoth would mate away from Mnementh. There were, to be sure, bronze dragons and bronze riders eager to do that service, but Lessa had no interest in them.

T'ton and Mardra occupied her with the many details in organizing the exodus, so that no clues, past the tapestry and the Question Song that would be composed at a later date, remained in the Weyrs.

It was with a relief close to tears that Lessa urged

Ramoth upward in the night sky to take her place near T'ton and Mardra above the Fort Weyr Star Stone. At five other Weyrs great wings were ranged in formation, ready to depart their own times.

As each Weyrleader's dragon reported to Lessa that all were ready, reference points determined by the Red Star's travels in mind, it was this traveler from the future who gave the command to jump *between.*

The blackest night must end in dawn,
The sun dispel the dreamer's fear:
When shall my soul's bleak, hopeless pain
Find solace in its darkening Weyr?

THEY HAD made eleven jumps *between,* the Weyr-leaders' bronzes speaking to Lessa as they rested briefly between each jump. Of the eighteen hundred-odd travelers, only four failed to come ahead, and they had been older beasts. All five sections agreed to pause for a quick meal and hot *klah* before the final jump, which would be but twelve Turns.

"It is easier," T'ton commented as Mardra served the *klah,* "to go twenty-five Turns than twelve." He glanced up at the Red Dawn Star, their winking and faithful guide. "It does not alter its position as much. I count on you, Lessa, to give us additional references."

"I want to get us back to Ruatha before F'lar discovers I have gone." She shivered as she looked up at the Red Star and sipped hastily at the hot *klah.* "I've seen the Star just like that, once . . . no, twice . . . before at Ruatha." She stared at T'ton, her throat constricting as she remembered that morning: the time she had decided that the Red Star was a menace to her, three days after which Fax and F'lar had appeared at Ruatha Hold. Fax had died on F'lar's dagger, and she had gone to Benden Weyr. She felt suddenly dizzy, weak, strangely unsettled. She had not felt this way as they paused between other jumps.

"Are you all right, Lessa?" Mardra asked with concern. "You're so white. You're shaking." She put her arm around Lessa, glancing, concerned, at her Weyrmate.

"Twelve Turns ago I was at Ruatha," Lessa murmured, grasping Mardra's hand for support. "I was at Ruatha twice. Let's go on quickly. I'm too many in this morning. I must get back. I must get back to F'lar. He'll be so angry."

The note of hysteria in her voice alarmed both Mardra and T'ton. Hastily the latter gave orders for the fires to be extinguished, for the Weyrfolk to mount and prepare for the final jump ahead.

Her mind in chaos, Lessa transmitted the references to the other Weyrleaders' dragons: Ruatha in the evening light, the Great Tower, the inner Court, the land at springtime. . . .

A fleck of red in a cold night sky,
A drop of blood to guide them by,
Turn away, Turn away, Turn, be gone,
A Red Star beckons the travelers on.

BETWEEN THEM, Lytol and Robinton forced F'lar
to eat, deliberately plying him with wine. At the back
of his mind F'lar knew he would have to keep going,
but the effort was immense, the spirit gone from him.
It was no comfort that they still had Pridith and Kylara
to continue dragonkind, yet he delayed sending someone back for F'nor, unable to face the reality of that
admission: that in sending for Pridith and Kylara, he
had acknowledged the fact that Lessa and Ramoth
would not return.

Lessa, Lessa, his mind cried endlessly, damning her
one moment for her reckless, thoughtless daring, loving her the next for attempting such an incredible feat.

"I said, F'lar, you need sleep now more than wine."
Robinton's voice penetrated his preoccupation.

F'lar looked at him, frowning in perplexity. He realized that he was trying to lift the wine jug that Robinton was holding firmly down.

"What did you say?"

"Come. I'll bear you company to Benden. Indeed,

nothing could persuade me to leave your side. You have aged years, man, in the course of hours."

"And isn't it understandable?" F'lar shouted, rising to his feet, the impotent anger boiling out of him at the nearest target in the form of Robinton.

Robinton's eyes were full of compassion as he reached for F'lar's arm, gripping it tightly.

"Man, not even this Masterharper has words enough to express the sympathy and honor he has for you. But you must sleep; you have tomorrow to endure, and the tomorrow after that you have to fight. The dragonmen must have a leader. . . ." His voice trailed off. "Tomorrow you must send for F'nor . . . and Pridith."

F'lar pivoted on his heel and strode toward the fateful door of Ruatha's great hall.

> Oh, Tongue, give sound to joy and sing
> Of hope and promise on dragonwing.

BEFORE THEM loomed Ruatha's Great Tower, the high walls of the Outer Court clearly visible in the fading light.

The claxon rang violent summons into the air, barely heard over the earsplitting thunder as hundreds of dragons appeared, ranging in full fighting array, wing upon wing, up and down the valley.

A shaft of light stained the flagstones of the Court as the Hold door opened.

Lessa ordered Ramoth down, close to the Tower, and dismounted, running eagerly forward to greet the men who piled out of the door. She made out the stocky figure of Lytol, a handbasket of glows held high above his head. She was so relieved to see him that she forgot her previous antagonism to the Warder.

"You misjudged the last jump by two days, Lessa," he cried as soon as he was near enough for her to hear him over the noise of settling dragons.

"Misjudged? How could I?" she breathed.

T'ton and Mardra came up beside her.

"No need to worry," Lytol reassured her, gripping her hands tightly in his, his eyes dancing. He was actually smiling at her. "You overshot the day. Go back *between,* return to Ruatha of two days ago. That's all." His grin widened at her confusion. "It is all right," he repeated, patting her hands. "Take this same hour, the Great Court, everything, but visualize F'lar, Robinton, and myself here on the flagstones. Place Mnementh on the Great Tower and a blue dragon on the verge. Now go."

Mnementh? Ramoth queried Lessa, eager to see her Weyrmate. She ducked her great head, and her huge eyes gleamed with scintillating fire.

"I don't understand," Lessa wailed. Mardra slipped a comforting arm around her shoulders.

"But I do, I do—trust me," Lytol pleaded, patting her shoulder awkwardly and glancing at T'ton for support. "It is as F'nor has said. You cannot be several places in time without experiencing great distress, and when you stopped twelve Turns back, it threw Lessa all to pieces."

"You know that?" T'ton cried.

"Of course. Just go back two days. You see, I *know* you have. I shall, of course, be surprised then, but now, tonight, I know you reappeared two days earlier.

Oh, go. Don't argue. F'lar was half out of his mind with worry for you."

"He'll shake me," Lessa cried, like a little girl.

"Lessa!" T'ton took her by the hand and led her back to Ramoth, who crouched so her rider could mount.

T'ton took complete charge and had his Fidranth pass the order to return to the references Lytol had given, adding by way of Ramoth a description of the humans and Mnementh.

The cold of *between* restored Lessa to herself, although her error had badly jarred her confidence. But then there was Ruatha again. The dragons happily arranged themselves in tremendous display. And there, silhouetted against the light from the Hall, stood Lytol, Robinton's tall figure, and . . . F'lar.

Mnementh's voice gave a brassy welcome, and Ramoth could not land Lessa quickly enough to go and twine necks with her mate.

Lessa stood where Ramoth had left her, unable to move. She was aware that Mardra and T'ton were beside her. She was conscious only of F'lar, racing across the Court toward her. Yet she could not move.

He grabbed her in his arms, holding her so tightly to him that she could not doubt the joy of his welcome.

"Lessa, Lessa," his voice raggedly chanted in her ear. He pressed her face against his, crushing her to breathlessness, all his careful detachment abandoned. He kissed her, hugged her, held her, and then kissed her with rough urgency again. Then he suddenly set her on her feet and gripped her shoulders. "Lessa, if you ever . . ." he said, punctuating each word with a flexing of his fingers, then stopped, aware of a grinning circle of strangers surrounding them.

"I told you he'd shake me," Lessa was saying, dashing tears from her face. "But, F'lar, I brought them all . . . all but Benden Weyr. And that is why the five Weyrs were abandoned. I brought them."

F'lar looked around him, looked beyond the leaders to the masses of dragons settling in the Valley, on the heights, everywhere he turned. There were dragons, blue, green, bronze, brown, and a whole wingful of golden queen dragons alone.

"You brought the Weyrs?" he echoed, stunned.

"Yes, this is Mardra and T'ton of Fort Weyr, D'ram and . . ."

He stopped her with a little shake, pulling her to his side so he could see and greet the newcomers.

"I am more grateful than you can know," he said and could not go on with all the many words he wanted to add.

T'ton stepped forward, holding out his hand, which F'lar seized and held firmly.

"We bring eighteen hundred dragons, seventeen queens, and all that is necessary to implement our Weyrs."

"And they brought flamethrowers, too," Lessa put in excitedly.

"But—to come . . . to attempt it . . ." F'lar murmured in admiring wonder.

T'ton and D'ram and the others laughed.

"Your Lessa showed the way . . ."

". . . with the Red Star to guide us . . ." she said.

"We are dragonmen," T'ton continued solemnly, "as you are yourself, F'lar of Benden. We were told there are Threads here to fight, and that's work for dragonmen to do . . . in any time!"

Drummer, beat, and piper, blow,
Harper, strike, and soldier, go.
Free the flame and sear the grasses
Till the dawning Red Star passes.

EVEN AS the five Weyrs had been settling around
Ruatha Valley, F'nor had been compelled to bring forward in time his southern weyrfolk. They had all
reached the end of endurance in double-time life,
gratefully creeping back to quarters they had vacated
two days and ten Turns ago.

R'gul, totally unaware of Lessa's backward plunge,
greeted F'lar and his Weyrwoman, on their return to
the Weyr, with the news of F'nor's appearance with
seventy-two new dragons and the further word that he
doubted any of the riders would be fit to fight.

"I've never seen such exhausted men in my life,"
R'gul rattled on, "can't imagine what could have gotten
into them, with sun and plenty of food and all, and no
responsibilities."

F'lar and Lessa exchanged glances.

"Well, the southern Weyr ought to be maintained,
R'gul. Think it over."

"I'm a fighting dragonman, not a womanizer," the

old dragonrider grunted. "It'd take more than a trip *between* times to reduce me like those others."

"Oh, they'll be themselves again in next to no time," Lessa said and, to R'gul's intense disapproval, she giggled.

"They'll have to be if we're to keep the skies Thread-free," R'gul snapped testily.

"No problem about that now," F'lar assured him easily.

"No problem? With only a hundred and forty-four dragons?"

"Two hundred and sixteen," Lessa corrected him firmly.

Ignoring her, R'gul asked, "Has that Mastersmith found a flamethrower that'll work?"

"Indeed he has," F'lar assured R'gul, grinning broadly.

The five Weyrs had also brought forward their equipment. Fandarel all but snatched examples from their backs and, undoubtedly, every hearth and smithy through the continent would be ready to duplicate the design by morning. T'ton had told F'lar that, in his time, each Hold had ample flamethrowers for every man on the ground. In the course of the Long Interval, however, the throwers must have been either smelted down or lost as incomprehensible devices. D'ram, particularly, was very much interested in Fandarel's agenothree sprayer, considering it better than thrown-flame, since it would also act as a fertilizer.

"Well," R'gul admitted gloomily, "a flamethrower or two will be some help day after tomorrow."

"We have found something else that will help a lot more," Lessa remarked and then hastily excused herself, dashing into the sleeping quarters.

The sounds that drifted past the curtain were either laughter or sobs, and R'gul frowned on both. That girl was just too young to be Weyrwoman at such a time. No stability.

"Has she realized how critical our situation is? Even with F'nor's additions? That is, if they can fly?" R'gul demanded testily. "You oughtn't to let her leave the Weyr at all."

F'lar ignored that and began pouring himself a cup of wine.

"You once pointed out to me that the five empty Weyrs of Pern supported your theory that there would be no more Threads."

R'gul cleared his throat, thinking that apologies—even if they might be due from the Weyrleader—were scarcely effective against the Threads.

"Now there was merit in that theory," F'lar went on, filling a cup for R'gul. "Not, however, as you interpreted it. The five Weyrs were empty because they ... they came here."

R'gul, his cup halfway to his lips, stared at F'lar. This man also was too young to bear his responsibilities. But . . . he seemed actually to believe what he was saying.

"Believe it or not, R'gul—and in a bare day's time you will—the five Weyrs are empty no longer. They're here, in the Weyrs, in this time. And they shall join us, eighteen hundred strong, the day after tomorrow at Telgar, with flamethrowers and with plenty of battle experience."

R'gul regarded the poor man stolidly for a long moment. Carefully he put his cup down and, turning on his heel, left the weyr. He refused to be an object of ridicule. He'd better plan to take over the leadership tomorrow if they were to fight Threads the day after.

The next morning, when he saw the clutch of great bronze dragons bearing the Weyrleaders and their wingleaders to the conference, R'gul got quietly drunk.

Lessa exchanged good mornings with her friends and then, smiling sweetly, left the weyr, saying she must feed Ramoth. F'lar stared after her thoughtfully, then went to greet Robinton and Fandarel, who had been asked to attend the meeting, too. Neither Craftmaster said much, but neither missed a word spoken. Fandarel's great head kept swiveling from speaker to speaker, his deep-set eyes blinking occasionally. Robinton sat with a bemused smile on his face, utterly delighted by ancestral visitors.

F'lar was quickly talked out of resigning his titular position as Weyrleader of Benden on the grounds that he was too inexperienced.

"You did well enough at Nerat and Keroon. Well indeed," T'ton said.

"You call twenty-eight men or dragons out of action good leadership?"

"For a first battle, with every dragonman green as a hatchling? No, man, you were on time at Nerat, however you got there," and T'ton grinned maliciously at F'lar, "which is what a dragonman must do. No, that was well flown, I say. Well flown." The other four Weyrleaders muttered complete agreement with that compliment. "Your Weyr is understrength, though, so we'll lend you enough odd-wing riders till you've gotten the Weyr up to full strength again. Oh, the queens love these times!" And his grin broadened to indicate that bronze riders did, too.

F'lar returned that smile, thinking that Ramoth was about ready for another mating flight, and this time, Lessa . . . oh, that girl was being too deceptively docile. He'd better watch her closely.

"Now," T'ton was saying, "we left with Fandarel's crafthold all the flamethrowers we brought up so that the groundmen will be armed tomorrow."

"Aye, and my thanks," Fandarel grunted. "We'll turn out new ones in record time and return yours soon."

"Don't forget to adapt that agenothree for air spraying, too," D'ram put in.

"It is agreed," and T'ton glanced quickly around at the other riders, "that all the Weyrs will meet, full strength, three hours after dawn above Telgar, to follow the Thread's attack across to Crom. By the way, F'lar, those charts of yours that Robinton showed me are superb. We never had them."

"How did you know when the attacks would come?"

T'ton shrugged. "They were coming so regularly even when I was a weyrling, you kind of knew when one was due. But this way is much, much better."

"More efficient," Fandarel added approvingly.

"After tomorrow, when all the Weyrs show up at Telgar, we can request what supplies we need to stock the empty Weyrs," T'ton grinned. "Like old times, squeezing extra tithes from the Holders." He rubbed his hands in anticipation. "Like old times."

"There's the southern Weyr," F'nor suggested. "We've been gone from there six Turns in this time, and the herdbeasts were left. They'll have multiplied, and there'll be all that fruit and grain."

"It would please me to see that southern venture continued," F'lar remarked, nodding encouragingly at F'nor.

"Yes, and continue Kylara down there, please, too," F'nor added urgently, his eyes sparkling with irritation.

They discussed sending for some immediate supplies to help out the newly occupied Weyrs, and then adjourned the meeting.

"It is a trifle unsettling," T'ton said as he shared wine with Robinton, "to find that the Weyr you left the day before in good order has become a dusty hulk." He chuckled. "The women of the Lower Caverns were a bit upset."

"We cleaned up those kitchens," F'nor replied indignantly. A good night's rest in a fresh time had removed much of his fatigue.

T'ton cleared his throat. "According to Mardra, no man can *clean* anything."

"Do you think you'll be up to riding tomorrow, F'nor?" F'lar asked solicitously. He was keenly aware of the stress showing in his half brother's face, despite his improvement overnight. Yet those strenuous Turns had been necessary, nor had they become futile even in hindsight with the arrival of eighteen hundred dragons from past time. When F'lar had ordered F'nor ten Turns backward to breed the desperately needed

replacements, they had not yet brought to mind the
Question Song or known of the tapestry.

"I wouldn't miss that fight if I were dragonless,"
F'nor declared stoutly.

"Which reminds me," F'lar remarked, "we'll need
Lessa at Telgar tomorrow. She can speak to any
dragon, you know," he explained, almost apologeti-
cally, to T'ton and D'ram.

"Oh, we know," T'ton assured him. "And Mardra
doesn't mind." Seeing F'lar's blank expression, he
added, "As senior Weyrwoman, Mardra, of course,
leads the queens' wing."

F'lar's face grew blanker. "Queens' wing?"

"Certainly," and T'ton and D'ram exchanged questioning glances at F'lar's surprise. "You don't keep
your queens from fighting, do you?"

"Our *queens?* T'ton, we at Benden have had only
one queen dragon—at a time—for so many generations that there are those who denounce the legends
of queens in battle as black heresy!"

T'ton looked rueful. "I had not truly realized till
this instant how small your numbers were." But his
enthusiasms overtook him. "Just the same, queens are
very useful with flamethrowers. They get clumps other
riders might miss. They fly in low, under the main
wings. That's one reason D'ram's so interested in the
agenothree spray. Doesn't singe the hair off the Holders' heads, so to speak, and is far better over tilled
fields."

"Do you mean to say that you allow your queens to
fly—against Threads?" F'lar ignored the fact that
F'nor was grinning, and T'ton, too.

"Allow?" D'ram bellowed. "You can't stop them.
Don't you know your Ballads?"

" 'Moreta's Ride?' "

"Exactly.'

F'nor laughed aloud at the expression on F'lar's face
as he irritably pulled the hanging forelock from his
eyes. Then, sheepishly, he began to grin.

"Thanks. That gives me an idea."

He saw his fellow Weyrleaders to their dragons, waved cheerfully to Robinton and Fandarel, more lighthearted than he would have thought he'd be the morning before the second battle. Then he asked Mnementh where Lessa might be.

Bathing, the bronze dragon replied.

F'lar glanced at the empty queen's weyr.

Oh, Ramoth is on the Peak, as usual. Mnementh sounded aggrieved.

F'lar heard the sound of splashing in the bathing room suddenly cease, so he called down for hot *klah*. He was going to enjoy this.

"Oh, did the meeting go well?" Lessa asked sweetly as she emerged from the bathing room, drying-cloth wrapped tightly around her slender figure.

"Extremely. You realize, of course, Lessa, that you'll be needed at Telgar?"

She looked at him intently for a moment before she smiled again.

"I *am* the only Weyrwoman who can speak to any dragon," she replied archly.

"True," F'lar admitted blithely. "And no longer the only queen's rider in Benden. . . ."

"I hate you!" Lessa snapped, unable to evade F'lar as he pinned her cloth-swathed body to his.

"Even when I tell you that Fandarel has a flame-thrower for you so you can join the queens' wing?"

She stopped squirming in his arms and stared at him, disconcerted that he had outguessed her.

"And that Kylara will be installed as Weyrwoman in the south . . . in this time? As Weyrleader, I need my peace and quiet between battles. . . ."

The cloth fell from her body to the floor as she responded to his kiss as ardently as if dragon-roused.

From the Weyr and from the Bowl,
Bronze and brown and blue and green,
Rise the dragonmen of Pern,
Aloft, on wing; seen, then unseen.

RANGED ABOVE the Peak of Benden Weyr, a scant
three hours after dawn, two hundred and sixteen dragons held their formations as F'lar on bronze Mnementh
inspected their ranks.

Below in the Bowl were gathered all the weyrfolk
and some of those injured in the first battle. All the
weyrfolk, that is, except Lessa and Ramoth. They had
gone on to Fort Weyr where the queens' wing was
assembling. F'lar could not quite suppress a twinge of
concern that she and Ramoth would be fighting, too.
A holdover, he knew, from the days when Pern had
had only one queen. If Lessa could jump four hundred
Turns *between* and lead five Weyrs back, she could
take care of herself and her dragon against Threads.

He checked to be sure that every man was well
loaded with firestone sacks, that each dragon was in
good color, especially those in from the southern Weyr.
Of course, the dragons were fit, but the faces of the
men still showed evidences of the temporal strains
they had endured. He was procrastinating, and the
Threads would be dropping in the skies of Telgar.

He gave the order to go *between*. They reappeared above, and to the south of Telgar Hold itself, and were not the first arrivals. To the west, to the north, and, yes, to the east now, wings arrived until the horizon was patterned with the great V's of several thousand dragon wings. Faintly he heard the claxon bell on Telgar Hold Tower as the unexpected dragon strength was acclaimed from the ground.

"Where is she?" F'lar demanded of Mnementh. "We'll need her presently to relay orders . . ."

She's coming, Mnementh interrupted him.

Right above Telgar Hold another wing appeared. Even at this distance, F'lar could see the difference: the golden dragons shone in the bright morning sunlight.

A hum of approval drifted down the dragon ranks, and despite his fleeting worry, F'lar grinned with proud indulgence at the glittering sight.

Just then the eastern wings soared straight upward in the sky as the dragons became instinctively aware of the presence of their ancient foe.

Mnementh raised his head, echoing back the brass thunder of the war cry. He turned his head, even as hundreds of other beasts turned to receive firestone from their riders. Hundreds of great jaws masticated the stone, swallowed it, their digestive acids transforming dry stone into flame-producing gases, igniting on contact with oxygen.

Threads! F'lar could see them clearly now against the spring sky. His pulses began to quicken, not with apprehension, but with a savage joy. His heart pounded unevenly. Mnementh demanded more stone and began to speed up the strokes of his wings in the air, gathering himself to leap upward when commanded.

The leading Weyr already belched gouts of orange-red flame into the pale blue sky. Dragons winked in and out, flamed and dove.

The great golden queens sped at cliff-skimming height to cover what might have been missed.

Then F'lar gave the command to gain altitude to

meet the Threads halfway in their abortive descent. As Mnementh surged upward, F'lar shook his fist defiantly at the winking Red Eye of the Star.

"One day," he shouted, "we will not sit tamely here, awaiting your fall. We will fall on you, where you spin, and sear you on your own ground."

By the Egg, he told himself, if we can travel four hundred Turns backward and across seas and lands in the blink of an eye, what is travel from one world to another but a different kind of step?

F'lar grinned to himself. He'd better not mention that audacious notion in Lessa's presence.

Clumps ahead, Mnementh warned him.

As the bronze dragon charged, flaming, F'lar tightened his knees on the massive neck. Mother of us all, he was glad that now, of all times conceivable, he, F'lar, rider of bronze Mnementh, was a dragonman of Pern!

Dragondex

THE WEYRS IN ORDER OF FOUNDING

Fort Weyr
Benden Weyr
High Reaches Weyr
Igen Weyr

Ista Weyr
Telgar Weyr
Southern Weyr

THE MAJOR HOLDS AS BOUND TO THE WEYRS

Fort Weyr
  Fort Hold (oldest hold), Lord Holder Groghe
  Ruatha Hold (next oldest), Lord Holder Jaxom,
    Lord Warder Lytol
  Southern Boll Hold, Lord Holder Sangel

Benden Weyr
  Benden Hold, Lords Holder Raid and Toronas
  Bitra Hold, Lords Holder Sifer and Sigomal
  Lemas Hold, Lord Holder Asgenar

High Reaches Weyr
  High Reaches Hold, Lord Holder Bargen
  Nabol Hold, Lords Holder Fax, Meron, Deckter
  Tillek Hold, Lord Holder Oterel

Igen Weyr
  Keroon Hold, Lord Holder Corman
  Parts of Upper Igen
  Southern Telgar Hold

Ista Weyr

Ista Hold, Lord Holder Warbret
Igen Hold, Lord Holder Laudey
Nerat Hold, Lords Holder Vincet and Begamon

Telgar Weyr

Telgar Hold, Lord Holder Larad
Crom Hold, Lord Holder Nessel

Southern Weyr

Southern Hold, Holder Toric

THE PRINCIPAL LORDS
(AND THEIR HOLDS)

Asgenar (Lemos)

Banger (Igen Plains)

Bargen (High Reaches)

Begamon (Nerat, 2)

Corman (Keroon)

Deckter (Nabol, 3)

Fax (Nabol, 1)

Groghe (Fort)

Jaxom (Ruatha)

Larad (Telgar)

Laudey (Igen)

Lytol (Ruatha Warder)

Meron (Nabol, 2)

Nessel (Crom)

Oterel (Tillek)

Raid (Benden)

Sangel (Boll)

Sifer (Bitra, 1)

Sigomal (Bitra, 2)

Toric (Southern)

Toronas (Benden 2)

Vincet (Nerat 1)

Warbret (1st)

CRAFTMASTERS AND MASTERCRAFTSMEN

Crafter	Rank/craft	Location
Andemon	Masterfarmer	Nerat Hold
Arnor	Craftmaster, scrivenor	Harpercraft Hall Fort Hold
Baldor	Weyrharper	Ista Weyr
Belesdan	Mastertanner	Igen Hold
Bendarek	Craftmaster, woodsmith	Lemos Hold
Benelek	Journeyman machinesmith	Smith Hall
Briaret	Masterherder	Keroon Hold
Brudegan	Journeyman harper	Harpercraft Hall, Fort Hold
Chad	Harper	Telgar Weyr
Domick	Craftmaster, composer	Harpercraft Hall, Fort Hold
Elgin	Harper	Half-Circle Sea Hold
Facenden	Craftmaster, smith	
Fandarel	Mastersmith	Smithcraft Hall, Telgar Hold
Idarolan	Masterfisher	Tillek Hold
Jerint	Craftmaster, instruments	Harpercraft Hall, Fort Hold
Ligand	Journeyman tanner	Fort Hold
Menolly	Journeyman harper	Harpercraft Hall, Fort Hold
Morshall	Craftmaster, theory	Harpercraft Hall, Fort Hold
Nicat	Masterminer	Crom Hold
Oharan	Weyrharper	Benden Weyr
Oldive	Masterhealer	Harpercraft Hall, Fort Hold
Palim	Journeyman baker	Smithhall

Crafter	Rank/craft	Location
Petiron	Harper	Half-Circle Sea Hold
Piemur	Apprentice/journeyman	Harpercraft Hall, Fort Hold
Robinton	Masterharper	Fort Hold
Sebell	Journeyman/Masterharper	Harpercraft Hall, Fort Hold
Sharra	Journeyman healer	Southern Hold
Shonegar	Craftmaster, voice	Harpercraft Hall, Fort Hold
Sograny	Masterherder	Keroon Hold
Tagetarl	Journeyman harper	Harpercraft Hall, Fort Hold
Talmor	Journeyman harper	Harpercraft Hall, Fort Hold
Terry	Craftmaster, smith	Smithcraft Hall, Telgar Hold
Timareen	Craftmaster, weaver	Telgar Hold
Wansor	Craftmaster, glassmith	Smithcraft Hall, Telgar Hold
Yanis	Craftmaster	Half-Circle Sea Hold
Zurg	Masterweaver	Southern Boll Hold

OWNERS OF FIRE-LIZARDS

Owner	Lizard(s)
Asgenar	brown Rial
Baner	—
Bargen	—
Brand	blue
Brekke	bronze Berd
Corman	—

Deelan	green
Famira	green
F'nor	gold Grall
Groghe	queen Merga
G'sel	bronze
Kylara	gold
Larad	green
Menolly	queen Beauty; bronzes Rocky, Diver, Poll; browns Lazybones, Mimic, Brownie; greens Auntie One, Auntie Two; blue Uncle
Meron	bronze
Mirrim	greens Reppa, Lok; brown Tolly
Nessel	—
Nicat	—
N'ton	brown Tris
Oterel	—
Piemur	queen Farlir
Robinton	bronze Zair
Sangel	—
Sebell	queen Kimi
Sharra	bronze Meer, brown Talla
Sifer	—
Toric	queen; two bronzes
Vincet	—

SOME TERMS OF INTEREST

Agenothree: a common chemical on Pern, HNO_3.

Between: an area of nothingness and sensory deprivation between here and there.

Black rock: analogous to coal.

Day Sisters: a trio of stars visible from Pern.

Dawn Sisters: an alternate name for Day Sisters.

Deadglow: a numbskull, stupid. Derived from glow.

Fellis: a flowering tree.

Fellis juice: a juice made from the fruit of the fellis tree; a soporific.

Fire-stone: phosphine-bearing mineral which dragons chew to produce flame.

Glow: a light-source which can be carried in a handbasket.

High Reaches: mountains on the northern continent of Pern (see map).

Hold: a place where the common people live; originally they were cut into the mountains and hillsides.

Impression: the joining of minds of a dragon and his rider-to-be at the moment of the dragon's hatching.

Interval: the period of time between passes, generally
200 Turns.

Klah: a hot stimulating drink made of tree bark and
tasting faintly of cinnamon.

Looks to: is Impressed by.

Long Interval: a period of time, generally twice the
length of an interval, in which no Thread falls and
Dragonmen decrease in number. The last Long Interval is thought to herald the end of Threads.

Month: four sevendays

Numbweed: a medicinal cream which, when smeared
on wounds, kills all feeling; used as an anesthetic.

Oldtimer: a member of one of the five Weyrs which
Lessa brought forward four hundred Turns in time.
Used as a derogative term to refer to one who has
moved to Southern Weyr.

Pass: a period of time during which the Red Star is
close enough to drop Thread on Pern.

Pern: third of the star Rukbat's five planets. It has two
natural satellites.

Red Star (sic): Pern's stepsister planet. It has an
erratic orbit.

Rukbat: a yellow star in the Sagittarian Sector, Rukbat
has five planets and two asteroid belts.

Sevenday: the equivalent of a week on Pern.

Thread: (mycorrhizoid) spores from the Red Star,
which descend on Pern and burrow into it, devour-
ing all organic material they encounter.

Turn: a Pernese year.

Watch-wher: a nocturnal reptile distantly related to
   dragonkind.

Weyr: a home of dragons and their riders.

weyr: a dragon's den.

Weyrsinger: the Harper for the dragonriders, usually
   himself a dragonrider.

Wherries: a type of fowl roughly resembling the domestic Turkey of Earth, but about the size of an
   Ostrich.

Withies: water plants resembling the reeds of Earth.

PERNESE OATHS

By the Egg

By the first Egg

By the Egg of Faranth

Scorch it

Shards

By the shards of my
   dragon's egg

Shells

Through Fall, Fog, and
   Fire

THE PEOPLE OF PERN

Abuna: Kitchen head at Harpercraft Hall, Fort Hold

Alemi: Third of Seaholder's six sons, at Half-Circle Sea Hold

Andemon: Masterfarmer, Nerat Hold

Arnor: Craftmaster scrivenor, at Harpercraft Hold

Balder: Harper, at Ista Weyr

B'dor: at Ista Weyr

Bedella: Oldtimer Weyrwoman, at Telgar Weyr; dragon queen Solth

Belesdan: Mastertanner, Igen Hold

Bendarek: Craftmaster Woodsmith, at Lemos Hold

Benelek: Journeyman machinesmith, Smithhall

Benis: one of Lord Holder Groghe's 17 sons, at Fort Hold

B'fol: rider, at Benden Weyr; dragon green Gereth

B'irto: rider, at Benden Weyr; dragon bronze Cabenth

B'naj: rider, at Fort Weyr; dragon queen Beth

Brand: steward at Ruatha Hold; blue fire-lizard

B'rant: rider, at Benden Weyr: dragon brown Fanth

B'refli: rider, at Benden Weyr, dragon brown Joruth

Brekke: Weyrwoman, at Southern Weyr; dragon queen Wirenth; fire-lizard bronze Berd

Briala: student at Harper Hall

Briaret: Masterherder (replaces Sograny), Keroon Hold

Brudegen: Journeyman of chorus, at Harpercraft Hall, Fort Hold

Camo: a half-wit at Harpercraft Hall, Fort Hold

Celina: queenrider, at Benden Weyr; dragon queen Lamanth

C'gan: Weyrsinger at Benden Weyr; dragon blue Tegath

Corana: sister of Fidello (holder at Plateau), Ruatha Hold

Cosira: rider, at Ista Weyr; dragon queen Caylith

Deelan: milkmother to Jaxom, at Ruatha Hold

Dorse: milkbrother to Jaxom, at Ruatha Hold

D'nek: rider, at Fort Weyr; dragon bronze Zagenth

D'nol: rider of dragon bronze Valenth, at Benden Weyr

Domick: Craftmaster composer, at Harpercraft Hall, Fort Hold

D'ram: Oldtimer Weyrleader, at Ista Weyr; dragon bronze Tiroth

Dunca: cot-holder, girl's cottage, at Harpercraft Hall, Fort Hold

D'wer: rider, at Benden Weyr; dragon blue Trebeth

Elgion: the new harper at Half-Circle Sea Hold

Fandarel: Mastersmith, Smithcraft Hall, Telgar Hold

Fanna: Oldtimer Weyrwoman, at Ista Weyr; dragon queen Miranth

Fax: Lord of Seven Holds, father of Jaxom

Felena: second to the Headwoman Manora, at Benden Weyr

Fidello: holder, at Plateau in Ruatha Hold

Finder: Harper, at Ruatha Hold

F'lar: Weyrleader at Benden Weyr; dragon bronze Mnementh

F'lessan: rider, at Benden Weyr, son of F'lar and Lessa; dragon bronze Golanth

F'lon: Weyrleader, at Benden Weyr, father of F'nor and F'lar

F'nor: wingsecond at Benden Weyr; dragon bronze Canth, fire-lizard gold Grall

F'rad: rider at Benden Weyr; dragon green Telorth

Gandidan: a child at Benden Weyr

Gemma, Lady: First Lady of Fax (Lord of the Seven Holds) and mother of Jaxom

G'dened: Weyrleader-to-be, at Ista Weyr, son of Oldtimer Weyrleader D'ram, dragon bronze Baranth

G'nag: at Southern Weyr, dragon blue Nelanth

G'narish: Oldtimer Weyrleader at Igen Weyr; dragon bronze Gyamath

G'sel: rider, at Southern Weyr; bronze fire-lizard, dragon green Roth

Groghe: Lord Holder at Fort Hold; fire-lizard queen Merga

H'ages: Wingsecond at Telgar Weyr; dragon bronze Kerth

Horon: son of Lord Groghe; Fort Hold

Idarolan: Masterfisher, Tillek Hold

Jaxom: Lord Holder (underage) at Ruatha Hold; dragon white Ruth

Jerint: Craftmaster for instruments, at Harpercraft Hall, Fort Hold

Jora: Weyrwoman preceding Lessa, at Benden Weyr; dragon queen Nemorth

J'ralt: rider, at Benden Weyr; dragon green Palanth

Kayla: drudge, at Harpercraft Hall, Fort Hold

K'der: rider, at Ista Weyr; dragon blue Warth

Kenelas: a woman of the lower caverns, at Benden Weyr

Kern: eldest son of Lord Nessel (the Lord Holder of Crom)

Kirnety: a boy, at Telgar Hold; Impresses dragon bronze Fidirth

K'nebel: Weyrlingmaster, at Fort Weyr; dragon bronze Firth

K'net: rider at Benden Weyr; dragon bronze Pianth

K'van: rider, at Benden Weyr; dragon bronze Heth

Kylara: a sister of Lord Holder Larad and a Weyr-woman at Southern Weyr who moved to High Reaches Weyr when Oldtimers were banished; dragon queen Prideth

Lessa: Weyrwoman at Benden Weyr; dragon queen Ramoth

Lidith: Queen dragon before Nemorth, rider unknown

Ligand: Journeyman tanner at Fort Hold

L'tol: rider, at Benden Weyr and, as Lytol, Warder of Ruatha Hold; dragon brown Larth (dies)

L'trel: father of Mirrim, at Southern Weyr; dragon blue Falgrenth

Lytol: Lord Warder for the underage Lord Holder Jaxom at Ruatha Hold; dragon brown Larth (dies)

Manora: headwoman at Benden Weyr

Mardra: Oldtimer Weyrwoman at Fort Weyr, banished to Southern Weyr; dragon queen Loranth

Margatta: senior Weyrwoman at Fort Weyr; dragon queen Ludeth

Mavi: Seaholder's (Yanis) Lady at Half-Circle Sea Hold

Menolly: Journeyman at Harpercraft Hold, Fort Hold, fire-lizards (10): gold Beauty, bronzes Rocky, Diver, Poll; browns Lazybones, Mimic, Brownie; greens Auntie One and Auntie Two; blue Uncle

Menolly: youngest child (daughter) of Seaholder (Yanis) of Half Circle Sea Hold

Merelan: mother of Robinton (Masterharper of Harpercraft Hold)

Merika: Oldtimer Weyrwoman, at High Reaches Weyr; exiled to Southern Weyr; dragon queen

Mirrim: greenrider, fosterling of Brekke at Benden Weyr: dragon green Path; fire-lizards: green Reppa, green Lok, brown Tolly

Moreta: ancient Weyrwoman at Benden Weyr; dragon queen Orlith

Morshall: Craftmaster for theory, at Harpercraft Hall, Fort Hold

M'rek: wingsecond, at Telgar Weyr; dragon bronze Zigith

M'tok: rider, at Benden Weyr; dragon bronze Litorth

Nadira: Weyrwoman, at Igen Weyr

Nanira: *see* Varena

Nicat: Masterminer, Crom Hold

N'ton: wingleader at Benden Weyr on dragon bronze Lioth; then Weyrleader at Fort Weyr (after T'ron), fire-lizard brown Tris

Oharan: Journeyman harper at Benden Weyr

Oldive: Masterhealer, at Harpercraft Hall, Fort Hold

Old Uncle: great grandfather of Menolly, at Half-Circle Sea Hold

Palim: Journeyman baker at Fort Hold

Petiron: the old Harper at Half-Circle Sea Hold

Piemur: Apprentice/Journeyman, at Harpercraft Hall, Fort Hold; fire-lizard queen Farli; runner-beast Stupid

Pilgra: Weyrwoman, at High Reaches Weyr; dragon queen Selgrith

P'llomar: rider at Benden Weyr; dragon green Ladrarth

Pona: granddaughter to Lord Holder Sangel, Southern Boll Hold

P'ratan: rider, at Benden Weyr; dragon green Poranth

Prilla: youngest Weyrwoman, at Fort Weyr; dragon queen Selianth

Rannelly: nurse and servant of Kylara

R'gul: Weyrleader before F'lar, at Benden Weyr; dragon bronze Hath

R'mart: Oldtimer Weyrleader, at Telgar Weyr; dragon bronze Branth

R'mel: rider, at Benden Weyr; dragon Sorenth

R'nor: rider at Benden Weyr; dragon brown Virianth

Robinton: Masterharper at Harpercraft Hall, Fort Hold; fire-lizard bronze Zair

Sanra: supervisor of children at Benden Weyr

Sebell: Journeyman/Masterharper, Robinton's second, Harpercraft Hall, Fort Hold; fire-lizard queen Kimi

Sella: Menolly's next-oldest sister, at Half-Circle Sea Hold

S'goral: rider, at Southern Weyr; dragon green Betunth

Sharra: Journeyman healer, at Southern Hold; fire-lizards bronze Meer and brown Talla

Shonagar: Craftmaster for voice, at Harpercraft Hall, Fort Hold

Silon: a child at Benden Weyr

Silvina: headwoman at Harpercraft Hall, Fort Hold

S'lan: rider, at Benden Weyr; dragon bronze Binth

S'lel: rider, at Benden Weyr; dragon bronze Tuenth

Sograny: Masterherder, Keroon Hold

Soreel: wife of the First Holder at Half-Circle Sea Hold

Tagetarl: Journeyman at Harpercraft Hall, Fort Hold

Talina: Weyrwoman at Benden Weyr; queenrider

Talmor: Journeyman teacher, at Harpercraft Hall, Fort Hold

T'bor: Weyrleader at Southern Weyr, later moves to High Reaches when the Oldtimers are exiled; dragon bronze Orth

Tegger: holder at Ruatha

Tela, Lady: one of Fax's ladies

Terry: Craftmaster smith, Smithcraft Hall, Telgar Hold

T'gran: dragonrider at Benden Weyr; dragon brown Branth

T'gellan: wingleader at Benden Weyr; dragon bronze Monarth

T'gor: rider at Benden Weyr; dragon blue Relth

T'kul: Oldtimer at High Reaches Weyr, exiled to Southern Weyr; dragon bronze Salth

T'ledon: watchdragon rider at Fort Hold; dragon blue Serith

Tordril: fosterling at Ruatha Hold, prospective Lord Holder at Igen

Torene: ancient Weyrwoman at Benden Weyr

Toric: Lord Holder of Southern Hold

T'ran: rider, at Igen Weyr; dragon bronze Redreth

T'reb: rider, at Fort Weyr; dragon green Beth

T'ron: Oldtimer Weyrleader at Fort Weyr; banished to Southern Weyr; dragon bronze Fidranth; also called T'ton

T'sel: dragonrider at Benden Weyr; dragon green Trenth, fire-lizard bronze Rill

Vanira: see Varena

Varena (also called Vanira): rider, at Southern Weyr; dragon queen Ralenth

Viderian: fosterling (Seaholder's son) at Fort Hold

Wansor: Craftmaster glassmith, Smithcraft Hall, Telgar Hold; also called Starsmith

Yanis: Craftmaster and Seaholder at Half-Circle Sea Hold

Zurg: Masterweaver, Southern Boll Hold

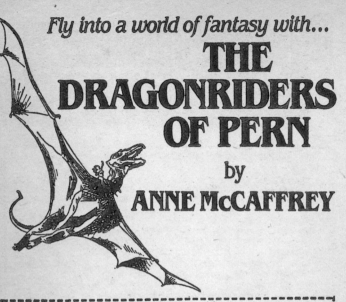